A SHIFT
IN MY WORLD

Johnny A. McDowell

The House Of Legacy Publishing
T.H.O.L.
The House Of Legacy Publishing
tholpublishing.com

First edition
Published by The House Of Legacy Publishing
P.O. Box 154086
Waco, Texas 76715
Design by Creative Man Studio

ISBN - 978-0-9898489-0-9

Library of Congress Control Number 2013952662

Dedicated

to

Mrs. Karen D. McDowell

You are constantly teaching me the true meaning of 'UNCONDI-TIONAL' and though our lives have taken us through some trying times, wavered you have yet to do. Though this is not my first book, I saved this special time to dedicate this book to you because it is the first book published by me. It would be silly of me to think that I could stand at the tallest peak in the world and tell the world how much I love you, so I decided to bring everyone that came in contact with this book, into our world. I thank you for holding our family together when I couldn't. Out of the few promises that I've vowed to you, I pray that you are proud of who I am today.

Orange juice and cinnamon rolls in this life and since we worship an awesome God, surely He will allow us the pleasure to dine on such, in the next life.

I love you.

Acknowledgments

Without God's favor upon me, none of this would be possible. To my staff, family and friends, you guys are the GREATEST. Special thanks to Stephanie Watson-Swan, we're here!!! My best friend, Former U.S. Speaker of the House, Jim Wright (There will never be another you), Terry & Elaine Stevens (Priceless!), Joe Barrow, Lesly Roscoe, Sherlyn Johnson, thank you for trusting me. The Mrs. Billie Davis (Miss Chicago Ill.), Peter Redmon, Michael Moncrief, Todd Orman, Veronica Campbell (Miss Alabama), Carol Price-Lofton (Miss Mississippi), Linda Mason-Crawford, Curtis Bunn for putting me on at the Nation Book Club Conference, Reflections Book Club, The Black Pearls Book Club and to EVERYONE OF YOU WHO ACCEPTED ME AS ONE OF YOUR FAVORITE AUTHORS.

A good writer is one that leaves the reader wondering if the content is real or fiction.

Former U.S. Speaker of the House, Jim Wright.

Contents

Chapter ONE

SUNRISE

As crazy as it may sound, for ten years now I've been wrestling with the idea that God and His entire heavenly host have plotted a conspiracy against me. I'm finding it easy to believe that theory since the only being that has all the control over my life is "God." Since the birth of my son Devon ten years ago, Mother's Day has been the only day in the year that has seventy-two hours in it. With Devon being born on Mother's Day, it meant that my wife and I would be bouncing back and forth between her parents' house and my mother's house.

We weren't married a good nine months when she broke the news of her pregnancy to me. From my wife's and her doctor's calculations, Devon was due to start raising hell the first week of June. I guess the Man upstairs really had a way of showing us all that we weren't running shit!

Mother's Day weekend of 1998 was the beginning of my building a foundation for a case against God. Surely, I had no intentions on making my feelings known to my wife. Hell, she would have immediately concluded that I was not grateful or thankful about Devon being born on that day. I wasn't given the privilege of doing my early morning ablutions before the drama started about which parents' house we would be blessing for Mother's Day.

My mother wanted her first grandbaby in church with her, and the same desire was the wish of my wife's parents. Of course, I ended up being the cruel, heartless bastard in a good Christian kind of way because I made the decision that the feud would be ended between my mother and my wife's parents by our staying at home that weekend.

It was Friday morning, and since we lived in East Point, Georgia, neither my mother nor my in-laws were prepared to catch a flight that late in the weekend to crash my one-on-one time with Devon; so that meant bliss for me.

I personally made sure that the little episode never happened again by having my wife choose a number between one and one hundred. Then I called her parents first to choose a number. They chose sixty and my mother chose twenty-two. It was settled that Devon would spend Mother's Day at my mother's house the following year.

Ten years later, I found myself peeling potatoes with Devon at my mother's on Mother's Day. I made it a point not to ever cut corners with my son, but I don't think I was really prepared for the question he asked me Mother's Day of 2008.

"Daddy, can I ask you a question?"

"Devon, you know you can ask me anything you want, son."

"Daddy, how did you and Mama meet?"

In just that split second, the knife I was using found an entry into my thumb.

"Daddy, you're bleeding!" Devon screamed.

I looked down and noticed my blood dripping slowly to the floor. I immediately thought of my wife.

It wasn't even noon yet, and being in El Paso, Texas, in June meant a sweltering 110 degrees in the shade. Thinking back on those days, I know and understand that Mama faced some real hard times. Whatever her burdens, the hardships that Marie and I were going through started to take their toll on us.

Though I can't remember what day it was, I do remember that it was early one summer morning when Marie and I left our home and began walking to our grandfather's house. What amazes me, even to this day, is how cruel society was at that time to allow two children to walk such mean and heartless streets without stopping us and asking us where our parents were or to at least assist us in reaching our destination.

I shiver with fear when I think about how vulnerable Marie and I were, and how we could have been taken across the border into Juarez and sold to a drug lord to work in the drug fields. The only sign of Marie knowing how to get to my grandfather's house stood towering over El Paso like a skyscraper. There was a Texaco refinery that had a fiery smoke stack that stood so high you could see the fire raging from the top of it, day and night.

We found ourselves zigzagging in and out of streets and alleyways to keep us in line with the smoke stack. Moving as fast as our feet would carry us, we knew that the sun would soon begin to rise, and we were about to come face to face with Mother Nature; and we knew we were no match to deal with her fury. After a good hour of walking, the area I knew as my "hood" had vanished behind us. With every turn that we made, we were introduced to fears that neither of us had ever experienced as a child growing up in our neighborhood.

Marie never showed a hint of fear as huge dogs charged the fence lines in the alleys, and at times, some of the more aggressive ones even climbed to the top of the fence, only to be dragged back down by the chains that held them captive. We ran across a man who lay lifeless in one alley. He had a syringe dangling out of his arm and was literally being eaten by the huge red ants that dominated El Paso. We never slowed down long enough to see if the man was dead or alive.

More than once we ran across young and old men who yelled out to Marie in flirtatious manners, and some of them even exposed their private parts as they spoke. There was no shame in their game as they beckoned for the attention of a child. As we passed through certain areas, the colors of the houses and the clothes that people wore began to change; an all-out indication of a shift in gang turfs. I was so thrown by all the shit that we encountered my staring almost got us into some real serious trouble.

There was a group of more than twenty Mexicans huddled in the driveway of a house, drinking beer and smoking weed. That wasn't an uncommon sight for me, but it was the two dudes going at each other with knives in a mock fight that made me do a double take. As soon as one of the guys saw me staring too hard, he yelled out, "What you looking at, puto? You want some, Negro?" I quickly learned to keep my gaze straight ahead.

Every few minutes Marie would tug at my arm, trying to get me to walk a little faster. After a short while, the welcoming committee of the sun's rays began to beat down on us. Our pace began to break down, and Marie stopped at every, safe shaded area that she could find so that we could rest.

Even as children, the law of nature prevailed because we found ourselves taking two bottles of soda off a Fanta delivery truck that was parked outside of a convenience store. We waited until the man loaded up his dolly and proceeded into the store, and once he did, we made our move to steal our sodas. The fact that we didn't have a bottle opener didn't matter at all to us because we already knew how to manage that feat with ease. Whether we used the corner of a brick building, a car bumper or the car rim that we found in the alley, we gained entry and drank the warm soda under an apricot tree.

As we drew nearer to my grandfather's, we began to see more oil tankers on route to and from the refinery. The smokestack began to grow larger as we got nearer to it, and that alone gave us the strength to push on. I cannot speak for Marie, but the sun sliced through my clothes like a sharp knife and even more so, the rubber that was holding my tennis shoes together was heating up and had my feet feeling the heat too.

The moment we crossed into the colors of my grandfather's neighborhood, we knew we were close and safe. Though we still had some way to go, if any harm came to us from anybody in that hood, his neighbors, as well as other family members would have intervened, and the punishment would have been strict. So we had very little fear due to our sense of security at being in safe territory.

Finally, Tampa Street appeared on the street sign above our heads, and Marie and I looked at each other in relief. We dared not to rest because we knew we had seven more blocks to go. The first two blocks were filled with frowns on the faces of people who knew us and our grandfather. Though the people never said anything to us, they knew where we were headed. It was evident that someone on Tampa Street had called down to my grandfather's house to inform him that his grandchildren were headed his way because he stood in the middle of the street looking in our direction as we made our way towards him.

The closer we got to him, the faster he ran toward us, mumbling, "No, not my babies sweet Jesus! Lord, no!" As soon as he wrapped his arms around us, we collapsed in the safety of his embrace because we could not take another step. With every step he took, my grandfather, being the spiritual man that he was, thanked Jesus for delivering us to him safe and sound. The moment he got us into the house, he quenched our thirst, fed us and made sure that we had a cool bath. Granddaddy never said one negative word about my mother or asked us any questions. He just kept on singing his spiritual songs as he wiped his tears away. Then again, my grandfather wasn't the type to say anything bad about his only child. Hell, my mother couldn't do any wrong in his eyes.

It wasn't long after my grandfather laid us down for a much needed nap and right before I fell asleep I heard my grandfather swear to someone on the phone that his babies would never ever have another day like this one. He vowed that he would make sure that this kind of fearsome trip would never happen again in his lifetime.

Two days went by and still no sign of my mother. Each night I lay awake as long as I could, hoping that she would come through the bedroom door; but that never happened.

At my age, I couldn't see the harm my mother was imposing on Marie and me. I know now that my mother's down fall was self-inflicted by her drive to consume all the alcohol and prescription drugs she could get her hands on.

Deep down inside I honestly felt as if someone put Marie up to convince me that Austin, Texas, was the most fun place to be on earth. Marie was only a year older than I was, but I let her describe the place as if she was an expert on Austin. What puzzled the hell out of me was the fact that she had only one photograph of herself standing right outside of someone's home as the single means of justification for her stories about Austin.

Her description of Austin was centered on the city being half an amusement park and half a junk food haven. I should have known that was some bullshit, but since Marie had been there before, I had to go with the flow.

Whether or not Marie had won me over on the joys of Austin life, it was my grandfather's turn to inform me that he was sending us away to live there. This news wasn't sitting too well with me because there was no mention in his plans of my mother being in the picture. My grandfather had explained that my mother's oldest brother, Thomas, would be coming from Austin to take us back with him. Knowing that I was unsettled about this, my grandfather did everything he could to ease my doubts.

As I look back on how my grandfather was struggling on a fixed income and suffering from various health issues, I can understand now that he knew the best thing to do for us was to send us off to live with my grandmother. Nevertheless, we ate out, had our fill of countless junk foods, and were buttered up to cushion the shock of having to leave the only home we knew. Upon his arrival, Marie and I were totally skeptical of the relocation. Leaving with an unknown member of the family didn't set well with either of us. Marie and I really didn't have too much conversation for our Uncle Thomas when he arrived because he was a complete stranger to us. We tried to feel comfortable around him, but apprehension about our future scared us both.

It's funny as hell right now, but my uncle was very upset when he found out that I had pissed on the floor of the backseat of his car.

Going through the vast mountain ranges of West Texas, people had given life to a rumor that a bunch of wild, evil monkeys invaded and had taken over a small church up in the mountains and had killed all the priests. Uncle Thomas had just passed the ruins of that church when he decided he would pull over to get some rest right where those wild monkeys must have lived. I couldn't understand why he would pick that point to rest since everything about the area was anything but restful. That desert area was also known for its infamous whip snakes that would stand up to any man. It was pitch black and only the chirping of crickets and other insects of the night could be heard. The stars that shined and the glow of a full moon provided the only light in the middle of the desert.

I kept my sights on that ruined church just in case some of the evil monkeys decided to come down the roadside. I wasn't about to be added to the rumors. Whether they were true or not, I wasn't taking any chances. About an hour passed and I had to piss!

Get out of the car and piss with the evil monkeys and whip snakes? I asked myself. It really wasn't a hard ass decision for me to make. Pissing on the floor of Uncle Thomas' car meant living to see another day, and to me, staying alive was the only option.

We pulled into the long, winding parking lot of the projects where my grandmother lived in Austin. As I looked around at the surroundings, the city was far from what Marie had described and I was mad as hell. The complex was deserted of all human life at 5:00 a.m. that Saturday morning. With all of the anger that was built up in my Uncle Thomas due to my piss, he was quick to unload us and all of our belongings out of his car.

It was my first time meeting Honey, who refused to be called Big Mama, Grandmamma, or anything else that would suggest she was old. So, "Honey" it was. Saturday was spent sleeping, and the only time we actually placed our feet on the floor was when Honey woke us up to eat some fish sticks, French fries, and corn, and for trips to the restroom.

Sunday morning came rattling our hunger cages with the smell of eggs, sausage, and pancakes. We didn't have to be reminded what time it was, and although the familiar smell of an authentic Mexican breakfast wasn't in the air, the aroma of sausage cooking said it all. After breakfast, Honey showed Marie and me where to place our belongings. Though we all were short on words with each other, Honey knew she had to give us some time to get used to our environment. After yet another small nap, Honey woke us up for lunch.

I have to admit that whatever Honey had waiting for us, it was minus the Mariachi music that Marie and I were accustomed to. Instead, we pulled up a chair to a complete culture shock. Everything was foreign to us. Instead of lunch in our original hood with extra helpings of frijoles, flautas, tamales, enchiladas, sopas, pico de gallo, menudo, and pozole, our new hood was served up with the soulful sounds of Marvin Gaye. To complement the repeated request to "Get it on", Marie and I stared down at a plate of fried chicken wings, a mixture of mustard and collard greens, some candied yams, hot-water cornbread, and red beans.

Honey had taken her plate in the living room so that she could watch her favorite program on TV. Five minutes had passed when Honey decided to come see how we were faring, and the look she gave us was disconcerting.

"You all eat your food," she said. Marie and I just looked at each other and back down at our plates.

"I said you all can eat now. Eat your food!" she demanded.

Marie and I remained steadfast. Honey walked back into the living room and dialed up my Uncle Thomas. Although he lived on the other side of the projects, you would swear he lived next door. He came through the door with his 6'3, 250 pound stature, still wearing that you pissed in my car look on his face.

"I want the both of you to understand that if you don't mind your grandmother, I'm going to spank your tails." Uncle Thomas ordered us to eat and we refused. Marie saw that Uncle Thomas was at a boiling point with us and finally broke her silence.

"We don't eat this," she stated softly, but held her ground by looking directly at him. I sat there waiting to see what the response would be and what form it would take.

"What do you mean you don't eat this?" replied Uncle Thomas, with a confused look on his face. He looked over at Honey, and she looked just as confused as he did.

"We don't eat food like that," Marie said as she pointed to the food on her plate.

"Thomas, maybe these babies never ate food like this," Honey mentioned with a still puzzled look on her face. "Marie, do you know what's on the plate?" she asked.

"Yes ma'am, some beans."

"What else?" Uncle Thomas angrily asked.

"Some beans," Marie replied again.

"Lord, Jesus Christ, these babies have never eaten any real food before," Honey said shocked. Honey brushed Uncle Thomas to one side and took the center seat between me and Marie.

"Marie, baby, just taste a little bit of this for me, sweetheart, and if you don't like it, you won't have to eat it," Honey reassured her.

Marie picked up her fork and placed just enough greens between its grooves to justify a tad bit. She slowly placed the fork in her mouth and hesitated before chewing. You could see the apprehension in her eyes. I guess the seasoning, fresh onion, pieces of beef neck bone and that old school "sho-nuff" must have kicked in as soon as they hit her taste buds because she reached for something classified as a smidgen more.

"Now try some of that," said Honey, pointing to the candied yams. Marie only went as far as to taste the sweet nectar that gripped the potatoes. She looked over at me and spoke to me in our native language.

"Esta bueno la comida," uttered Marie.

"Thomas, what did she say?" Honey asked with raised eyebrows.

"Mama, how am I supposed to know?"

"Marie, what did you just say, baby?" Honey posed her question to the source of her curiosity.

"I told Stephon the food was good," Marie explained.

I didn't need any other signal to commence eating. Marie's elbows were up like wings, and she was eating as if she was a lost, starving child.

"Stephon, baby, is the food good?" asked Honey.

"Si, I mean, yes ma'am," I said in my deep-rooted accent.

Honey looked up at Uncle Thomas with a glaze of mist in her eyes, "Thomas, these babies been down in that city way too long."

Two days had passed and Marie and I weren't prepared for what we were about to experience. For the first time in my life, I saw fear in my sister's face as she stood in the window looking down at whatever had a grip on her. I eased up beside her and just like Marie, I was not ready for what I saw.

Marie and I looked at each other and spoke a language that was speechless. She knew what I was feeling, and I knew her concerns. She placed her arm around my shoulder as if to say, "it's going to be all right".

"What are y'all looking at down there?" asked Honey. She came to the window to see what had captivated both of our attention, and with a smile on her face, she immediately thought our amusement was a good thing.

"Oh, you all want to go out there and play?" she asked us both the question as we backed slowly away from the window.

We had never seen so many black people in our whole lives. We had only known three, or maybe five black families in the whole city of El Paso, and if there were more, they were military brats on the Fort Bliss Army Base.

"Honey," Marie whispered, "a lot of black people."

Honey chuckled. "Little girl, this is the eastside projects. What you expect?" Honey had no idea that we were experiencing more culture shock. If she knew that there were only four black children who attended Douglas Elementary School with us and I was the only black child who starred in a Mexican Mariachi dance program, or even more so, if she only knew that I considered Mexico's culture as my own, she would flip out!

The first day we decided to test the water and go outside. We stood on the porch for two hours with our backs up against the door. Two days later, we made it to the bottom of the stairs, and the following day, the police were called for a major domestic disturbance. Marie and I were already being teased and sized up because we refused to speak English when we were away from Honey. We had become a circus act to some in the neighborhood because our English was so broken, and we didn't like that.

We decided to go outside early to shoot marbles. We enjoyed the solace that the early morning brought without the other kids around. We were so deep into our element that it wasn't until we noticed about sixteen kids watching from a short distance that we realized that some shit was about to go down. I knew that when the biggest boy out of the bunch made up his mind to come our way, the others would follow. I was so busy keeping an eye on them, that I didn't realize that Marie had placed what appeared to be an old, worn out, coffee table leg in the tallest part of the grass to conceal it.

"I want to play," the boy stated. Marie and I continued with our game, but she instructed me in Spanish not to keep my back to the boy or the others. Her guard was up which alerted me that mine needed to be up as well.

"They don't know what you said Lil' Marcus," said a small-framed girl out in the crowd. Lil' Marcus reached down and grabbed a hand full of marbles.

"Give them back!" I ordered. Lil' Marcus turned to look back at the crew that had followed him over to us, and they all laughed at my cultural accent.

"Give them back, for the last time," I ordered again.

"Shut up black meskin," he uttered with a sense of self—proclaimed authority.

Marie and I had already spoken about how peaceful the apartment complex was compared to the one we lived in back home. The fact that they didn't know us gave us an edge. There was one rule that we lived by in El Paso, "Hurt them first!" I hadn't been much of a fighter and

I contribute that to my style of fighting, or maybe I should just keep it real and state that fear always forced me to end my fights as quick as I could.

It was either the nut sack or the Adam's apple for me; and if I didn't get it right the first time, I knew I was most likely going to get my ass kicked. Since Lil' Marcus was taller and bigger than me, I struck hard and fast and brought him to his knees with one hand and took my marbles out of his hand with the other.

"Get 'em," one of the other boys ordered. He was the first to receive Marie's thrashing across the head with that table leg. It was another nut sack victory for me, and then an Adam's apple. It took four bleeding and badly injured boys to set the tone for the others; and I realized that Marie had no idea that she could have killed one of them. There were no mild or fair blows delivered by her. Every one of them was meant to maim. It wasn't until one of the mothers started loud talking in an irate manner that drew Honey to the window to see what the commotion was about.

"You little bitch. I don't know who the hell you are, but you don't put your…" were the last words the woman uttered at Marie because Honey was on the scene with a .38 revolver in her hand.

"If you threaten my grandbaby again, I'll kill you dead!" Honey warned her with assurance.

"Look what she did to my baby and to these children!"

"Well, if you or those other women had any sense, you would be tending to them instead of trying to beat up on an eleven-year-old child," said Honey.

"Marie, Stephon… upstairs now!" Honey ordered. I refused to leave my marbles.

"Stephon!" shouted Honey. I saw a look on Honey's face that made me say, "To hell with the rest of the marbles!"

At least ten squad cars were immediately on the scene, and three policemen were in our apartment investigating the incident. One of the officers jokingly told another officer, "The other children ran up on some guerilla warfare that was out of their league and from a tougher neighborhood than theirs!" After finding out that a ten and an eleven-year-old caused all the damage, it pretty much ended up being an acknowledgement to everyone involved. You all keep your distance and we'll keep ours.

After the police left, Uncle Thomas came up to the apartment after cleaning the blood stains off the sidewalk, and just looked at us with a smile on his face. "Well Mama, at least we know they ain't no push-overs," he stated with pride.

It was clear that Marie and I were being targeted for a beating, and that meant a wave of more violence. It was either Honey killing some-one or Uncle Thomas being killed, so we all moved out and the move was a good one.

We moved from the east side of Austin to the far west side. However, Honey made the whole move happen. The new neighborhood was above standards, and Marie and I were very thankful.

Our new neighborhood didn't bear the burden of being all black, white, or Hispanic. Moving into a house gave us the comfort of our own space, individual bedrooms, and a yard to play in. Living off of William Cannon Road gave me a new understanding to the meaning of life. It wasn't my life in El Paso that I questioned, but the life that was kept away from me.

I made up my mind that I was not going to live below the new stan-dard of living that Honey had provided for us at that time.

Chapter *TWO*

WHO AM I?

It wasn't too often that the doorbell rang, and when it did, it was usually a stranger. The chimes lasted about five seconds in a funny rhythmic tone that got on Honey's nerves, so everybody knocked at the door instead.

Nine months had passed since we last saw Mama. When Honey asked me to see who was at the door, peeping out of the window onto the porch was all I could do because I wasn't tall enough to see out of the peephole. Seeing Mama on the front porch with her suitcase in hand left me speechless.

"Stephon, I said who is it?" Honey demanded as she began walking towards me and the front door. I really wasn't trying to ignore Honey, but before I could run into the kitchen to grab a chair, race back to the front door to take the chains out of the cylinders and open the door for my mother, Honey stepped between me and the door. She displayed the meanest attitude and used the most frightening and abusive speech I had ever heard come from a woman's mouth. Trying to run into my mother's arms was out of the question at that time. Having a bonding moment while Honey was chewing on Mama's ass was like getting in the middle of a lion and his fresh kill.

Honey lit into her by questioning the nerve she had to even step within five feet of her house, knowing that she had abandoned her kids for her addiction. It didn't matter to Honey that Mama had gotten her life together and had finally felt that she was ready to regain the responsibility of raising her own children. Honey still considered my mother trifling, and called her that at least four or five times before mother could begin to explain her new-found life.

All Honey knew, or was concerned with, was the fact that we had been through more hell and high water than any two young children should have ever experienced. It was as if Mama, through her actions, had disgraced Honey and the meaning of being a real mother. Honey didn't hold back from telling Mama how low down and worthless she was even at the expense of me and Marie standing there listening to it all. Even with Honey's attacks, Mama was able to grab me. She placed her loving arms tightly around me and told me to stop crying.

The warmth of her arms was instantly soothing to that place deep down in my soul that had begun to freeze over.

"Baby, stop crying. I'm not going to leave you anymore." Marie came running to comfort her mother. She was a big girl about seeing Mama and wasn't dramatic like I was, which was just a sure indication that I missed my mama. After Honey readjusted her attitude and came to the deep-down realization that having Mama back in our lives was probably a good thing, she still was a bit apprehensive about allowing us to get too comfortable with having her around. Her actions indicated that Honey had a fear that Mama would once again jump ship and return to her old ways, leaving me and Marie as casualties of war.

After a week had gone by, Honey let me know in a very cruel way that I was being silly for following my mother around the house the way that I was. She told me I was acting like a love sick puppy; and I let her know that I wasn't going to let my mama's ass out of my sight ever again. If she went to the bathroom, I was standing outside the door. I slept where she slept. Where she went, I went.

"Stephon, you bring your narrow behind here," demanded Honey. I walked up to her cautiously, only to be apprehended by her. "I've been watching you trail behind your mama since she walked through that door. You gettin' on my nerves with that mess. Your mama is here to stay, so stop that before I give you a whippin'!"

I looked towards Mama, waiting for her to rescue me from Honey's grip, and Honey snapped.

She snatched me up by the front of my shirt. "Boy I don't care that your mama is sitting over there. I used to spank her ass too. Do we understand each other, Stephon?" Honey asked, waiting on my response.

"I won't do it anymore, Honey," I said with tears in my eyes. I knew right then and there that Honey was the H.N.I.C. (Head Nigga In Charge) in that house. A knock at the door broke up Honey's fussing and until I saw the man's face clearly, I thought my mother had a boyfriend with all the hugging they were doing. I couldn't put a fix on where I had seen the man before, and my mind began to scramble fast for who, when, why, and where? The closer he and my mother got to me, the tighter my fist balled up.

"Stephon and Marie, this is your Uncle James. Your daddy's brother," Mama said with pride.

"Hi Marie," he said as he bent down to hug her. "Hey Stephon," he said, attempting to greet me with the same hug. I refused to greet him and sought protection under my grandmother.

"Stephon, stop acting silly, boy!" Mama ordered.

"Betty, he's okay. The boy just ain't accepting any wooden nickels," Uncle James stated, winking at me. My dislike for him wasn't genuine, but it was for my father. We stared at each other off and on the whole hour he was in our home. Staring into his eyes and seeing my father in the bone structure of his face, sent me back in time.

I remember Marie and I playing a game called kick-the-can with some of the other neighborhood kids in the projects in El Paso. I couldn't have been any more than five when I severely cut my leg on a broken beer bottle. I found comfort in my mother's bed after Mama and I returned home from the Emergency Room. It was way into the night when my father came knocking at our door. He and Mama spoke for a few minutes before I saw his face.

"Stephon, are you going to speak to your daddy?" my mother asked. I remained silent. My father and one of his cousins had broken into a store and came to our home for refuge. For some reason, Mama was glad to see him and I couldn't for the life of me understand why. You would think a child at five or six would have full knowledge of his father; but for me, that was the first and last time I ever saw him. He never mentioned or asked about Marie or cared to see her, and that had been etched in my hate file for life.

My Uncle James reached into his pocket and pulled out a hand full of money. "Marie, Stephon, before I leave I want you two to know that you can count on me for anything you need. All you have to do is call me," he said. "Marie this is for you." He handed her a hundred dollar bill. "Stephon, this is for you," he said. He reached out to hand it to me, and I stood my ground with a cold stare into his eyes.

"Uncle James, I'll give it to him," Marie told him, and brought the hundred dollar bill to me.

"Boy, you're the most stubborn child I have ever seen in my life," Honey said as she rubbed my head.

"James, he's a good boy, but when he's uncertain about something or somebody, NASA couldn't move him," Honey said.

"He'll be all right, Honey," James stated and walked toward the front door.

It took a few weeks of Uncle James coming to visit with me before I gave in to his politeness towards me. A few visits before I gave in, I heard him tell my mother, "You take care of Marie and I'll take care of Stephon."

Hearing that caused me to frown because Mama was so quick to agree and what I heard next was a bit overwhelming. "I missed you."

"Hell, if you missed me that much James, why didn't you come see about us?" asked my mother. Uncle James quickly told her that they would discuss that at a later date.

I couldn't move away from the door fast enough, and immediately I was looking eye to eye with Uncle James when he stepped out of the room. He knew I had been listening all along and he acknowledged it by the cold stare he gave me.

"Well, Stephon, where would you like to go, since this will be our first outing together?" asked Uncle James.

"I don't know, Uncle James," I said.

"Before we go anywhere, you and I are going to make a promise to each other. After I get through talking, if you tell me you and I can't be the best of friends, I'll just remain being your uncle. Stephon, look at me, son," Uncle James said. "I'm not your father, and I'm not trying to be your father, but I want to be better than your father has been to you, son. I don't have to know about all of the hurt or anger you have built up in your heart because of your father, and you'll never hear me make an excuse for his ass either. From the time you were three days old, I was there to feed you and change your diapers. You are my first and favorite nephew. I can't fill the void a father can, but because I love your little stubborn ass, I want to be everything you want and need me to be in your life because you deserve that opportunity just like any other child."

He then said, "I would be a low down son-of-a-bitch to sit back and watch you or Marie struggle the way you have and not do anything about it. So, will you let me be your friend, son?"

"Yes, sir," I said.

"First of all, we're going to drop all the formal shit. When we're together, it's yes, no, okay, cool or not cool. Are we straight?"

"Yes," I told him.

"Now that we got all that out the way, I want you to look me in my eyes and you promise me that whatever we do together stays between you and me. Not even your mother needs to know."

"But what if she asks me what did we do, Uncle James? What do I tell her?"

"Stephon, you'll know what to keep between us, so don't worry about that," he said. "Do you promise to keep our business between us?"

"Yeah, Uncle James!"

He extended his hand and we shook on it to seal the deal.

"I want to be very clear on this promise. I won't stop being your uncle and I won't stop loving you, but we'll stop being cool like this if you betray me. Do you understand me, Stephon?"

"I understand, Uncle James," I promised. I stood up straight and proud, feeling important to my uncle. It would good spending time with him; especially since I was the only male in the house.

"I want our first trip to be something you'll treasure all of your life, Stephon."

I had been in and out of the eastside so much that it didn't make a difference if we were taking the long way around or taking M.L.K. or First Street, I knew the area well. It took us over fifteen trips back and forth when we moved out of the projects, and Uncle Thomas had taken more than nine different routes out of the eastside to shake off any would-be fools. We were four blocks away from the projects, and my gut feeling told me that whatever Uncle James had up his sleeve, existed within the vicinity of those projects. I was hoping like hell he would just pass them up, but he pulled right up in the driveway of the projects and all eyes were on us and his Mercedes.

"Get out and walk with me, Stephon," Uncle James stated as he placed a revolver in his waistband. I hesitated until I saw he was standing outside of my side of the car. I slowly opened the door and stepped out reluctantly.

"Uncle James, I don't want to be here," I told him.

"Why don't you want to be here, nephew?" he asked.

"Because I don't like it here!" We continued to walk without saying a word for more than ten minutes. I saw all of the kids who Marie and I got into the fight with. Two of them went so far as to run in the house to inform their mothers of my presence.

"How come we're not leaving, Uncle James?" I asked. I was so nervous I put my hands in my pockets to try to calm down. Uncle James wasn't nervous at all. He just walked slowly with his head high and arms to his side.

"Because I want you to feel enough of this in your heart that you never, ever, want to return to this. I want you to remember this walk and this conversation until you have a dislike for this lifestyle. These are your people, Stephon. I never want you to hate them, but I want you to ask yourself why they continue to live like this when they have a choice."

We continued to walk full circle until we made it back to the car.

"Where are we going now, Uncle James?" I asked, anxious to get in his car and drive away.

"That really depends on you, son," he said. We left the eastside and began traveling in a direction in Austin that was new to me. The closer we got to wherever we were headed, my gut feeling of uneasiness was replaced with awe in every direction that I looked. The streets weren't filled with broken bottles or empty containers that gave way to fast food restaurants or convenience stores. Old model cars were now replaced on every street we turned on with cars ranging in prices from fifty thousand to...shit I couldn't put a price on them if I tried. We pulled up to a granite building that was way over twenty-eight stories high.

"Get out, nephew," was all Uncle James said. He handed a well-dressed white man a ten dollar bill, and he drove off with Uncle James' car. I just stood there wondering why.

"Nephew! Let's go, son," Uncle James commanded as he walked through a set of tinted glass and brass framed doors. The first thing that caught my attention was the transparent walls of the elevators that were shaped like large capsules, and the people riding on them staring back down at me through the glass as they rode from floor to floor. Uncle James and I boarded one of them, and though I wanted to take a glance down into the lobby, out of fear, I couldn't convince myself to step toward the back of the glass elevator. Being able to see the lobby disappear as I ascended was all I needed to see.

Exiting the elevator into a well-lit hallway, I felt as if I was visiting my very first art gallery. A signature of prestige lingered so thick that any first-time visitor would be breathless. We stopped. Brass numbers, 1521, hung from the door. Uncle James unlocked the door, looked down at me and then pushed the door open to usher me into his home. I was so stunned at what I saw that I just stood there in the doorway in awe.

"Stephon, before you take another step, I want to ask you a question, young man. Who are you, Stephon?"

I looked at Uncle James with an expression on my face that clearly said, You got to be joking!

"Stop playing, Uncle James," I told him as I took a step into his apartment. Before I could take a second one, I was stopped by his firm grip on my shoulder. My smile left immediately.

"Who are you?" he asked again. From the tone of his voice, this time I knew he was serious.

"I'm Stephon, Uncle James."

Uncle James released me and motioned me into the apartment. Even scarier than thinking about approaching the clear view of the elevator, was the view from left to right in his apartment. I could see Austin, Texas, in a way that I could never have imagined. I cautiously approached the ten-foot wall of glass with a sense of uncertainty with each step I took. "Stephon, it's safe boy," Uncle James assured me, laughing at my hesitance.

"Where is Honey's house at Uncle James?" I asked as I desperately scanned the city to see if I could recognize a familiar place.

"Honey's house would be on the other side of the building, and if we were on that side, you probably wouldn't be able to see it anyway because we're too far away from that section of the city," he explained. I continued to stare out, totally amazed. I had never seen anything in my life like what was before my eyes.

"If I took the name Stephon Wilkerson from you, who would you be, son?" He stood back with his arms folded, waiting on my answer.

"I don't know, Uncle James!" I was confused because I didn't know what he wanted me to say.

"Does that even matter to you, Stephon?"

I just stood there staring back at him because I didn't know how to respond to the question. Seeing the confused look on my face, Uncle

James knew he had my attention.

"From this day forward, son, that will be your job—to know and understand who you are; and most importantly, know where you fit in this world. I'm not going to baby your ass or lead you around by the hand. So if you want something from me, you'll have to earn it." His voice was firm and commanding.

"Uncle James, why are you mad at me?"

I saw something in Uncle James that startled me; and the uncertainty of not knowing how to filter the face I was getting from him, made me stand on guard for his next move. It wasn't the fact that I was afraid of him harming me physically, but I needed to understand why he even came to me like that.

"Son, I'm not mad at you. I'm mad at your father," he said. Hearing that "father" word changed my whole demeanor and Uncle James saw it. He placed a strong hand on my shoulder and gave me an encouraging grip.

"That's it, boy. You chew on that dislike until it festers deep in your soul," he muttered then he walked into an adjacent room. "Come here, Stephon," he ordered. "Do you like this room?"

"It's nice," I said as I contemplated why he would even ask me a question like that. The room was larger than my room at Honey's. The walls were somewhere between not quite white but not brown either. There was a big bed with a brown, blue and white bedspread with oversized pillows on it. There was also a dresser, a small table by the bed with a clock and lamp on it, and a desk. A picture of African kings hung on the wall.

"Then this is your room," Uncle James stated.

"I'm staying with Mama," I quickly said and proceeded toward the entrance to his apartment. I was ready to go.

"I'm not taking you from your mother, boy! Whenever you decide you want to come spend the night over here, that's where you'll be sleeping. Follow me so that I can show you around the rest of the place," he said, and as I heard his words, I relaxed.

"I have some do's and don'ts you need to get into your head, so pay close attention because I'm only telling you this one time." He used a drill sergeant's voice as he began to show me the rest of his apartment. "This is my room, my office, my space, and do not enter it unless I ask you to or you're coming in here to save my life. Is that understood?" he barked, not waiting on my reply.

We walked to another room, smaller than mine, but with the same pieces of furniture. The colors were yellow and red, and the walls were clearly white. "This is a guest room in case you want to bring Marie with you. This is the laundry room, study room, and the kitchen. Whatever you mess up, you clean up. Is that understood?" he asked. The tour was quick and we were back in the living room.

"I understand," I said.

"You will not speak of this apartment to anyone outside of your mother, Thomas, Honey, or Marie. Are we clear on that?"

"We're clear," I confirmed. It was clear that Uncle James didn't want any company and commanded his privacy.

"Uncle James, who are you?" I asked him. My question caught him off guard. He did an about face in slow motion, and knew that I was waiting on a legitimate response.

"Take your right hand, Stephon, and place it on the left side of your chest," he instructed me. "What do you feel son?"

"I feel my heart beating."

"What kind of rhythm does your heart make, Stephon? I want you to make that sound on there," he said, pointing to the counter top. I balled up my fist and gave him what he wanted; creating a sound that came from beneath my fist. Boom boom, boom-boom, boom boom, boom boom.

"I'm the other boom in that boom boom," he stated. "The quicker you grow up and learn the rules of the game called 'life,' the quicker you can have that 'boom' back. It's all right for a boy your age to have a lifeline, but a man ain't shit if he doesn't know who he is and has to rely on someone else to keep his ass afloat in this world. You're either going to control your own life Stephon, or someone else is going to control it for you. Right now, it's you and me. So if you want to know who you are, you have at least nine good years to take control of your own life," Uncle James lectured, and like a good student, I listened.

"Stephon, don't you want to live like this?" he asked as he made his way back into the living room, holding his arms wide open and staring out over Austin.

"Yeah!" My response was soaked in enthusiasm. Uncle James turned to face me with a cool look on his face.

"You need to learn to be greater than I am and want more than this, Stephon."

"You don't like all of this, Uncle James?"

"No," he said as he turned back to face the view of the city.

"Why not?" I asked him with much confusion.

"I didn't have good teachers, Stephon, and because of that, I didn't do well in school. What happens if you don't make good grades in school, Stephon?"

"You flunk, Uncle James."

"You're very correct, nephew; you flunk! I flunked for a long time, and when I finally got tired of being labeled as a 'flunky,' son, I started learning how to make good grades. Though I started late, I'm doing pretty well for myself, but I'm not satisfied." He continued to stare out the windows as if he were looking out on Austin for the very first time. He didn't smile and his thoughts weren't in the room.

"I grew up watching my brothers go to school for a few hours a day, and then your father made them work in the fields until sundown. Shit like that made them half of who they are and the other half of them was lost."

I asked, "What do you mean by 'lost,' Uncle James?"

My eyes were stuck on him and my face was twisted with confusion. How a man could lose half of himself was a mystery to a boy my age. He faced me, and I could tell that he was glad I had asked that question by the look on his face. He pointed to the huge leather sofa and told me to sit down.

"I didn't have to be around you to know that you were being told to make good grades so that you can go to college and get a good job.

Don't get me wrong, son, I still think that that's the right thing to do; but it's not the only thing you should do. To hell with going to school all your damn life just to be a good worker. I want you to be larger than just a good worker, Stephon. I went to school from the time that I turned five and didn't stop until I was out of college. Ten years after I graduated from college, I woke up asking myself, 'Who am I?' When I finally admitted to myself that I was just another educated flunky who failed to understand the rules of the game, I got off my ass and went back to school, son."

Uncle James' revelations came covered in frustration.

"I may be up in age, son, but I'm not out of the game just yet. Plus, maybe I'll get to see a little of myself in you before the good Lord sets me on the bench." He rubbed my head after his last comment.

"Okay, nephew, school is out for now. Consider yourself fortunate to have a good teacher like me." He smiled slightly and continued, "Now, let's go get something to eat, and in the process I'll introduce you to some people you need to know if you're going to start hanging out with your uncle."

We started towards the door and Uncle James asked, "Do you have any questions you need to ask me about the rules concerning this apartment?"

I asked him if I could eat whatever I wanted to eat. He started laughing, and I had to smile at him because I had never seen him do that before.

"From this day forward, before we come this way, we can stop off at the grocery store to do some shopping because I eat out all the time," he said in a humorous tone making sure we were both on the same sheet of music.

As we proceeded towards the elevator, a very well dressed lady stood waiting for the elevator, and once she looked around to see me and Uncle James walk up, she began to smile. We all stood waiting silently. We allowed the beautiful woman to board first as the elevator doors opened and gave its view down into the lobby. She was dressed in a burgundy two-piece skirt set and a silk rose colored blouse that shined just a little brighter than the bronze tone of her cleavage. With all the smiling she was doing, deep down inside I knew there was a connection somewhere down the line between her and Uncle James.

"The garage please," she uttered in a smooth, silky whisper. Uncle James pushed the button marked "G" and before his finger could come up off the button, she spoke again. "Thank you." Her smile was mischievous.

"You're welcome," Uncle James said.

"He is a handsome young man," she said softly as she looked at me through beautiful hazel-colored eyes. As he pushed the button marked for the lobby, Uncle James said proudly, "It runs in the family." He cut his eyes just enough to catch her reaction, and never changed his posture.

They both remained quiet the rest of the way down, and when I knew the elevator was about to come to a stop, I looked up at the lady for my last glance. As beautiful as she was, I was just about to give her that flawless award until I saw the scar on her neck. You would have to be looking very closely to notice it hid by her makeup. Whether or not she knew that I noticed it, I had questions concerning who did it and why. Coming from where I did in El Paso, Texas, I recognized old battle scars when I saw them. The "ding" sound from the elevator system broke my thoughts as the doors opened.

"You have a nice and productive day," Uncle James said to the lady before we got off the elevator. I couldn't help looking back and she smiled at me.

"We'll see," she said as the elevator doors closed behind us. We walked up to the front desk in the lobby where a fair-skinned man stood. There was no mistaking that he was born and raised on some island in South America and he had an accent to match his ancestral breed, which he wore with pride.

"Ahhh, Mr. Wilkerson, and this is the young Wilkerson you spoke about, I presume, sir?"

"Yes, Carlos, this is Stephon Wilkerson," Uncle James told him. Carlos held out his hand in good fashion and I shook it.

"Carlos, if this young man ever wanders through doors of this building, day or night, without me, I would appreciate you securing any situation that might need my immediate attention," instructed Uncle James.

"Oh, Señor Wilkerson, please sir, say no more." Carlos assured him with a firm understanding. Uncle James turned to me and continued, "Stephon, if you ever need me and I'm not at home, you ask to speak with Mr. Carlos and he'll take care of the rest. Are we clear on that?"

I looked back and forth between the two of them and said, "Uncle James, I don't have the number."

Carlos quickly pushed his personal company card in my direction but Uncle James stopped him.

"No paper trails for him, Carlos. He'll learn to store the numbers in his head or not have them at all." His statement was firm.

"As you wish, sir," Carlos said, placing the card back into his pocket.

Everything about my uncle was intriguing to me. The way people gravitated towards him showed me that he was indeed a very powerful man. As we drew closer to the dining area of the hotel, there was clear evidence that the playing field was indeed balanced out. The residents of the Tower over Austin were all rich. As we stepped into the restaurant, my perception of Uncle James being "the shit" in that big ass building was shattered because all the residents received the same star treatment that my uncle was receiving.

"Good evening, Mr. Wilkerson and Mr. Wilkerson. Your table is ready."

It was apparent that Carlos had already informed the lady that we were coming to dine.

"Thank you, Melissa," Uncle James stated as he handed her a ten-dollar bill. A waiter stood at the secluded corner table with menus in hand.

"Good evening, Mr. Wilkerson," he said.

"Good evening, my good man," Uncle James replied as he received his menu.

"I'll give you gentlemen time to look over the menu." The waiter nodded in our direction as he waited on Uncle James' approval.

"That will be fine, sir." Uncle James nodded back at the waiter as an indication that he could leave.

"Pay attention, Stephon. I'm giving you two things to remember today, and I expect you to remember them before we leave this table," Uncle James demanded. "804-3171 and 804-2763." Uncle James repeated the numbers five times in a row. I sat there mumbling the sequence of numbers under my breath during the entire meal.

Uncle James stared at me as I finished my dessert of key lime pie with a graham cracker crust. "Repeat the numbers, Stephon." I had learned a long time ago a form of memory building consisting of spelling a word backwards after learning to spell it correctly. It was a game Marie and I had shared since we were in grade school.

"1713-408 and 3672-408." I uttered them so quickly that it threw Uncle James for a loop. I sat looking at him with an innocent look on my face, but inside I was smiling because I knew I had him stumped.

"What the hell was that?" he demanded to know with a frown on his face.

"1713-408 and 3672-408. That's 804-3171 and 804-2763 backwards," I stated again as quickly as I could roll the numbers off of my lips.

"What's the apartment number, Stephon?" he asked curiously.

"That's your personal business, Uncle James."

He looked at me and smiled! I knew he was proud.

"How much money did I give the lady out front?"

"You gave Melissa ten dollars," I said.

"If I told you to walk home from here, which way would you go?" Uncle James wanted to know. It took me a few seconds to think back on the turns we took to get to our table, but I gave it my best shot.

"Behind you," was what I came up with.

"What!" I caught him in the process of trying to swallow a bite of his food and my on-cue response caught him so off guard that he began to choke.

"Behind you," I repeated as I pointed behind him.

"How in the hell would you come up with that, boy?"

"Uncle James, you said that Honey's house was on this side of the building," I stated as I pointed at him again. He got up from the table, threw some money on it, and ordered me to get up.

Once he made it out of the entrance of the restaurant, he looked back towards his favorite table area, back towards the lobby, and back at me.

"Ain't that some shit!" He chuckled.

His rubbing the top of my head meant that I had done a real good job at memorizing things. As we slowly walked through the lobby, a person would have to be lacking in three of the six senses God gave them not to know that prestige and power were breathing off of the aura that the people around me manifested. You didn't have to know it to understand it, because it was felt above all knowledge.

I looked down at my attire and I felt ashamed. I was ashamed of the clothes that I wore, the shoes that I had on, the way that I was raised, the way I talked, and the way that I walked and stood. As I walked out of the lobby, I didn't know if I should have been pissed off at Uncle James for introducing me to the very reason of my shame or because I was sheltered from a life I should have known.

It was clear that everything that I was feeling was manifested on my face and my entire demeanor.

"I want to go home, Uncle James," I said as demanding as I could. Carlos already had Uncle James' car parked out front, running with the air condition on low. Uncle James refused to speak to me or respond to my demand of wanting to go home until we got in the car.

"I don't want to know what's wrong. I want to know what you're feeling," Uncle James declared as he made his way into the oncoming flow of traffic. I really couldn't just come out and tell him how I was feeling and why I was feeling the way that I was, because I didn't know where to start so I just said the closest thing to my discomfort.

"I hate who I am, Uncle James!" I couldn't even look at him. I kept my head turned toward the window to avoid his seeing my watery eyes.

"Boy, I don't ever want to hear you say that again. If you want to hate something about yourself, hate the conditions you've been in, and hate it enough to want to change that shit. But don't hate who you are. Do I make myself clear?" Uncle James was so heated up about what I said that he had forgotten I was a child. "Yes, sir," I said through my tears.

"You might as well stop all that cryin' shit too. I told you I wasn't babying your ass, and I meant that!" he affirmed without remorse. "I'm swinging by in three days from now, and I expect you to be ready at one o'clock sharp. I'm taking you shopping for some dress clothes and some things every man should have. Do we need to go over anything?" he asked as he handed me some tissue to clean up my emotions.

I was excited at the news. I couldn't remember the last time I had gone shopping for new clothes; plus I knew shopping with Uncle James would be the bomb.

"How come we can't go shopping tomorrow?" I asked.

"Be ready at 1:00 sharp, Stephon, and when you get to the point to where you want to start taking care of my business, let me know. So, for now, let me work my business the best way I know how. I have some advice for you, nephew. You stay young as long as you can and enjoy the pleasures of somebody caring enough about you to shield you from a lot of bullshit, and enough to teach you how to fend for yourself."

Chapter THREE

STANDARD PROCEDURE

Getting to know Uncle James, in my later years, became second nature to me, and when he said he wasn't doing anything he felt I should be doing for myself, it was real talk and I was on my own. Whether I wanted to or not, my opinion or outlook on whether I wanted to work every summer for the last eight years meant nothing. It was Uncle James' decision. Each time I looked in his eyes, I was instantly taken back to when I was fourteen and tried to use some weak ass "reverse psychology" on him and pretended to be eager to start a job he had lined up for me that summer. The reality of it all was that I really didn't want to work at all because I wanted to hang out at the pool, go to the movies; hell, just the shit normal kids do at fourteen. My attempts to fool Uncle James didn't work back then and he had a way of showing me that I couldn't pull anything over on him even now.

There was one incident that comes to mind, when I was acting like LaVar Burton in his role as Kunta Kinte in the movie Roots, when it came to giving in to Uncle James and working. One reason was that I was only receiving fifty dollars out of my pay every two weeks, and all the shit about saving my money for a rainy day was not computing at all. Like Kunta, I gave my soul to Master James and me trying to act like I was over-enthused about going to work that one year landed my ass on a grown man's working schedule from 8:00 a.m. to 6:00 p.m. for six days a week under Carlos' watch.

If I would have known my deadline of enjoying childhood would be at the age of twelve, I would have dragged Uncle James' ass through the mud. Carlos reminded me of the Negro slave who the master used strictly for hunting and running down runaway slaves. I labeled Carlos as being "Rochester." Rochester would be on the hunt for that runaway brother, and if Rochester went through hell to catch him, he would beat the slave for the hard work he had to put in to catch his ass. If the master gave him until sundown to bring him back and he did not, Rochester knew he was getting the whip too; so he beat the runaway slave for that too.

When Rochester finally brought the runaway slave back and Master saw that he damaged his goods, Rochester was waiting on Master to say, "Nah Rochester, you know I'm gonna have to whip your nigga ass for bringin' this here nigga back this way." And the only thing Rochester would say was, "Ah, it's okay, Massa; wouldn't have it any other way!"

Whatever Uncle James had on Carlos or whatever Carlos owed him, Carlos didn't swagger to the left or right when it came to Uncle James' demands. I had begun living in the towers with Uncle James. I started out working with the housekeepers cleaning toilets, mopping floors, dusting, polishing silver, and some more shit at age twelve. While all of the adults thought that shit was cute, it was just the opposite in my book.

Carlos was checking on me every thirty minutes on the hour, and like Rochester, he wasn't letting me make it all. My being eighteen didn't mean a thing to Carlos and though I wasn't trying to hear most of the shit he brought my way, Carlos was my boss. I was his personal assistant and I might as well view the title as Carlos' slave. Every time I came close to making up my mind to cut his throat, all I could see was

Uncle James saying, "If you disgrace me in my front yard, boy, I'm going to personally put my foot in your ass!"

There was only one time in my history of ever knowing or seeing Uncle James get rough or gritty with anyone. There were these two petty thugs who tried to push up on him down on Chicon Street. Uncle James had a frat brother living there who had gotten caught up using drugs, so life was hard for the brother. Nevertheless, every first and fifteenth of the month, Uncle James would go by to check on him and try to talk him into getting some treatment. Uncle James would always take groceries to him on those days and whether he shared with the other addicts or not, at least someone was eating.

I guess these two chumps had been sizing up Uncle James for a while, and decided to get stiff with him. Well, Uncle James had always told me to play the hardcore roll and be very passive until within arm's length of your subject. It took the first fool to be an example for the next, and even if the other fool wanted to flex, Uncle James' frat brother was ready to fire a round in the brother's ass. Hearing the heavy emphasis being placed on Uncle James putting his foot in my ass if I disgraced him and how he handled that fool, I wasn't about to do a damn thing against Carlos. For me to complain to Uncle James about how Carlos was handling me would only mean that I was trying to get served some special treatment.

It took me a while to figure out how in the hell Carlos would always know where to find my black ass in a skyscraper with over twenty-five floors in the damn place!

My weekly schedule was always school, work, homework, and sleep. I had excelled in my studies so well that I was going to class four hours a day and working eight hours since the eleventh grade.

Even though I had a heavy schedule, I decided to run down this super-fine ass dime piece from Honduras, and I knew I had to find her on her normal trail. I faded into the employee break room for the first time. The moment I walked in, it was like a black man entertaining a honky tonk bar full of Klansmen down in Mississippi during the Jim Crow days.

The only sound I heard was the hum of electricity flowing from the vending machines. I was caught off guard so tough that me frontin' like I was there to buy a Coke turned into an embarrassing moment. Reaching into my pocket and pulling out a fist full of twenty-dollar bills didn't make shit any better for me either. It wasn't intentional but for me to have done that made me an arrogant bastard.

Even though I didn't know Ms. Honduras' name, she came to my rescue by handing me a dollar bill and in her Central American accent, told me to use it. Conversation started back up in Spanish after she found her way back to her seat, and I was on top of every word within hearing range as I walked out of the door. I soon found out her name was Catalina. From one end of the large break room to the other, Spanish heritage occupied the it, and though I hadn't seen a lot of the women and a few of the men, I knew that Carlos was their lifeline.

I had my afternoon meal delivered up to Uncle James' pad every day that I would work, and I would spend a full hour eating and looking over the city in peace. Once I walked out of the apartment one minute over my scheduled break and found Carlos standing down the hall looking at his watch. That was a sign that the dude was playing me too damn close. Catalina and I had been seeing each other in various spots in the Tower, and not knowing who to trust, I allowed her to pick and choose our meeting sites.

Over the next four to five months of playing the cat and mouse game with Catalina, our emotions began to rise to a level that was new to me. And though I had other puppy-love ass encounters with a few girls at Austin High School, nothing was stronger than what I was feeling for Catalina.

The fact that Catalina was near her mid-twenties, with a lovely five-foot six body frame, with beautiful long naturally curly brown hair, bronze-tone skin, hazel-colored eyes, curvaceous waistline, and an ass that was on the borderline of being labeled in my hood as damn!; caused her body to appear in my dreams so often that I had to keep clean sheets on standby after a long lonely night of dreaming.

As bad as I wanted to finally get Catalina up in the apartment for some extracurricular activity, Carlos was always too close for any of that; as if he had a Lojack placed under my skin. Life with Catalina was crazy because she had gotten to the point where telling me she loved me was natural. Then when I wouldn't respond with an, "I love you too," she would gently kiss my lips and tell me that one day I would feel for her what she felt for me.

To throw Carlos off, I decided to start picking my meal up myself so that he could see me board the elevator. When I got on Uncle James' floor, I would exit the elevator and take the stairs up to one of the other floors that had a conference room, pool, gym or banquet hall and eat my meal there. Carlos was always there to see if I was going to be late getting back down to the lobby.

I decided to spend some time at Uncle James' place and since Marie was attending college at Spellman in Atlanta, my days of kickin' it with her on the weekends were over. It took me three times to see a repeated commercial about DeVry Technical College before I made up my mind. I was on the phone with Mama fifteen seconds later. Though I had made up my mind about it all, the notion of leaving what I considered as home didn't settle well with me and the fuzzy feeling that I felt in my gut wasn't making things any better.

"Mama, I'm moving to Irving, Texas before the summer ends to attend DeVry Technical College."

"Stephon, baby, why don't you just enroll at U.T. and stay home, sweetheart? You won't have to worry about paying rent or any other bill."

"Mama, I'm not concerned about bills."

"You and your sister act like you're tryin' to get as far away from me as you can."

"Mama, I can't believe you said that."

"Where is this damn place at anyway?" she asked.

As soon as she asked that question, I knew I had either her approval or she knew that I wasn't backing down from my decision.

"Mama, Irving is a suburb of Dallas, and it's not far away from you either."

"So you're just going to leave your job just like that?" She acted like the thought was absurd.

"Mama, this job is not what I want to do all of my life."

"Baby, do you know the possibilities at that place?" She conveniently reminded me of how much bullshit people had to put up with once they settle.

"Mama, please keep reminding me how a good Negro can keep catering to people."

"Boy, shut your silly ass up, and that's a horrible way to look at a good opportunity, Stephon," she said in her attempt to campaign for the good folks who ran the Suites Over Austin.

"Have you discussed this with James?" she asked.

"Mama, this is my life, and while we're on the subject, you didn't sell me to my uncle or anything like that, did you?" I asked jokingly.

"Boy, don't have me come up there and whip your ass!" she snapped and I thought she was about to come through the receiver after her comment.

"Let me know you're still my mama then!" The way Mama had repeatedly mentioned my uncle and spoke as if he ultimately had the last say, I had to ask her if she had sold me to him.

I had to laugh because Mama never let me forget that I was never going to be too old for her to threaten to whip my ass. I had to ensure her that I would inform my uncle of my decision as soon as he got back into town.

"Now, Stephon, would Mama even go there?" she stated in a way that I didn't know whether to believe her or not. I knew she wanted the best for me, but I also knew she wanted me close to home and near her.

It wasn't long before the predicted rain moved in. Living high up off the streets of Austin, I had the pleasure of enjoying rain and lightning storms in a manner that someone else would fear. It was the water cascading down the glass wall of the living room that captured a part of my heart. There was an unexpected knock at the door that led me to question who and why, to the point that I went to one of Uncle James' hiding places and brought a .38 pistol to the door with me. No one had ever knocked on his door in the eight years that I'd been around, so hearing knocking was foreign to me.

I stared through the peep hole. It was Catalina, my Honduras mommy. In just the time that it took for me to peep out the hole to see her, she had looked left and right up the hallway which meant she wanted to stay undetected. I quickly opened the door for her. I allowed her to stand there for a few seconds as we stared into each other's eyes with a silent form of communication that needed no explanation. I extended my hand to her, and she gently gave me hers. I brought her in from the rain in her world.

After I closed the door and turned to give her my attention, she stood about five feet away from me. She had a look on her face that was hollow. While she fought all she could to hold her head down, she just couldn't take her eyes off mine. I already knew what she wanted. She wanted me to let her know that I wanted her just as bad as she wanted me.

"For me to ask if you are sure that you want to be here with me would be a silly question, wouldn't it?" I asked.

"I'm concerned about what you may think about me, Stephon," she said.

"Why would that concern you, Catalina?" I was curious.

"I would like nothing better than to give you my very soul, but I am afraid of what my people would think."

"Catalina, is it your people that you have fallen in love with or me?

"You, mi amor," she said. "So, do you want me here with you, Stephon?" Her seductive Central American accent stirred up something in me.

There wasn't a need for further conversation, and I made that clear by walking up to her, placing my arms around her waist, and pulling her close to me. I slowly kissed her lips softly, nibbling on the bottom lip about five times while holding back my tongue. I could tell that she wanted to release her whole heart and soul into my world. The heaviness of her breathing along with the force with which she pressed her body against mine confirmed it. Every time I teased her lips with my tongue and stopped, her breathing would raise her breasts up and down with a build-up of whispers in my ear.

"Please take me, Stephon!"

I gave her what she wanted to taste by kissing her deeply and passionately. Her head tilted back, allowing me full access of her mouth. I allowed my tongue to take full advantage of the sweetness that lay just beyond her lips. Since I was in my bathrobe and boxers already, she didn't hesitate to let me know what she wanted by reaching and caressing between my legs. Her touch was soft at first, but with each movement her grip became firmer and firmer causing me to rise uncontrollably.

"Come with me, Catalina." I led the way to my bedroom. As soon as she entered my room, she turned to face me and started removing her clothes innocently, staring deep into my eyes, never releasing me from her thoughts. She walked into the bathroom, turned on the shower, and called for me in a way that almost brought me to my knees.

"Venga aquí, Poppi," she ordered, clearly informing me that she was about to introduce me to her heritage.

By the time I walked into the bathroom, Catalina's figure was no more than a silhouette moving behind the hazy Plexiglas. I stood still for a moment. Even as a silhouette, her breasts showed their firmness and her nipples were detailed to the very point that only the perkiness of young breasts possess. I slowly moved into the shower to look upon her beauty. As she turned to face me, my last glance was that of the perfect heart shape of her ass.

"Can I tell you what is in my heart?" she asked.

"Will it mean a lot to you?" I asked her.

"Ohh, very much, Stephon," she replied never breaking the direct eye contact between us. I kissed her as my hands rested on both of her hips. Though I wanted to feel the firmness of her full breasts, I knew she was eager to get something off her chest before she spoiled me.

"I do not have a boyfriend for nine months," she said as she held up nine fingers. "Me boyfriend leave me before I come to your country and I see no man but you in my heart, Stephon." As she was explaining her boyfriend situation to me, she placed my right hand as close as she could to her heart. "Me family...me sister...tell me not do it because Carlos get mad—fire me."

"Why did you come to me if you are afraid of what Carlos might say or do?"

"Stephon, I come because I do not give one shit about what Carlos has to say."

"Why do you like me, Catalina? What draws you to me when you fear what your actions may cause?" I asked.

"Me like you for the reason you like me, Stephon. It is in the hearts of us." Her response was wrapped in a certainty that I had not heard spoken by a woman before.

"I'm leaving for school in a few months in another city," I informed her.

"No, Stephon. Please, no go," she begged as if her very life depended on changing my mind. Her beautiful brown eyes pleaded with me and tugged at my heart, but my decision was made. She dropped her head and I knew things were moving like lightning, but everything was surreal for me and Catalina.

"I have to leave, Catalina," I said, placing two fingers under her chin to raise her head back up. Doing so, I saw that she had tears building up in the corners of her eyes. I felt like not only was I breaking her heart, but I was ruining her dreams.

"I will come home on the weekends." I tried to sound reassuring in my words as I kissed her on the forehead.

"You will come see me, Stephon, si?" she asked hanging on to a promise I was not sure I could keep.

"Only when I can, Catalina," I replied. I changed my wording because the way she reacted made me want to ensure there wouldn't be any trippin' if I didn't come home every weekend.

"Next year, Stephon, I go back to my country again. They make me file the papers again for the work visa. Sometime I get it, the papers one week, sometimes six months, but I come back again," she explained.

"It's okay, Catalina," I reassured her that I was cool with whatever.

"Stephon, you go and come home to see me, I promise my heart to you. I go to my country and come back, my heart still for you if you like, Stephon." The words, though broken in form, reached out to me as she looked in my eyes for approval.

"Is that what you want, Catalina?" I asked.

"Si Poppi, that's what I like!" Her smile returned and my body began to respond to the warmth behind it. There was no need for further dialogue, and because Catalina was about twenty-five, I wanted her to teach me more than a few things.

"¿Hará el amor a mí como un extranjero o como mi mujer? I asked her. (Are you going to make love to me as a stranger or as my woman?) She was so shocked to hear me speak in her native tongue that it brought a sexual peak to her demeanor. She didn't care to know how, when or where I had learned her language; she was just content with the thought of me being able to converse with her as a part of her foreplay.

"I want to make love to you in ways that will show you that my heart is yours and only yours if you will accept it." She ran her hands across my chest.

As our tongues began to dance in each other's mouths, I allowed my hands to run slowly along the sides of her body, enjoying the smooth softness of her skin. She arched her back with each movement of my touch and I knew she was ready to feel me inside her. I knelt slightly down at the same moment that my hands reached the small of her back. The water beating down on her body and mine lessened our control. In between kisses and lustful sighs, Catalina began to raise her behind higher in the air welcoming my hands to explore areas I had dreamt of traveling to. I locked my hands around the base of her ass and picked her up into the air. The sound of her exhaling in anticipation was my clue to continue on my mission. At the moment I had her where my piece met the entry point to her wet slit it brought me to a firmness that I had not experienced before. I entered her with ease and I didn't stop until her body had accepted all of me. I positioned her back up against the shower to gain leverage and my thrusts, which were slow and methodical at first, became more forceful and animalistic in nature. The mere act of having sex was exciting, but she and I both knew that I wasn't receiving it in the way Catalina wanted me to have her.

"Baja mi, mi amor," she commanded under deep and heavy breaths. (Put me down, my love.) I stared at her with so much anticipated passion that she felt my staff yearning to continue without interruptions.

"Baja mi, mi amor," she softly repeated as she kissed my lips.

I pulled my man out of her unwillingly, but I knew she had something better in mind for me and had no plans to deny me the depths of her wetness. The moment her feet touched the tile in the shower, she gave me her tongue again and again. I was amazed at her ability to be aggressive and submissive at the same time. She had a way of "giving" herself to me and guiding me at the same time. Catalina quickly turned her back to me, grabbing my hands and placing them on her fine ass hips. I cupped both cheeks with my hands and the firmness of her backside made my blood begin to boil once again.

"Esta manera es más cómoda para usted y yo lo quiero mucho," she said submissively. (This way is more comfortable for you and I like it a lot.)

I slid myself into her and though my experiences with a girl or a woman consisted of Catalina being number four in my eighteen years of living, the depths of her chamber defined all that I imagined doggy style was supposed to be. I can't speak for all men, but I knew that my piece was more than God's standard issue. Seeing her pant the way she was doing as I slid myself into her until my jewel sack touched the rim of her chamber was a moment that was so serene that I paid close attention to what her body was calling for.

I slid out of her until I felt her muscles firmly tighten around the tip of my manhood as she exhaled. Slowly, I descended to the depths that made her moan. Hearing her sighs of pleasure gave me an indication that what she was feeling each time I pressed myself deeper into her was desired. So, I fed each moan with a rhythm of deep, slow and constant thrusts that turned into a dance of pure precision. Her moans were long, soft and soothing like the sounds of sweet jazz.

"Oooh, oooh, oooh," came with the walls of her chamber gripping every inch of me. It was the overdose of moisture that informed me that she had reached ecstasy. Knowing that she was in her moment, I searched her depths for mine in a fashion that pleased her even more. I don't know if it was the firm grip that I had on her waistline or the strong, deep thrusts that I delivered in rapid successions, but the motivation she was feeding me was fuel to my fire.

"Si, si, si Poppi!" she uttered with much approval in my quest to give her my seeds. (Yes, yes, yes, Daddy!) "Oooh, oooh, si, Poppi," came from her in a way that brought me to climax. As I drained my manhood deep within her, we both found air to breathe as we came back to calmness. I pulled out of her, and she was very eager to turn and give me her tongue once again. She released me only to start covering my body with rich lather and bathing every inch of me. When she finished her sensual bath of my entire body, I returned the favor by bathing her as well. During the whole process, neither one of us mumbled one single word. As I watched the suds race down to her feet, I became fully conscious of Catalina's beauty. Her natural bronze tone skin held its balance until I saw the deep brown tone around her nipples.

It was easy to figure out that she had prepared and groomed herself for me once I noticed how neatly manicured her hair was around her garden.

"Stephon, take me to your bed and make love to me as your woman," she said very softly as she held my hand.

Drying off was never an option for either of us, and once we made it to my bed, she felt the need to bless me before I honored her request. We kissed several times before she found her way down on her knees, face to face with my manhood. She looked up at me with a look that needed no explanation as to what was about to happen.

"Para ti Poppi." (For you, Daddy.) The words dripped off her lips before she began taking me inch by inch into her mouth.

Slowly, she took my tip into her mouth until I moaned and trembled uncontrollably as she worked my pride over like a prize fighter. She ran her fingertips up and down my shaft, playfully licking the top with her tongue. Her eyes were fixated on me in between light licks and strong suction. A slow and steady pace dictated her movements at first, but as my body gyrated in acceptance of her actions, she gained both speed and momentum.

Once she felt I was content, she stood up, pulling me on to the bed. She positioned herself on her back and motioned with her finger for me to come in closer. I let my tongue lead me as I slowly kissed and licked a trail up the inside of her thighs. The smell of her sex guided my lips to her honey spot and I blessed it while taking in all of the nectar that resided within her walls.

With each flicker of my tongue, I gently massaged her spot, taking on each side of her clit so as not to miss a drop of her juices. Her legs were bent at the knees and spread in a butterfly position which gave me full access. I knew once the language of passion came up out of her, her river was about to over-run its banks.

The sounds coming from her mouth had me fueled to burn down every structure she had built up between her thighs. It was sheer desire to catch her in the midst of her climaxing which forced me to move from using my mouth to please her and repositioning myself so that I could penetrate her with my stiffness. As I entered her over and over, she held her thighs pressed tightly up against her chest, accepting every inch of me.

"Oooh, oooh, oooh, Daddy, don't stop my love, don't stop! She begged for more with each thrust I delivered into her. I knew once the muscles around the walls of her cave constricted, it was my turn to self-destruct, and I did so in a raw way.

For more than five minutes, she refused to let me move from on top of her. She had a death grip on me, holding me firmly in place on top of her as if her life depended on it. Finally, I had to demand my release.

"Catalina, let me go, baby," I whispered tenderly in her ear.

"Stephon, please stay with me and no go away to school. Good school here in Austin, Poppi," she pleaded with me as she slowly began to loosen her grip.

"I'll come back on the weekends to see you and spend time with you. I have to go use the bathroom now," I stated as I forced myself up off of her.

I came back to her with a warm, soapy towel and cleaned her up. Whether she found pleasure in how I was wiping her down or getting off as I kept running across her clit, the smile on her face let me know that she was very pleased with it. I climbed back into bed with her, and she nestled herself in my arms, and we both laid there in complete silence until sleep over took us.

The smell of fresh baked rolls, candied yams, grilled meat, garlic, and flowers brought me out of a deep sleep. Catalina hadn't moved an inch and had her arm wrapped around me in a way that left me no room to free myself from her. Seeing my bedroom door closed, I knew Uncle James was back in town and two days early at that. Something deep down inside of me went 40 North all of a sudden. Carlos! I thought, with some gangster shit on my mind. The fact that I had made up my mind to leave Austin made finding the opportunity to check that punk high on my list.

"Catalina," I whispered, trying not to fully wake her. Hell, with the apartment smelling like a restaurant, it would take a stopped up nose not to smell all of those aromas.

"Si, Poppi," she said.

"Roll over, baby," I instructed her just to see if that was going to disturb her sleep and it didn't.

I had to remain still for about three to four minutes, and when I heard that sure sound of a deep sleep, I was on my feet and putting on my bathrobe. Uncle James kept a pistol in every room in that apartment. My thoughts of Carlos made me look back at the stash spot in my room where a .9mm was hidden. I shook the thought off and opened my door to see a makeshift mini buffet being kept hot by a low flame underneath each pan. Seeing Uncle James' bedroom door open and unlocked, I released Carlos from the wrath I had in store for him.

I raised the lids on two of the pans to ease my curiosity.

All my favorites, I said to myself. I walked up to Uncle James' door and stood in the doorway watching him work on his computer. He sensed me standing there and turned to meet my stare.

"Sleeping Beauty," is all he said before returning back to his work.

"How come I couldn't be a strong black character or at least a weak white male instead of a white female character? Come on, Uncle James!" I waited for him to respond, but after a few seconds we both just laughed.

"You're home early," I pointed out.

"Sometimes my work is hectic and, when it's going well, I have the choice to come home early," he replied.

"Are you going to be around for a few days?" I tried to pick his brain for a minute.

"Yeah, you want to do a little something together?" he asked.

"I really wanted to talk to you about a decision I've made."

"What? About you going away to school?" he asked with a smile on his face.

"Damn, does Mama tell you everything?" I asked with a sense of curiosity mixed with irritation.

"Stop your fussing son and I don't want to find out that you got on her about that either." He made his statement in a joking manner, but I knew he was dead serious.

"Are you sure that's what you want to do?"

"I'm sure, Uncle James," I emphasized.

"Listen to me son, I haven't been a perfect man and won't ever claim to be, but do you think that I've spent these past years with you so that you can run off to some damn school?"

There was a stiff tone in his voice that surely spelled out disappointment and trying to get in one word to ease him would be disrespectful of me while he was trying to relay his message.

He stood up from his desk and brushed me aside as he walked toward the windows in the living room.

"There are people out there wanting to see the end of me because of the work that I do. I'm not proud of what I do or what I've become, but if it wasn't me, it would be someone else. Do you think I have all these guns around you for mere amusement?"

"No sir." I responded very cautiously.

"I want you to understand what I'm about to tell you," he stated as he turned to face me. "I was hoping that you would one day step into my shoes, but the right way and do something good with everything that I screwed up. It's a very unforgiving world out there boy. You either use or be used and I didn't waste my damn time for you to be the later."

"For the last time, is this what you really want Stephon?"

"Yes."

"Then there's nothing I can say or do about it, but to be behind you one hundred percent. Have you started gathering information, talking to anyone, finding something out about the city, the living space, et cetera, et cetera?" He began spitting out questions to me quicker than I could answer as he looked over the edges of his glasses at me.

"For what! That's why I have you. Besides, you're going to over-see everything anyway," I told him.

He turned back around in his black leather swiveled chair, smiling with a sense of confidence a father would have and said, "I have to make sure your behind stays safe from any harm or bullshit. Your mama would be torn up to know something was wrong with her 'baby'."

"Aren't we full of jokes this afternoon, dear uncle?" I smirked and shifted my weight to my left leg. "I've contacted admissions, and they're sending you an enrollment package. I've contacted the leasing agent at Pioneer Parkway Apartments that are located in a good area of the city, and it's time that you have your own car so that you can stay your ass out of mine."

"I was hoping you'd let me have the Benz to take with me," I said in a sly manner. Since he was taking care of everything else, it wouldn't hurt to ask. He looked over his shoulder at me and said, "Keep hoping, boy!"

"These apartments: Are we going to see them before hand or what?" I asked.

"As soon as the leasing agent faxes me back, we'll head that way and buy furniture that day," he stated.

"Uncle James, is there anything I need to do?" I chuckled.

"Yeah, go tend to your girlfriend," he suggested with a smirk on his face. "Don't tell me, Carlos, right?"

"Boy, you know I'm not going to lie to you: Carlos!" he said.

"Uncle James, I need a favor," I informed him with a serious tone and an emphasis on need. He turned to face me and took his glasses off.

"Boy, don't mind the look on my face. It's very rare that you ask me for anything and when you do, I give you my undivided attention."

"Her name is Catalina. She feels like Carlos is going to ride her ass about us being involved. Can you see that she gets her space and some respect?"

"Is this your girl we're talking about or just something to screw?"

"Uncle James, I'm claiming her as long as she's claiming me," I professed.

"Enough said!" With that Uncle James put his glasses back on and went back to work.

"Can I throw in the other half of the favor before we end this conversation?"

"Damn, son, how many halves are there?" His smile showed that he liked me asking for his help.

"Uncle James, work with me, baby, I'm on a roll here. I want Catalina to have my job and same pay."

"You got to be kidding, Stephon!" He jolted up, taking off his glasses again at the same time.

"What would I be joking about, Uncle James? The job or the pay?"

"How in the hell do you expect me to pull that off, Stephon?" The smile was gone.

"The same way I ended up working for Carlos at twelve years old, Unc!" I walked over to his desk and handed him the phone so that he could get that trick on the line.

"You're dead serious about this too, aren't you?" he asked with an I can't believe this shit look on his face.

"Uncle James, absolutely no static on Catalina. He trains her well, and not just to be his flunky like he's been doing me." After hearing me say that, Uncle James was up on his feet.

"You're telling me that Carlos has been using you as his personal flunky?" he asked. He was angry and the lines in his forehead, the look in his eyes, and the harsh tone of his voice proved it.

"Yeah, Unc! I really haven't learned shit, and he has never allowed me to be close enough to any of the residents or visitors to really learn how to be a public-relation staff member," I informed him.

"The son-of-a-bitch has given me good progress reports on you all this time. Saying stuff like, 'Oh, Mr. Wilkerson, he's been a great member of our staff'. The bastard just told me that shit four days ago." Uncle James was outraged. "Back to Catalina." He started to put away his work and continued, "I'll personally see that she gets your job, your pay and advances to any level she works toward, but I won't be holding her hand on this shit either." Uncle James stopped and turned to me. "Stephon, go tend to Catalina." His statement was more of an order than a request.

I walked out of his bedroom and found Catalina standing in the living room in a bathrobe crying. I grabbed her hand and took her back to my bedroom.

"Why are you crying?" I asked her. I wrapped my arms around her.

"I come looking for you and hear you talk to Uncle about me. Why do you do this for me, Stephon?" she asked through her tears.

"Do you want this, Catalina?" I pulled her closer to me to comfort her.

"Poppi, I do not know how to work the work you and Carlos do," she replied.

"Catalina, how much is your pay?"

"Three hundred, seventy-five dollars a week only."

"You will now make six hundred dollars a week, Catalina."

"Six hundred dollars, Poppi?"

"Yes!" I stated with much assurance. "Catalina, that's a lot of money for you and your family."

"Stephon, I hear you tell you uncle that I am your girl as long as I want you. That makes me cry because I like Stephon." Tears continued to run down her face accompanying her words.

"I will make you uncle very happy and will not, how you say, 'dispunt'?"

"It's 'disappoint' girl," I chuckled holding her tighter.

"Yes, disappoint you or uncle," she said trying to muster a smile on her teary face.

"Stephon, Carlos will not do me bad?"

"No, he will treat you right, Catalina," I reassured her with a flurry of kisses. I took her by the hand, and we headed to the shower. Catalina had sex on her mind, and me telling her "no" disappointed her because she wanted to express her gratitude to me. We were out of the shower and dressed with intentions of sitting down with Uncle James for dinner, but he was gone. Wherever he was headed, Carlos was going to be his final stop!

"Stephon you uncle…"

I stopped her before she could finish her sentence. "Catalina, look at me," I ordered her. I lifted her chin so she could look at me and looked down into her beautiful eyes. I took a few seconds. "Are you willing to let me help you?" I asked her.

"Yes, anything, Stephon," she replied.

"I want you to take a class." Saying that confused her. "School, esquella Catalina, para tu langua," I explained. "For your speech."

"Will you do this for me?"

"I will do this for you. This esquella will make me better; no?"

"Yes, it will make you better," I said but couldn't help laughing at her.

"Why do you laugh at me?" she asked as she threw a piece of bread at me.

"Because I like you the way you are, but the people want you to be like them," I stated.

"Carlos once talked like me and he go to the school too?" she asked.

"Yes, he probably did mi ruca," I said in a sexy way (my girl).

"Stephon, you know Spanish very, very well, and you trick me when you talked to me," she said with a flirtatious look on her face.

Suddenly, the door to the apartment was slung open as if someone kicked it open. From where Catalina and I were seated at the dining room table, I couldn't see what or who was coming our way. I quickly grabbed Catalina and headed towards the kitchen stash spot to retrieve a weapon. I opened the dishwasher, took the .45 automatic off safety and waited on whatever was coming our way.

"You get your sorry ass in there and apologize to my nephew before I lose my damn cool," came from Uncle James' mouth.

"Mr. Wilkerson, I meant no harm or disrespect sir," Carlos pleaded.

"Haven't I been good to you? I got you where you are today, and this is the treatment I receive from your punk ass!" Uncle James never gave Carlos time to respond. He snatched him by his tie and drugged his ass to the living room. "You disrespected me and my family, Carlos!"

"Uncle James," I called very calmly to remind him that Catalina was still in the apartment.

"What!" he shouted in my direction. Seeing the frightened look on Catalina's face, he released Carlos. Uncle James looked at me and saw that I was placing the pistol in my back waistband as Catalina stood behind me to shield what I was trying to do from Carlos. What came next really caught me by surprise because it came from a side of my uncle I had never heard. "Perdóneme por favor y mi genio la Sra. Catalina. Soy trastornado muy con este hombre porque me faltó al respeto y mi sobrino. Es un hombre muy malo," Uncle James explained. (Please forgive me and my temper, Ms. Catalina. I am very upset with this man because he disrespected me and my nephew. He is a very bad man)

"Por favor señor, pregunto que usted no hace daño a él como un favor a mí. Ha ayudado muchas de a mis personas encuentran trabajo aquí en este lugar; para mí, señor," (Please sir, I ask that you do no harm to him as a favor to me. He has helped many of my people find work here at this place; for me, sir.) Catalina begged Uncle James sincerely.

"Do you care for my nephew the way that he cares for you?" Uncle James asked her.

"He has always been very kind to me and never has he disrespected me because of who I am or because of where I come from. Yes, I care for him in ways that he is not ready for me to do so," she explained with watery eyes.

"¿Catalina, Se fía de él?" asked Uncle James. (Catalina, do you trust him?)

"Sí, hago!" (Yes, I do!)

"Entonces usted se fía de mí," stated Uncle James. (Then you trust me.)

"Carlos," Uncle James called out, giving an indication that it was his floor.

"Mr. Stephon, I apologize for treating you the way that I did, and please know that I didn't mean you any harm. I apologize for disrespecting you and your uncle, and ask that you forgive me for overstepping my authority," Carlos pleaded with a great sense of fear. As he explained himself to me, Catalina stared at me. I knew this was not the time to put on an I'm hard with my shit show to impress Catalina or to finally get back at the punk ass dude whose life was in jeopardy. Whether or not Uncle James wanted me to assert some authority, I kept Catalina in mind.

She knew this was an opportunity I could take advantage of, but hearing her beg Uncle James not to do the fool, and her compassion for his welfare caused me to be the bigger gentleman. I made it my business not to say a word to Carlos because I knew my frontin' would not go over well with Uncle James. So, I did a gangsta move neither one of them was expecting. I extended my hand with an ice-cold look on my face. On the cool, I was saying to myself as I stared at him, Bitch ass dude, I really want to kick your ass for handling me the way you did.

"Thank you, Mr. Stephon," Carlos sighed with much relief.

Catalina sat looking pleased, and was satisfied to know that I had a heart.

"Carlos," Uncle James looked at him in a way to let him know he was clearly not forgiven.

"Yes sir," he responded to Uncle James and took a few steps toward Catalina."Catalina, you will have his job, and I will teach you everything I know." Carlos took a deep breath and continued.

"I will not be mean to you or disrespect you ever; this I promise you. You will also get his pay as well."

"Carlos, please leave my home, and if you ever disrespect me, my nephew, or this lady again, I'll send you back where I found you. If I find out that you are not teaching Catalina as she should be taught, I swear to you Carlos…" Uncle James stressed his promise to Carlos. "Please leave my home," he ordered him.

"Yes sir," Carlos said as he walked out with his head down like a dead man walking.

As soon as Carlos shut the door, Catalina came to me quickly. She stood behind me, lifted my shirt, and removed the pistol from my waistband. She held it carefully in both hands, looked up at me and said, "No, too much trouble for you," and walked over to Uncle James and gave it to him.

"You are very kind sir. I thank you and I won't let you down," she told Uncle James before finding her way back to my side.

"Stephon, yo tango hombre," announced Catalina. (Stephon, I am hungry.)

"Hey, no more Spanish around me unless I ask for it. Do you understand?" I conveyed to her. "If you are to do better with your speech, you start now, okay?"

"Okay, okay. I understand, Mr. Man," she jokingly stated. We all turned our attention toward Uncle James' bedroom door. The sound of his fax machine caught all our attention.

"I have to get to work." His demeanor immediately changed as he looked at me. "I don't expect Catalina to be spending a lot of time up here since you will be leaving soon; but I want her to know the rules, and put this back where you found it," Uncle James instructed as he handed me the pistol.

"Catalina, do you have to work tomorrow?" he asked, speaking directly to her.

"No, me not work until Monday."

"Damn boy!" Uncle James said as he had taken a quick glance at Catalina's hips while she wasn't looking. "You're in for a long ass weekend boy!" He chuckled walking towards his room.

"Catalina!" he shouted from the doorway of his room, "You stay here for the weekend if you like."

"Thank you, but only if Stephon want me to stay," she answered back keeping her eyes locked on mine.

"Catalina," Uncle James shouted as he laughed, "believe me, lady, Stephon says it's okay!" We all laughed.

Chapter FOUR

CROSS ROADS

Three months had passed since I decided to move to Irving. Deep down inside, I was tired of the whole Austin scene without my best friend being around me. Although Marie and I talked every other day, shit wasn't the same anymore. I had two weeks of paid vacation time built under my belt, and I spent both the time and the money on Catalina. I did for her what Uncle James did for me, but on a peewee baller's budget. I took her to see the "Lioness", a.k.a. Ralph Johnson. He wanted to be called "Lioness" because he had a style of his own for a gay brother. Not only did he represent that lifestyle, but his clients ran the streets as his personal calling card.

For every gay brother who decided a process perm was his calling and wanted an edge, it was done and created by the Lioness. Ralph had two spots and two levels of clientele: the millionaires of Austin and those who paid a grand. Uncle James made a phone call to get Catalina a spot in the Lioness' book uptown. The standards weren't going to be bent for him, so he settled for a squeeze in appointment downtown. Catalina went from being the shit to being top-flight shit! At

every stop we made, she cried. Shoes…tears. Dresses…tears. Suits…
tears. Manicure and pedicure…tears. Dinner back at the crib…more
tears, and a lot of sex.

Catalina and I met with Carlos and reassured him that the confronta-
tion that went down wouldn't leave the apartment. Catalina had told
me soon after leaving the meeting with Carlos that her main objective
was to move Carlos out of his position and out of the building.

Asking her why brought our conversation to a heart-to-heart talk
and on some shit that Uncle James should have told me. Carlos came
to the states illegally looking for work. He was only fourteen at the
time, and his willingness to work caught Uncle James' heart. Carlos
started washing towels at both of the Lioness' locations; washing and
ironing clothes and shining shoes for every frat brother who was connected with Uncle James in the Austin area; sometimes until about
four o'clock in the morning.

Uncle James would give him fifty dollars a week out of all the money
he made, and every six months, Uncle James would give him five thousand dollars to send to his family back in Honduras. Every time Carlos
would ask him about the amount of his savings, Uncle James would
show him his bank statements. Carlos and five other people shared a
rented house that belonged to one of Uncle James' frat brothers; and
because the brother vowed out of the goodness of his heart to give
back, he never charged anybody rent. It's been twenty years since then,
and people are still coming and going from that same house. Although
those same frat brothers are now in the corporate world, they are still
helping Catalina's people.

Catalina's reason for wanting to drive Carlos out was because he had
forgotten where he came from and was insensitive to the needs of his
people. Carlos handled me the way that he did out of a fear of losing
his position and the influence over his people to me.

The Tower Over Austin was more than just fine upscale living for the
able bodies. It was a beacon for immigrants who wanted fair working
wages as regular citizens and an employment outreach center. Carlos,
having full contact with "nay" and "yay sayers" of the city, could get

up to fifty requests a week for maids, gardeners, builders, painters, and any other position that his people could fill.

I asked Catalina what made her feel she could do a better job than what Carlos had been doing for more than ten years. Her response was that her people often passed on rumors about Carlos being a tyrant towards his people and that there were some who wanted to bring numerous threats to the front door of his lavish home, hoping he would change his ways.

"Plus," she added, "I'm prettier than he is."

Understanding why she was head strong on seeing Carlos out of the way, I personally mapped out what I thought would help her achieve her objective. To me it was more than just obtaining work and a place for her people to lay their heads at night. I made her understand that she had to build a world for those who were here legally, and continue to provide for them.

I showed her the importance of creating an allegiance for the people she would eventually help who would become citizens one day. She had to become bigger than Uncle James' frat brothers for the sake of her people's existence and well-being in this country.

I explained to her the difference between a slave and a flunky, and she ran into the bathroom, locked the door, and started crying. It took me twenty minutes to get her out of there; and that was due to me explaining that I was trying to get myself out of a flunky level.

Nevertheless, I'd been in Irving, Texas, for three weeks, and although class didn't start for another two months, Uncle James was paying me seven hundred dollars a week to work out at the gym two times a day. It was under the watchful eye of a personal trainer and nutritionist for five days a week.

It was six o'clock in the morning and I was standing out on my balcony watching the city come alive. I had a view of the Irving Mall and also Highway 183, which led fifteen miles into Dallas one way and twenty miles into Fort Worth the other way. Working out the way that I was and traveling to Austin to see Catalina, I hadn't had the energy to get out and check out the city.

For the first two weeks, Catalina had begged me to come home every day. She kept me in between her legs when I did go. I would leave Austin at midnight, pulling up to my crib at 2:45 in the morning; which wasn't about to happen this weekend. Hell, my answering machine only held fifteen calls, and nine of those were from Catalina. I had to admit the loving was excellent, but I needed some "me time".

The fact that Uncle James had paid my rent for the year, along with my cable, phone, electricity, gym fees, and had also given me a gas card, meant that I hadn't spent or checked on the account I had at Irving National Bank because I had been living out of my pocket.

Though I had clothes and shoes in my closet that I hadn't worn yet, I made up my mind to get out and hit the city, and my starting place was the mall.

I missed the hell out of ordering my meals up from the restaurant; even more so, after Catalina started her new position. The older ladies who were either from Honduras or Mexico City took turns coming up to the apartment to cook me home-cooked Mexican food. I hadn't eaten such deep-rooted food since I left El Paso. Catalina told me that refusing their generosity would be a form of disrespect to the ladies, and once Uncle James found out about it, like he does everything else, he would surely be upset about that. He was always telling me to allow Catalina's people to show their gratitude. He stated that the smallest gesture is big to them and means a lot if we accept it. Well, it was now all about eating trashy tasting take-out and cooking up my own version of bullshit.

I was the first one in the bank and I felt kind of funny standing in the lobby trying to decide which teller to go to. They all looked at me with a look that said, Man, just choose one and bring your ass on!

One cute redbone waved me to her counter, and I didn't hesitate to move. "Can I help you with something, sir?" she asked.

Being six feet, five inches tall, I was able to see more of her body than the average height brother.

"Nice outfit, and being that we might be close in age, we can get past the formal issues if you don't mind," I suggested.

"I get paid to address even a child as 'sir' in the bank," she said with a smile.

"So by me being a client in this joint, I have the right as a client to be addressed in a manner that is comfortable with me. Yes or no?" I asked. She started giggling and answered yes.

"My name is Stephon Wilkerson. What's yours?" I asked.

"LaShonda Conners," she replied.

"I'm glad to have met you LaShonda Conners."

"The same here, Stephon Wilkerson. Now what can I help you with, Stephon?" she asked amongst cheeks that were beginning to turn red from her blushing.

"I would like a statement of my account for last month, please," I stated, handing her my savings book and exposing my account number. She typed my number in the computer and her eyebrows rose. She hit a key on her pad and the copy came out. I saw why her eyebrows were raised after she handed it to me. Uncle James had opened up the account with fifty-thousand dollars, and just as he promised, I had a total of twenty-one hundred dollars for the three weeks of working out.

"I would like to withdraw the twenty-one hundred please," I requested.

"How would you prefer your bills, Stephon?" she asked, her professionalism steady.

"Any way you want me to have it, LaShonda."

"You all throw some nice parties," she stated as she counted out the money in hundred dollar bills.

"I'm lost on that statement, LaShonda."

"Your apartment complex."

"Well, I've only been living there for three weeks, and things have been pretty dry."

"I'm very surprised to hear that because it's usually a weekly thing at your complex." She gave me the 411 as she continued counting bills.

"Well, I guess me moving in kind of killed that, you think?" I jokingly stated.

"If another three weeks go by and they haven't thrown one, I'll agree with you on that," she replied laughing slightly, never missing count.

"May I have an envelope please?" I asked.

"Sure, would there be anything else I can help you with, Stephon?" she asked.

"As a matter of fact, there is. The name of a very nice place to have dinner. I'm new in this city, and today is sort of my breakout day to do the city."

She became enthusiastic, smiled and said, "I know a very romantic spot that you'll enjoy, and the food is off the chain."

"You visit the place quite often?" I questioned her reaction.

"I wish. My brothers took me there for my birthday last year, and I haven't been back," she said.

"Why not?" I was curious to know why, since she liked it so much.

"On what I get paid? Please!" She had no problem about revealing her financial issues.

"Where can I find this joint?"

"It's connected to the Four Seasons in Las Colinas."

"LaShonda, is that supposed to ring a bell for me or is this your way of testing to see if I'm lying about just moving here?"

She started laughing. "I'm sorry, Stephon. I forgot just that quick."

She started drawing me a map on the back of the envelope she was giving me.

"This is where you live, and you won't get lost if you follow my directions," she said as she slid the envelope toward me.

"Now that you wrote all over my envelope, can I have another one?" I requested.

She smiled. "Oops, I'm sorry."

I placed two hundred dollars in the second envelope and gave her a warning as I slid it back to her.

"If the food isn't good, I'll be going to another teller whenever I come back in here," I told her as I turned to walk off.

"What is this for, Stephon?" she said with a curious smile.

"You said you hadn't been back to the place. Well, dinner's on me."

As I found my way back on Beltline Road, which was a main drag through the newly built area of the city, I saw that Uncle James had made sure that I was within distance of everything. Beltline Road was part restaurant row, three or four grocery stores, gas stations, shops and apartment complexes out the ass.

I went all the way up Beltline Road until I got up to Highway 114 just as LaShonda instructed me, just to know that I was on point. I busted a U-turn at the light, and saw DeVry College as I made my way back down the other side of Beltline Road to get closer to what I needed to know about my area.

Finally, I caught a spot in the parking lot of the mall that was in view of my apartments. Since Dillard's was a main store where I shopped, I started on familiar ground. As soon as I made my way past the makeup counter, it was all eyes on me, and I was in my element.

I made it a habit to size up every brother I ran across on my mental scale, and if his dress code was fresher than mine, I was adding his shit to my forte. I was introduced to a style or dress code that made an average full-grown man envious. It just wasn't about cotton or silk button downs, ties, slacks, or shoes, but more about the details in my attire. I had passed up six brothers who kept it real and threw up the nod or said, "What's up" and they all rocked the typical jeans and T-shirt.

Was I over-dressed? I wore a pair of half-baggy-pleated, one-inch cuffed emerald green slacks, a white, silk, pinstriped shirt, which I wore open to show a white silk tank top. Along with my diamond-stud earring, olive green, tinted glasses, white on white Nike low- quarter tennis shoes, and a fresh cut from one of the Lioness' barbers; hell, I was the mall!

The fact that Irving wasn't predominately any color had me feeling like I was in the hood and the hood was out. I was being watched by every ethnicity God created for man, and I was pleased.

"We have some new perfume from Lagerfeld. Would you like a test?" a sister at the lady's perfume counter asked.

"Are you receiving a commission on the sale?" I asked.

"Of course," she said with a smile.

"In that case, I want two bottles; one in the box and the other gift wrapped," I instructed her.

"But you haven't even smelled it yet," she said, puzzled.

"I enjoy anything he comes out with. Are you going to sell it to me or not?" I asked with a smile.

"Walk this way, sir, and I'll be happy to fix you up."

"It's Stephon."

"This way, Stephon, and if you don't mind me saying so, you have a nice name. It fits you," she added.

"Is that part of the sales pitch?" I asked.

"No it is not… and I'm serious. It's a nice name, Stephon."

"So if my name was Rufford, you wouldn't be saying this?"

She started laughing. "No, I wouldn't be telling you this," she said. "Please have a seat." Her grin widened as she pointed at the counter stool.

"I'll just take my items and leave since you're being rude," I said with the intent of getting her attention.

"Rude? I'm not, nor have I been rude to you, Stephon." She placed her hands on her round hips, bringing out a bit of "sista girl" in her stance.

Somewhere between twilight and the norm, I flashed back to some of the finest sisters out of the hood in Austin. The ones that claimed their own status outside of the so-called "want-to-bes" or so they were called. One thing that stood stiff as a difference between the women in El Paso and the women here was the thickness and sexy sass of my fine ass sisters.

"I don't hear you telling me your name, and you've practically drug me by my feet to this counter," I said as I sized her up from head to toe.

She started laughing as she told me her name, which was Monica.

"Now I'll feel better about giving you my money."

"Stephon, you need to stop!"

"Okay, I'm cool now, but I try not to deal with strangers," I told her in a fly ass tone. "Sixteen ounces," I said.

"Both of them?" she asked, as if I didn't know what I was asking for or questioning my ability to pay for the shit.

"Are you selling me the items or not?" I asked, letting her know that I was fully aware of what I was getting.

She started scanning the boxes, punching in some numbers, and finally gave me the total.

I had a habit of placing my expected spending money in my right pocket so that I wouldn't be pulling out a wad of money. I handed her three, one hundred-dollar bills, and she gave me my change.

"What time do you get off?" I asked her.

"Now that's personal information, Stephon," she said as if I was trying to get my flirt on.

"Listen, Monica, I would like to swing back through on my way out, and pick them up if it's not a problem because I don't want to sit around waiting on the gift wrap," I explained. Once I killed the flirting notion, she put on a fake-ass smile.

"Oh, that won't be a problem. I don't leave until four p.m.," she said and I could sense a bit of disappointment in her voice.

"I'll be back then," I said, walking off.

"Stephon!" she shouted, "What color wrapping?"

"I trust your judgment, and by the way, nice outfit and shoes you have on." That brought her spirits back up.

Dillard's was Dillard's no matter where you went; so I moved on. The more I stopped and looked, a lot of brothers were average, dedicated mall shoppers because more than a few of them had worn the same outfits that were on the mannequins. Seeing the store employees wearing their own products was crazy. I ended up buying a few suits, some linen wear for the next party at my complex, some nice suede loafers, and some sandals. Going up the mall was like I was walking the red carpet in Hollywood, and coming back down, it gave way to everyone who was waiting on me to come back their way.

On my way up I saw a few things that I thought Marie would appreciate. Living in Atlanta made her picky about certain shit, and her calling a few of my gifts too "Texan" meant that they were country; all except the shit that came in green with pictures of dead presidents on them anyway.

I had more telephone numbers weighing me down than my own bags after picking out some things for Marie, Mama, Honey, and Catalina. I was amazed at how a woman would go the distance to put it down when she wanted you. Monica was eye to eye with me as I walked back into Dillard's.

"You find what you were looking for?" she asked in a flirty way.

"I'm not the hunting type, Monica."

"I'll say!" she said. "Around here they don't mind hunting you down," which was her way of insinuating that she wasn't a part of that crowd.

"Would you consider their actions as knowing what they want or doing whatever it takes?" I asked.

"I can't speak for them."

"I was really referring to you, but I didn't want to violate a code of yours and get hit with 'I'm asking about your personal business.'"

"I'm from Arkansas and as country as I am, I'll say that I'm used to being pursued. I don't do the pursuing," she said.

"So, how long have you lived in Irving?" I asked.

"I don't. I live in Arlington."

"Well, I have no idea where that is."

"Either you're full of shit, Stephon, or you just moved to this area."

"Consider yourself a smart woman, and I'm not full of shit either."

"Welcome to Irving!" she said and gave me a smile so warm I could feel her sincerity.

"It's past noon. Can I buy you some lunch, Ms. Arkansas by way of Arlington?"

"Are you serious?" she asked surprisingly.

"Damn, did I just violate another rule?"

She started laughing. "No you didn't, and stop going there. I only have an hour."

"You're not allergic to seafood are you?"

"No, Stephon," she said smiling.

"Do I need to go to my pad to retrieve my pistol in case I need to bust your man in the ass?" I asked with a serious look.

"I'm happy to say that I'm single right now."

"Now that sounds like some bullshit right there, girl!" It was hard to believe that the beautiful woman in front of me was without a man to provide and take care of her wants and needs.

"I'm serious, Stephon."

"I guess I don't have a choice but to take your word on that." Now I was smiling.

"Talking about me...what about you? Do I have to worry about a woman running up on me?" she asked.

"You can fight, can't you?" I asked jokingly.

"Since you don't have but an hour, find a Red Lobster that's close; tell them you want the special and a bottle of white wine."

"What is the special?" she asked.

"Ask about the grilled cod, shrimp and broccoli."

"You tell them what you want, how you want it, and it's done. Have them reserve a table with a five minute arrival time," I instructed.

"Give me a few minutes to make the call and to get my purse. By the way, here are your items, and I hope you like the wrapping."

Lunch with Monica turned out to be a venting event for her, and she really appreciated my being a good listener too. The fact that I wasn't trying to push up on her meant a lot to her, and she had much respect for me. Hell, it seems like Irving was a breeding ground for hunters, both male and female; brothers putting their mack down and the ladies doing likewise, from the gas stations to the grocery stores. It was going down.

On my way to my apartment, I decided to do a drive through my entire complex just to find out where everything was. My complex had two pools, but only one had a clubhouse attached, and after seeing the size of the damn thing, I could imagine the size of the parties thrown there.

There were two parts to my complex, Phase I and Phase II. By the time I made it out of the maze of my side, I crossed the median that separated them and discovered even more. Tennis courts, ponds, and large hot tubs were the highlights in Phase II. From what I was seeing, there was going to be a party going down tonight. Sound systems were being tested, balloons being blown up, lawn chairs being positioned. Hell, even the Budweiser van was unloading.

The first person who came to my mind as I looked around was LaShonda. I hadn't made up my mind if I was going to crash the party or not, but I was definitely going to run by after I sampled the cuisine LaShonda talked about.

I had had enough of my personal tour of my surroundings and had some sleep on my mind. I noticed this middle-aged sister who could pass for an aging Lisa Raye, with the salt and pepper style working like she had just fallen out of the Lioness' chair. She wore a burnt orange silk pajama short set while she stood on her tiptoes to water a plant in a hanging basket. I was caught up between how her shorts complemented the roundness of her ass and the tank top that only came down a few inches past her breasts. Hell, if I was walking down the sidewalk I would have had a good look at her goodies under those loose fitting shorts. I could see her breasts clear up to her nipples the way she reached up to water the fern. The first thing that came to mind was, "store bought".

She caught me looking, and to add some humor to the situation, I placed my left hand over my eyes for a quick second just to let her know that I was busted. When I looked back up at her, she just smiled and kept doing her thing.

I wasn't in the door good when the phone rang. I saw that I had seven messages flashing and though I couldn't review them just yet, I had a feeling my little South American Queen had been on her daily.

"Hello," I said as I waited to hear "Poppi" on the other end.

"Damn, your ass move away from home and you get too grown to call your sister; huh?"

I smiled with joy when I heard her voice. "Hey, baby! I miss you like crazy. Where are you?"

"Atlanta! Where else would I be? We have Keith Sweat, Babyface and some group I've never heard of opening for Sweat and Face tonight,"

She bragged on with a level of excitement that was off the scale.

"Just stab me in the heart, Marie. I thought I was your favorite brother."

"Boy, you're my only brother and stop trippin'. I've been calling your ass all morning to see if you could make this gig. It was a spur of the moment purchase, and I had to call the big gun to get the tickets."

"Who the hell is the big gun?" I was curious.

"Uncle James silly!"

"If he had to step in, the tickets were a grip."

"Only four hundred," she said.

"For one?" I know she could tell how shocked I was by my tone.

"Yeah!"

"You could have paid me to beg for your ass for that change," I told her. "When are you coming to see me, girl?"

"I'll try to make it before your classes start up. I heard you got you a bangin' Mexalina," Marie teased. "Trying to hold on to your roots, boy?" she teased and I could tell she was enjoying every minute of it by her laugh.

"Shit just happened like that, Sis."

"So how do you like your apartment and your freedom?"

"I'm feelin' this shit, but it ain't right without you here to kick it with me."

"You'll get used to it, little brother. Just keep your company limited and enjoy your privacy," she advised. "I'm surprised Mama and Honey haven't crashed in on you yet. That's all I've heard... 'My baby this, my baby that.' I cut all that whining shit short and reminded them that you are grown now."

"Now you see what I had to put up with for months after you left the crib," I told her.

"You got plenty of rubbers?" she asked without the humor.

"Some rubbers?" I replied. "Why would you ask me some shit like that?"

"Boy, a fine ass young buck with money. And you're probably out dressing everybody in the city. And by the way, I heard about your Jag.

Boy, you're breakfast, lunch, dinner, and a late night tidbit for 40% of those women. Don't let your, 'cross the border sister' have to come down there and regulate some shit!" she said laughing.

"Sis, I got this."

"Okay, you got this," she quickly replied.

"To hell with all that, you need money, girl?"

"Stephon, now you know when I called Uncle James about the tickets, he tripped on me. Not about the tickets, but because I couldn't spring for them myself. He wired me five grand on top of all the shit he talked."

"I know you're not broke?" I asked her.

"What? You referring to my savings? Boy, I'm not touching that shit until I finish the quest. So yeah, I'm broke. For the record, I know Uncle James opened up an account for you. Just to let you know, he keeps tabs on your spending to see if you're a fool."

"How'd you find out?" I wanted to know.

"Hell, I arrived here with six suitcases filled with some brand new country shit, and when I saw that I was Elli Mae, I hit the mall and got my shit right. It wasn't two good weeks and his ass was up here in the flesh raising hell about me withdrawing eight thousand dollars the first day I was here. I made him take all of my clothes back to Texas, and he returned it all plus sent me the amount of the money to put back into my account."

"Thanks for the heads up, girl. Listen, I bought you a few things and they're not country."

"Hold it for me and I'll pick them up when I get there. I have to go, young buck. I have to find something to wear that nobody else will have on," she said.

"Well, you can always shop the country stores in Texas," I teased.

"Bye Stephon! I love you, boy."

"Show me you love me by giving me that ticket to the show."

"What did you say? My connection is breaking up." She hung up the phone but I heard her laughing at me before we disconnected.

I checked my messages and come to find out, Catalina only called once.

"Hello Poppi. I'm a little sad right now because I'm not looking at you face. I mean looking at 'your' face, but I just wanted to tell you that I love you and miss you. Call me tonight." Her voice started some tingling down below, but I had to shake that feeling.

I popped in some Frankie Beverly and Maze and hit the shower to relax myself. I microwaved some barbecue brisket I had bought at the grocery store two nights before. As I stood in the kitchen butt-ass naked, some yester-year flashed across my mind that I wasn't ready for.

Go to school. Get good grades so that you can get you a good job. Educated flunky came into my thoughts.

Why are you here, Stephon? I asked myself. You're either going to control your own life or someone is going to control it for you, were the thoughts that replayed in my mind. Am I here to find out who I am? I asked myself. "This shit is crazy," I whispered to myself.

Suddenly I heard someone right outside my apartment door. Some old habits don't change. I opened the oven door, grabbed a .38 pistol Uncle James had given me, and walked to look out the peep hole.

A white girl came across my sights with some papers in her hand. I moved to my front living room window to catch her next move. She was dropping off notices about tonight's party. I glanced at the clock on the wall as I headed back to the kitchen to put the pistol back.

I made up my mind to just chill after dinner. I set my alarm to go off about six o'clock, and laid down. I must have fought that beep, beep, beep, beep from my alarm for thirty minutes without knowing it because it was 6:30 p.m., and I still felt cheated out of my rest. I stared up at my ceiling for another thirty minutes before I finally dragged my ass out of bed to get dressed. Keeping in mind where I was headed to dine, I was undecided about a full suit and tie or just a blazer. I had to remind myself that I was eighteen years old and needed to relax a bit.

I ended up doing the fool anyway and whether I was overdressed for the joint or not, Uncle James wouldn't have had it any other way. It was 8:00 p.m. when I stepped out the door, and the sun was setting with a fiery glow. My complex was alive and functioning on all cylinders. I drove passed Lisa Raye's apartment and noticed her lights were on. However, there she stood in the yard as I passed by, waiting on her dog to finish doing his business. She didn't wave and neither did I.

I followed my "you are here" marked with an X map that LaShonda had drawn for me all the way to the front door, and the girl was right; it was high end. It took me twenty minutes to get seated, and my wine was on the house because I had to wait on a table.

Every time a table came open, it was always a seating for four or more. I respected the game and allowed a group to take the table. It didn't make sense for me to hog a spot just because I could; so I waited on a booth. By the time I was seated, my table was swarmed by the manager and my waiter introducing themselves and apologizing for the delays.

They say good things come to those who wait and from my point of view…it was storming and lightening good things.

The manager of the joint gave me a voucher for my next meal. I received one hundred dollars from the first couple whom I let take my spot the first time, an envelope with two hundred dollars in it from the second group, and a business card from a third gentleman who was the Vice President of Operations at Zale's in Las Colinas. On the back of the card was written "next meal is on me". I was to present the card to the manager of the restaurant, and my meal would be placed on the man's tab. I instructed the waiter to place all of the cash on a tab for me. Dinner turned out to be at the top of my ultimate meals that had ever entered my body list, and although the bill was seventy dollars, I can honestly say that I'd do it again with my last piece of change.

Upon leaving, I couldn't help but take a look at what the Mandalay Four Seasons Hotel held in statute. One thing's for sure, I was glad that I got dressed because anything shorter than what I had on, security would have been all over my ass. I gave the place a five-star rating, and declared it a T.K.O. victory over the Tower that Uncle James lived in.

Like any other black man, I was full, developed niggaritis, and was ready for some rest. I would say that I was about a block away from the Phase II complex when I turned Kenny G. all the way down just to see if the party was crunk; and the closer I came, the more my hormones jumped for some play time.

I took a left turn into the driveway that would lead me past the clubhouse and pool, and shit was going off the chain. Looking at the dress code, the white linen piece would put me on the map. I sat there watching everybody do their thing, trying to convince myself that the party would be good for me; but I just wasn't ready for the crowd.

By the time I made it upstairs, I saw a small platinum-colored box with a matching ribbon tied around it, and a card attached sitting on my doorstep. I picked it up and took it inside with me, curious as to its contents. The only person in Irving who knew my address was LaShonda. Nevertheless, I popped open the card to see if the identity was enclosed, but it only read, "Welcome to the neighborhood." I opened the box to find three chocolate-dipped strawberries.

As I walked towards the kitchen to trash the calling card, I saw that I had two messages. Hitting play, Uncle James stated he was just calling to check on me and Catalina was next. I didn't waste any time punching in her digits.

"Que pasa sexy?" I delivered with some sugar on top.

"Hey, sweetheart, I was going to start crying if I didn't hear from you by the end of the hour," she said.

"Stop it, girl. One weekend away from you and you're in a panic."

"What is panic?"

"That means to worry—get scared," I explained.

"Now you really make me cry, Stephon."

"Baby, you call me more than once a day."

"I miss you so much, and then you break my heart when you didn't come to me this weekend." I could hear the tears in her voice.

"Catalina, I was just tired, baby."

"Is that why you haven't been at home all day?" she asked.

"Catalina, let's get one thing straight. From this point on you don't question my time, and there is no checkin' me." I felt my temper rising and knew my tone let her know it.

"Baby, I don't understand what you say," she said. I could hear the tears coming, but I didn't let that stop me.

"You understand clearly, so don't give me that shit. If we have to live with conditions that I don't want in the first place, then I'm going to stop this. Am I clear?"

She didn't answer me.

"Am I clear?" I made sure that the tone of my voice left no need for questions about my seriousness.

"Yes Poppi." I could hear remorse in her tone.

"I'm eighteen years old and you are twenty-five. You want certain things in your life that I am not ready for, baby. I like you a lot, girl, but you have to give me time to grow. Am I not good to you, Catalina?"

"Oooh, yes. Very good, Stephon." She was almost apologetic in her response.

"Then what's the problem? What's wrong, Catalina?"

"Baby I'm just scared to lose you to another woman, Stephon."

"Catalina?"

"Yes, Stephon?"

"Ask me if I want to leave you." I began to relax and let my words soothe her fears.

"Do you want to leave me, Stephon?" I could tell that although she asked the question, she was afraid of the answer.

"No, Catalina, I don't want to leave you," I assured her. "I am not a full man yet."

"Oh, yes you are, Poppi!"

"No, Mami; not yet."

"Poppi, please tell me that you will give me the first chance to be the wife in your life when the time comes for you," she said.

"Catalina, you are the most beautiful woman my eyes have ever seen, and you are good to me; but when I'm ready for that, and if you're still down with me…then, 'yes'."

"What is this, 'down' thing, Poppi? I no understand that word."

"If you are still by my side."

"Oh, Poppi, I stay. This I promise you and I stay loyal to you also, Stephon."

"So, we are okay now, yes or no?" I asked her.

"Si Poppi, esta bien," she said. (Yes, Daddy, we're good.)

"What did I tell you about speaking in Spanish when we talk?"

"Stephon, I can't help that sometimes, I have spoken Spanish all my life, stubborn man," she chuckled. "Why is it that you only allow me to speak Spanish to you when we are making love or when we are intimate?" she asked.

"Because I always want to feel Catalina Marie Malano in my soul when it's just you and me," I said. "Do you have a problem with that?"

"Catalina Marie Malano will be yours until you no longer need her in your life, black man." I loved the bold way she answered.

"I appreciate that, Catalina."

"Poppi, do you eat good? I worry because I am not there to bring you food like you like it."

"Yes, I eat good, woman."

"The ladies ask about you all the time, Poppi."

"How is Carlos treating you?"

Her voice changed, becoming more intense. "Very well. He teaches me too much sometimes, all day long, and with the college every day, I am tired and want my Stephon," she confessed.

"Are your classes helping you?"

"Yes, baby, they are very good for me."

"Are you moving closer to your plans on Carlos?"

"Yes, Poppi. Every day and the people like me. First the ladies don't like me because the men smile at me, but I give the ladies my loyalty as another woman and they know it."

"So, you're cool, right?" I asked.

"Yes, Poppi."

"Catalina, tell the ladies I would like some tamales next week when I come home."

Catalina got quiet and I heard her sniffle, so I knew she was crying again. "I will tell them, Poppi."

"Why are you crying?"

"I'm happy that you are coming home to me, Stephon, and I am very happy for that," she replied. "I have a surprise for you, Stephon." "

"What is it?" I asked.

"No, when you come home. Okay?"

"Catalina, are you pregnant, girl?"

She started laughing. "No, Poppi! I get pregnant with your baby when Stephon says he's ready for our baby, crazy man," she said. "Just come home, mi amor."

"I'll call you tomorrow."

"Okay Poppi. I love you, Stephon."

"Yes, I know, Catalina."

I already knew that not telling her that I loved her cut like a knife, but she told me that I would come around to saying it one day.

My muscles were sore as hell from those two-a-day workouts, and I needed to relax before Monday came around. I went over to close my patio blinds and I saw just what I needed. From where I stood, I could see the hot tub bubbling, and the fact that no one was around made it perfect in my book.

Catalina had talked a little trash about me not bringing my clothes home for cleaning, and doing so would give the ladies something to give back to me for getting Catalina set up. So to avoid her raising hell, I started gathering my dirty clothes instead of taking them to the cleaners. Every time I would go into my dresser drawer, I had to search it for yet another pistol. I had found three so far around the apartment, and Uncle James wanted a full account of all of them when he came to visit. I had put the hunt on hold several times, but needed to get on top of it for my sake and not his.

A fully loaded .9mm handgun, two towels, and a bottle of water accompanied me to the hot tub; and being that it and I were all alone made it all good. I did about five hundred pushups and squats to expand my soreness before getting in the water, and I hoped like hell that it would end my discomfort.

I wasn't in the water ten minutes when I heard the latch on the gate to the hot tub pop. Keeping my cool, I placed my hand under my spare towel and on my pistol. After seeing who it was, I relaxed. Lisa Raye smiled at me.

"I don't mean to disrupt your solitude, but I have a lot of questions I would like to ask you. But if I can't start with the first one, I'll be disappointed." she stated.

"Disappointed in whom? You or me?" I asked.

"Me of course," she replied.

"And why would you be disappointed?"

"A sister my age still likes to know that she's still in the game one way or another," she replied as she slowly turned in a complete circle to show me her graceful package.

"I'm listening," I stated.

"First, is there room for me in your tub?"

I stood up and offered my hand to her. Before she took it, she pulled the bow that held her wrap around her waist, which cascaded to the ground revealing more than I imagined.

"Nice color," I said referring to her thong.

She took my hand as I helped her into the hot tub. I sat back down as she stood in front of me with a bottle of wine and two glasses in her hand.

"Second question. Can I offer you a drink?" She teasingly toyed with the ends of the wine glasses in her hand.

"Is it cold?" I asked.

"Of course! A moment like this requires the coldest touch," she stated in a way that brought my curiosity to attention. She handed me the bottle. I opened it and filled both glasses as she held them.

"Where would you like for me to sit?" Her question was dripping in innuendo.

"Where I can see the best," I replied in a touché manner for the comment she made about the coldest touch.

"So, do you have a name?" she asked.

"Please call me Stephon."

"My name is Fran, Stephon."

I started smiling and she had to ask me why.

"When I saw you on your patio earlier today, and after getting a good shot at such a beautiful body…"

She interrupted me. "Well, thank you," she commented on my compliment as if I was telling her something she didn't already know.

"I labeled you Lisa Raye."

"Lisa Raye? As in the actress? Hell, I think I'm finer than she is and better looking at that!" she boasted.

"I guess that's my bad, isn't it?" I said.

"You meant good, though. The girl does have a nice body," she admitted. "So where are you from?" she asked as she continued shifting her body in the water.

"Next question."

"Are you single?" she asked.

"Next question."

"What's the use if I keep asking the wrong questions?" She looked at me puzzled.

"I feel that you already know the answers to the questions, Fran. Thank you for the gift you left me on the porch."

"You're very welcome. Can I cook you dinner tomorrow?"

I wasn't ready for dinner with Fran so I said, "What about lunch?"

"Is there something special that you prefer, Stephon?"

"I'll let you surprise me," I said. "So tell me, Fran, why me?"

"I'm picky. Is that a crime in this state?"

"Am I going to regret this?"

"If you give me half the chance, I think you will enjoy me, Stephon," she said, lifting her glass up for another refill.

"So what do you do for a living, Fran?"

"I'm a consultant for a group of female investors."

I told her it sounded interesting, and she could tell just how thought provoking I found her line of work to be.

"My clients are very picky and too demanding at times; but they are very good to me."

"What is your schedule like?"

"Twenty-four hours a day, six days a week," she reported.

"Seriously?" I asked.

"Baby, Sundays are the only days my phone doesn't ring, and that's the only day I can really sit on my fine ass!"

"That it is, I might say," I agreed.

"I'm usually on a flight some damn where trying to take care of them and then back in town by Friday night or Saturday morning."

"So who cares for the pooch?" I asked, even though I wasn't a bit concerned about the mutt. I really just wanted to see who was coming around her apartment.

"Ooh, that's such a harsh word to call my baby, Stephon. Her name is Gee-Gee and when she's not traveling with me, I leave here with a sitter. Where do you work?"

"Nowhere at the moment, but I'll be looking in about a month."

"A month!" she exclaimed, surprised at my answer. "You must be doing pretty well not to be looking for work right now."

"I'm doing all right; but I still need a job."

"What was your last job like?"

"I was an assistant to the concierge at some high-rise condos."

"Baby, I have a perfect job for you, and you'll fit in just right with your tall, fine ass," she declared and began eyeing me up and down.

"And what would this job be, if you don't mind me asking?"

"An assistant hotel front desk manager. There's no question you have what it takes. Hell, that's all a concierge is, a hotel manager on the cool!" she stated.

"I might consider your offer, Fran."

"Nonsense, Stephon, I'll give you the name and number of my contact. You two talk and that will be the end of it." She waved her hand in the air as if to indicate that she was finished with the whole topic. Her mind was made up.

"Just like that?"

"Just like that!" She grinned at me with a look of power that assured me she liked being in control.

"It's getting late, Fran, and I need some rest. Please let me walk you home."

"And a gentleman too." She stood up, took a step up on the first stair inside the hot tub, exposing her goods in the sweetest of forms. Being the young man that I was, her actions worked because my manhood stood at attention like a true soldier. I wore my stiffness with pride. She raised both eyebrows and smiled.

As I got back to my pad, I glanced slightly over my shoulder toward Fran's place and saw her standing in the shadows of her balcony watching me.

"Shit, she can watch my every move," I said to myself. I didn't like it. My privacy was being compromised. I went to sleep thinking about my options. My asking for another apartment behind an old school who wanted to put me between her thighs wasn't bad at all, but it's the after drama that worried me.

I didn't bother setting the alarm last night because there was no way my body would let me sleep past ten o'clock. After my much needed piss, I had to do my Sunday ritual of calling the house because not doing so meant I messed up somebody's whole day.

"Good morning, Honey."

"Hey, whatever your name is." Her reply was cold.

"Now what's that supposed to mean, Honey?"

"That means you and your sister act like you don't want to fool with your grandmother since you all's hot asses moved away from home!"

"Honey, you need to stop it! I don't come home for one weekend and all hell breaks loose."

"Hell, when you're here, you're with Catalina all damn day. You don't want me to cook for you on Sundays like I've been doing for your black butt since you left little Mexico; but that's all right though."

"Honey, I'll be home next weekend."

"Yeah, you comin' cause I'm raisin' hell about how you and Ms. Thang just threw me to the curb."

"So, what are you planning to cook for me?" I asked her.

"You just bring your tail home, boy. Here's your mama."

"Hey, baby."

"Hi, Mama. Man, did she wake up raising hell?"

"Child, your grandmamma has been raisin' hell since you left. She just misses you coming by doing lunch with her and bringing her those little fancy desserts."

"Mama, I call Honey at least five times a week."

"Baby, Mama knows. Just stroke her ego, child. As soon as she gets her fussing ass in church, she'll talk her sisters' ears off about how her grandbabies call before church."

"Well, you know Marie went to a concert last night, so call her before Honey leaves the house," I informed Mama.

"Child, your sister can be in a coma, but Sunday morning she'll wake up out of it to call home. Don't worry about her."

"How are you doing, Mama?"

"I miss my babies too, but I would rather see you two doing what makes you happy no matter where it is."

"I'll be home next weekend, Mama."

"All right, baby. I hate to run you off, but Honey's almost dressed and you know what that means."

"I love you, Mama."

"I love you too, Stephon."

Man, let me call this girl before we both get disowned, I thought to myself as I dialed Marie's number.

"Yeah," Marie answered as if she had been dragged through the mud all night.

"Damn girl, you sound ugly as hell this morning."

"Stephon, you missed it, boy," she said with a crackling voice.

"We'll talk later. Honey is about five minutes away from walking out the front door for church," I reminded her.

"Shit, bye, boy," she said and hung up.

804-2763 is a number I've only dialed three times since I was told to store it in my memory.

"Carlos speaking."

"Carlos, where is my uncle this very minute?"

He was very reluctant to tell me for a second. "He's in Miami, sir."

"When is he coming back?"

"I do not know the exact hour, but it will be sometime today, Stephon."

"Tell him to call me as soon as he pulls up, and this is not an emergency Carlos," I stressed.

"Yes sir."

Now to Ms. Sentimental. The phone didn't get a good full ring in before it was answered.

"Hello," came through the receiver in an authentic Mexican swagger.

"Catalina por favor," I asked in a language I knew the person would understand.

"Espeda te por favor," I was told (Please wait). A few seconds later, Dellia, Catalina's sister was on the phone. From the time that I found out that the two of them were sisters, I quickly questioned the bloodline because Dellia's figure was built up like an avocado.

"Hi Dellia."

"Oh, Stephon, how are you today?"

"Fine and you?"

"Just fine, Stephon. Your Catalina is busy working on a surprise for you. You call her later please, okay."

"Thank you, Dellia."

Now I was really curious about what Catalina was doing, but I wasn't going to worry about that. It was almost eleven o'clock, and I had to get ready for Fran. I thought about the job offer at the hotel, and though Mr. Ellington, the Tower of Austin's manger, and I weren't good associates, I had to get Uncle James to make sure I received a good recommendation.

I reached in the cabinet to get a fresh towel and ran into the fourth pistol, another .38, with a pearl handle.

This shit is out of control. I saw having all this armor around to be unnecessary, but I grabbed a pen and wrote the location of the discovered ones down, and made up my mind to talk to Uncle James about it when I saw him.

I found just enough time to tidy up the place before heading over to Fran's. As I opened the door to take the trash out, a small personal envelope fell from the crack.

"What do we have here?" I whispered as I glanced across the street to see if Fran's patio blinds were open.

I guess she didn't have a need to put the big eye on me if I was going to be there in the next thirty minutes. I waited until I got down to the trash bin before I opened the envelope.

I guess you cancelled the notion of being the reason why a party hadn't been thrown. I thought you would have considered showing up, but maybe next time. Hope to see you again.

LaShonda

I ripped the note up and tossed the remains in the trash bin with a mental reservation to see the red bone early in the week.

Well, I guessed lunch was ready because Fran was on watch, and I wasn't dressed yet. The wind was blowing so lightly that there was no way it could cause several of her blinds to move. Their movement let me know she was watching me. I was back out of the apartment and headed her way ten minutes later.

As I passed her patio, she told me that the door was unlocked. I couldn't get up the stairs good without fighting my way past the aromas she had set loose on the neighborhood. As soon as I opened the door, I was met with growls from her dog, Gee-Gee.

"Gee-Gee, be polite and get out of the way. Don't mind her, Stephon."

"I would hate to lose a leg up in here behind a jealous ass dog," I stated.

Fran began to laugh. "Baby, my girl weighs about four and a half pounds on a full stomach, and if she was that bad, I'd be selling puppies to the U.S. Marines by morning."

"Damn, you look good in anything you put on, Fran."

"Stephon, are you trying to flatter me?"

"Call it what you want, but I'm calling it like I see it, lady! Whatever you have cooking ain't legal."

She started laughing. "Are you referring to my food or what's on my mind?" she asked.

"Both on the cool," I replied.

"Stephon, have you ever had a woman who was able to be straight forward with you?"

"Only one," I said.

"How did you like that?" she asked.

"So far, you're doing okay, Fran." I knew she wasn't expecting my answer, which brought a smile to my face.

"So, it doesn't bother you at all?"

"I would prefer it that way."

She took me by the hand, led me to the dining table, and even pulled my chair out for me.

"Do you treat all your guests in such good manner?" I inquired.

"Baby, I hadn't done or had time to do anything for a man in six months. I hope you don't mind me taking full advantage of this situation."

"I'm curious now," I stated, and we both smiled knowing what was ahead. Fran fixed my plate. I quickly knew that she was accustomed to eating at restaurants by the looks of the silverware setting, the water and wine glasses, and the position and amount of food on the plate she brought me. The rolls were wrapped in a cotton cloth and placed in a basket.

First, it was fillet mignon, asparagus with a cream sauce, thin slices of yam topped with a sweet syrup, and red wine. Second, there was lobster tail, steamed broccoli florets, and white wine.

"I hope you don't mind, but I took the pleasure of cooking you two types of dessert; one cold and a hot one. The question is which one you would prefer?" she asked as she cleaned my hands with a warm, damp towel.

"Whichever one you'd like to give me, Fran," I teased.

"I hate to ask a man if he's sure about what he just said."

"Then why are you asking?"

"I want you to have the hot one first," she said as she took me by the hand and led me into her bedroom. She took off my shirt as I slipped out of my sandals. As she looked into my eyes, she asked, "Stephon, have you ever made love to an older woman?"

"Any woman older than I am is an older woman to me, Fran."

"Okay," she said as she pulled my pants down and patted my legs, signaling for me to step out of them so that she could hang them up with my shirt. She then slipped my briefs down and kept her eyes glued on my piece.

"I'm talking about a woman my age, Stephon. Ooh Lord! And you're healthy all over too." Her eyes were fixated on my pole and she began to caress it with both hands.

"No, I haven't," I confessed while she pulled her dress off, revealing her naked body.

"There are special guidelines you should know about us and how we prefer things; and if you would like to learn what those things are, just kiss me and I'll teach you," she promised. I knew I was in for a deep, intensive learning session, and I was willing and eager to learn.

I moved in on her lips slowly and hesitantly as I came within tasting distance. We made our connection leisurely, off and on. I gave her the chance to advance her tongue into my mouth, and though we teased each other with only the tips of our tongues, I was cool with it. She pushed me back on the bed and began to school me as only an older woman could.

"Stephon, never assume what she wants, but allow her to ask for what she wants or wait on her to advance on where she wants to take both you and herself. Never be in a rush or too physical because we are past the age of the rough shit. We want it slow, long, and deep." She knelt down and took the head of my manhood deep within her mouth. Her motions were slow and deliberate as if she were savoring every inch. As she worked her mouth and tongue around my stiffness I felt my eyes roll back in my head. Her attention and suction were like none other I had felt before. After about two minutes, she was back to the lesson of the day.

"I already know that you wanted me to take in as much as I could, but we don't kick it that way because we enjoy savoring the meat and its strength, Stephon." With direction and demand from her eyes, I scooted up in the bed and she climbed on top of me. As she slowly slid down on top of my piece, she just sat there with her eyes closed as her muscles contracted around the tip of my piece.

"Can you feel that, Stephon?" Her voice was labored as she asked the question.

"Yes," my reply was simple because it was all that I could muster.

"My muscles are adjusting themselves to your measurements, and you have to give us a few minutes before the dance can begin. You see, a younger woman wants her's used as quickly as you can beat it up, as long as it's constant. Us, on the other hand—we want it slow, long, and deep." She placed her hands on my chest for leverage and raised her body slowly towards the edge of my tip and slid back down slowly.

"Always allow us to move on our own without all the grabbing and handling, Stephon. We like using the tool in a way that better suits us instead of the tool 'using' us. A lot of men don't know that the more they stay out of the picture, the longer the dance is," she explained with an air of confidence.

"You see that small timer on my night stand?" she asked.

"Yeah," I moan in rhythm with her movements.

"How much time has elapsed from zero?"

"Nine minutes," I stated.

"I want you to keep an eye on it from time to time. Relax. Lay your hands to your side and let me borrow you for a while," she said as she slowly rode up and down on my swollen piece. Her breathing was paced and smooth. I would tighten my ass muscles to help give her more every time it got good to me; but she would stop, open her eyes and let me know that my actions were in error.

"Stephon, relax baby. I don't need you right now. Again, I just want your piece."

She continued her ascending and descending motion, and closed her eyes again, finding her rhythm when she felt that I was relaxed.

"Slow, long, and deep, Stephon, that's how we like it," she whispered. "What does the timer say?"

"Eighteen minutes," I said wanting to be a good student.

"Oooh that's good," she said. She came to a stop, climbed off me, and asked me to stand up. My stiffness was yearning for some relief and she had exactly what I wanted.

She reached over to her nightstand, grabbed a towel, and cleaned me up.

"This is a real test for you, Stephon," she cautioned. She then turned and got in the doggy style position. "Put it in slowly, baby, and I want all of it. When I feel your nuts touch my ass, don't move." I slid my soldier all the way in her as she requested. "Place the palms of your hands on my back," she further instructed. "Pull halfway out of me slowly and put it all back where you started." She was clear in her demands and I did exactly as told.

"Again," she directed. I did as I was instructed, waiting on my next command.

"Now, do it five more times the same way," she ordered. Her juices were flowing so thick. Every time I went in and out of her, her body gave up a mating call of pure joy between her legs as she continuously accepted me with every slow thrust.

"Stop, Stephon!" she barked out.

"What's wrong?" I asked.

"Do you know how I know you are doing you and not doing me?"

"How?" I questioned.

"Your hands are around my hips, and you have a firm grip on me. Put your hands back where they are supposed to be and relax. If you're pressing down on my back just slightly, I'm going to stop you again. Now, halfway out and put it back where you found it. Do that ten times. Stop and look at the timer. Slow, long, and deep. Slow, long, and deep." She chanted ten times and I stopped to look at the timer.

"Forty-one minutes."

"Ten more times, Stephon, and I want your palms barely touching my back—go!" she ordered. I fed Fran slow, long, and deep. I knew she was coming because her muscles tightened up around my piece, never wanting to let go.

"Oh, baby, you're doing good, Stephon," she moaned.

After a few more thrusts from me, she grabbed another towel and cleaned my pole up again. As an incentive, she placed as much of it as she could take into her mouth fifteen times. She stopped, laid back on the bed, raised her knees up and opened her legs.

"Pass this test for me, baby, and I'll let you have your way with me until you get enough," she promised.

She took two fingers and parted her lips, causing her clit protrude out. "Do you see that little piece of meat right there?" she said, pointing with her other index finger.

"Yes."

"This is what makes us happy," she smiled as she continuously played with it while I watched intensely. She reached her orgasm, and started class again.

"Come to me. Put it in slowly, and I want it all." With every inch, I felt her muscles eating and eating me the deeper I went.

"Ooh, I love feeling your nuts up against my ass like that. I want you to lie down on top of me, and place your arms under my back. Now, the trick to making us happy is to make love to me—not screw me, Stephon. The difference between screwing and making love is when men screw, it's all about you going in and out of me without giving that piece of meat the attention that it needs; but when you make love, I get all the cock you can feed me and I get my spot massaged while you're feeding me. Look at the time, baby. I want you to give it to me until the hands get back to zero. That's ten minutes, Stephon, and then you can have your nut. I don't want you to start holding me tight or trying to get aggressive. Just let me borrow your tool for nine minutes beginning right now."

I started my flow in one direction, and switched it up another way. Every time I fed her that way, I brought forth an "aaah" which let me know that she wanted just that. The timer went off and I refused to release her clit until her muscles tightened around my cock. Slow, deep, and long, I whispered in her ear twice. I kept feeding her for several more minutes until her walls contracted, and I didn't stop feeding her until she relaxed.

I pulled out of her and stood up.

"What do you want, Stephon?" she asked, fully and completely satisfied.

"I want you to clean me up."

She grabbed another fresh towel and did as I requested. After she finished, I led my piece straight into her mouth, and she didn't hesitate to accept it. I let her continue until she was full. She stared up at me waiting on my next instruction.

"I want it from the back, Fran."

"Oooh, you're going to kill me," she said, positioning herself in the manner I desired.

"Stephon, baby," is all she could say when I slid into her. I slowly fed every inch into her, and placed my hands in the center of her back like she had instructed me to do. She had one thing to say, "My baby." Little did she know it wasn't about to be the halfway shit. I wanted it to the tip and back to my sack in medium motions and not slow.

"Aaaaah, aaaah, aaaah, baby, please don't stop," she begged between my thrusts. About twenty strokes later, her muscles contracted, and I acted a fool with it.

"Ooh , ooh baby," came from her until she felt my climax. She wanted to lie down after I exploded, but I refused to release her until I was completely done. The moment I released her, she laid there in a fetal position with a smile on her face.

"Do you think you could remember everything I just taught you?" she asked.

"Thank you, Fran," is all I said.

"Can you remember it, Stephon?"

"Fran, every word, every do and don't; the works," I assured her.

"By the way, you can have the job if you can start next Monday," she said.

"In a week?" I replied.

"Yes or no, Stephon?"

"I'll take it!"

"There's an envelope on the dresser with all the information you'll need concerning your contact and directions to the hotel."

I walked over to the dresser, opened the envelope, and saw five one hundred dollar bills in it.

"So, what's the money for?" I asked. I was trying hard to keep a straight face.

"Final lesson Stephon, and I don't mean it lightly. If one of us pursues you, you make sure they bless you for blessing them."

"So, I'm a whore now, huh?" I didn't know if she heard the fumes beginning to boil in my voice or not, but I didn't know what to feel. Disgust. Disrespected. Proud. Numb.

"Aah, baby. Never that, Stephon. I just want you to know that if you're going to let me or any other woman use your piece the way I did, make sure you're appreciated. That's all. A lot of men don't want to take the time to spoil women my age the way you just did; and when we find someone who will care for us in that manner, it's only right that we take care of you. Baby, I make fifteen thousand dollars a month. Do you think a mere five hundred dollars will make or break me? I'm only home Saturday nights and all day on Sundays, whether you have time for me or not. All I want is to cook you a meal, put my timer on and bless you for blessing me. Stephon, I don't care about personal lives and won't ever meddle in yours. One day a week for a few hours. And if that's all the time you want to give a sister, I promise you, baby, I won't complain."

"Just like that?" I asked her.

"Just like that, baby!" she said, snapping her tangerine painted fingernails. "As a matter of fact, sweetheart, let's take a shower because I have to start packing and I have to take Gee-Gee to the sitter's. I don't mean to rush you, but that's how my life is, Stephon."

"I'll just wipe up and catch a shower when I get to my pad." School was over for the moment, and I was ready to leave.

She got up, wrapped her arms around my neck and kissed my check. "Thank you, Stephon, I needed that so bad. Are you coming by next Sunday for lunch?

"Pack your things early so that you won't have to be in a rush. I'll be here by 3:00 p.m., I have a meeting to go to."

"Fine, Sunday at 3:00 p.m. Now, get your fine ass out of here before I forget that I have priorities." She slapped me on the ass as I walked away from my first lesson in cougar seduction.

Chapter FIVE

STRAIGHT IN

I had been in the shower just long enough to soap up when the phone started ringing. Everybody knew that I was close by if the answering machine didn't pick up the call after the third ring. Dripping with soap and water, I had to get the call.

"Damn, boy, are you on top of something strange?" asked Uncle James.

"I was in the shower."

"What's so urgent that it can't wait until I can get up into my own damn house to take care of?"

"I knew Carlos was going to put some emphasis on you calling me. I specifically told him to tell you that it was not an urgent call Uncle James."

"Doesn't matter now, what's up?" he asked.

"I got hooked up with a job at a hotel as an assistant front desk manager. I thought I needed a letter of recommendation, but that may not be necessary now."

"So what, you're straight in?" he asked.

"Hell, come to think about it, you took the words right out of my mouth. Yeah, straight in. I'll be talking to my contact in the morning because I start in a week."

"So where is this place?" he asked.

"About ten minutes from here," I replied.

"Well, consider it a good thing, son. You'll have the opportunity to save you some money. So, when are you bringing your ass home to see about this whining ass woman of yours?"

"How would you know she was whining, Unc?"

"Stephon, she's the first person I saw when I stepped in the damn building!"

"I'll be there this weekend. Are you going to be around? I have an interesting story to tell you."

"What day are you coming into town?" he asked.

"I'm coming early Friday because I need to be back in Irving before two o'clock."

"I'll be home Saturday morning. That will give you enough time to deal with your girl," Uncle James said.

"Unc, tell her to give me time to get out of the shower, and I'll call her back."

"I'll talk to you later, son."

I'd have to put an end to Catalina putting Uncle James in my business like that. It was twenty minutes before I got back to her, and I knew she was waiting impatiently.

"Hey, Mommy."

"I don't feel like Mommy, more like a stranger, Poppi."

"Damn, baby, why are you sounding so down, Catalina?"

"I have to wait another week to show you your surprise. That's why," she admitted.

"Well, I'm not sounding down, and I have to wait to give you some gifts that I've bought you," I told her.

"Poppi, you buy me gifts!"

"Yeah, crazy girl."

"I'm crazy because I am in love, Stephon."

"With who?" I asked trying to sound irate.

"Stephon, don't make me come down there and kick your ass, black man!"

"Damn, baby, I was just playing."

"Not like that, Poppi," she stated seriously.

"How much do you love me, Catalina?"

"I am ready to have your children, Poppi. Is that not enough?"

"Yeah, that would be enough. I have some good news and some bad news for you," I told her.

"I want the bad first."

"I'll be leaving Austin about eleven or twelve noon Sunday."

"Baby, noooo!" she shouted as if she were in physical pain.

"Can I finish talking, woman?"

"This better be good, Stephon, or I will cry!"

"I'll be there Friday in time to have lunch with you. How good is that?" I asked her.

"Do not play with my heart."

"The right word Catalina is, 'emotions'."

"I am learning as fast as I can, Stephon, she cried in frustration. Baby, don't play. We will have lunch together. Yes?"

"Yeah!"

"Now I am happy again," she said joyfully.

"So you understand that I am leaving early Sunday?"

"Poppi, you told me and I hear you, but I do not want to ask you why because I don't want you to be upset with me."

"I am starting work next Monday, not tomorrow, but next Monday at a hotel." I only gave her half the story.

"Poppi, you do not have to work, I will take care of all your needs, just go to school and come home to me."

"Catalina, don't start girl!"

"Yes, Poppi," she stated in a defeated tone.

"Just for you my crazy-in-love Honduras, Mommy. I am telling them that I want whatever your off days are so that we can be off at the same time."

"Now I am even more happy, Stephon. Can I call you sometimes on your job?" she asked with a need to be closer to my world.

"Only in an emergency. I don't want anybody in my business. You know how I feel about my privacy, Catalina."

"This I know and understand, Poppi."

"Catalina, we need to talk when I get in."

"You worry me now, Stephon?"

"I want to talk about Carlos."

"Why him?"

"Because I worry about you, too, Catalina."

"I, too, worry sometimes. Poppi, if you don't mind, can I get some protection for me? Yes?" The way she asked, I assumed she meant a gun.

"I gave you two guns, Catalina."

"No, Poppi; man protection," she said and got very quiet.

"You mean a bodyguard, Catalina?"

"Yes, like the Lioness has."

"Catalina, are you afraid of Carlos?"

She didn't respond quickly. "This is why I want you to come home. I am not comfortable when you or your uncle are away, Poppi."

"Are you afraid of Carlos?" I asked again.

"Yes, Stephon, I am afraid of him!"

"I'll be home Thursday night. No, in fact, I want your ass on the bus to Dallas before five o'clock Thursday. Are we straight?" I demanded.

"Yes, Poppi," she said as if relieved by my demand.

"I don't want anyone to know that you are coming besides Dellia. Do you understand?"

"Yes!"

"We will be back in Austin by noon so that they won't trip about your work."

"You let Catalina worry about these people," she said.

"I'll call you again tomorrow, girl."

"I love you, Stephon."

"I know, Catalina," I said and hung up with a lot of frustration behind Carlos' punk ass.

Not knowing what the dude was capable of had me worried. I had to find out how deep in the game the fool was, and see if he had some loyal people behind him. If Catalina asked about some protection, I knew Carlos had some heat too. I dialed Uncle James thinking that I couldn't just sleep on the new twist in things.

"Talk to me," he said when he answered the phone.

"How do you know who this is?" I asked.

"I don't give a shit who it is, you called, talk."

"I want to talk to you about Carlos."

"Not over the phone. I'll see you when you get here, son."

"Do I need to worry about Catalina Unc?"

"I thought about that two weeks ago, boy. She'll be all right, and we'll talk when you get here. So get off my phone."

"Later, Unc."

Sleep didn't come easy, and when I finally got in good, the alarm was calling out my name. It was seven o'clock in the morning, and traffic coming out of the complexes was like fighting for a position on the interstate. It was bumper to bumper. Since I didn't have a job to go to, I respected the game and stayed my ass out the way by sitting idle in the parking lot until it emptied out. The traffic was worse, but I had to learn how to fight in the area sooner or later.

The gym was clear across the other side of town, and it gave me the opportunity to experience the old and new of the city. Shit like passing up an elementary school and being made to wait on the kids to cross the street to attend their summer school programs brought back a lot of memories that took me back to El Paso. So, I enjoyed going through that part of the city.

I had yet to beat my trainer to the gym, and I was totally convinced that the dude lived in the damn joint.

"Yeah, I'm late again," I said to Tye as I handed him my wrist wraps so that he could wrap them before the workout.

"What time are you trying to catch some z's?" he asked.

"Hell, about eight o'clock," I said.

"Still tossing huh?"

"Tye, I have to creep up on the tossing first." We both started laughing.

"Well, give me five laps around the track, ten minutes on the rope, and I'll be at the bench waiting on you," he said.

"Damn Tye, you ain't making shit any easier."

"Look around you, youngster. These a.m. dick stalkers aren't jockin' me; it's you they're trying to catch slipping. Now hit the damn track because I have a meeting to go to after this session."

"Pushy this morning, aren't we?" I muttered as I took off to start my run.

"I've been in here two weeks and a day, and I still haven't passed this fatigue yet. Hell, it couldn't have been Fran because she did all the screwing and not me. Tye was closing in on me, and I hadn't been on the rope but five minutes.

"Stephon, I got some vitamins for you, if you want some."

"Tye, for the last time, no pills, man!"

"Timers up. We push this morning, and we're doing it for forty-five minutes straight," said Tye.

"Remind me to tell you to kiss my ass when we're done, Tye."

"Sounds personal, Stephon, but I'm not into shit like that!"

Tye was the shit when it came to a workout, and it was straight business and no talking.

"We made good time today, but if you can get here twenty minutes earlier, I'll introduce you to some new techniques to strengthen your lower ab section to give you some thrust power in your bedroom," he said.

"Tye, I'm struggling to do the shit I'm doing now. Plus, I start work next Monday on top of it all."

"School, work, and workout. Welcome to the real world, playa," he stated as he gave me a hug. "Tomorrow, and don't be late," he said as he walked out the door.

It was nine o'clock and a perfect time to call the hotel and see how straight in I was. Walking up to the check-in desk at the gym, I caught a white girl trying to do the damn thing with me, but dealing with Fran I decided to take her advice. Little Susie was looking for a fresh morning bang, but I had other things on my mind.

"Excuse me, Miss, could I possibly use the phone please? It's local."

"Sure, and would you like to try one of our many juices or water? They're free to members," she said.

"Please, whatever flavor you choose," I told her while getting a good shot of her package as she walked off. We were eye to eye with each other the whole time she was coming back with my juice. "Thank you," I said grinning and trying to glance at her nametag, but the problem was I couldn't get my eyes past looking at her breast. Well, that is until she took her index finger, and raised my head up by lifting my jaw.

"It's Tammy," she said, laughing. "You're welcome, Stephon," she said and walked away giving me a show by which to remember her.

With a high level of optimism, I dialed up the number at the hotel.

"Thank you for calling The Bay of Las Colinas. This is April. How may I help you?" was the introduction that came flowing into my ear.

"Good morning, April. My name is Stephon Wilkerson, and I would like to speak with Steve Pennington, please."

"He's been expecting your call Mr. Wilkerson, and welcome to the Bay. One second and I'll transfer your call. You have a nice day, Sir."

"Thank you and you have the same, April."

"Stephon, I'm glad you called, son. You've got to be one of the most important employees I've had on my staff in a long time. From what I am told, you are a good looker, polite and a snappy dresser," he said.

"Well, sir, that sounds a bit over-rated if you ask me; but I'll go with the flow if the job requires it."

We both started laughing.

"I'd like to meet with you on the formalities of your position here at the Bay. Being one of my managers, you're free to wear what you want as long as it consists of a jacket and a tie. From what I hear, you won't have a problem with that! All I ask is that you have some mercy on me and the rest of my crew," he kidded.

"What day and time, Mr. Pennington?"

"First things first, it's Steve, and tomorrow morning will be fine. I walk through the door at eight o'clock Monday through Friday."

"Tomorrow it is then, Steve."

"Have a nice day, Stephon."

"You too."

Fran must have been scoping me out from the moment I pulled up. How in the hell would she know anything about my dress code? Hell, I really hadn't had a reason to put on anything outside of the trip to the mall and to dinner the other night. I really hope that the broad wasn't some kind of damn stalker. It would be my luck that Fran would see Catalina one Sunday and turn into a drama granny.

Marie had dropped some pearls at my feet the other day that I needed to check on, and I hoped like hell LaShonda could help me out without giving Uncle James a warning. Then again, he had probably blessed somebody in the bank. I was on a mission; it was to the house, a shower and a trip to see LaShonda. As I was pulling out of the driveway, I was flagged down by the manager of the complex.

"Well hello, stranger," she called out to me.

"Stranger?" I said, surprised.

"I throw one of the biggest parties for my tenants and you don't show up."

"I thought I would sit that one out until I'm more familiar with my surroundings."

"I'm feeling you on that, but maybe the next one then. How is everything going for you?" she asked.

"Fine, but I have a question for you if you don't mind me asking, Debra."

"Shoot," she said.

"Will it be asking too much if I chose another apartment?" I asked.

"You're not happy with that one, huh?" She spoke with a suspecting of why I was asking for another one.

"You know, I thought about asking you that when you came to pick up your keys. It really didn't give you much of a choice, being that your uncle came in to take care of everything. To answer your question though, come in when you're ready, pick out what you want, and I'll get my staff to help you move your things. On one condition, though."

"I'm listening," I said giving her my full attention.

"That you allow me to escort you to our next party."

"Are you going to introduce me as your friend or as your tenant?" I asked her.

"As my friend, of course," she said, grinning.

"I'll get with you on the apartment issue at another time, Debra."

"Don't wait too long, Stephon, they come and go like hotcakes."

"Talk to you later," I told her as I drove away.

I chose a far side entrance into the bank instead of the conventional front door to avoid all eyes on me. There was a board on the wall that listed the names, positions and offices of certain staff members in the bank. I was interested only in who was over "New Accounts" and the bank manager's name. I stood where LaShonda would notice me while I filled out my deposit slip. She watched me, and I kept an eye on the line that was leading to her counter. Waiting on her line of people to thin out was a waste of time, and we both knew it. She held up a finger indicating to give her a minute, and she jumped on the phone as she continued to take care of her customers.

Soon after she hung up her phone, a sister came over her way and looked at me with a smile on her face. They spoke briefly and LaShonda motioned for me to come down to the opposite end of the counter. I looked towards the sister who relieved LaShonda and mouthed, "Thank you." She winked her eye at me as I walked towards LaShonda.

"Good morning, lady."

"Well hello, Mr. Stephon Wilkerson."

"I'm sorry I didn't show up Saturday, but I have this thing about being somewhere or around people I don't know."

"I was there and looking pretty, I might add."

"When do you not look pretty, LaShonda?"

"Flattery will get you nowhere, Stephon."

"Is that why you're smiling?" I asked.

"And you know this," she said with great enthusiasm. "Are you going somewhere special? Did you get dressed up just to come to the bank or is this normal for you?" she asked rapidly.

"All of the above with a heavy dose of the latter. Is that bad or good?"

"What! Look around you. You got all my co-workers questioning me on some telepathic shit."

"Tell them I'm your cousin from Utah," I kidded.

"I will not! That would be lying. What's wrong with me telling them that you are my new friend?"

"I thought friendship was something that was earned."

"You're right," she said.

"I need a favor, LaShonda."

"I guess this is where brownie points start, huh?"

"Would you prefer that they did?" I asked her.

"It's either that or lie to my co-workers about you being a lost Mormon cousin from Utah," she said laughing.

"You have ten minutes of my time left, Stephon. I'm on break as of five minutes ago."

"If I called up here to inquire about the status of my account who will I be directed to?"

"Two people, or bitches, for better words," she said.

"What would they ask me for?"

"Well, for one, they shouldn't be giving out that type of information over the phone anyway. Two, I know that they will if they know the person and their voices. What's wrong, Stephon?"

"I have a family member checking on my statements, and I don't like that. Hell, from what you are telling me, one of the ladies listed on the bulletin board under 'New Accounts' is leaking my business."

"Well, you can't go checking them, Stephon, if you don't know who it is for sure," she said.

"I guess I'll have to test the waters real soon then, huh?" I announced my challenge.

"Well, if you need me for anything, just holla," LaShonda said.

"Have you had dinner at your spot yet?" I asked her.

"Since you mentioned it, I'm taking my mother there Wednesday night, courtesy of my new friend, Stephon Wilkerson," she said with a big gracious smile.

"So, what's your mother's name, if you don't mind me asking?"

"Her name is Ms. Gloria Stevens."

"I hope she enjoys the food. You think you'll need some more change?" I asked as I dug into my pocket.

"You better not!" she said in a good hood fashion.

"Wednesday night, huh?" I asked again curiously.

"You keep bringing it up. Are you going to be there or something?" she asked.

"You never know, my friend. Guess I'll let you get back to work before you get you fired," I said.

"Boy, please! These people need me too much."

"So you're saying you got it like that?"

"And some!" she said boastfully.

"By the way, no promises, but I'll try to make the next party," I told her.

"Yeah, yeah, promises, promises," she replied.

"Take this five hundred dollars, and deposit it in my account for me if you don't mind."

"You'll have to get in line."

"I thought we were friends, woman?"

"You still have to get in line, Stephon."

"Oh, hell naw; that's Mr. Wilkerson to you!" We both laughed on the way back to her counter.

It was five minutes before I made it up to her, and the wait was good because I got a chance to see some of Irving's finest women.

"Damn, Stephon, you lonely or something?" LaShonda was being a straight nosey ass.

"Why you ask?" I said.

"You jocked every woman that walked by you up and down."

"Hell, I did you the same way when I saw you, LaShonda."

"I guess," she muttered, barely audible.

"Can I get my receipt please?"

"Bye, Stephon," she said smiling as I walked off.

With Catalina coming down for the first time, I had to find out what time her bus would arrive Thursday afternoon and find the damn bus station. I got back to the house and heard some Kenny G. seeping through the cracks under my front door. I looked out in the parking lot and saw the rental car.

"You could get your ass shot messing around a brother's music collection like that," I told Uncle James.

"You call that a collection, boy?"

"Some of the best," I said as I gave him a hug.

"You been here long?" I asked.

"You must have just left, because I smelt fresh cologne."

"So what's up Unc?" I asked.

"You said you wanted to discuss Carlos, Didn't you?"

"Does Carlos have enough juice to have you killed?" I asked him.

"Have me killed? What the hell are we discussing here, Stephon?" he demanded.

"Does he have enough juice to kill you, Uncle James? Yes or no?" I said again.

He got up and brought Kenny G. to silence, then flopped back down on the sofa. "Yeah!" he said, as if he had seen a ghost.

"You can talk your shit to me."

"You watch your tongue, boy."

"You told me anyway I wanted to express myself," I reminded him. "You can talk your shit to override your pride, but before you leave this apartment, I want a list of all of your frat brothers, names, addresses and numbers."

"Who the hell do you think you're talking to?" Uncle James asked me as he sprung to his feet with anger. I stood my ground and I didn't flinch or blink. I wanted him to know I was coming to him as a grown ass man. An agitated grown ass man who wanted answers.

"Again, you can talk your shit, but I said what I said! Not one time have I asked you what your line of work was because that's your business, but when an immigrant has to tell me some shit my brother's keeper is supposed to tell me, then that places me at a disadvantage. You and I both know that's a no-no with me, and that's by the standards you taught me. If Carlos will have you killed, I'm not shit! I want to know what Carlos' weak and strong points are. I want to know about his most loyal and who they are. For almost ten years I've been living around enough artillery to arm a small militia, and I didn't snap until last night. Carlos has turned into a tyrant amongst some of his people, and just like any other situation, it's either use or be used. Isn't that what you taught me, Uncle James?"

His voice let me know that he was furious. "Who the hell do you think you are?" The veins in his head were clearly visible and his nostrils were flaring. I stood my ground.

"I'm glad you asked, Uncle James. I might not be the brightest eighteen year old, but if I continue to live, I'm going to be greater than you."

He started laughing. I didn't.

I went to my makeshift bar, grabbed a bottle of his favorite brandy and a glass, and poured him a drink. He practically snatched it out of my hand when I handed it to him.

"Thank you," he muttered. "So what... you want to wear my shoes now, boy?" he asked as he sipped on his brandy.

"Wrong size, Uncle James and you taught me never to settle for a pair of used shoes; not even if they're yours. That's what you said."

"Touché, nephew." He continued sipping on his drink. "So what's wrong, Stephon?" he asked.

"I'm not big enough to start fixing shit that's malfunctioning or that could end up broken by some freak-ass accident, Uncle James. I don't run to Mama, but I do come to you for shit my Mama don't have a clue that's going on in my life because I'm loyal to the only man I love as a father," I said as I poured him another drink. Right now you're sitting up here pissed off at me because I'm vulnerable and so are you, Uncle James. You told me that you made certain moves in your life because you got tired of flunkin'. Now the flunky has grown stronger. What do you think Carlos' next move is, Uncle James?"

"Sit down, Stephon!"

I did as he commanded.

"I don't know, nephew. I've been going and coming so long, I failed to stay on top of my game," he confessed. "I'm being told that he's been meeting some dudes that have never visited the Tower before. I don't know if he has been anticipating you, me or Catalina to leak the little episode that went down at the crib. That would be an embarrassment to him."

"Uncle James, just so you know, Catalina is driving Carlos out of the Tower and taking control of his operations as we speak," I said.

"Says who?" he asked, as he extended his glass for another shot.

"Says her and her people!" I said.

"Are you in the middle of this, Stephon?"

"Am I coaching her you mean, Uncle James?"

"These people play for keeps, boy."

"So why did I have to learn this from Catalina?"

"I apologize, boy" he allowed himself to say with sincerity.

"What have you done for Catalina, Uncle James?"

"The girl is very smart, boy. She won't allow me to do shit for her. If it ain't coming through you, it's not happening," he explained.

"Uncle James, answer the question."

"I helped her get into the building. She said she didn't feel safe at her sister's or at the house when we both are away."

That was the surprise she talked about, I thought.

"She asked me for approval on some bodyguards."

"How would that work?" I asked him.

"The girl has enough juice, not just in Austin, but across the damned country and the borders. Her people are all around her. She doesn't take an elevator without somebody from a department moving with her," Uncle James told me.

"Catalina's sister works as a sitter for a well-off couple and Catalina's pad is next door. Carlos, or anyone else, would be crazy to try to pull some shit off on that floor. Plus, the assistant chief of police lives across the hall from her," Uncle James informed me.

"Thank you," I told him.

"Shit, don't thank me. I just set up the meeting, and she did the rest. She never would have made it on that floor or in the building for that matter, if it wasn't for the women residents liking her. I'm sure Carlos already feels the pressure that Catalina is applying on him, Stephon. It's just a matter of time," Uncle James said as he took his last sip of brandy.

"Catalina is about to come into a lot of power, Stephon. The girl loves the shit out of you too," he added.

"Don't remind me, Uncle James."

"Now the real question is, how do we keep the both of you safe, boy."

"There's no question that her people accept you, and expect both of us to keep her safe."

"Hold up. Let me get this straight right now. That's my girl true enough, but bodyguard I will not be," I said as I stared at Uncle James in a way that caught his attention.

"What is it, Stephon?"

"I want everything you have on Carlos and that list I asked you about."

"You can have Carlos, but the brothers I can't do. If anything ever happens to me, they'll get with you. There's too much going on for a young man your age to be knowing. I want you to know and understand, I might not be on top of everything, but never underestimate the fight in this dog," he stated.

"Who else knows my whereabouts, Uncle James?"

"You're a sitting duck, Stephon."

"I gathered that much with all of the weapons around me, and since you're here, let's cut the guessing game and show me where they are located please!" I asked him.

Two hours later Uncle James was on a flight back to Austin. I had time to ponder everything we'd talked about, and more so, the shit that made him boil. Catalina had more power than Carlos, and we'd been together such a short time. How was this affecting Uncle James and the invisible frat squad? Carlos wasn't worried about me moving in on his job, he was trying to keep Catalina from getting to me! Was this a way for Uncle James and his frat brothers to get rid of Carlos and step their game up with Catalina? I better start trying to figure out something.

I decided to just play along with everybody and see what panned out. For one, moving wasn't going to do me any good. I needed to withdraw my money out of Uncle James' bank because that was exactly what it was, and find my own bank.

I grabbed the phone to call Catalina, and I thought about her asking me for approval on some bodyguards. She knows she's in the game and she's scared of her own people. They won't dare attempt to harm her as long as Uncle James or I are close by, and I wonder why. Okay Catalina, let's do this. I thought to myself.

"Catalina, please."

"Who may I tell her is calling?"

I was hesitant to answer that question, but I didn't have time for the bullshit. "It's Stephon!"

"Please hold, sir."

About twenty seconds later, she responded. "Hey, Poppi, I have been waiting on your call. I love you, Stephon." She sounded like she was full of joy.

"Are you busy, sweetheart?" I asked her.

"I am always doing something if I am here in the Tower. But when you are here, I do nothing except be with you, Poppi."

"Do you feel safe with me?" I asked her.

"I will not lie to you Stephon; Dellia has been here many years before me and people who she thinks don't change, they change on her. I worry about people changing on me when all I do is help, Stephon," she said.

"Do you need my help, Catalina?"

She didn't respond right away. "I am afraid for you too, Stephon," she said.

"Catalina, do not discuss too much on the phone. What time is your bus coming?"

"I will arrive at 4:25 p.m., Poppi. I will see your face before I get off the bus or I will not get off," she announced. By her tone, I knew she was smirking her mouth like she would whenever she wanted me to know she wasn't taking any foolishness. I couldn't help but smile.

"Baby, I'll be there. Catalina, no one must know that you are coming except Dellia. Do you understand?"

"Yes, Poppi."

"You are a brave lady," I told her.

"No, I am not brave; I'm a scared lady, Stephon!"

"Tell me something, lady; who do you trust the most, me or my uncle."

"You," she said.

"Why?" The question shocked her.

"Stephon, please don't," she pleaded.

"Why, Catalina?"

"Because your uncle is a liar, and he too is a bad man, Poppi!" she blurted out.

"So, why should you trust me, Catalina?"

"Because of what you have done for me, Stephon."

"How do you know I won't change on you also?"

"Because I know your heart better than you do Stephon," she said.

"And what is that supposed to mean?" I asked.

"When my people first saw me smile at you, they get real mad. They say that the Negroes with money are the worst kind. They say look at your uncle. For years that you work at the Tower, my people wait to see if you will be like your uncle. When you grew up, they see different. You never stop smiling at me, so I make up my mind to love you, Stephon. No matter what my people say," she told me.

"And what do your people say?"

"A lot respect you, Stephon, but there are still some who don't because of your uncle."

"Are you in danger, Catalina?"

"Yes, especially after Carlos is forced to leave the Tower."

"Am I in danger also?" I asked her.

"I don't know, Poppi, that's why I would rather be with you," she insisted.

"What you are doing for your people is good?"

"Oh yes, Stephon!" She sounded proud of herself.

"Is it worth your life?" She was hesitant to answer.

"I'll be at the bus station at 4:00 p.m., waiting on you."

"I love you, Stephon."

"We'll see, Catalina," I said before hanging up.

Uncle James had been a bad boy under my nose, but I blamed that on me. It was time to eat and I couldn't help but think about Monica. I guess I'll see if she would like to talk and eat again.

"Thank you for calling Dillard's, how may I help you?"

"I would like to speak with a lady that I bought some cologne from yesterday please. I believe her name is Monica."

"Please hold, sir."

About twenty seconds went by before she was on the line.

"Monica speaking, how can I help you?"

"Is that your Hollywood voice or what?" I said.

"Stephon, boy what do you want?" she asked in a happy-to-hear-from me way.

"Evidently, I'm thinking about you, if that's cool?"

"What's up, handsome?"

"Lunch is what's up! Can you get away?"

"Are you serious?"

"Woman, are you coming or not?"

"I'll be off in one hour and don't have to come back," she said.

"So, what, you taking off for something?"

"Naw, boy, it's my short day today."

"So does that mean I can kidnap your country ass for a while?"

"Country!" she barked out. "I is a city gal now, boy." She mustered a country accent for emphasis.

"Bullshit!"

We both started laughing.

"Yeah, I'm down," she said. "Would you like me to meet you or are you coming to pick me up?" she asked.

"I'll be there to pick you up. Do I have a time limit on when I need to have you back at your car?" I asked her.

"I don't like driving at night. How's that?"

"I'll be there in an hour. By the way, what do you have on?" I asked her.

"A very cute summer dress and some pumps. Why?"

"I'm trying to relax too," I said. "Bye, woman."

Chapter SIX

TOSSED UP

Thursday couldn't get here quick enough for me. I hated like hell that I told Uncle James about the job at the Bay Hotel. Then again, Mama or Honey would have leaked my whereabouts anyway. The more I drilled Catalina, the more I saw that she would do more than just die for a humanitarian reason and would protect me without hesitation!

It's 3:55 p.m. and I'm double parked out in front of the bus station in downtown Dallas. Though Catalina wasn't due for another thirty or forty minutes, moving meant stopping traffic on Jackson Street. The thought of my going to jail for a pistol would cause too big of a ripple in the water right now. I've had winos jockin' me for change, prostitutes trying to put in some work, hustlers looking for a quick come-up, carjackers sizing up my ride, and I've only been stationary for fifteen minutes.

I was parked in a position where Catalina would pass me up on the way into the terminal and when she got off the bus, all she had to do was walk to the car. Several police officers passed me up more than once, and I knew that my plates had been ran just on general principle.

If I would have left the car for any reason, it would be towed or stolen. So frontin' like someone was about to run out at any second will have to do.

Finally, I saw my girl's face pressed against the window as the bus passed me by. She had a grim look on her face. I may as well been ready for some crying as soon as she got in the car. Taking the bus alone could have been costly, and we both knew it.

"Hey! Hey! Yeah, you! You want to make some money playa?" I asked this brother who had undoubtedly been living on the streets.

"What we talking about, my good man?" he asked as he felt on the body of my car. "Oooo-weee, this is a nice car, black man," said the wino.

As the bus door opened, then and only then, did I expose my money. "Peep game, soldier. You see that lady right there?"

"Damn. Hell, yeah, I see her. A brother would have to be blind and stupid not to see all that, fool!"

"I need for you to bring her bags and toss them in my back seat, and this is yours," I said, showing him a hundred-dollar bill.

One glance at the money and off he went. Car horns began sounding like crazy. Buump, Buump! Beep, Beep! "Get the hell out of the way you crazy bastard! You trying to get killed, fool?" came from moving vehicles as the dude bobbed and weaved in and out of traffic to retrieve Catalina and her luggage. The dude literally ran in the middle of the street, suitcases in hand, stopped all the traffic and signaled for Catalina to come on. I had both the front passenger and the back door open to receive what was rightly mine.

"Pay up, rich boy," the wino demanded as he snatched the money from my hand, and ran off to do his peddling. Before Catalina could start sobbing, I secured the doors, locked her in her seatbelt, and darted into traffic to get out of harm's way. Neither one of us made a sound because I was concentrating on getting us to safety.

After I was on Stemmons Freeway, I reached over and released her from her seatbelt. She was like a horse leaving the gates at the Kentucky Derby.

"Stephon, please Poppi, no more buses," she stated under uncontrollable tears of fear. Catalina knew that Carlos has pull in all of Texas to bring trouble to Stephon and to her, because she knew of the awful deeds going on between him and Uncle James.

"I won't ask you to do that again, Catalina. I promise."

"Poppi, take me home please," she begged me through her sobbing. I knew right then the effects this shit was having on her. It was clear that she was not mentally prepared for her task, but instead of passing the torch to somebody else, her pride was in the way.

Well, I had twenty-four hours to work on her, and if we would have to pull back into Austin on the same mission, I was going to be on some more shit! It was either be down with her crazy ass or turn her loose. Simple as that!

Traffic was starting to flow as we approached Beltline Road, and that meant everybody coming home at the same time. Outside of Fran, I really wasn't trippin'; but it was Debra who would be the one to receive a phone call from Uncle James as soon as he discovered that Catalina was nowhere to be found. This was going to be a test for him. Even if he did call Debra at the front office of the complex and ask her to report or acknowledge Catalina's presence in Irving or if he didn't, I knew that he would know that she was with me.

"Baby, clean up your face. I can't have you being seen like this because someone might call the police and tell them that I was hurting you in some way," I said.

"That's crazy talk, Stephon," she said and continued to sob.

I pulled down the sun visor on her side so that she could get a good look at herself. "Look Catalina," I said.

" Ah mi Dios," (Oh my God) she said once she had a good look at herself. "I'm sorry, Stephon."

"Stop apologizing, Catalina."

Instead of me taking the loop to go South on Beltline towards the apartment, I took the north exit and headed toward Highway 114 until she got straightened out. I drove down 114 until we ended up on the north exit of the Dallas-Ft. Worth Airport; paid my toll and kept driving until I ended up at the south end exit.

I looked at my watch to catch the time and like on any other job, Debra, her assistants and the maintenance workers would race to leave the complex at five o'clock. It was 5:45 p.m. and I was fifteen minutes away from the house. If Debra was still on the grounds of the complex, she was there for Catalina. Traffic was at an even flow as I took the south Beltline exit; and as I turned on Pioneer, I had to know how Catalina started her journey towards me.

"How did you leave out of the Tower?" I asked.

"I told Carlos that I was going to get my hair done."

"How did you get your luggage to the bus station?" I asked her.

"I placed it all in a locker at the bus station two days before."

"So, how did you get to the bus station today?"

I saw a taxi parked, asked Dellia to stop, and paid the driver to drive around the city until I had five minutes before it was time for the bus to leave.

"So you're telling me that Dellia is the only one who knows you're here?"

"Yes!"

Well, I was about to find out if that was true or not. As soon as I passed the complex office, there she stood looking out through the blinds. As soon as she saw Catalina, the blinds closed. I purposely waited to see her leave her office, and about three minutes later, she was leaving. That was just enough time to make her call to Austin.

"Poppi, why we wait in the car, baby? I want to go inside please."

"I'm sorry, sweetheart," I said to her leaning over to kiss her. "Come on, let's go. Here, you take the keys and go on up while I get your bags."

"Baby, I help too," she insisted.

"No, you go!" I snapped. I tried to smile to cover myself.

As she sashayed up to the apartment, I thought about Uncle James being in the apartment the last time. It's a forty-five minute flight from Austin to the D.F.W Airport. I'd been gone for two hours, and Catalina, coming from the Tower, had been gone longer than I had.

"Catalina!" I shouted up at her before she made it all the way up the stairs. "Baby I'm sorry, come help me out."

"I tell you all the time about trying to be the perfect gentleman. Sometimes even a perfect gentleman needs a woman's help," she fussed. I grabbed her around her waist, pulled her near to me and kissed her.

"That will not excuse you, Stephon Wilkerson."

"I love you."

She kept on with her powder-puff fussing as she bent down to retrieve her suitcase and froze. She slowly rose back up to meet me eye-to-eye and stared into my eyes.

"Poppi, what did you say to me?"

"I said I love you, Catalina." Her eyes became watery as she stared into my eyes a few seconds more before bending down again to retrieve her suitcase.

She walked off toward the apartment with her head held high.

"Come, Mr. Wilkerson," she said to me as she looked back over her shoulder. I had to have some spare time to retrieve my pistol and have first view inside the apartment. If she knew what I was feeling, we would end up at an undisclosed location instead of my apartment.

She sensed that I was cautious about something by the way I moved throughout the apartment.

"Poppi?"

"You stay right here," I told her as I placed my index finger on her lips. She remained quiet as I darted in and out of each room.

"So why don't I get an 'I love you too' back from the woman I love?" I asked her as I slowly walked up to her. Seeing her hand deep down in her purse meant that she was on high alert, so I had to be very creative to break the edginess.

"Because you only hear those words that come from my heart two times a day when you call to speak to me, but I tell you those words all day long, Stephon, and even before I close my eyes to sleep. Now that I am with the man that I love, I show him why I love him so much," she said as tears ran down her cheeks.

"So why do you cry now?" I asked.

"I'm happy to be with you alone and not with everyone in the Tower too."

"So what's up with all these damn suitcases? Are you running away?" I asked her in a joking manner as I dried the tears from her face.

"Stephon," she called my name and placed her hands on her hips. "You know how picky you will be when I put on clothes before we go somewhere, so I bring enough for you, not for me, black man."

"Girl, I'm not that bad." She looked at me, rolled her eyes, and had one word for me, "Bullshit!" We both started laughing as we hugged and kissed on each other.

I looked down at my watch and she immediately asked, "Poppi, why do you watch the time?

"You said you wanted to show me why you love me so much. You know Daddy has to have all of that," I stated as I pulled her close to me.

"And you know this Honduras bullet"

" It's bombshell, woman." I said laughing.

"Okay, bombshell, bullet, whatever! I bet you understand this language," she stated as she lifted her dress over her head and spun around slowly, showing me her body.

"You comprehend this, black man?" she said as she shook that ass towards the bedroom. "Come and let me speak my language to you like you like it, Poppi."

When she ordered me into her world, I brought the Isley Brothers with me for back up. There was no sense in going to a gunfight with a knife, but with Catalina, shit was the other way around. She wanted the Isley Brothers, Luther or this dude from Mexico. I tried making love while the brother was getting his paper, but he stopped me from getting mine! So the Isley's were the shit for her and past her statement, "I want to love you." I was deep into her forest and didn't give a shit about Ron!

I called and made reservations at my spot, and either they were happy to reserve a table for me so that I could close that open account or I was becoming a good regular. Nevertheless, I ordered flowers to be

delivered to Catalina to compliment the one carat necklace and matching dinner ring that I bought her the week before.

"Poppi, are you sure this dress is all right for you?"

I just stood there in the living room with my hands placed together
as if I was praying, saying, "Please God, let her learn just a little more
English. I still want the 'Poppi' and the part that…well I won't go there,
but you know."

"Stephon, I know you hear me talk!"

"Catalina, for the last time…" she interrupted me by walking out to
show herself to me and I was speechless.

"Yes, Catalina, you are beautiful my Honduras bullet."

"Aaah, you want to play!" she said as we laughed. We left the house
with enough time to spare, and I showed Catalina the beauty of Dallas
at night before we made it to Las Colinas. A few minutes after we were
seated, her flowers were delivered, and I threatened her by promising
to leave if she started crying.

"I will save my tears for the car, you mean man," she said.

"So, I'm 'mean' now, huh?"

"Yes, because you stop me from shedding tears of joy."

"Do all the women in your country cry about everything?"

"You have to understand that me and my people live in very bad conditions, Poppi. The money that you spent for this beautiful necklace,
this ring, silk shoes that adorn my feet, the price of my dress, all of that
together would feed one family for a year, Stephon. So there are many
reasons that my people cry for, and I have so much to thank God for,
that I cry."

"I guess I am a 'mean' man then, huh?"

"I will let you pass this time," she said.

"It's let you make it, girl!"

"Aah, quiet, Poppi. I will get it right before I bring your sons into this
world."

I looked at her sideways.

"No, I am not with child, Stephon. Again I tell you, when Stephon
says so, Stephon will have his children by this Honduras bombshell. I

got it right this time!" she said with a smile.

"Poppi, we talk, yes?"

"Are you sure you want to do this right here?" I asked her.

"We eat and we talk. It will be good for us, Stephon."

"The minute you show me signs that we can't eat and talk, we leave; understand?"

"I understand," she said.

"Why did you look around the apartment today?"

"Are we here to lie to each other, Catalina?"

"Stephon, look at me face." I glanced up at her and back down at my food. "No, no you won't," she said as she grabbed my chin and raised my face back up. "I will never lie to you, Stephon. One day you ask me something and I tell you the truth and it still hurt your heart, but I still tell you the truth, Stephon. Now, do you understand?" She stared at me with my face still in her grasp, waiting on my response.

"Yes," I said with a look that told her that she had better be standing true to her word.

"My uncle was in my apartment Monday when I came home from working out."

"He told you he was coming to see you?" she asked.

"No," I replied.

"So why he come to see you, Poppi?"

"Because of you!"

"Me!" she said as she dropped her fork in her plate. "Poppi, I do nothing wrong, I promise you!" She was defensive with her response.

"Catalina, calmate." (Catalina, Calm down.) I told her.

"I wanted to know if Carlos had the power to have you killed."

"I could have told you that myself," she stated.

"What does Carlos control that you will be getting in the way of, Catalina?" She looked at me and paused before uttering a single word. I laid my knife and fork on my plate and sat back as I reached for my wine, never taking my eyes off her.

"Carlos is receiving thirty percent of the people's money, and when your uncle found out that this was going on, at first he was very upset,

Dellia tell me. Then James wanted half of the money. He told Carlos to tell everybody that the money he was getting was going towards helping in many other ways. You and me know Poppi that a good man would stop Carlos many years ago, and a good man would not take the people's money."

"What else?" I asked her.

"Carlos has allowed the drugs to flow through the Tower."

"What else?"

"Your uncle helps the bad of my people open businesses, buy land and houses for double the price of the house."

"What else, Catalina?" I did not elaborate on any of her statements; I just wanted to know everything that I was dealing with.

"Carlos has upset the cartels because he has misused their money in foolish ways. He is now taking it out on the people, making them pay more or he sends word to the immigration, and they take everyone in the house to NIS Detention Center."

"How strong is Carlos, Catalina?"

"I do not understand the question, Poppi."

"Carlos, his power…only in Austin?"

"Oooh no, Poppi, maybe in this city too! Texas is his state only, and others like Carlos have states too."

"Why you, Catalina, and not another man from your country?" I asked.

"There are no more of my family left in my country. Either they join with the rebels or the cartels have them killed, or they die of bad sickness. If you betray the cartels or big family that the cartels help, they kill somebody in your family in Honduras. I only have very little family left in the world, Poppi, I have nothing to lose," she said.

"What about me?" I asked her.

"You will not give me you, Stephon!"

I didn't want to go there so I asked her what she was going to do about all the shit that was going on.

She slowly took a sip of ice water before responding. "I am asked to go to secret meeting in San Antonio to meet with big, big people that want to see Carlos out, and your uncle's hands released from around the necks of my people, and all the drugs away from the Tower."

"How are you to get there and who will keep you safe?" I tried to keep my voice calm.

"There are people who have devoted their lives to me; because with Carlos gone, I will see that their children, wives and parents will find refuge in the form of work at the Tower. The people who live in the Tower are very rich and some are very powerful people, and they provide work for my people all across the United States. Now they have not been wanting to help my people because many go to jail for the drugs and the killing of innocent people that get in their way. I will clean the Tower up and the people at the meeting will help protect me and you, if you like," she presented seriously. The look on her face was so intent.

"Where do I fit into all of this Catalina, and if you lie to me I swear..."

She stopped me, pointed her steak knife at me, and said, "I will not ever tell you again you son-of-a-bitch, I will never lie to you." I didn't know if she had lost her mind, but I let her continue without interrupting her.

"I'm tired of seeing people die, Stephon, for nothing. Before I knew that your uncle was a bad man, our hearts had begun the courtship. Two days after I give you my love, I hear that a part of my people want to kill Carlos and your uncle. I tell Dellia that I have given my love to you and ask these people to spare both Carlos and your uncle, and told them that I would clean up the Tower if I had their protection."

"What the hell does that have to do with me, Catalina?" I asked.

"Carlos found out about my love for you, and he thinks that you and your uncle will help shift him out."

"Squash that!"

"Please, Poppi!"

"Don't do me right now, Catalina!" I told her with a cold voice and a look to match.

"We must leave now, Stephon," she said as she began to slide her chair back.

"You sit your ass down!" I ordered her.

"Yes, Poppi," she stated as she sat with her head held down.

"Did you use me to get yourself in the position that you're in?"

"No, Stephon. I love you too much, Stephon. I love you before this bullshit. I too receive letters that they kill me because I love the nephew of the bad man, but I tell them that I did not care. I would not stop loving you." She started crying.

"So what do they say now, Catalina?"

"Forget what they say, Stephon. This position is like the president's position. I tell them what I want, and if a black ass Negro that I'm in love with is going to hinder them or stand in the way of the parents, children or wives from finding refuge, then find someone else to do this job. That's what Catalina Marie Malano says! No more questions for me, Stephon. I have only one for you," she said as she dried her eyes. Are you going to stand by my side as my man? Yes or no, Stephon?"

"Yes!" I stated.

"Catalina." She looked up at me, "Don't mess with me! On top of all this, you don't go anywhere unless I know about it and if you go, I go. Is that understood?"

"Yes Poppi!"

"You let them know that I don't want to talk and I'm out of their way, and nobody messes with my uncle. If they stop Carlos, they stop my uncle. Are we clear?"

"Very clear, Stephon. Thank you, Stephon."

"For what?"

"For being my man when I need you the most."

"Can we finish eating this meal please?" I stated as I stood up to kiss her. As we returned back to the apartment, we both were cautious about what the shadows of the night concealed. The first thing I did when I made it into the apartment was check on any incoming calls. There was only one from Marie talking about a party. I slid a chair up under the front door, went into the kitchen, grabbed the .44 semi-automatic pistol, took the .38 out of the oven, and then went into the bedroom.

"Catalina, we sleep tonight," I stated with some authority. I knew once I got into Austin, I wouldn't get any.

"This I have to see myself." She chuckled with her words.

"What is that supposed to mean?" I asked.

"Be serious, Stephon. Poppi always wants some loving before sleep," she teased. She made it a point to slide out of her panties and bent over to show me the well-kept manicured garden.

"Sleep, Catalina."

"Whatever you say, Poppi," she said as she strolled throughout the apartment naked while she pinned her hair up.

By the time she stepped back into the room, the Isley Brothers filled the whole apartment again.

"Oooh, you're wrong for that tramp," I teased back. I grabbed her and threw her in the bed.

"We sleep after the Isley Brothers, black man."

"Shut up and take this," I told her as I slid into her.

"Anytime, black man...anytime," she said in a whispering voice.

I left a message to cancel my appointment with Tye about five o'clock that morning to ensure that as soon as he walked through the door he would get it. Uncle James told me that if you wanted the jump on someone, catch 'em before they pissed in the morning.

I had pulled over in Waco, Texas to call Tye about forty-five min-utes earlier, and seeing the Pflugerville sign up ahead let me know that Catalina and I had exactly twenty minutes before pulling up in front of the Tower Over Austin. Carlos wouldn't be on duty until 8:00 a.m., but that didn't mean that somebody wasn't going to wake his ass up; or Uncle James for that matter.

As soon as we pulled up, a Hispanic male ran out to valet park my car and Catalina immediately told me not to allow him to park the car. I didn't ask any questions because I was on her turf now. Once this other Hispanic guy saw Catalina, he started her way. She pointed to me and he ran to the other side of the car to park it. She told him in Spanish that she wanted the keys and the luggage to arrive at her apart-ment together by him and him alone.

We took the elevator up with a Hispanic man I knew worked in the laundry department, along with a luggage handler. Both of the men waited until the elevator doors closed.

"Good morning to you, Mr. Wilkerson."

"No more 'Mr. Wilkerson' with me. The both of you have children my age. Are you fair men?" I asked.

They both replied, "Yes."

"Then I expect to get treated as fair as I treat you, not because of this Tower or Catalina; but as men first, and second, I respect my elders. That's what my mother taught me, not my uncle. Can the two of you live with that?" I asked as I stuck out my hand. They looked me in the eye and shook my hand.

"Today is a good day," one of the men stated as we all just kept looking forward. Catalina looked over at me, smiled and winked her eye at me in total approval of what I had done with the men who helped watch over my girl. Catalina was making it clear that the men had to talk to her without the whispering or secrecy. To her that was a form of disrespect, and they had to accept that it was "us" and not just "her"!

The men were gone, and she stood at the door with her back up against it looking at me.

"What's up, girl?"

"I hate that your uncle tell you about our apartment."

"Our apartment!" I stated.

"Stephon, don't start playing around, asshole."

"Damn, where did you get that one from?" I asked her.

"I hear one of the ladies tell her husband this when she is mad at him."

"So you're mad at me?"

"No, but you keep it up and I will be. So, are you going to see your uncle this morning?"

"First I want to go see Mama and Honey, eat me some breakfast, and be back to do lunch with you. So what are your plans for us?" I asked her.

"I would like the two of us to have lunch downstairs in the open so that all my people will know your face and Carlos' people will know that my man is standing behind me."

"This is good for us because the people that want to see me will know that I am not, for nothing, leaving my man. Are you pleased with that, Poppi?"

"On the cool, girl, the only thing on my mind is that I'm eighteen years old and in the middle of some serious shit that can get you killed and me too. So, hell no, I'm not happy, Catalina, but this is your battle, not mine! Don't start that sad face shit either. Where is your man?" I asked her.

"My man is here with me," she replied.

"Does anything else matter, Catalina?"

"Yes!" She replied. "That you love me."

"I love you, girl. Call and have my keys picked up and my car brought back around."

"Si, Poppi," she said.

As I made my way over to see my girls, showing up at that time of the morning was going to bring about much shit talking from Honey, but it was going to be the ultimate conversation for her at church. It didn't do me any good trying to sneak in the house because Honey was already up when I came through the door.

"Boy, what are you doing, comin' up in here at this time in the mornin'?"

"Come to see my favorite girl, that's what I'm doing!" I replied as I hugged and kissed her. "So are you cooking your boy some breakfast or do you want me to cook you some?"

"Boy, you know you couldn't cook an egg over an open fire if you had to, so just sit your tail down, child."

"By the way, I bought you something special. I figured a good breakfast from my Honey is a fair exchange for these," I stated as I pulled out two jewelry boxes from my pocket.

"Boy, let me see what you got there," she ordered, reaching for the boxes.

"Ooh, nooo! Give me my breakfast first," I said as I pulled the boxes away from her. "I don't mean no disrespect, but you are a woman, and when women get a taste of this kind of stuff, they just forget everything else."

"So that's how you handle Honey, huh?"

"Honey, business is business, girl. Do what you do with those pots and pans, and I'll just sit these right over here until you fill my plate up," I stated. I sat both boxes in the center of the dinette table and left out of the kitchen to go wake my mother.

Since her door was already cracked, I just went on in and sat at her side as she quietly slept. I tapped her on the cheek a few times before she started to stir around.

"Hey, sleepy head," I cooed leaning down to give her a hug.

"Baby you are traveling early in the morning or you pulled in last night and didn't tell anybody."

"Now that sounds like you're trying to get in a grown man's business, Mama."

"Nonsense, child, your ass can live to be seventy-five, you still going to be my baby and I'm still going to be in your business. So which one did you do?"

"I got up early since you handling me so tough!"

"You didn't know that's what mamas do, young punk!" We both started laughing.

"So what's really happening?" Mama asked. As she sat up in her bed, I realized how pretty she was and that I missed her.

"I start work this Monday, and thought I'd drop by to give my girls some gifts. I don't know when I'll be dropping in on a regular. But if unannounced is what it takes to see you two, then unannounced it is."

"So what did you bring your mother, young punk?"

"Mama, you know it's always money for you." She was satisfied and hugged me to let me know.

"Good, son. What about Honey?" she asked.

"I wanted to get you both the same thing, but that wouldn't have been too special to her. It was a matching canary yellow diamond earrings and necklace."

"That was sweet, baby. Boy, she's going to talk those poor sisters to death all day Sunday."

"Baby, do you smell something burning?" Mama asked.

"Yeah, I do!"

"Boy, go in there and check on Honey."

"Honey, the eggs are burning, woman. You're going to burn down the neighborhood, and I told you to fix my food first, cheater."

"Just put the pan in the sink and run some water over it baby; hell, that's a cast iron skillet," Honey stated as she put on her earrings. "Baby you sure know how to brighten Honey's day, and such a pretty color in these things too," she said as she admired the earrings in a small hand-held mirror.

"So your boy don't get breakfast this morning, huh?"

"Child, have a seat and don't get all riled up. I don't know what it is about my cookin' that have ya'll men folk keep comin' back for more," Honey said with a smile on her face.

I looked at Mama as she stood next to the refrigerator and she whispered, "Mr. Roberts just left before you got here."

"Aah, shucky-ducky now! If I would have made it here about thirty minutes sooner, I would have seen my old fishing buddy, huh?" I asked Honey.

"Boy, stop meddling me. Your Honey might be old, but she ain't dead!" We all just busted out laughing and gave each other high fives.

After my early morning feed, I curled up in the only safe place- my old bedroom- for some much needed sleep. Honey never removed or touched anything. I set my alarm to go off at eleven o'clock. I was only fifteen minutes from downtown, and it was written in stone that lunch had to start at noon straight up! By the time I pulled up for valet parking, a Hispanic guy jetted over to my car.

"I hear there's no more Mr. Wilkerson for you…only Stephon?" the guy said while we looked face to face. There were only four of us who heard that in the elevator this morning. I guess the word was out.

"That's the only way I want it to be known, my good man." I told him and I tried to give him a ten-dollar bill.

"Oh no, Stephon. Our days of taking money from each other will soon come to an end," he stated with a smile.

"Until that happens, you take my money and help feed your family."

"Catalina has left instructions for me to bring you your car keys to the dining area around one o'clock personally, if that is what you prefer, Stephon."

"Listen, I am not in the middle of anything, so I don't dictate or make any rules or tell you or your people what to do. Catalina is my girl, and she is the captain of this new coming. So, if that's what she wants, do it, and do it for her."

"I understand, Stephon."

"You make sure everybody else does too," I said as I shook his hand. As I turned to start towards the lobby, Carlos was right inside the brass and glass doors doing his public relations thing.

"Carlos," I said as I passed him by.

"Mr. Wilkerson!" he yelled out to stop me. "Mr. Wilkerson would like to meet with you for lunch."

"Is he in the Tower?" I asked.

"Not yet, sir," he replied.

"He'll have to fall in line. Tell him I said, 'first come, first served'!" I walked off.

I saw Catalina making her way toward me from the front desk dressed in the traditional Tower Over Austin colors; navy blue, white and gold buttons.

"I thought you decided not to work today?"

"Since you were not in the building, I decided to make my rounds. It is very important that I do this, Stephon."

"I understand, Catalina," I said to her while I was in the act of intimately placing my hand on her ass as we traveled up the elevator.

"Okay, Poppi, you starting it, not me." She chuckled.

"Hush! You don't have time anyway," I said.

"You better be glad." She returned my gesture by intimately grabbing my ass.

"How much time do we have?" I asked.

"Just shower, Poppi. I already have your navy blue pinstriped suit out with your blue silk shirt and your cuff links too. I had your shoes polished as well," she stated.

We exited the elevator.

"No tie?" I asked.

She smiled at me as we walked hand in hand towards the apartment.

"No tie! That's how I want you to kick it today," she said in a fly ass way.

I looked at her and said, "You can't be using the shit I say. You have to get your own, woman."

"But I like your shit too, Daddy."

"Okay, your shit is out of control, girl."

"No, that's love, Poppi," she said as she was grabbing my ass again.

"All right, you keep that shit up and I'll be putting on some Isley Brothers."

"Oooh, stop crying, black man."

My girl had on a navy blue dress that exposed her shoulders, hair pinned up, the diamond set I had bought her, and some alligator skin pumps that jumped straight out of the swamp. She was off the clock, so we entered the place as any normal king and queen would—hand-in-hand. The whole Tower stopped to pay homage to the up and coming overseer of affairs at the Tower.

"Very beautiful, Ms. Malano." "Stunning, Catalina." "You go, girl." "I love your outfit, Catalina." "Just absolutely gorgeous, Ms. Malano." The ladies of the Tower complimented her as we made our way to the restaurant. Her people were in total awe, from the floor maids to the valets.

"I wouldn't be here today, Poppi, if you wouldn't have joined me. These people don't realize that I am nothing without you, Stephon."

As I pulled her chair out to seat her, I whispered in her ear with sternness, "Don't ever let me hear you say that again. You are more than somebody. For starters, you are Ms. Catalina Marie Malano, and second, you are my woman. Are we clear on that?"

"Yes, Poppi," she whispered with a smile on her face, a smile that sent tingling sensations through my body, especially my piece. Luckily, I was able to control myself and him for the time being.

"I guess you chose the right table to get some attention stirred up," I said. I pointed out how her people, on every floor that I could see, were either peeping over the balconies on each floor, or coming through the lobby just to see us. Catalina signaled for the waitress, who was also from her country.

"Yes, ma'am, can I help you?"

"I want them all back to work right now. What they do in the eyes of the residents is embarrassing. Everybody back to work at once," she said very gracefully and in a tone of voice that she would use when she talked to me.

"Si senorita," the waitress stated as she left us to get on the phone.

Sixty seconds later, Catalina's request spread like a California wild fire on a windy day. Within three minutes, traffic in the Tower was back to normal.

"Do me a favor?" I asked Catalina.

"Anything you ask, Stephon."

"Never, ever, raise your voice at your people. To sound like a dictator is not good Catalina."

"This I know first-hand, Poppi, and I will never do that."

"So, tell me the real reason you have me down here," I asked with curiosity.

"Since you asked, Stephon, they are coming through the front doors as we speak."

I looked over my shoulder, trying not to draw too much attention, and saw five Hispanic men making their way through the door of the Tower.

"Stephon, you said don't move without you, so I stop the meeting in San Antonio and brought it to me."

"Good move, girl!"

"You like, yes?"

"If I had time, I would kiss your ass, my Honduras mommy," I said.

"Oooh, you freaky man, you save that for later."

"One last rule, Catalina: never get out of your seat when they come or go."

"Why is that, Stephon?"

"Because that's what queens do Catalina; and it is seen as power and they respect that!"

"I understand, Poppi."

"Are you ready for this?" I asked her.

"Hell, no!" she replied.

"Well, you should have been."

"Mr. Stephon Wilkerson, I presume?" one of the gentlemen inquired. He candidly stuck out his hand for a greeting.

"No disrespect to either of you or your people, but let's drop the 'Mr.' shit and just stick with 'Stephon'. I'm still learning how to become a man," I said as I shook his hand.

"Please, let me introduce you to everyone, and I'll give you our full names because we have nothing to hide from you or Senorita Malano." He pointed to each man during the introduction. "This is Mr. Hector Gonzales, Mr. Miguel Ortiz, Mr. Eddie Punto, Mr. Jesus De La Rosa, and I am Juan Sias." As they each shook my hand, they took Catalina's hand and kissed it as a formal greeting of royalty.

"I want to explain to each of you that I am in no way influencing Ms. Malano in her decisions today, nor will I do so in the future; what she does for her people, your people, and the country that holds your people—she does this from her own heart. I asked Ms. Malano if she would put her life on the line for her people and she said, 'yes'. The minute she told me that, I knew that what she was about to do was something I could not hinder or get in the middle of. Today, I assure you that if either of you are not willing to protect this woman with your lives, don't ask her to put hers on the line. I am no more than a young boy, but I assure each of you if I find out that harm has come to her or death, and it was through any of you, I will kill you." I was calm and straightforward, but the look on my face let them know I was dead serious. They all looked at each other in total amazement from what I had just said, and Catalina grabbed my hand.

"Stephon, as you prefer," said Juan Sias, "We do not take your words as threats, but as a promise to us. Whether you know or not, Senorita Malano was ready to risk her life for you as well. You, sir, are a very big man in some little shoes, and along with Senorita Malano, you, too will have our highest respect and protection until this thing is finished, or for life, if you want it."

"Please, gentlemen, take your seats and if there is anything you would like, your money is no good as long as you are in the Tower." I looked over at Catalina, kissed her cheek and told her to take care of her business.

"Out of respect gentlemen, I will leave you to your business; Catalina..."

"Baby, I'll be fine," she stated as she patted me on my hand. I made my way to the bar and saw Carlos headed up on the elevator with shit on his face. It was clear that he knew who the men were, and what they were at the Tower to do. I signaled for Catalina's personal luggage handler and valet.

"Stephon, what's up?"

"You have some people on Carlos' floor?"

"Men and women, what's up?" he asked again.

"I want to know if Carlos is ever on Catalina's floor or my uncle's; and if the snake is going up to his floor by elevator or catching the stairs anywhere in this building, I want to know about it," I instructed.

"As you wish, Stephon," he stated as he walked back to his station and got on the phone.

The meeting went on for three hours before I saw those at Catalina's table shake hands. As soon as the gentlemen stood, I approached them and Catalina. I walked up, kissing Catalina on her cheek.

"Are you okay?" I asked her.

"Yes, Stephon, and things will start getting better," she replied.

"Gentlemen, I pray that all went well for you and your trip was not wasted," I said.

"Oh, no, Stephon, this trip was well worth it because we had the pleasure of meeting you face to face. It is very important that Senorita

Malano has a strong man—not behind her, but at her side," stated Mr. De La Rosa. "I repeat; I am here because I understand the humanitarian effort that Ms. Malano is trying to set forth and to ensure that she is respected."

"No disrespect, but can I steal her away from you now?" I asked. They all laughed.

"She is all yours, Stephon," said Mr. Ortiz.

"No sir, Mr. Ortiz, she is not all mine. Her life is dedicated to God first, her people second, then I get the rest Mr. Ortiz." I could tell that they all liked hearing that by the way they shook my hand before I dragged Catalina back upstairs.

She couldn't wait to get me in the room; tearing the buttons off my shirt as she undressed me in the hallway.

"Damn, Catalina. Give me some time to get the door open."

"When you say what you say to those men about me, you cause me to wet between my legs with love, and I wanted you right then and there, black man. So get the damn door open and allow me to serve you like a queen should."

It was nine o'clock when I rolled over to look at the clock, and I had put Uncle James on hold long enough. After a quick shower and a few kisses on Catalina's face as she slept, I was headed down to the next floor. As I walked into the living room, Uncle James was standing in the window looking over the city.

"So how did everything go today?" Uncle James asked.

"To be honest, it's been a lot of sex and no talking," I replied.

"Don't you want to know?" he asked.

"It's not my business to meddle in, Uncle James."

"So that's how it is, huh?" he asked.

"Uncle James, it's not my business, and I have no intentions of making any of it my business either."

"So, you've made your choice?" he asked.

"This is not about picking and choosing with me, and if you place me in such a category, it's because you've placed me there and not because I asked to be there."

"I ain't mad at you, nephew. You do what you have to do," he said, but then whispered, "And I'll do what I have to." He didn't intend for me to hear the last part of what he said.

"I'll be out on business. Shit ain't changed just because Catalina has an apartment. If you're in the building, check on the crib off and on," Uncle James said.

"I will," I replied. "Got to get back to my business before she wakes up."

"Tell her I said, 'hi'," he requested. I knew war had started as soon as I closed the door behind me. I had to be inside of the bank if I wanted to hold on to the money I had, because Uncle James would drain the account ASAP.

I knew I was on my own from there on out. There was no sense in me asking him about my savings or how much I had left. A new Jaguar, lease paid up, utilities paid up, tags still on my clothes, and a questionable fifty thousand dollars. He owed me nothing! Screw him, I said to myself as I walked down the hallway to board the elevator. As I approached the doors, Catalina was heading towards me.

"Hey, Poppi. You have been to your uncle's, yes?"

"Yeah, baby, and what are you doing up out of bed?"

"Really wondering if I should let you come in here and kick your ass."

"For what! What did I do?" I asked.

"You tell me to tell them to fix you food, remember?"

"Damn, baby, I forgot and it's your damn fault anyway," I shot back at her.

"Oooh, no, black man, do not blame me for nothing."

"Did you not drag me in here with this Isley Brothers shit?"

She started laughing. "You could have told Catalina no!" she stated.

"What?"

"You don't know how to handle a woman from Honduras or what?" she taunted and then put her hands on her hip waiting on my response.

I had only two words for her, "Fuck you!"

"No, that is why you got in trouble with the ladies, black man." She walked up and started kissing me.

Sunday morning came around and after explaining to Catalina what I felt about Uncle James, she was upset that I wanted to leave early. She wanted my advice on receiving a paycheck from the five wise men that paid her a visit. They felt that she should get compensated for the work that she was putting in for her people. One thing they made clear to her after she had repeatedly declined their offer was that she worked for the Tower, and her time that she put in on a 24-7 basis earned her the right to be compensated. The money was made legally through their companies, and for her to refuse it would be disgraceful. I told her to save every dime of the money in case she wanted to give it back.

When my car pulled up, I noticed that it was washed and waxed. I looked inside and saw that it was spotless and had a full tank of gas in it already. She smiled at me. "You like how I take care of my man, Poppi?"

"Yeah, I like that," I replied as I drew her near to me. "How long is this shit going to take, Catalina?"

"We cannot rush change, Stephon," she said.

"Something come up, you call me at the hotel, girl."

"Poppi, there is no need to worry about me. I am safe."

"I love you, girl."

"You know every time you tell me this, I want to put on the Isley Brothers. Yes, I love you too, my black man."

"I'll call you tonight, baby," I told her and kissed her goodbye.

I pulled back into Irving about one o'clock, taking the south bound exit to Beltline Road, and passing up the mall made me think about Monica. I vowed to call her once I was done with Fran. As usual, she was on her patio doing her thing with her plants, in some Daisy Duke ass shorts, and a tank top that barely held her breast in. I was glad to see her in that outfit because I really wanted to relax.

"What's up, lady?"

"I was just thinking about you," she said.

"So that means that I hadn't been on your mind prior to that thought?" I asked her.

"Hell, a whole lot of times before then," she replied.

"So what's on Fran's agenda today?"

"Have you forgotten about our little arrangement?" she asked.

"I really just stopped by to see if that's what you wanted."

"Are you busy now?" she asked as she continued to water her plants without looking down at me. I took that as a "come on with it" and went home to check on the place and put up my things.

I was passing her balcony when I heard her say, "It's open." I was expecting Gee-Gee to be at the door, but all I received was a naked Fran. "I've been waiting on this all weekend, sweetheart. I hope that your week hasn't been too stressful on you because I need you to give Fran a good repeat," she said as she undressed me. I gave Fran more than what she asked for, and not one time during the encounter did she instruct me.

When it was my time, I looked over on the dresser and saw my payment in the same tan-colored envelope. I purposely gave her all that I had, pulling out all the stops in a way that would guarantee a request for an encore performance.

"Please tell me that we have an appointment next week?" Fran asked.

"If that's what you want," I replied, nonchalantly. I was cleaning myself up while she laid in her king-sized sleigh bed in the fetal position.

"Stephon, wait, baby. Hand me my handbag, please." She reached in it and handed me another five hundred dollars. "Baby, you were excellent. I swear you truly deserve this."

I opened her legs and used my fingers to play with her clit for a few seconds. She thought I wanted some more.

"Ooooh nooo, baby, Fran can't take no more of what you're issuing out. Hell, I'm doing good to be accepting what you're giving now at sixty-three years old."

When she barked out her age, I looked over at her body and said, "Bullshit!" I sat there for a few seconds trying to accept the sixty-three jolt. Nevertheless, we made plans for the next Sunday and discussed the job at the Bay Hotel. In less than fifteen minutes, I was out of her crib and at home showering her leftovers off of me like it never happened.

For some reason, Monica was on my mind, so I called her up. After having to go through the usual rigmarole with the store's switchboard operator, Monica was on the phone.

"Stephon is this you?"

"How come it couldn't be another brother or sister for that matter?"

"Because out of the four years that I've worked here, the only person that has called me on my job was my mother."

"So how are you doing today?" I asked.

"I won't do any frontin' today, but I'm blessed, Stephon."

"You hungry?" I asked her.

"You stay your ass away from me Stephon Wilkerson. Fooling with you I've gained six pounds. No, I don't want to eat!"

"Damn, you gettin' on my ass like I forced you to eat all that food."

"Stephon, the food was so damn good, I couldn't help it."

"Four years, how come you haven't moved to Irving?"

"I wish I could, but things just ain't right for me yet; but I plan to."

"So what's your off day this week coming up?"

"Tuesday and Wednesday. Yours?" she asked.

"They told me to choose my own days and I haven't yet."

"Must be nice," she said.

"We'll see. I'll call you later in the week with the scoop. Are you the type of woman that will allow her pride to get in her way?"

"Sometimes I will." At least she was honest in her reply.

"Let me come by before you get off and give you a blessing."

"Why?" she asked.

"Because I got it like that, and if you give me any bullshit, about some past shit you went through with some other chump, I'll never call you again or buy anything from you. As a matter of fact, if you mention anything about paying me back, I'm through with our friendship. I'm not in the habit of doing this, but when I like you and I can help relieve some burdens…girl, just say okay."

"You kill me with your kindness, Stephon."

"To hell with that. Yes or no?" I did not want explanations or excuses from her…just an answer.

"Okay, okay. You don't have to get crazy, boy."

"I'll be there in about thirty minutes; bye."

I decided to make my move toward Monica, and as I walked to my car, I saw Fran leaving as well. We just looked at each other as she drove past me. I met Monica in record time. She was waiting on me to park and step inside of Dillard's.

"Stephon, you look good in blue jeans and a tee-shirt." She looked me up and down.

"You just watching a brother's ass that's all."

She just started laughing. Stepping in closer to her, I gave her the thousand dollars I made doing Fran.

"Say, hold up. Wait until I leave before you look in the envelope because I don't want to hear the sentimental conversation."

"Can I at least give you a hug?" she asked.

"Yeah, as long as you don't be feelin' on my muscles or my ass," I replied.

I noticed tears building up in her eyes and was ready to go after the hug.

"Thank you, Stephon."

"You don't even owe me that, Monica. I have to get me some sleep, woman. I'll check on your sentimental, country ass in a few days."

"You gon' stop callin' me country 'cause I's from the city now'." We both smiled at her imitation of a country accent.

"Bye, Monica," I said as I walked out of the store.

Chapter SEVEN

SHIFTED

Though my alarm was set to go off at seven in the morning, combating Uncle James was going to take more than just an early rise. It was 5:30 a.m. and the only thing that ran through my head was, Boy if you want to get the jump on somebody, you have to catch them before they piss in the morning. Well, Uncle James, we'll see if your words stand true. One thing I knew for sure, I had to leave the complex before the rush started up and before Debra drove up. Being in the parking lot of the bank when LaShonda drove up was my main objective. As much shit as she talked about her employer needing her, I was counting on her "employee of the week, the month, and the year" skills.

Five minutes to explain why I needed all my money withdrawn at 7:59 a.m. was all I needed, and her running late this particular morning would place the beginning of some major burdens in my world. The bank was twenty minutes across town and it was just six o'clock; but something inside of me was ordering me to leave that apartment as soon as possible. With all the shit going on with Catalina, Carlos, and Uncle James, the thought of me being an innocent neutron-plus the

•153•

possibility of losing my life- wasn't registering too well with me.

I rode around in circles of the blocks that were minutes from the bank, looking for some form of breakfast after catching the first wave of traffic out of the neighborhood. After getting coffee, juice and a doughnut at a 7-Eleven, I found a spot in the parking lot where I thought LaShonda and other bank employees might park. Finally, I spotted her yellow-bone ass pulling onto the lot, swaying back and forth to an unknown tune. I had been standing outside of my car to make sure my presence was known in case she came in another way. I knew that if I missed seeing her, at least a rumor of me being out in the lot would have made its way back to her and she would have come looking for me.

As soon as her double take concluded that I was who she thought she was seeing, she pulled up.

"Boy, what are you doing here so damn early?"

"How much time can you spare and I need to know right now?" I said with a serious look on my face. She looked down at her watch. "Eight minutes," she replied. As soon as I explained what was going on, she had nine words to say to me before rushing off, "Give me your bank book and meet me inside!"

It was 8:00 a.m. straight up, and I had my hand on the handle of the entrance door of the bank when one of the bank guards turned the key to unlock the door.

I flew past the gentleman, disregarding his salutatory, "Good morning" to me, and went searching for LaShonda. The same sister that gave her a break so that she could talk to me the last time I was in the bank signaled for me to come to her counter. Looking at her as she tried to put in a quick primp on her hair, told me she wanted to put her shot in at hollering at me, and I didn't have time for the shit.

"LaShonda, please...where is she?" I asked.

There was a lot of urgency in my voice. Though disappointed, she quickly said, "Up those stairs, to the right and two doors down at new accounts. My name is Cathy by the way!" she shouted as I took off in LaShonda's direction.

As I pulled the door open that read "New Accounts", LaShonda stood on the other side of the desk from a Hispanic sister speaking a language that was clearly not classified as "banking language".

"Bitch, I'm telling you for the last time to place that account back the way you found it or one of us is going to leave this bank today in a bad way," LaShonda said stepping out of her five-inch high heels.

"LaShonda, this isn't your department, and you don't run a god-damn thing up here, hoe!" replied the Hispanic girl.

"Correction, bitch, Stephon Wilkerson is my business. I'm giving your scank ass five seconds to put that account back the way you found it, bitch, or I'll fuck your world up, and I put this on my mama's life," LaShonda promised and took two steps towards the girl.

"Bitch, just because I'm doing this don't mean that you sold me shit. I need my job, but as soon as you get your funky ass off work, bitch, I need to have a word with you," said the Hispanic girl as she typed on the keypad of her computer. And when she was done, LaShonda put her shoes back on.

"Bitch, anywhere, anytime, because there won't be that much to dis-cuss," LaShonda said to the girl as she pushed half the stuff on the girl's desk onto the floor. "Now clean this shit up bitch and holla at me at 5:01 p.m. and don't be late, hoe!" LaShonda told her. She adjusted her feet in her shoes, lifted her head high, and gracefully walked out the door of the office.

"I won't ask you if all of that was necessary, but is it where I can close out my account?"

"If Cathy is taking care of her business like I asked her to do, your money is waiting for you. What are you doing up here anyway? I told Cathy to call you to her counter, and as soon as I got up here to take care of my business, she could close you out."

"I thought she was trying to get her play on with me."

"She probably was, but she's cool though."

"I need a cashier's check."

"For what?"

"I need to open another account at another bank," I replied.

"Your uncle will have that hoe upstairs to track that check to its destination the minute it clears," LaShonda explained. "Take the cash and open up the account with special conditions that would prevent your uncle from even knowing that you're even at whatever bank you choose."

LaShonda and I hadn't made it all the way down the stairs when Cathy threw the thumbs up in our direction.

"What do I owe you, red bone?"

"You've already paid me in full, Stephon, and I want to thank you for sending my mother those flowers. She's still telling me that I need to wrestle your fine ass down with a choke hold if necessary, and force you to marry me."

We chuckled behind that shit as we walked up on Cathy.

"I didn't wait to ask you how you wanted your money, Stephon; but I gave you all one hundred-dollar bills, if that's cool with you?"

"I can't get my friend here," I said, pointing at LaShonda, "to accept a token of gratitude, but I hope you will allow me to give you something for your help in this matter."

LaShonda stood back on her legs, placed her hands on her hips and said, "Girl, you better not!" Cathy looked at LaShonda, smiled, and put her face within inches of LaShonda's face and said, "Girlfriend, I love you like a sister, but talk to the hand right now cause Cathy is too busy to hear that shit you talkin' about."

Then she looked at me.

"Now before we were rudely interrupted, I would like a dinner date with your fine ass, but if I can't have my cake and eat it too, I'll settle with a dinner at the joint Ms. Thang here keeps telling me about."

I looked over her counter in a playful gesture to see how fine she was and LaShonda popped me on my shoulder.

"Look, Cathy, I'll have to pass on the date invitation with your fine ass because I'm already dealing with a conspiracy to get me married off, so I'll stay neutral and respect my friend," I said, while hugging on LaShonda.

"Damn, Shonda, get out the way," Cathy said as she slid me fifty thousand dollars to count. "Cathy, can I get you to do something special for me?"

"If it has something to do with getting naked with you, you don't have to ask, baby." She winked her eye along with her comment.

"Girl, stop with your hot ass," said LaShonda, as they gave each other high fives and laughed.

"Okay, on the serious side, will you treat my girl to dinner for me?" I asked as I slid five hundred dollars to Cathy. She looked at LaShonda for about ten seconds and smiled.

"Bitch, you better be glad I love your short red ass. Plus, I wouldn't waste this opportunity on any no-good-ass-Negro anyway. Okay, Stephon, I'll take her!"

"I have to run, ladies; but I'll call you later, 'Red'. And thank you for everything. By the way, LaShonda…don't get your ass kicked today."

"Kiss this," she said as she pointed at her perfectly round ass.

"I'm not into that kind of shit yet, but I might be willing to learn, little mama," I said as I walked off.

As I headed towards my ride, there was something that LaShonda said earlier about conditions preventing someone from obtaining information about my account that made me do an about-face back into the bank. LaShonda saw me come back in, but since she had three customers already standing in her line, I went to Cathy.

"You change your mind about me?" she asked with a smile on her face.

"I need to make two calls, Cathy. Both long distance. Can you make that happen for a brother?"

"Keep them short as possible and it's done! Come; follow me," she said as she walked me into an empty office and closed the door. I immediately dialed Catalina at the Tower.

"Good morning and thank you for calling The Tower Over Austin. This is Lucy; how can I assist you?"

"Morning, Lucy, this is Stephon and I need to speak with Catalina like yesterday!"

"Hold on," she stated.

"Stephon, what's wrong, baby?"

"Don't I get a good morning, Poppi?" I hoped she could hear my smile through the phone lines, even if it was forced.

"Yes, but Lucy made it sound like it was very important."

"I am, aren't I?" I stated.

"Stop playing, Poppi."

"I need to speak to whichever one of your visitors it was who had a friend at a bank in Irving."

"Mr. Sias would be the one, Stephon."

"I need to talk with him right now, Catalina."

"I cannot say the number over the line, but if you can give me the number where you are, I will contact him and ask him to call you right back," she said.

"214-555-2131; and the extension is 743."

"Call me soon, Poppi," she said before she hung up.

Two minutes had ticked off of the clock when the phone rang.

"Mr. Sias," I asked.

"What can I help you with, Stephon?"

"My uncle opened up a fifty thousand dollar account for me and after finding out about your meeting with Catalina, he has decided to punish me for choosing to stand by my girl. He tried to remove the money out of the account, but I withdrew the money first. He has influence where I bank, sir, and I need to be at a bank where he, or no one else for that matter, can get on the phone and find out that I do business with a certain bank. Can you assist me, sir?"

"First Commerce Bank of Irving. Go see a lady by the name of Ms. Lupe Montoya, and she will take care of you. I will make sure that you and your business remain as if you were a ghost."

"Thank you, sir," I said.

"Irving is a very productive city for many of my people, if you understand me, Stephon."

"I'll keep that in mind, Mr. Sias. Now you know where I stand with my uncle?" I emphasized my words to make sure he got my message.

"Remain stern, Stephon," he said as he hung up.

After seeing Lupe, I was reassured that my dealings at First Commerce would be above personal. As I walked through the door of my apartment, I wasn't expecting a message from Uncle James because his calling card came in a way of attempting to take my money. Though I wasn't due in at the Bay until two o'clock, I needed to find some peace, so I got dressed and showed my face early.

"Well, well now... everybody meet the King of the afternoon shift," said Steve.

"Stephon, this is my morning crew starting with Sam, my pick-up guy; Sally, my desk manager and Dennis, my luggage guy; and crew... meet Stephon."

After the formal greetings were over, I was dragged into Steve's office.

"So, why the early bird, Stephon?"

"I'd like to know something about my crew."

"What would you like to know?" he asked.

"Who can I depend on the most?"

"Lora; if I had to choose one out of the three."

"Why her?" I asked.

"She's been here longer than I have," he replied.

"So why didn't she get this job, Steve?"

"She's turned it down three times in the past seven years. I guess if you decide that you've out-grown the place like the other guys that were here before you did, I'll be asking her again."

"If I wanted to stay out of her way to allow her to do what she's used to doing, what would you suggest I do?" I asked.

He laughed slightly and responded, "Give her the desk and stay out of her way. She enjoys working her desk, and if you take that away from her; well, just don't shorten her duties and we won't have to call an ambulance for you. You have a good crew, Stephon; you'll see."

"Say Steve, my phone has been ringing off the hook with 'when are you coming home' from my whole damn family. What do I have to pay for a hide-out for a few days?" I asked as I pulled out about fifteen hundred dollars.

"Stephon, son, you're a manager here. You pay for the maid service, which is fourteen dollars a day, and stay as long as you want."

"Get off the bullshit!" I replied.

"Have it your way, son; you asked; I told you."

"Well, if you don't mind, I'd like to walk the hotel from top to bottom, inside and out, before my crew gets here. I would like a complete roster of everybody from the gardener to the cook on my shift, and a list of everything that has been reported, but hasn't been fixed."

"You are good, son. Give me a few minutes and I'll get you everything you need. Sounds like you're after my job," he said with a questionable smile on his face.

By the time I made my rounds, which was a front to pick out what I felt was the safest room in the building, my crew was coming through the front doors of the Bay, and I greeted them as they came in.

"Ben Colby, my pick-up guy; Doug, my luggage guy; and Ms. Lora. For the record, Lora, I'm your right-hand man, and if you need me, just holla. It's nice to see all of you again, and since I'm told I can structure this shift as I please, I have only one rule—just show up!"

I had to break the ice that stood between me and my crew. The best way I knew how to bring about some positive feelings in a man or a woman, was by doing what made me feel good, shopping for new clothes!

I received my copy of a memo from the owner of the hotel asking for ideas that would bring a new look to the place. I can say that I was lucky to have accepted the job when I did because each manager was receiving a bonus. I wasn't planning on accepting the money for my personal benefit, but I asked Steve to allow it to be sent to me anyway. Six thousand dollars was some nice shopping money; plus, I refused the manager's raise, but opted to have that money to be given to my crew instead. So on my third day, I gave each of them a check for seven hundred and fifty dollars and informed them of my plans to take them shopping the following day before our shift started.

I visited Monica about the whole thing. I picked out what I thought Lora would be banging in since she had an ass on her, but I needed Monica to help me influence her dullness in the dressing department.

I wasn't worried about Ben and Doug, the way they jocked my style, anything I said "yes" to was a go for them!

We all met at Dillard's at 9:45 a.m. sharp, and I turned Lora over to Monica and a white co-worker of hers while the rest of us went to the men's section. In three hours, my team was strapped with enough confidence to take on the runways of New York.

I made it back on the job while the others went home to dress for work, and I couldn't wait for the infamous first shift to see the "new crew on the block"! You might as well say my team rolled up in limousines because they even washed their cars. The way they strolled through the doors, you would have sworn they all bought a can of "Swagger" to compliment the new rags. I stood with my arms folded across my chest as they each signed autographs for the groupies of the first shift. After Steve finished drooling over my crew's makeover, I gave him the receipts for every dime I spent on my crew.

"Stephon, you didn't have to do this, son. Hell, that was your money."

"I did what I felt was right, and since I didn't earn it, I gave it to the people who did!" I replied. "I would appreciate it if you would file those receipts under 'company purchases'."

"But this wouldn't be classified as one," he replied.

"Steve, once headquarters finds out that 'you' did this for your crew, they're going to stroke your pale ass, chief."

"You'll do that for me, son?"

"When I earn mine, Steve, just make sure I get mine." We shook hands and he accepted the receipts.

At that moment, a goddess of a white woman, who had everything working for her, came through the front doors. I mean, from head to toe. I got my ass out of Lora's domain and was headed back to my office when the woman stopped me.

"Excuse me, young man, would you happen to be the manager of this establishment?" she asked.

"At this moment, yes ma'am, I am. How may I assist you?"

"I have some personal items that I would like to secure in your care until I leave," she stated.

"Would you like to secure those items at this time, ma'am?"

"Yes, please," she stated.

"Ma'am, if you would please step around the corner, I'll let you in and we can take care of this in my office, and I'll register you at the same time," I told her.

Once we got in my office, she dug in her purse and pulled out three jewelry boxes and opened each of them, exposing their contents. "Very impressive Mrs. ...."

"Just call me Amanda and please drop the ma'am. It makes me sound old," she said with a smile. We got into a conversation about the sandy, black beaches of South Africa after signing all the necessary paperwork and locking up her jewels. The lady had me and my spirit cruising those shores by yacht while I personally took her bags up to her room.

"I see why you keep such a beautiful tan, Amanda," I told her as I tried to end my travels with her to get back downstairs.

"Well, Stephon—such a beautiful name," she said, "I won't keep you from your duties with all my talking. I do have a favor to ask of you, though."

"Please ask, and if I can make it happen, it's done," I said.

"I'm a bit embarrassed about sitting in a bar, but I enjoy a shot of brandy before I retire to bed. It's sort of a sleeping pill without the narcotics, if I may. Would you mind bringing me two personal size shot bottles of your best brandy please?"

"What time would you like them delivered, Amanda?"

"Oh, I can wait until you get off, if you don't mind, that is," she asked.

"No problem, plus I'm just up the hall from you, so I'll drop them off on my way through. Please enjoy your stay at the Bay, Amanda."

"I plan to, Stephon, and don't work too hard," she said as I closed her door.

By the time I made it back to the office, Lora was moving her fingers around as if she was using sign language. "You trippin' on the juice again, girl?" I asked her.

"I know the old woman talked your ears off, so I thought about telling you some lady by the name of Catalina Malano called about thirty minutes ago, but I didn't want to interrupt your trip to Africa. She stated it wasn't urgent, but she needed to speak with you."

"Thanks, Lora."

"No problem, boss."

It's not urgent, but she needed to speak with me. She's trippin'! It was crazy that she had her own phone in the apartment and yet was never there until it's time to call it a day. I got tired of hearing, "Thank you for calling The Tower Over Austin" primer, so without being a rude ass, I quickly ask for Catalina.

"Catalina, please."

"Hold, please."

"Ms. Malano speaking."

"When can I call my woman at her house?" I asked her.

"When you get ready to call it a day. I call it a day and I make sure that I am at home to receive your calls, do I not?"

"I guess I lose that one, huh?"

"Of course you do!"

"So what's up?" I asked her.

"Your uncle has been in a meeting with four men at his place for six hours now, and they didn't look too happy as they came into the Tower. Hell, your uncle never speak to me as he passes."

"You tell someone to inform you when the men leave the building and I want your sexy ass off the clock and in the apartment when I hang up this phone. Clear?"

"Yes, Stephon!"

"I don't want my uncle to point you out to the other men."

"This bad for me, Poppi?"

"Hell no! I just don't want them to see you. Don't worry, Mommy. Now get off and go home."

"You call me later, yes?"

"Always, lady," I said and hung up.

So the "frat brothers," have come down from the mountains, finally!

Crashing the Tower with some unappealing looks on their faces was a good sign that the pressure Catalina and company were applying was about to invade their grounds. I hadn't spoken with Uncle James since Sunday; and I had no reason to. I thought about him making a bitch out of himself by crashing my pad just to take some things, but that would be little of him. I had been clock-watching for two hours, torturing myself. I wanted to call it a day, drop Amanda's juice off, and get the scoop on the five shystie Negroes.

I waited until my crew was off the lot before I swung around to the bar to pick up the single shot bottles for Amanda. I was running ten minutes past my promise, and if she didn't come to the door after my first knock, I was on my way to my own cave. I tapped on the door as lightly as I could and got a reply.

"Stephon?" she asked.

"Yes, it's me, Amanda."

"Are you alone?"

"Yes," I replied as I stood back far enough so that she could see me through the peephole. As soon as she opened the door, she walked back into the room.

"Just don't stand there, Stephon. Come in and sit the bottles on my nightstand, please."

I stood there in awe because Amanda came to the door in a total see-through nightgown that was thigh length and showed she had a nice tanned ass. My mind shot back to our conversation of her being in South Africa lying out on the deck of a yacht. Now I knew it was in the nude. I wasn't trying to do any trippin, but saw my whole life flash before me and ending with a prison sentence of life without parole because some old lady said I raped her.

"Stephon, please come in and close the door." I did it just to please the woman's conscience.

"Look, Amanda, I'm not trying to get myself caught up." She came over to me and silenced me by placing her index finger on my lips.

"I'm trying to get caught up, Stephon. You have no reason to be afraid. Look at me. Do I not have a beautiful body?"

"Amanda."

"Yes, Stephon. I'm old enough to probably be your grandmother, but I'm still a woman." Instantly she had my hand in hers and began using it to caress her breasts. "Will you stay with me for just a little while, Stephon?" Her words seemed to be said out of necessity as she unfastened my pants.

All I could think about was Fran telling me, "Never take charge or assume what we want; allow us to choose what we want."

"Will you stay with me, Stephon?" she repeated her request.

"This is what you want, Amanda?"

"Yes it is, Stephon." Her fingers continued to undress me until I stood before her naked.

"You are strong; and very healthy for a young black man. Do you know what this is, Stephon?" She held up a small bottle of honey.

"It's honey."

"Oh no, my strong black man, this is a gift for you and me both." Slowly she started to pour it all over my cock until it dripped down onto a towel she had laid beneath me. She continued to pour the honey until every inch of me was dripping with the thickness of nature.

"Yes, yes, yes!" Excitement seemed to grow inside her as she knelt down on her knees and started catching the drippings of honey in her mouth.

Never speak or control the conversation, Fran's instructions whispered in my head.

"Yes! Yes!" Amanda said as evidence of missed droppings of honey ran down the sides of her nose and chin.

I remained absolutely quiet and still for Amanda and allowed her to feed on my stiffness until she was satisfied. What really turned me on was to watch her play with her own body as she entertained me. She was so wet between her legs that sometimes I heard her wetness speak out to me in a smacking sound. She placed her hand in mine, "Please help me up, Stephon," she begged as she looked into my eyes the whole time getting up.

She took my hand and led me to the bed. As if dancing to a song playing only in her head, she raised her gown over her head rhythmically before crawling onto the bed and showing me her honey spot from the back. Once she chose the spot that gave her the most pleasure and me the easiest access, she took a pillow and placed it under her butt and reached out for my hand to usher me into her private world.

Placing myself between her legs, I waited on her to take my piece in her hand and lead me into her depths. Slow Stephon, and find her depths, I reminded myself.

"Ooooh. Aah. Yes. Yes," she moaned until I couldn't go any deeper.

Give her time to adjust to you, Fran had told me. Once Amanda's hips began to gyrate in circular motions, I knew she was ready. Slow, long and deep ran through my mind as I placed my arms and hands in position just like I had been instructed by Fran.

Her body was calling me. Begging for my stiffness. I started singing a song to block out her moans that only had three words to the hook; slow, long and deep…never raising up off her clit.

"Oooh, I can't believe this. You've got it just right." I drove deep as I could to silence her before she broke my concentration.

"Oooh. Aaah, Yeah—careful, baby."

Slow, long and deep, I repeated to myself until I felt her muscles tighten all around my shaft with a death grip that only good sex can muster.

"Don't you dare stop, Stephon!" Her instructions got louder as she pulled her legs up and locked them around my waist.

Slow, long and deep, I sung while another gripping moment surrounded my man. Her legs released me, and she gently asked me off of her by pushing me at my chest. I obeyed. She rolled over onto her knees, and showed me her golden bronze lips that yearned for every inch of me.

"Stephon," she called out to me, never looking back at me.

"Yes?"

"Be gentle with me?" she asked. I entered her slowly, until my sack touched her outer walls, I waited on her permission to start my delivery, and when she started to rock her body back and forth slowly, I knew what she wanted.

Halfway out, put it back where you found it Stephon. Again, Stephon, slowly. Now do it ten times and stop, Fran's voice said as I followed her instruction.

"Nooo, nooo, don't stop, I can take it, baby," Amanda begged.

Hearing her beg for me like that made my hands lock around her hips like the jaws of a pit bull.

"Stop, Stephon!" I was really ready to tell the voice of Fran's ghost to get the hell out of my business until I heard Amanda's voice remind me to be gentle with her.

Halfway out, put it back where you found it, lasted through two hard grips from her inner walls.

"Harder, Stephon!" Amanda ordered.

There's a difference between making love and screwing Stephon, came to mind as I visualized Fran.

"I said harder, damn you, Stephon!" Amanda said with a sense of frustration because she had to ask me the same thing twice.

I gave it to her as ordered, and Amanda accepted every stroke of the pounding I put on her. I watched her grab as much of the sheets as her delicate hands could hold as I tightened my grip around her thin waistline. The moment I came and emptied myself into her, she knew it was over.

"Take it out, Stephon," she ordered. As I removed myself from within the warmth of her walls, Amanda laid down on her side. I got a glimpse at her face and saw that she had been crying; a reality that frightened me.

"I'm not crying because you did something wrong, Stephon; I'm crying because I miss my youth. I asked you to give me what you just gave me because it takes me back forty years—back to when life was good to me. I'm not ashamed of this; I cherish every moment of it, and you should too." She reached under the other pillow, grabbed my hand and placed a roll of money in it that was held tightly by several rubber bands. "Thank you, Stephon, now please hand me my Brandy, get dressed and leave." I did as she requested and left.

The moment I made it into my room, I closed the door and placed my back up against it and asked myself one hell of a question—who am I?

Listening to Amanda's last words had me shifting from right to left. I fell to the floor with my legs folded underneath me. But in my deepest self-judging moment, whether my actions with Amanda were good or bad, I arrived at my crossroads. I couldn't help thinking about Honey when she stated, "Honey might be old, but I ain't dead." Just to keep it real with myself, I began grasping for reasons, or one, maybe just one "reason" to justify what I had just done. My actions placed me at war with my conscience. My shift to the right was my choice and my stand with all the shit going on in and around my world.

My standard of choice was far from that of Dr. Kevorkian, and if I am to be judged for what I have done, then so be it! I opened up my hand and stared at the roll of money that Amanda had placed in my hand. I placed a firm grip around that money and lifted my ass off the floor. You either use or get used in this world, came to mind and it was clear that I allowed myself to get used, and from where I stood, fair exchange wasn't a robbery.

Seeing the light blinking on the phone let me know that Catalina had called. I showered as quickly as I could because I knew she would call again. The phone rang as I was in the process of drying off, and I answered it to avoid annoying Catalina.

"Hi, lady."

"You worry me at times, Stephon," she said.

"Is that a bad thing or a good thing, Catalina?" I asked.

"Because I call the apartment and leave sweet, sexy messages for my man, and someone pick up the phone. I say 'Poppi, is that you?' and they hang up. That's why you worry me tonight, Stephon."

"What time was this, Catalina?"

"Ten, ten on the clock!"

I looked at my watch and saw that it was almost midnight.

"You listen to me, Stephon—and I do not play either—if you tell me, or I even feel you go to the apartment tonight, I will get into my car and come to you."

"You sit your ass still, girl."

"No!" she snapped.

"Catalina!"

"No, I say to you again."

"My uncle?" I asked.

"He has not left the building, and I have my people watching all night, Poppi."

"What time did the other men leave his apartment?" I asked.

"They leave about one hour after we talk last."

"I want you to call Mr. Sias and tell him that I'll be pulling up at the apartment at 6:00 a.m. I need a safe passage to the apartment."

"Stephon, you come home this weekend, yes?"

"Too much going on right now."

"Oh, I forgot to tell you, Poppi, I put money for you in the compartment of your car before you left."

"Girl!" I said.

"I want to take care of you, Stephon. Do not fuss at me for that."

"Don't do that, and if I need you for something, I'll ask you, cool?"

"No, not cool!"

"You are going to make me spank your ass, ornery girl!"

"What is this, 'ornery' that you speak of, Stephon?" she asked.

"It means, 'hard headed', 'stubborn'."

"Like you, Stephon?" she asked. "Anyway, Poppi, I hear about the spanking of the ass. I may like it too, if you feel me!"

"Stop using my words, girl. Get your own words for the last time."

"Stop hating, playa," she mocked.

"So you want to play now, huh?" I asked her.

"Stop trippin, daddy." She impressed me with her advancement in the English language.

"As soon as I get home, girl."

"I'm just playing, Poppi."

"Call Sias, woman, and I'll get back with you sometime tomorrow." I let a small chuckle escape my lips.

"You better not have me worry, Stephon."

Hell, you'll get all you need to know from Sias before 7:00 a.m., so stop trippin'."

"I will call right now, Poppi." Her assurance was all I needed.

We ended our conversation and hung up at the same time.

Well, that was yet another step that I had to secure, and I couldn't avoid asking, or wondering, whether Uncle James would allow harm to come to me or if he would have me hurt. I got dressed and went down to the bar for some of that non-narcotic sleep aide Amanda spoke about. It was a good night for some much needed rest.

It was 6:02 a.m. when I pulled onto the parking lot of my apartment. Before I left the Bay I noticed the lawn service truck parked on the lot with two Hispanics sitting in it. I knew they were either Mr. Sias or Carlos' people. As soon as I walked to my car, they nodded a few times, and I did the same in good gesture. I knew then that Catalina had taken care of her business.

There was a store on the corner of Beltline and Pioneer called, Wiki-Wiki, and as I passed up the store by taking the right turn, three more Hispanics raised their hot, steaming cups of coffee at me as they watched me pass. I nodded at them as well. Being that the lawn service truck kept straight and didn't make the right turn with me on to Pioneer, I knew someone was waiting on me at the apartment.

A van was parked in my usual spot with a large Hispanic man sitting sideways in his seat watching me as I drove up.

It's either you or me, I said to myself. I took my .45 automatic handgun out of my glove compartment.

Catalina's envelope fell to the floor of the car, and I thought about her telling me about the stranger in my home. Traffic was flowing out of the complex reckless as ever, and I didn't play the chances down that I couldn't, or wouldn't get hurt with all the people moving out of the parking lot. As I got out of my car covering my pistol with some old newspaper, the Sumo-sized Hispanic man got out of the van and waited on me to come his way.

"Stephon?" he asked.

"That depends on who's asking," I replied as I exposed the tip of the barrel of my gun.

"They call me 'Baby' and my father is Mr. Sias. I personally asked to take care of this for you because of the stance you're taking with my people. Either your nuts are the size of a bull, or you're the stupidest fool on this planet," he said. "As soon as my people heard about the flack your uncle was placing on you, and the bullshit that happened last night at your pad, we stopped questioning your stupidity and concluded that you needed to see a specialist about your over-sized nuts," he roasted on me.

I shook Baby's hand and placed my pistol in my waistband.

"Nobody in or out of your place since my boys got here at 12:45 last night. You need me to go up with you?" he asked.

"No, just chill. There's a white-on-white Cadillac that's going to pull up in front of the office very soon. I need to know if she's taking an interest in the direction of my pad," I told Baby.

"I gather this person is on your uncle's team?"

"Smart man, Baby," I said walking towards my apartment. The only thing that concerned me was the firearms in the place as soon as I walked through the door. I didn't have to look any further, or concern myself with the other spots when the one in the oven was gone.

Uncle James had disarmed me! There was a note in the oven that read, "Touché again." No secret he was talking about the withdrawal of the money. Nothing else was taken or disturbed except the pistols and the answering machine. There wasn't a need for me to stay any longer, so I left.

"You were correct about the lady in the Cadi; she's peeping every move you make brother," Baby informed me.

"Screw her, Baby; she's doing what she's told to do," I vented.

"You need me anymore?" Baby asked.

"I'm good, Baby. It would be very disrespectful of me to ask you if I owe you something for this favor, so I'll just say, 'Thank you'. Please pass that all the way down and up to your father for me."

"It's done, Stephon."

It had been some days since I pushed or pulled anything under Tye's direction, so I had to drop by to see him.

"So look what blew in," said Tye.

"A lot of shit going on in my life right now, Tye."

"What does that have to do with your workout?" Tye asked.

"I'll get back on it in about a week."

"A week?! Shit, you might as well start over then. At least do you some damn push-ups and save me some time so that I don't have to baby your ass."

As soon as Tye said that, it struck a nerve inside of me. I'm not going to baby your ass; I'm not going to baby your ass, played over and over in my memory until it stopped with a picture of Uncle James and me standing face to face when I was eleven.

"Tye, I have to go," I barked at him. I grabbed my bag and walked out of the fitness center in a rush. Tye stood watching me leave, his mouth hanging open, wondering what the hell was wrong with me.

I reached for the envelope Catalina left me, opened it and counted the money as soon as I closed the door to my car. Five thousand dollars. She was coming up a little too fast for me, but I needed the money. I was headed back to the Bay to unwrap what Amanda gave me last night.

When I pulled up in my parking spot, Steve came out to the lot, calling for me.

"One of the guests checked out and left a thank you card for you. Told me you were the perfect gentleman."

"I'm always that, Steve," I stated, taking the card out of his hand.

"I'll let you go, youngster. Looks like you have a few things on your mind."

"Thanks, Steve," I said. I walked off reading Amanda's note. All she had written was that she would see me in thirty days. She had pressed her black cherry painted lip print on the card.

I tore the card and envelope up and trashed it in the hallway trash bin. As I walked into the room, I was glad that the message light wasn't flashing on the phone because I didn't feel like dealing with Catalina right then. I untied the roll of money and smiled at the fact that Amanda had given me two thousand dollars for my services. I grabbed my monthly planner to search for the day that Amanda said she was coming back. I marked it by placing 10:00 p.m. on that day to remind me.

It was almost 9:00 a.m., and I needed to discuss some business with "Ms. Country Bumpkin" and offer her a deal she couldn't refuse. I showered again, dressed, and headed to see Monica before ten o'clock. The doors to the store were being unlocked by the time I parked my car. She was stocking her counter up with more cosmetics when she spotted me.

"I'll pay you two week's pay to get sick, just to kick it with me for four hours on business; yes or no?" She saw that I was serious.

"I'm sick already!"

"I'll meet you at your car and you can follow me back to my job."

"Five minutes," she said as she walked towards the manager's office.

A few minutes after I got back to my car, Monica was headed to her car. I pulled up past her and she followed me back to the Bay.

I lowered my window and instructed Monica to park her car in the spot I pointed at, which was my parking space.

"You're riding with me." She got out and locked the doors.

"Whatever it is, you got some serious stuff on your mind, boy," she said as she got into my car.

"Am I looking that bad, girl?" I asked as I looked at myself in the rearview mirror.

"Hell yeah, and then some!" she replied. "So are you going to start talking, or do I just throw this seventy thousand dollar car in park while you're driving like a bat out of hell, just to get your attention?" she seriously inquired.

I was about five miles from my spot at the Four Season's Mandalay.

"You can wait a few more minutes. I'm trying to grab a booth at our spot before reservations suck them up."

By the time we made it inside, we were just in time to get in before the calls came in. After seating, I gave the waitress time to set our water and menus down before I started talking. Monica was so impatient that she started the conversation.

"Stephon, you're killing me with the suspense, boy."

"Look, after I finish explaining, you'll understand why I need a favor from you," I explained.

After fifteen minutes of dodging around the whole "Catalina situation", I gave just enough info on Uncle James to make him out to be a cold-hearted bastard in Monica's eyes, even though she had never met him.

"So what are you going to do about all this shit?" she asked.

"Monica, I need to get me a place where I can lay my head down and rest without worrying about his antics. My place is paid up for a year, and since I didn't pay for it, I'm not worried about it."

"Shit, I'll live in it!" she quickly made it known.

"I have a better proposal for you, Monica."

"I'm listening," she said. Her eyes got big and she looked like a little girl waiting for a rabbit to jump out of a hat.

"Let me find a place right here in Las Colinas, pay it up for two years, same for the electricity and a phone. If you would put the lease and everything else in your name, you can have the place if we can share the space."

I kept eye contact with her, making sure she knew I was serious. I continued, "I want to be straight up about something." Her eyes dropped down to the napkin in her lap. It was like she knew what was coming next.

"I'm seeing someone back home, so you need not worry about me making a move on you. Hell, between my room at the hotel and going back home sometimes, I'll be lucky to spend a couple of days in the place. You'll have the chance to save your money and be close to your job." She lifted her eyes to look at me and gave me a weak-ass smile.

"I can't, Stephon," she said putting her head down even lower.

"Why, what's wrong, Monica?"

"I have a baby, Stephon." I saw something in Monica that I used to see in a lot of women in the projects when I was growing up.

"Monica, you don't need to be ashamed about that girl." She raised her head and I saw a new look on her face.

"I wouldn't give a damn if you had ten children. Never put your head down because of your children, woman. If a man can't accept you for who you are, or what comes with you, forget that dude. Now that I know you have a child, I'll have to decline on the offer," I said with a half-smile.

"I thought you just said..."

"Don't get your panties caught up in your ass, girl! Now it's a three bedroom and two years of paid daycare and some toys. How's that?" I asked.

Monica got up from the table and ran to the ladies restroom. The waitress gave me a look and I knew I was being called a bastard in her mind. I had to clean that shit up quick.

"It's not what you think...wedding blues."

My small, white lie made the waitress smile.

"Would you like for me to check on her?" she asked through a grin that exposed all her teeth.

"Please do!"

A few minutes later, they came out laughing and smiling. Monica came and hugged me.

"You told that girl we were getting married, crazy ass man."

"That was the best that I could come up with on such short notice."

"What about my stuff in Fort Worth?" she asked.

"What do you have?" I asked.

"On the cool, I'm living with my aunt, and I only have my son's baby bed, clothes and his shit."

"Look, pack your clothes, his shit, leave everything else...because I got you. I'll furnish the place and make sure your son has everything he'll ever need. You can keep it all and you'll owe me nothing. All I want you to do is say, 'yes' without running your ass in the bathroom again."

"Thank you, Stephon."

"Screw that, 'yes or no'? Why do we have to go through this every time we get together?"

"Stephon, I've been knowing you for some months now, and you have turned my whole life upside down, boy. So be patient with me when I'm hesitant. I'm far away from home with a one-year-old son, and I'm scared at times," she confessed.

"Stop being scared, Monica. You have a friend in me, and I ask for nothing in return. Fair warning though."

"What?" she asked with her arched eyebrows raised high.

"When his ass goes to teething and starts chewing on my shoes and shit, I'm putting his ass out!"

"You'll put my baby out?"

"Quicker than his ass can say, 'Mama'!" We both started laughing.

"So, all bullshit aside; can we do this by the end of the month?" I asked her.

"Yeah, and I'm oh so ready to get away from my aunt."

"I want you to find the place, the daycare, take care of the phone and the electricity. Here's seven thousand dollars to start. Give me time to get to the bank and I'll get you some more."

"Boy, I'm not taking that kind of money with me in my purse. Are you crazy? Now, what I'll do is, I'll find everything and you can take me to pay for it all, and then I'll feel safe," she explained.

"Well, just keep in mind, I like to live very well, and don't trip about the price. Just find a nice place," I stated.

"Can we eat?"

"I'll just have a salad," Monica said.

"I'm telling you now, don't ask me for my food, girl."

"Stop bringing me here, Stephon. You know damn well I'm going to eat up some shit. Hell, I'm trying to get, my fine on so that I can find me a man...and you crashing all my good efforts."

"Go wait in the car then." I laughed under my breath.

"This is for you," she said as she threw me the finger.

Once we made it back to the Bay, I gave Monica two thousand dollars to start her off on our project, and I was back on the clock. For a

Thursday, things were moving pretty fast and the place was jumping. Ben had made at least ten trips to pick up commuting guests, and it was just 6:00 p.m. Doug was doing the best he could to deliver our guests' luggage, but they just kept coming and coming.

"Excuse me, young man," came from above me while I was bent down, trying to help Doug tag luggage.

I stood up with an overload of frustration written all over my face and the lady knew it.

"Yes ma'am, how can I help you?"

"I appreciate the Southern gentleman that you are, but please call me Hillary."

"What can I do for you, Hillary?"

"I'll be out roaming the city and won't be back here at the Bay until 10:00 p.m. or a bit after; can I have you to personally deliver my bags up to my room please? Being that you are the manager, I would feel more comfortable about opening my door at that time of the evening."

"I won't have a problem with that, Hillary."

"I'll call you..." she started.

"Stephon—Stephon is my name."

"I'll call you as soon as I get settled, Stephon," she said as she walked out the front door and got into a cab. We finally caught a break and like a good supervisor, I allowed my crew to take a break first and by the time they got back, I had an hour and a half to go before the shift was over. Seeing Hillary's luggage kept reminding me that I had one final thing to do. Steve had a policy posted about not drinking while on the clock, and after the day we'd had, I was ready to buck his ass. I pulled Hillary's registration to see what room she was in, and released a big sigh of relief to know that she was above me on the next floor.

Since I at least had time to enjoy a good meal, I ordered from the desk and waited on it to come my way.

"Stephon, you have a call on line three," Lora informed me.

"Hey, girl."

"Yeah, chief," she responded.

"You look very nice today," I told her because she wasn't receiving any compliments from her truck driver boyfriend.

"Thank you, Stephon," she said with a schoolgirl smile.

"Stephon speaking."

"I found the perfect place and you'll be surprised about the package. Daycare is about six blocks away, and, hold on to your shorts...I informed the leasing agent that I would be paying the lease up for two years, told her that I had a baby, and she agreed to give me the apartment for seven hundred and fifty dollars a month because I was paying the lease up in advance for twenty-four months."

"Damn, little mama, slow down and breathe, girl. So you have a total on everything you'll need?"

"No, because I did not know how much you wanted to put down for electricity or the phone, she said.

"Well, just say a hundred and twenty dollars a month," I replied.

"I'll fill out the application for the apartment tomorrow, and we can take the leasing agent a cashier's check before you go to work."

"What about your job, girl?"

"Baby, I talked with my super, told her I was trying to get away from a bad situation, and she gave me a week off."

"So does that mean you're going to be dragging my ass all over town?" I asked her.

"Now, Stephon, not little old me!" she replied in a deep country girl voice.

"I want to get the apartment, daycare, phone and electricity taken care of by noon because I need to call my mover about an overnight move. So, the quicker I can get my hands on the keys to this mansion you found for us, the better I'll feel and the quicker I can get our shit in it for living purposes. Can you manage to get your things moved or do you need me?" I asked.

"Stephon, let me handle me, okay! You have been so remarkable." Her voice started cracking.

"If you're going to start that sentimental shit, I'm hanging up on your ass, girl."

"I can't help it, Stephon."

"My meal just came in, can I eat please?" I asked.

"I'll be at the Bay at 8:00 a.m."

"No you won't. You'll be at the Bay at 6:30 a.m. so that we can have some breakfast," I told her.

"I'll be there, old mean ass boy."

"Bye, Monica," I said.

Dinner isn't the best of the best when all you're yearning for is some sleep. Every time the phone at the front desk rang, I was waiting on a "Boss, line three" response and finding Catalina on the other end sounding sad.

"Can we talk?" Lora asked.

"Sure, you want my seat?" I asked her.

"I'm cool. Just want you to know that I think you're cool, and I really wasn't looking for us to fuse like this when you came on board because I've never worked for a black guy, and especially not a damn eighteen year old. Another reason I'm in here is to tell you I think your girlfriend is pretty cool, and to kiss your ass in case you're mad that I didn't tell you that she called twice. She asked me if you were busy, and I explained how you were running around helping us do all our jobs and yours too. She said she was proud of you. Second time she called, we were on the down side of cleaning up after that storm of a crowd. Funny thing is, I asked her when the two of you were tying the knot, and she said it was hard getting you to commit to being her full-time boyfriend. I asked her how was she dealing with that, and she just said, 'You don't deal with Stephon, Stephon deals with you!' Stop being afraid of love, Stephon. Catalina said she wants to hear your voice before she goes to sleep. With that, I'm gone boss," she stated.

I sat back and thought about what Lora was saying, but I was too young for what Catalina wanted and not old enough to fulfill my own expectations. The next shift was coming on and they were late as always. The phone rang just about the time I was gathering Hillary's luggage up, and I expected to hear Catalina's voice, but it wasn't.

"This is Hillary O'Donald. Who am I speaking with?"

"Hillary, this is Stephon. I've been expecting your call."

"Would you please be so kind to bring my bags up?" she asked.

"I'm on my way up."

The closer I got to her room, I knew it wasn't right, but what made me toss what I was feeling aside was Hillary acting like all black people she came in contact with were supposed to cater to her needs. It was in the tone of her voice, like a privileged expectation to which she was entitled. I knocked on her door twice before hearing my name being called on the other side of the door.

"Yes, it's me," I said. When the door opened, the bitch stood in the door with a monogrammed robe on, pointed her finger towards a sitting area in her suite, as if to say, "Darkie, put those bags in there". I looked at her ass, rolled my eyes and took her bags where she wanted them placed.

Once the door closed behind me, I knew what was up. I turned around slowly and saw her robe hit the floor.

This shit is crazy, I said to myself.

"Stephon, do you like nice things?" she asked.

"Don't you?" I said.

"Well, of course; only the best," she stated.

"Do you believe in good business, Stephon?"

"Good business is always about supply and demand, Hillary."

"Bravo, Stephon! You are free to leave if you want. I'm a businesswoman, Stephon. I deal strictly with the best of products," she explained as she walked toward me, never taking her eyes off mine.

I stood there and let her completely undress me, and then she rubbed my entire body down in some imported body oil out of India. "Now me, Stephon," she said as she handed me the oil to massage her body in the same manner that she had done to me. I knew exactly what I had to do, how it was supposed to be done and how long. I had made up my mind that I was banging any and every old school that pushed up on me, after I got through with Hillary.

For a woman to want it strictly from the back, made me ask why. She stated it was to hide her shame. Hillary said she grew up being told to hate the black man, and it was when she tested the waters that her mind was made up. If she was to go against her upbringing to fulfill her desires, she wanted it in a way where history couldn't look her in her face while she received the root.

And that's just the way I gave my root to her, over and over again before calling it a night.

I counted out three thousand dollars after I came out of the shower, as the water helped me erase the traces of bigotry. The moment I came up with the idea about sharing an apartment with Monica, whether or not I was making the right judgment or not, was not going to be placed on a scale of consideration for someone else's feelings because I needed for things to be this way for now. The only question in my mind was, How far are the frat brothers willing to take their bullshit, and what is really at stake?

Whether or not Catalina understood my decision wasn't going to be a deciding factor for me, just as some of the decisions she had made disregarded factors on my end. If she won't understand, cool, I thought as I dialed her number. So be it.

"Stephon?" she asked in a drowsy voice.

"If that's who you want it to be," I replied.

"Are you mad at me, Stephon?"

"Why would I be?"

"Because I called you all day to see how you were doing,"

"I guess Baby didn't have enough information to ease your curiosity, huh?"

She started yawning. "Are you going to continue to badger me or tell me what you found?" she asked and yawned again.

"He took all my protection Catalina, and I already know that the apartment manager is in his pocket because it wasn't a break-in. Nothing else was taken. No jewelry, not even the little money in my jewelry box—nothing except the guns."

"What will you do, Poppi?"

"I don't want to tell you or discuss that with you for good reasons Catalina," I replied.

"Is this because you do not want to worry Catalina? If this is true, know that Catalina will worry still, selfish man!" She stated with some bite.

"No, it's not because you will worry, it's because I am doing what's best for my safety in this matter Catalina Marie Malano," I said in a calm tone.

"I do not want to upset you, Stephon," she said.

"I'm learning how to deal with your tantrums."

"What is this, 'tantrums', Poppi?" she asked.

"It's when you want something to go your way, Catalina."

She remained quiet for a while. "I do not mean to give you my 'tantrum' Stephon."

"Yes you do, so stop bullshittin' me," I said.

"Tell me one time I have questioned you about the decisions you have made," I said to her.

"No times, Poppi!"

"That's because I want you to do what's best for you. I don't complain about anything when I'm with you because you make sure I am comfortable in everything we do. Do I not see that the same is extended to you, every time you are with me?" I asked.

"Yes!"

"Then you stay clear of my decisions, just like I do when it comes to yours."

"I apologize, Stephon. Can I not shelter or protect my man?"

"I need Baby Sias to call me, and I will ask of you one time and one time only: do not ask Baby or any of your people about my business, simply because you are with them. Do you understand?"

"Yes, Poppi!"

"Catalina, do you understand me?" I asked her again, to let her know that I was very serious about what I said.

"I understand," she said.

"There won't be a need for you to call my apartment anymore because I am moving from there. From this day on, you contact me at the Bay. And Catalina…do you value our friendship?"

"That is a crazy question, Stephon."

"Yes or no?"

"Yes!"

"Then never tell a stranger about our business again! I'm in this city alone, Catalina. Sometimes the enemy can talk real good to you. Please, help protect me by keeping our business between us. I don't want the ladies to know when I will be coming to see you anymore because they race to prepare things for me, and each time they do it, Carlos knows that I'm coming."

"Ah, mi Dios Poppi; you are correct," she stated (Oh my God).

"Do you understand why it is very important for us to keep certain information from other people?"

"I see very clear, Stephon."

"Get Baby on the phone, Catalina," I urged her before hanging up. I had started securing my door by placing a chair under it the day that James, what I now call him, took my protection away from me. It was very unnatural that I had to carry the .45 automatic pistol around the suite with me, but I did so out of a "better them than me" mentality.

My phone rang, and knowing Catalina the way I did, it was Baby calling me.

"You are a very prompt, brother," I said.

"My jefe (father) taught me that lives depend on my promptness," he shouted over some loud Tejano music. "Talk to me, my friend," he stated.

"I need a moving crew that can move my shit out of the apartment and into an undisclosed location in the middle of the night. I didn't want to say anything about what I found in my place because I didn't want Catalina to worry about me, but my uncle took my fire power and left me a sitting duck."

"You've got to be bullshitting me, Holmes!" he replied.

"You strapped or you need some heat? I got you."

"I'll need two automatic handguns, Baby."

"Your uncle is playing a dirty game at the wrong time, Holmes."

"Can you get me moved from point A to B?"

"No problem brother, but I got a question though."

"I'm listening," I stated.

"Do you want the spiders too, because my people don't leave shit when they come out!" he proudly stated. We sat silent for a second, and both started laughing. I could picture him laughing, which made me laugh more. His whole body shook when he laughed.

"Everything that belongs to me, Baby, and because I am a good-natured man…leave the bottle of Dom and a shot glass on the bar for my uncle."

"All I need are the keys to both places and the address you want the shit delivered to."

"One more thing, Baby. Catalina knows that I'm breaking camp, but the location stays between you and me. If she ever comes to the place, it will be under your protection, and only by my request. I need a safe spot of my own, if you feel me," I explained in a way only another man would understand.

"Surely you don't think the girl will slip, do you?" he asked only to find out two things. One, if Catalina would drop the ball at any time, and second, if my loyalty to her was some part-time bullshit.

"Let me explain something to you, Baby, Catalina found out about the bastard being in my pad because she was leaving some love shit on my recorder, and whoever it was just hung up in her face. She didn't hesitate to call me to warn me, and she wasn't hearing shit I said about her having to sit down when it comes down to bustin' anybody in their ass behind me. So, it's not her loyalty, or the level of our relationship that's on the scale here, Baby. I know that she'll come to me on her own, and won't wait on you or your people if I'm in danger. So, for me, she only comes by your protection and on my request."

"You have my word on that, but you know I have to let my jefe know about this and your request, and he will make sure that your requests are honored. Keys and address when you're ready, and to avoid any future delays Holmes, here's my 911 number…."

My conscience wouldn't let me rest knowing that Catalina was high above Austin crying.

"Hello," she muffled out in a wounded tone.

"Tell me why you are crying."

"Every time I think I do the correct thing for you, I see another day that it was not good thinking, Poppi."

"You love me a lot don't you?"

"Yes!" she said amidst her crying.

"This is how we will do this, Catalina. You let me take care of me when I'm on my own; and when I'm on your grounds, I'll let you take care of us, okay?"

"This is okay with me, and I like it that you share with me, Stephon," she said.

"You will come home to Catalina when you have the time, yes?"

"As soon as I get straightened out. I don't need James knowing where I am all day."

"And what about your Honduras bombshell?" she asked.

"Just pick up a phone, girl. If I'm not at the Bay or won't be at the Bay, you'll know and I'll get another phone so that you can leave me sexy messages too."

"Thank you, Poppi," she said.

"I have to sleep now because I have to wake up early to take care of some business. I'll call you when I get some time, okay?"

"Be careful, Stephon," she begged before hanging up.

The morning came and I was up, dressed, and in the hotel's restaurant, looking out the window when Hillary walked by my table and placed an envelope on it.

"You have a nice day, young man," she said as she walked out of the hotel and got into the shuttle.

I opened the envelope to find the following:

I want to feel comfortable knowing that you will be behind me when I return next month.

I couldn't help but smile at the covert message of her "thank you" card.

Monica was ten minutes late when she pulled into the parking lot. Watching her in a panic was funny to me and I couldn't resist getting my play on early.

"Don't start with me this morning, Stephon. It's because of you that I haven't slept all night and when I did get to sleep, I woke up to go pee and wondered why my clock didn't go off at 5:00 a.m. After figuring out that it was set for 5:00 p.m., I was mad at you."

"Don't blame this shit on me. If you haven't figured out how to use conventional devices, start bringing that rooster in the house with you."

"Ohhh, you just had to go there, Stephon."

"You hungry?" I asked her.

"How do you expect me to have an appetite when something this big is about to happen for me?"

"You eat or we don't move."

"You get on my nerves with this food stuff, Stephon. I'm nervous, boy! Look at my hands," she said holding them up to show me how much they trembled.

"Eat some dry toast and drink some juice, and I'll be satisfied."

"Bring it on then!" she said as she settled in her chair.

"How about Sunday?" I said.

"How about Sunday what?" she asked.

"Me having the apartment ready for you and your son."

The only response that I got from her was in the form of tears streaming down her face as she stared back at me.

"You know what? I'm tired of you doing that."

"Doing what?" she said.

"Give me your driver's license."

"My license?"

"You heard me! Give it up," I said with my hand extended. "I don't know what you got going in Fort Worth, but you won't be going through that shit another day," I said as I signaled for a waiter.

"Yes sir, can I help you?"

"Take the lady's drivers' license to the front desk, tell Steve I said to place her in a suite as close to the restaurant as he can, and I'll pay for it when I come on. Wait on him to fill out the register and bring the license back to me," I said. I gave the waiter a ten dollar bill. "Get your clothes, his stuff, leave the crib and everything else. Forget the sheets, blankets, pillows and the toothbrush. I want you in and out. We clear?"

"Stop talking to me like you're my father!"

"Hell, if I was, you wouldn't be going through what you're going through; now eat so we can leave," I demanded as I pushed my toast and juice in front of her.

Monica and I had made our rounds and finished by eleven o'clock. I wanted shit to be right for her and her son before the move-in, so I went the distance to slip one of the clerks at the phone company fifty dollars to make sure Monica's phone line and another one for my bedroom were turned on by the end of the day.

On our way back to the Bay, I questioned the thought of her going back to Fort Worth alone. "Do you need some help getting your things?"

"No...I'll just swing around to my aunt's house to pick up my son and our things," she said.

"So can I expect to see you back here within the next four hours?" I asked.

"I don't have that much to grab."

"It's 1:00. I want to see your ass back in this parking lot by 5:00 or I'll stop foolin' with you."

"You wouldn't dare." I could tell she doubted my words because of the gaze she gave me.

"Come get your key to your room, and if you think I'm bullshittin', let 5:01 beat you here," I said sounding firm and looking serious. I got out of my car and left her sitting there.

Chapter *EIGHT*

SMILE NOW
FIVE MONTHS LATER

Before I could make it up the stairs to Fran's place, Gee-Gee was barking up a storm. "Stephon, are you out there?" Fran asked. I could tell that she was looking out of the peephole. "Baby, why didn't you ring the bell?"

"I don't have to as long as Gee-Gee is here. Ain't that right, little mama," I said to Gee-Gee as she jumped up on my leg, begging for my attention.

"Stephon, you have literally stolen my baby's love away from me." Fran made her accusation while she stood in the hallway with her hands on her naked hips, watching Gee-Gee go bananas.

"Gee-Gee needs love too, don't she?" I said to the dog.

"All right, tramp, get your miniature ass somewhere and sit down because it's Mama's time to play with Stephon," she told Gee-Gee then pulled me into her bedroom. I gave Fran her weekly "attention" and as I showered of the residue of our session, she laid in the bed fishing for information about my whereabouts outside of the Bay Hotel.

"Outside of your sensitivity, I would honestly say that you're being nosey, Fran."

"I'm being nosey because I'm concerned about you!" she said with an attitude. I stepped out of the bathroom to dry off so that I could listen to Fran's bullshit, only to avoid the yelling. "If you're that concerned, buy me a place on Turtle Creek," I told her.

"Hell, if I could afford to put you in a high-rise that would mean Fran has become a millionaire," she said.

I didn't waste time getting dressed because an uneasiness came over me about Fran. I grabbed the envelope on my way out the door, stopped, opened it to count the contents, and turned to look at Fran.

"Am I not giving you what you need, as you requested?" I asked her. My question caused her to sit up in her bed.

"What's wrong, Stephon?"

"Let me know you appreciate me sometimes," I said as I looked into the envelope she gave me.

"Stephon, baby, I'm sorry. Wait!" she said jumping out of her bed to grab her purse. She just handed me a wad of cash without counting it.

"Why didn't you tell me you wanted more?" she asked.

"At the start of this agreement, you said you just needed an hour of my time; but you also asked me not to stop after your timer goes off if you aren't done," I said. "My not stopping isn't a good thing for you?" I asked.

"Baby, you know it is."

"I just wanted to know," I said as I walked off. "Next Sunday?" I paused at the door, waiting on an answer from her.

"Until you don't want to come anymore, Stephon. Baby, I'm sorry," she apologized again.

"Next week," I confirmed in the process of walking out the door.

I was tired of going back to the Bay and just laying up watching TV. I hadn't been to the apartment to see Monica and my main man in about a month. I wanted to fire up the fireplace for Monica one time, but I thought that was a bad idea since the youngster was crawling all over the damn place. Nevertheless, it was time to make my presence a part of the place. I stopped back by the Bay to pick up a gift I had for her and her son, and on the cool, to call her to let her know that I was stopping by.

"Hey, Stephon."

"How did you know it was me?" I asked.

"Because I just got off the phone with Mama about thirty minutes ago and you two are the only people who have my number. Every time you call me sounding like you do right now, I know you're coming home. I wish you would stop that too, Stephon."

"Stop what?" I asked. Clueless to what she was talking about.

"I told you to stop calling me before you come home," she stated.

"I don't want to impose on your privacy, Country."

"Stephon, I've got the only two men I want up in this joint and I'm not ready for anything more right now."

I quickly had to shut her conversation down because I didn't want her to venture off into the sentimental zone. Especially since, in her eyes, the agreement between us was an opportunity for her to show her appreciation and prove her loyalty to me, which she had no problem taking!

"You can raise hell now or later, but I bought my boy another gift."

"Stephon, he has too much shit already. Hell, he don't know what half of it is, and doesn't know that the other half is even in the house."

"Yeah, yeah, yeah," I said. "Should I stop for some take out or what?"

"I don't want to talk to you about this because you've been lying about sitting on your ass doing nothing long enough, or coming home so that I can cook a meal for your black butt."

"Girl, you might be trying to feed me some possum stew or some coon!" I teased. "You can rustle me up some vittles today if you want to, Country."

"Stephon, don't be playin' with me. Are you staying here tonight? Your phone rings every night, and you need to at least find out what Catalina is saying anyway! For you two to be in a relationship, I don't see how the both of you have made it this far."

"Stay out of my business, Monica," I said, to put an end to the conversation. Catalina's trip back to Honduras was drawing near and she would have to be away until her work visa got approved; something that we both weren't feelin' too good about. I had been driving to Austin soon as I got off the clock just to ease her mind about a lot of shit. She'd been having meeting, after meeting, concerning the functions in her area, and most importantly…the Tower.

My leaving the Bay without letting her know meant Steve being in my business because of repeated phone calls from Catalina. So calling was essential!

"Hello."

"Hey, lady."

"And what do I owe the pleasure of having the opportunity to talk with my man at this time of the day?" she asked.

"I'm leaving the Bay for today to spend some time at the apartment."

"You need some sleep, Stephon."

"Oh, remind me to do that when you're wanting me between your legs for three hours off and on throughout the night," I said.

She responded, "Whatever," and I told her that I would call her later on.

The day that James had my belongings delivered to the apartment gave her some hope that I might move back to Austin since I'd decided not to attend DeVry, but I had the need to continue building my finances up…one favor at a time. I had befriended six ladies, whom I now considered clients. Since they became constant in my world, I made sure that I utilized each client to benefit my cause. I had over one hundred and twenty thousand in my savings account; four Rolexes; seven carats worth of diamonds; two fifty-thousand-dollar CDs with the bank, and some clients that wouldn't allow me to walk away from what I was providing them in the way of "services" without meeting me at the bargaining table for some serious negotiations.

As I made my way towards my safe haven, my thoughts stood stern on "what if" Catalina wasn't allowed to return back to the U.S. because of pressure being placed on the proper authorities by top rebels, or one of the cartels dangling her freedom in exchange for a favor? Subconsciously, that was the main reason why I hadn't allowed myself to be totally consumed with her. There was a rumor still growing cobwebs in my mind about her only wanting to marry me to stay in the country, and Honey didn't make shit any better when she found out how serious we had gotten.

"Boy that girl is tricking you into marrying her. What else would a twenty-five-year-old woman want with a eighteen-year-old boy?" she told my mother.

I had made up my mind to marry Catalina if she made it back, and I had our rings put up in my safety deposit box. If our relationship was just a ploy of hers from the beginning, then my objective was to shield myself; and holding off on proposing in order to protect myself from such wouldn't be in vain. Just thinking about all of this shit made me sick to the stomach. I had to sit in the car for a few minutes before I went upstairs to the apartment because I didn't want to take my frame of mind in there to Monica.

I knocked on the door three times and couldn't see if Monica's eye covered the peephole because I'd had it tinted. The door came flying open and she stood in the doorway with her hands on her hips. She slapped me on my arm twice before allowing me to pass.

"Stop knocking on this door and use your key," she said while delivering her blows. With a smile on his face, the little man of the house sat on the living room floor watching his mama assault me.

"When am I going to start receiving a hug when I come home? Come to think about it, that might be the real reason why a brother hasn't been this way, on the cool."

"Oh, you must want to get beat up for real. I'll show your frontin' ass what this country girl's holdin' if you keep lying on me."

"Hey, young prince," I said to the little man of the house as I picked him up. "I hope all this smiling you're doing is because you're glad to see me and not because that mean mama of yours was trying to handle me. Look, little man, I brought you something special. Your crazy mama fusses because I bring you too many toys, so I had to step my game up," I explained to him as I handed him his own savings account book. He grabbed it and went straight to his mouth with it.

"You like it?" I asked him, and he popped me in the face with it. "I'll just take that as a 'yes' because if I even thought that you were trying to handle me like your crazy ass mama, I'd be putting your butt out on the porch, boy." He just sat there on my lap, chewing on his account book. "You didn't understand anything I just said, did you?" I asked him and in return I got slapped with the book again. I turned to ask Monica when she was going to teach him how to talk, instead of assaulting me, while she stood in the kitchen watching me kick it with the youngster.

"Stephon, you're going to make a good father," she said with tears in her eyes.

"Just one drop from either eye, girl, and I'm leaving and I'm taking my boy with me." She turned her back to me and wiped her eyes with the dish towel she had lying across her shoulder. She walked into the living room to crash me and my boy's conference time and took his savings book out of his mouth, and he went slap off!

"Girl, can't you see how this brother is feeling about his money?" I asked her as I snatched it back out of her hand and gave it back to him. As soon as I gave it back, he went from pitching a fit to whimpering as he laid his head on my shoulder and hugged my neck.

"I know, my little man. She's just mean. Messing with a brother's paper like that." After the whimpering stopped, the little man was fast asleep. Once the savings book fell freely from his little grip, Monica and I knew he was out for the count. I took him into his room and placed him in his crib. Like a mother, Monica wasn't far behind, watching my every move.

"You just don't know when to stop, do you?" she whispered to me. I turned to respond back to her and saw the savings book in her hand and more tears flowing. She came to me and I gave her what she wanted, a secure, long hug.

"If you're crying because it wasn't enough, I'll put some more in it tomorrow morning," I said with some sarcasm.

She pulled the dish towel off her shoulder and started whipping me with it. "Just for that, your black ass will be eating skunk this afternoon. Stephon, ten thousand dollars—seriously Stephon! Was that necessary?" she whispered as quietly as she could.

"Start putting something with it, and by the time he gets our age, he'll be able to start a goat farm back home," I said, laughing and dodging the dish towel she threw at me.

The phone in my room started ringing and Monica and I knew who was on the other end.

"Go get the phone, boy," she said and pointed towards the room. I was busy trying to get my keys out of my pocket to unlock my door, and the phone continued to ring. I thought about James and the whole setup.

I answered the phone with, "Hey, sexy."

"That would be me, Poppi!" Catalina said.

"I know that you are okay there because no one knows where you are," she said.

"I sleep real peaceful here, Catalina. No chairs under the doorknob, no guns all around me; just peace, baby."

"I'm not worried about you when you are there," she said.

"When you get back from Honduras, I will have a very nice surprise for you."

"You promise, Stephon?"

"I promise you this!" I said.

"Thirty days is coming fast, Stephon, and I feel as if the sun and the moon race to get me back to my country."

"You have to go in order to get back here to me, girl."

"This is true, black man of mine. Listen, Poppi, I have a meeting later this week with my people. You can sleep in that day, instead of coming here."

"What day?" I asked her.

"Thursday."

"I haven't had a chance to listen to your messages yet, but I will before I go to sleep."

"Don't listen to them all at once, Poppi. Treat them like good food and wine. Have you eaten yet?" she asked.

"I'm working up on something now," I said.

"You eat, shower, listen to only two of my messages and call me before you sleep, yes?"

"I'll talk with you then," I told her.

As soon as I got off the phone, I was headed toward the aromas coming from the kitchen. I stepped inside the edge of the kitchen to check on the vittles, and Monica was in there doing her thing as if she had nine arms.

"Monica, I'm staying," I told her so that she could slow down.

"I just didn't want you to leave without eating."

"So what did you plan to do with this roast, broil it to death?"

"You helping?" she asked.

"I'll do the yams, muffins and greens," I told her.

"Hell, cook the whole meal then," she said. "Stephon, I want to go to school."

"Then go," I said.

"Is that all you have to say? 'Just go'?" she asked. She stopped seasoning her roast and put both hands on her hips.

"Damn girl, what more should I say?"

"How about what are you taking up, what school, etcetera, etcetera!"

"Woman, the only thing I want to know is the whereabouts of my little man while your schooling is going on. Period!" I announced.

"I'm trying to figure that out right now." I stopped doing what I was doing and walked towards her.

"If you have any plans to deal with Fort Worth again, I'll be very upset about that, Monica."

"Never that, Stephon." She took her hands off her hips and focused on the roast again.

"I'm listening," I assured her.

"I've been trying to talk Mama into coming to Texas to live and to watch my baby, but she's hesitant about it."

"Why is she so hesitant, Monica?"

"Boy, Mama has been in the hills so long that she's scared of doing anything else or living anywhere else. Hell, if she ever saw the inside of this place, she would swear by God that I was a millionaire."

"When did you want to start?" I asked her.

"After the summer," she replied.

"She can have my room."

"I don't think so!" she said in a sharp tone.

"I'm saving enough money to get her an apartment of her own, Stephon."

"Listen, before you get your panties in a bind, I might be leaving the city within the next six months."

"Stephon, please don't leave us," she said in a soft, wounded tone.

"The only reason I paid everything up was to ensure that you would be okay. My boy has some change. I don't have to worry about you going downhill because you work too hard. I'm buying you a new car for your birthday and you can keep the one you have now for a backup. So you need to press a little harder on your mother about coming to live with you in this apartment so that you can hold on to your money."

"Why, Stephon?" she asked me through her tears.

"Why what?"

"Why are you leaving?"

"I don't want to discuss that right now...put the meat in the oven, woman."

"If I ever find out that you're leaving because I brought up this school shit and my mother, or you trying to be nice, I'll walk out and leave everything you gave us. Do 'we' understand each other?" she shouted, raising her voice and working her neck.

Monica took a deep breath, and in a calm voice asked me to pass her the yams so that she could rinse them off for me.

"With that attitude you have, you might be gettin' your ass kicked out the kitchen, while you trippin'," I shot back at her.

"I get frustrated when I have the opportunity to do something for you, and you won't sit still long enough for me to show you my gratitude, Stephon."

"I'll give you one chance to do that if you're game," I said as I brought the potatoes and myself within inches of her face and body.

"Name it and don't play with me," she warned me as we looked eye to eye.

"Law school. I need an attorney I can trust. Take it or leave it!" I told her, still looking directly at her.

She never responded! She snatched the potatoes out of my hands and turned away from me.

"I guess a thank you will have to do then," I said in a backstabbing nature, and hoped she would feel the tip of my dagger in her back.

"What type of attorney?" she asked.

"I'll let you know next summer," I said.

"You make me sick, Stephon."

"Fuck that! Yes or no about law school?" I demanded to know.

"Yes!"

"You stay here, get up in enough time to go to S.M.U for class," I told her.

"Boy, that's all the way in Dallas, Stephon," she shouted.

I went in my pocket, pulled out all the cash I had and slammed it on the counter. "Do you need some gas money?" I said with an attitude.

"I'm going, Stephon, so let's drop this before you get your ass put out the kitchen." I walked over to her and kissed her on her forehead.

"You're still an asshole," she said.

"Correction: I'm an asshole with a top-flight lawyer who cares about my black ass."

She turned and chunked me the bird.

Dinner turned out to be a family setting with me feeding my boy and Monica smiling proudly. There was no question about who was running the household. It was 9:00 p.m. and all three of us were full; Monica had to be on the move at 7:30 in the morning, and the youngster wasn't trying to hear shit about sleep.

"Boy, it's time for bed and you are not going to have me up all night foolin' with you, so come on," she said to her son.

"Let him do his thing, Monica. He'll wind down soon." It was evident that he knew what time it was because he was ready to fight tooth and nail. "Girl, you see he doesn't want to go."

"Stephon, he ain't running nothing!"

"Okay, hold on! Leave him alone, you go shower and get ready for bed. I got him."

"You got him!" she said with her hands on her hips and her eyebrows raised.

She walked off mumbling under her breath about me and her son keeping her up all night. By the time she was out of the bathroom from doing her thing, the youngster was bathed and getting powdered down.

"Stephon, that's just too much powder on that boy," Monica said.

"I told him to tell me when to stop and he wouldn't say nothing, so I laced his little ass up."

"Got my baby looking like a powdered doughnut."

"I started to put his ass out on the porch a while ago for trippin' with me," I said.

"What did he do?" she asked.

"Don't worry about it!" I said with a frowned up face.

"Boy, what did he do?" she demanded to know.

"The chump pissed on me, Monica. I mean it hit me in the face too." She laughed something serious. "So that's funny, huh?" I said as I tried to hold a straight face. "I'm telling you, boy, if I wasn't cool with your mother, I would have put your little dusty behind out on the stoop."

"The stoop?" Monica stated. I looked at her sideways just to be funny.

"You know this boy is from the country just like you. Hell, he don't know what a porch is yet, so I have to kick it to him in his native language." She popped me on my head and demanded me to give her the young prince.

"Hold on! The boy pissed in my face. Can I at least get a hug before he goes to bed? I mean, I am emotionally distraught about the issue, you know."

"Give Stephon a hug, baby, for peein' on him," she said to her son.

"I wasn't talking about from him, but from you. First legal lesson for you as his mother, you are liable!" I said as I held my arms open and received both of them. "Trust in yourself, Monica. You're going to be a good attorney." I whispered in her ear.

"I hope so, Stephon," she said as she looked into my eyes and rubbed my face.

After a long, hot shower and a two-hour long conversation with Catalina, sleep became my best friend. I remained in bed until noon. It was Monday and my scheduled day to get used by Beatrice. She was the most generous one out of the seven with whom I was doing business. Leftovers really weren't what I was yearning for as a pick me up meal, and I knew I was running too late to get a seat at my spot, but I had to try since I was a couple blocks away. It took me four minutes just to get inside the door, and once the receptionist saw me, I knew she couldn't get me seated soon.

I raised my hands up, using my body language to inquire on me getting a seat. She read me.

"Sorry, Stephon, at least thirty five minutes. Try inside the hotel," she suggested.

The hotel was probably at thirty-five percent capacity, and it was just a one-minute walk to the front of the Four Seasons. It was the second time I had actually stepped foot in the place, so I tipped around until I spotted the restaurant.

"Table for one or two, sir?" I heard him repeat twice. "Sir, are you all right?" the concierge asked me.

I backed out of the restaurant as quickly and as quietly as I could. I was so thrown, shocked, and confused about seeing Fran dining with those who I had labeled, "my clients," that I panicked. I went to the Bay to regain my thoughts.

Come on boy, it doesn't take a rocket scientist to figure out some game, I said to myself as I stared in the mirror. There was this part of me that wanted to distance myself from the betrayal that overcame me the moment that I saw Fran and the other ladies together, but the rules of the game stood stiff as steel in my heart.

I replayed the events over and over in my head…I have a meeting to go to, she had said. No rush to take Gee-Gee to the sitter and no rush to shower and leave. This is how we like it, Stephon. I am a consultant for a group of demanding women. I'm always on the go because of them. My only off day is Sunday. There are special guidelines you should know:

Never assume what she wants.

Give her a few minutes to adjust.

Slow, long and deep.

Always allow us to move on our own.

Let us use your tool.

Halfway out, put it back where you found it.

Place your hands here, there and not like that.

The difference between screwing and making love.

Don't get aggressive.

Touché ladies, touché! Fran groomed me for the damn cause. Okay Fran and Company, I want to join in on the festivities too! I said to myself as I continued to look in the mirror. I went over to my mini-fridge and pulled out a bottle of water, opened it and did as they were doing when I encountered them. Let me also raise my glass in your toast to life ladies.

I had to go see a friend about some "fishing" equipment, but I needed some extra time.

"Front desk, this is Steve."

"Damn, Steve, how many times have I told you how dry and bland that sounds?"

"Okay, let me try it your way then, Stephon. Daddy's place, what's jumpin'?"

"That's what I'm talkin' about, playa. Be the shit up in your own house," I stated and we both laughed.

"What's up, Stephon?"

"I need a few hours before I take over the desk," I said.

"You want me to stay or you're letting me know that Lora's good?" he asked.

"Lora's good. Let her know that I'll be there at about four."

"Do your thing, playa."

"Thanks, Steve."

By the time I made it to the gym, Tye was on his way out.

"What's up, sleepy head?" he said jokingly.

"I need some help, Tye."

"You, the no nonsense guy, need help?" he said.

"Serious, Tye, I need to hire a private investigator, a P.I.!"

"Damn son, you got troubles?" he asked.

"If I had troubles, I'd handle the shit on my own or call the police, Tye."

"How am I supposed to know a P.I.?" he asked.

"Hell, you train some police officers, a doctor, a few lawyers; use your resources, man."

"I'll make a call or two. So show your ass up in the morning. By the way, if they ask what it's in reference to, what do I tell them?" he asked.

"Some personal shit back home," I said, since he was trying to be nosey. Depending on what I found out about my favorite girls, would my next move be determined. Since I couldn't do anything about that situation except continue to play along and wait on the possible hookup with a P.I.—finding Baby was next!

"Baby, please," I said to the voice on the other end of the phone.

"Who's calling?" she asked.

"Stephon Wilkerson." It took about a minute to get the brother on the phone.

"Stephon, talk to me."

"You sleep?" I asked.

"Had to shit, playa!" I frowned at that thought.

"T.M.I. Baby; T.M.I.!" It was easy for us to share a laugh, but I had to get serious.

"I need to meet with your father concerning Catalina."

"Something going down?" Baby asked.

"Come on, Baby, you know I'm not close to the action. I'm concerned about her finding her way back here without some bullshit."

"There's a Luby's Cafeteria down the street from Six Flags in Arlington. You can follow me from there," he said.

"I'm about fifteen minutes away, Baby."

"I'll be there, brother," he stated before hanging up.

I was surprised that Baby told me to come right on. That was a sign that I had been in quite a few conversations, and what level didn't matter to me because I wasn't on the shit list. It was a point A to point B drive to the Sias' residence, and as I expected, he was protected from head to toe! After properly being introduced to his family, Mr. Sias, Baby and I took to his office in private.

"What's on your mind, son?"

"Catalina, of course. I gave you my word that I would not meddle in her business unless it had something to do with her well-being. My question to you is, does Carlos' debts in Honduras carry over or will they affect the safety of Catalina in any fashion?"

Baby and Mr. Sias slightly glanced at each other.

"So we're bullshitting each other now?" I asked.

"Please forgive us, Stephon, but why would you ask such a question?"

"No disrespect to your family or to you, Mr. Sias, while I'm in your home, but this is my woman we're discussing. If you want to screw with my intelligence, do it on another subject matter, but not on Catalina."

"No, the debt is not carried, but she stands a good chance of being sought by the cartels because of rumors that she will stop the flow of their drugs," said Mr. Sias.

"From what she told me, it's past a rumor!" I mentioned.

"Well, it doesn't take a genius to know that Carlos has been allowed to continue to do his bidding, but only because of Catalina's safe return back," he stated. "We assure you, Stephon, we will use every resource available to see that she returns to you and for the betterment of our people," said Mr. Sias.

"No disrespect, sir, but I would be more inclined to believe that your resources are all that, but since you don't control the cartels, let's just continue to see that the girl stays out of hot water. Can you help with her paperwork?" I asked.

"Even if we have to pay out of our own pockets, Stephon." Mr. Sias assured me.

"Let me apologize for lying to you and your associates." As soon as I said that, both Baby and Mr. Sias glanced at each other. "Whatever happens to Catalina, I'll be in your business because of Carlos, and if I find out a single hair from my uncle fell in the middle of this, he won't be spared either. I thank you for your time, Mr. Sias. I don't mean to be a pest by calling you up like this, but I couldn't avoid it, playa. Catalina is my business."

"Any time, Stephon. I mean that, brother; anytime," he said hugging me like I was family.

Forty-five minutes later, I was back at the Bay, holding my composure because Beatrice would be walking through the doors very soon. It would cost me everything if I blew it simply because I had an attitude about getting played. Usually Doug would be the one driving up with Beatrice, but since her flight arrived at an earlier time, seeing her getting out of a yellow cab threw Doug off.

Neither one of us said a word about her arrival to the Bay, because it wasn't our business how our guests came or left. We made eye contact and I retreated to my office. Beatrice was the type of person who never came out of her room; she even took her meals there. I was very eager to get to her because I wanted to feel the top of the line essence that she brought to the game. I wanted to be fueled by her ability to use me with a steady hand and composure. Being that it was Monday and things were slow, I could send my crew home at 9:00 p.m. and run the desk myself. Third shift was running late, as usual, and I was like a greyhound in the gate, ready to chase the rabbit at the track when it came to Beatrice.

It was 10:10 p.m. when I walked through her door. Instantly, I had a flashback of all six ladies sitting at the table together and how they would either glance at the clock or their watch before doing what they did.

As I entered her room, she was in her usual nothing, and I remained speechless until I was spoken to. I gave her more than her usual service and because of that, she blessed me above measures with dead presidents. Knowing that a part of Fran's deception was up the hall from me, I showered, talked to Catalina and took refuge at my pad.

I beat Monica up for the first time since we moved in together; allowing me to see her in that early morning stage was taboo. Nevertheless, breakfast for her was all fresh sliced fruit, sliced turkey breast, and wheat toast with a bottle of water. Little man wasn't a morning person and I wasn't big enough to deal with him or his attitude during the wee hours of the morning. I saw them off that morning and went to the gym for my workout and the info about my P.I.

"I've got some good news and bad news for you, youngster," Tye said.

"Give me the bad first, Tye."

"She just got out of college, but a few detectives said the girl doesn't cut corners, and is out to make a name for herself. Get this; she's giving out discount rates, depending on the job."

"Good news, Tye!"

"The girl is bad!"

"So what about the damn hookup?" I asked.

"Oh, I'll give it to you after showers."

As soon as the workout was over and I had gotten dressed, I caught a vacant office and got the Denise chick on the line.

"Gray's Investigators, can I help you," came from a female voice.

"My name is Stephon Wilkerson and I'm in need of some information."

"Are you comfortable about talking over the phone, would you like to come in or would you like to meet me somewhere? We can do this however you like," she said in one stroke of her tongue.

"How about I buy you some lunch?" I said.

"Free food, any day!"

"Marriott Hotel at eleven, backside of the D.F.W Airport on Highway 114. Can you find it?"

"Mr. Wilkerson, is that a trick question or are you just trying to be cute?" she asked.

"Since you asked, both!" I said.

"Eleven o'clock Mr. Wilkerson, and how will I find you, sir?"

"You're the P.I.," I told her.

I made it to the Marriott about 10:30 a.m. to get a feel of the place and asked for a table for two. I wasn't seated but for two minutes when I heard her voice as she walked up to the table.

"You make it a habit of being prompt, Mr. Wilkerson?"

I got a good look at her from head to toe and got out of my seat to pull out her chair. This was a high-maintenance sister that walked on sand without leaving her foot prints. Her clothes had a sensuous way of cascading down the contour of her fine ass body. Trying not to be so damn obvious about massaging her upright breasts and her slim waistline with my eyes, I ended the exam before I became the typical male.

"Especially when it comes to business," I said.

"And a gentleman at that," she said.

"I got it from my mother," I said. I sat back down after she was seated. "So how did you find me?" I inquired.

"You have a driver's license, Mr. Wilkerson," she said showing me the enlarged photo that was on my license.

"Well, that's two," I said.

"What's that supposed to mean?" she asked.

"I was told that you were smart and beautiful."

"As hard as I try, I can't seem to shake bad slandering of my character," she coldly stated. Her eyes were piercing and unreadable, but I knew there was sadness in them.

"You promised me lunch. I'll eat and you'll talk, Mr. Wilkerson."

"For starters, let's drop the formal. Stephon will do," I said. I waited on the waiter to leave before I got back to her.

"It's new by Liz Taylor," she said.

"Excuse me!" I said.

"The perfume. You've taken in at least four deep breaths and exhaled slowly. Unless you get off on the smell of the food," she said sarcastically, though trying to hide her smile behind a menu.

"How much?" I asked.

"Try the eight ounce at eighty-five dollars, she'll love it." Her eyes barely left the menu as she spoke.

"We'll see," I said.

"So what's happening back home that needs my attention?" she asked.

"That was just to keep my trainer out of my business. I'm not too comfortable about telling you what I'm about to just yet, and, I'm sorry, but you won't get an explanation for that. Are you taking me on or what?" I asked before I spilled my beans.

"Yes." she said.

"Hold on to your skirt, lady." I gave her the disclaimer before I started giving her the low down of what was going on with me and my clients. After hearing it all, she looked me directly in the eyes and just smiled.

"So what the hell was that for?" I asked.

"I was asking myself if I would be willing to do what those ladies are doing."

"From your smile, I'll say your answer is, 'yes'!"

"You might be right, Stephon," she said with a smirk.

"So what do you want me to do?" she asked.

"They signed in on the register with first names," I said as I slid her the names of my six clients at the Bay as well as Fran's name. I also gave her the days that I saw each of them. "I want to know who they are; that's all."

"You're making this real easy for me, Stephon.

"So what do I owe you?" I asked.

"Three grand and another lunch," she answered without blinking.

"Hell, the way you eat, let me pay you four grand because you can eat, girl!"

"Ooooh no, you didn't! That's cruel, Stephon," she said surprisingly.

"I'm joking, girl. Hell, you're too high maintenance to worry about a sandwich or two, and I would rather feed you than clothe you."

"Give me two weeks from today and I'll meet you back here at eleven. I've just got to try those potato wedges," she said without another word before getting up and leaving.

Chapter NINE

CRY LATER-DAY 13

It's ten o'clock in the morning, and Catalina hasn't, and refuses to have any mercy on my poor, young and fatigued soul. Though the driving back and forth from Irving to Austin is weighing heavy on a brother, I can feel the girl's frustration about having to go back to a poverty-stricken country; and on top of that, having the cartels fighting over her soul is on the table, also. A sadness was brought on the more I thought about not ever seeing her again, but for her it was something far more devastating.

I hadn't been able to go do my regular deposits at the bank and I was riding around with over twenty-five thousand dollars in cash and two payroll checks from the Bay that I hadn't deposited. I couldn't avoid not making the deposit, as tired as I was. Every time I saw my personal teller, she reminded me that Monica was making her regular weekly deposits. She thought that Monica was my "in case shit go wrong girl". The teller counts my cash without raising a brow and just deposits the money. With all the illegal shit going and coming her way, my constant cash intake is nothing new to her. As I pulled up at the bank this morning, my intention was just to see if my personal teller would bend the rules for me. Mr. Sias assured me that she would keep my business safe and since I was a referral from the top dog, I took a step.

"Good morning, Senorita."

"Good morning to you too, Stephon," she said. "Ms. Monica came in yesterday. She is a very sweet girl. She tells me that college is on her agenda this summer."

"Yeah, I'm kind of proud of that myself. Listen, since we're on the subject, I'd like to deposit five thousand dollars into her account, if you don't mind. With college and a baby and no support from the dead-beat dad, she can use some extra help."

She looked up at me over her glasses for a split second, and she did it.

"I guess I can do that for such a special cause, you know. Will you be seeing Ms. Monica anytime soon?" she asked.

"Maybe before the week is out. I haven't seen my godson in about two weeks."

"Please, make sure she receives this added deposit balance for her records," she instructed.

"I'll call her at work and inform her of this," I reassured her.

"You are very kind, Stephon."

"I don't know if that's good or bad sometimes," I stated as I walked away. Making such a deposit brought me to thinking about Catalina, and a question I had asked her about what kind of money she would need while in Honduras.

She had picked up an old pair of tennis shoes that had four thousand dollars matted down and hidden in the soles of the shoe. She told me that she would take five hundred in cash as a front for the shakedown officers who somehow always got a manifest of those coming back home for renewals on their visas. Drumming up some trumped up charges to put you in jail versus giving up fifty dollars to appease them, what was there to consider? She had sixty thousand dollars in her savings account that she was leaving behind, but the money she had in those tennis shoes was enough to last her a year without drawing too much attention to herself. I went to the apartment to shower and punish myself with an hour's worth of sleep before walking through the doors of the Bay. I ran into a card, dated three days ago, Monica had left for me.

I understand that I'm not your woman, but you could at least check on me and "Your Boy" at times. You got me thinking that my cooking ran you off (Smile).

~Country

I jumped on the phone and ordered her some flowers from a floral shop a few blocks up the street. I left instructions for the leasing office at our apartment to place the flowers on the bar in our apartment. Then I called her on the job.

"Thank you for calling Dillard's, can I help you?"

"Cosmetics, please."

"Cosmetics, Monica speaking."

"Why don't you sound like this when you're at home?" I asked.

"I thought you'd prefer me for me, but if me frontin' will bring you home once in a while to check on us, I'll start."

"Are you okay?" I asked.

"Sometimes." she replied.

"What's wrong?" I asked.

"Your boy is talking now," she said.

"Get off the bullshit!" Her statement brought a smile to my face.

"I thought that would be some good news for you and a reason for the three of us to have dinner out somewhere," she said.

"Wherever you want to go, little mama."

"I received a phone call from the bank this morning. Thank you! I don't mean to sound ungrateful, but please stop! I don't want the money, the gifts or anything else, Stephon. I want you," she said in a soft spoken voice.

"Monica..."

"I know, Stephon, but it doesn't change what I feel or how I feel."

"I'm not doing it, Monica; so leave it alone and stay out of that zone."

"That's easy for you to say, Stephon."

"Saturday," I said.

"Saturday what, Stephon?"

"We'll spend the day together and you can talk all the shit you want to, but I'm getting my boy some toys."

"Child, I've realized that I'm fighting a losing battle, so I'll just stay out of your way and let you be you when it comes down to my son or me."

"Submit then woman!" I stated.

"I'm willing to, but that's not what you want, Stephon." Sarcasm dripped from her lips.

"You gon' make me slap you on your ass, girl."

"I've been waiting on you to do that since I met you," she said.

"Monica! Can we do this my way? If we can't, I'm gone! Please, don't get me wrong, you're all that and some more, but I refuse to destroy our friendship."

"Is this a one-sided conversation?" she asked.

"Yeah! I'm not releasing what I have going on right now, and when my life gets to the point where I can give you my time, then that's a sure sign that my current status is dead. So get your ass out of that zone and be my friend, please. That's what I want from you today."

"I'm not going to apologize for the way I feel about you, Stephon, but I will apologize for over-stepping my bounds concerning our friendship. Please forgive me, and that won't happen again."

"Do you think my boy will trip or go ballistic if I stop by the daycare to see him?" I asked.

"You know you can't do him like that, Stephon. That boy will have a fit and they'll be calling me on my job because he won't settle down."

"I'll be there right before you pick him up Friday for a few minutes."

"I guess I'll see you when I see you," she said.

"You're a good lady, Monica. I want to keep it that way," I said.

Today was Jacqueline's day to show up and I was always nervous when I dealt with her because she was a very loud moaner. She was so loud one night that the front desk called the room and asked her to please keep the noise down to a minimum because her neighbors were complaining; but that's how she got off.

My night ended with Catalina begging me to hit the highway, but my appointment with Denise was a long time coming. I left the Bay about midnight and went to the apartment. I had made up my mind to catch the young prince in babbling form before Monica dropped him off.

I peeped in on them when I got in and found them both sleeping. I had stopped off at Kroger's for fresh fruit because Monica preferred that type of breakfast. I cut up some red and green apples, tangerines, hothouse strawberries and grapes before going to bed. I saw that she had left me another card. I plucked it from the grasp of the paper clip that held it to the vase of roses I sent her.

You're still an asshole, but I love you just the same, my friend.

~Country

I knew that seeing the card missing and the fresh fruit in the fridge, she'd come by my room to wake me or drop the youngster off on me to feed and dress while she did her thing. I had tried dropping him off at the daycare once before, but the boy did so much damn crying and reaching for me to rescue him from the arms of his care tech, that I couldn't leave him in such a state. Once I'd got him back in my arms, he was straight. We had both showed up at Dillard's around Monica's lunch-time and that had made her day. I guess the lunch thing with her two favorite men was cool, but my getting handled by the youngster was funny to her. I was known as "tender ass" for a week.

Morning came and my boy was dropped off to me just as I had called it. I was awakened by short and stubby fingers digging into my nose and poking me in my eyes.

"Trying to take me out this morning with your judo moves, huh?" I asked him, but he just smiled back at me. I laid there listening to baby babble for a while and then the "Fef-fon, Fef-fon" came rolling off his tongue and it was on.

I was off to Monica's room with my boy hooked under my arms with news of him trying to say my name, and I ended up running into a butt-ass naked Monica. She didn't flinch to cover or hide.

"That's what you get for not knocking," she said.

"The door wasn't locked either," I hit back. "He tried to say my name," I made known with a huge grin on my face. I continued to stare into her eyes, withholding myself from looking down.

"I've been teaching him how to say it," she said as she slid into her panties.

I turned and walked off and she began to laugh.

"That's not funny, girl!" I said.

"It is to me," she shouted back at me.

"The middle finger, Monica."

"You don't want me to comment on that, Stephon."

I stayed behind to chill for a bit longer. It had been a while since I had put on some C.M.D.'s (Clothes of Mass Destruction) and being that Denise out-shined me, I thought I would knock her on her ass and be the shit at the Bay all day. By the time I was a good five steps into the restaurant at the Marriott, Denise was licking her fingers from the potato wedges she had spoken about two weeks before.

"Damn, Daddy, you doing a photo shoot for G.Q. today?" she asked.

"Something like that! What, you spent the night here for the wedges?"

"The two-week waiting period was killing me, Stephon. Hell, I dreamed about these damn things. I know it's not lady-like to be sucking my fingers like this, but as long as there's a spud left on this plate, I'm a beast!" She pushed a large envelope my way. "That's yours," she stated.

"Very nice," I said as I saw the photos of all seven women and an information sheet attached to each photo.

Mrs. Beatrice Ferguson, Co-Owner of Ferguson Meat Companies; Home Office...New York.

Mrs. Ciara Williams, Owner of The Marina Bay Hotels of Florida.

Mrs. Hillary O ' Donald, Co-Owner of O'Donald Import Motors, Mercedes Dealerships of Florida.

Mrs. Jacqueline Summers, Owner of Summer Realtors of Atlanta.

Mrs. Karen Danelle, Co-Owner of Abram's & Danelle's Fine Furnishings of Dallas.

Mrs. Amanda Brooks, Co-Owner of Brook's Wineries of New York.

Frances Oliver, Marketing Consultant, Home Office…Highland Park, Dallas.

"According to one of the waiters, they meet once a month at the Mandalay. The Hyatt Regency East and West Hotels are really their primary stops when the visitors come to Texas. They catch a hotel shuttle back to the airport and your staff picks them up," she explained.

"At times, they make it back to the Hyatt before sunrise, and at times before eight. Well, there's something to feel good about."

"What's that?" I asked.

"I did some cross checking and it's apparent that they do the same thing in Atlanta, New York, and Florida. So you might not be the only 'good' piece of ass they knock off. These girls are aging nymphos with money to play with," she continued. She looked at me trying to guesstimate my vibe.

"Looks like your girl Fran is the sampler, and from what you told me, an instructor too!"

"Ain't this a bitch!" I snapped.

Denise reached over and patted my hand and asked if I was all right.

"I'm cool," I said but kept glancing at the photos. I'm making twenty thousand dollars a month, replayed in my conscience. "Is this package mine, Denise?"

"You paid for it, brother."

I got up, paid for our food, and walked back to my car without a "goodbye" or a "thank you". Fran was running back and forth through my mind like crazy, and I desperately fought to slow it down.

What's out of place with all this that I keep running over or past? I thought. Then it hit me like a ton of bricks. The black bag! The last thing in the car and always close by her computer in the spare bedroom. The keyboard is always pulled out too, like she's keeping it ready for action. I just realized that the only phone in the house is in the spare room. "I got you girl!" I said with a cunning smile on my face.

I knew only one person who would help me gain entry into Fran's apartment, and that was Baby!

"Baby on the line, talk to me," he said.

216 • Johnny A. McDowell

"I need a favor, Baby."

"Stephon, my man. Call it, brother."

"I need to gain entry into an apartment of a new adversary of mine."

"Me personally, brother... I don't ask my people to do shit like that, but what I can do is get you a bump key and you can go in on your own."

"How long?" I asked. I gained more respect for Baby.

"Hell, when do you need it?" was all he needed to know.

"Before night fall!"

"It's going to cost you, Stephon. Nothing personal, but I have to pay the toll fee, baby."

"Talk to me," I said.

"One grand."

"Just tell me where," I said.

"I'll be at Hooter's on Collins Street in Arlington in about an hour. You take a seat, you pay the girl and she'll give you your hot wings to go," he said before hanging up.

It was Hillary's night tonight, and I couldn't wait to see her either! One thing that I found out about Hillary; it was her intention to belittle my subconscious prior to our business. The more hate I had in my heart and on my mind for her and her bigotry, the harder my delivery would be into her. I could count on her calling me a nigga real soon. She'd resorted to placing raw and vivid thirty-two by forty inch pictures of slaves around the room. In each picture, the slaves were beaten to a bloody pulp, exposing their bones where the whip had bit down to the white meat. There were also black babies being marched to the auction block in chains.

I had to admit that it disgusted me. The angrier I got, the more I tried to punish her body; but the more I punished her, the stronger she climaxed. She knew that her racial tactics were losing its grip and wearing off, and that my anger was diminishing because my delivery wasn't punishing her spot like it had been in prior weeks. I've been a black bastard, coon baby, porch monkey and tonight might be the 'darkie' night. Tonight, there would be no need for any tactics because

I was going to run the show!

Tonight was a fair exchange: You give me what I want and I'll see to it that you see your chiropractor as soon as you touch down in Florida. I was seven thousand dollars to the good, and with a little help from four shots of Napoleon Brandy, the bitch begged me to stop before her hour was up. I was back in my room and in the shower before the eleven o'clock hour struck. The fact that I was a known visitor over at Fran's dummy-home, no one would question me or my Jag being there for about an hour.

I was straight into her parking space and into her apartment. The screen saver glowing from her computer was all I needed to lead me straight down the hallway and to its keypad.

Okay Francis, how sloppy are you? I asked myself. Within a few minutes, I was searching for access codes to get me into a program that was marked "Gee-Gee." I tried everything from cities to states, initials, first and last names, hotels, and then it hit me on the head. As a last ditched effort I typed in, "Stephon." The damn computer started doing shit that even frightened me. Once it stopped, I started smiling because Fran had got down and was winning off my black ass and ten other men from every state that the ladies came from.

From the looks of it, old Stephon was riding the range in Texas as the "Lone Ranger." Fran made twenty thousand dollars every time my pants came down. In fact, the bitch made twenty thousand dollars every time the past brothers who came before me dropped their pants too! "Ohhh, mercy me," I said when I found her personal calendar for the past six months and up to February of the following year. From what Steve told me about Highland Park, if you weren't a millionaire, you didn't live there, and if you were black, there was no doubt you had mega money because blacks were scarce in Highland Park.

"I'm not mad at you, Francis Oliver, and don't be mad at me," I whispered as I began transferring everything I found onto my own disk. Before leaving I made sure that I deleted her files just to let her know that someone had been up in her ass. I was out of the apartment and in bed in two hours. Daybreak came and it was like waking up on

Christmas morning to me. I wasn't doing any traveling until Monday night, and though Catalina was warm about that, I needed the rest. Monica cooked breakfast and planned our entire day. Our first order of business was the Dallas Zoo. It was a rather warm seventy-degree day, and since the wind wasn't blowing, the youngster was about to come face to face with nature.

I really wasn't depending on my boy to start recognizing certain things, but it was the ferocious animals in the gift shop to which I wanted to introduce him. Hell, it wasn't a secret that the whole outing wasn't for Monica anyway. I fronted past the "Oooh look, a baby lion," coming from Monica as if the youngster knew what the hell a lion was. We finally made it full circle and it was on!

"That's all you wanted to do was get my baby in this gift shop so that he could act a fool!"

"Girl, you know I just paid to get inside the gates to bring him straight in here. You steady saying 'look baby, a monkey' and he's playing with my ball cap."

"Now it's Stephon time!" I said proudly. "Excuse me, ma'am," I said directly to a woman working in the gift shop.

"Yes sir."

"Whatever he puts his hands on and goes crazy behind, sack it up for the young man," I instructed the cashier. The zoo manager gave us some nylon net, tied a knot at one end to act as the bottom and then filled the net until it was full. Ordinarily, a mother would have been happy, but Monica was hot.

"Look at all this shit, Stephon. You can't even see out the back window. Just silly," she said. I looked back at my boy and he was all smiles.

"Fef-fon, Fef-fon," was all he was saying.

"That's right, recognize your boy," I told him with the pride any father would or should have for a great kid. He was happy and that meant I was happy.

"Okay, where to now?" I asked.

"Let's go to that Luby's Cafeteria," she said pointing up the highway. I looked at her like, I don't think so! From that point on, I knew she was just wanting to hang out with me. I took them to the top of the Dome for lunch, a movie and did some shopping for her. It was when we pulled out of the theater's parking lot that I noticed a white Mustang on our tail. I only decided to take on the Red Bird Mall just to see if the person was a fluke or not.

I turned, the tail turned. We spent three hours in the mall and so did our tail. We left the mall and so did the white Mustang. It was time for me to get Monica and my boy to safety. I chose the quickest route to the Bay. Once I got them upstairs in my room, I ran downstairs to jump on the phone to call Baby.

"Baby. Talk to me," he said.

"Anybody you know drive an all-white Mustang?" I asked him.

"Not a part of my crew. You need some help right now?"

"Yeah, playa! It followed me all the way back from Dallas and I'm back at the Bay."

"Sit tight for thirty minutes, then go wherever you need to go. You in your car?" he asked.

"Yeah!"

"If the fool is still on you when you leave the Bay and you see my people pull the son-of-a-bitch over, keep going and I'll fill you in later." We ended our conversation.

Whoever it was had been on me since we left the apartment, and knew that I spent too much time at the Bay. I snaked my way up to my room, hoping to catch a glance at the character before I got back to Monica, but whoever was following us wasn't as big of a fool to catch a spot on the lot. Thirty-five minutes went by and the more I moved about frontin' like I was gathering some gear to take back to the apartment, the more Monica raised an eyebrow.

"Let's roll up out of here. Having you in close quarters like this is bad for your equilibrium," I told Monica with a cheesy smile, trying to act like all was cool. She threw me the finger and remained focused so as to catch the last part of a movie she was watching.

"Sure is a lot of clothes," she commented.

"It's time that I trade them for something else anyway," I said.

"Can I ask you a question?" she asked nonchalantly.

"What's up?"

"Where do you plan to put all that stuff?"

"Damn!" I shouted after thinking about all those stuffed animals. "In your lap," I said. I waited for some trash talk about the stuffed animals.

"Boy, do you see this dime-piece making a statement in this outfit to those who come within eyesight of this here?" she said, as she turned around to display her whole package.

"Girl it's not going to blemish your groove to put this in your lap for a few minutes," I said.

"Just so you don't make a habit of it, playa," she kidded.

I wasn't going to feed into her playful mood because Baby's people were waiting on me to leave the Bay. I had been around the Bay long enough to spot anything that was out of place, and spotting Baby's people was easy.

No one moved out of the lot behind me as I turned onto the service road of Highway 114. As soon as I made the loop to jump on 114, I spotted the Mustang sitting idle on the shoulder of the highway, about a quarter of a mile back. Come to papa, you bastard, I said in my mind when I merged onto the highway. Though I wasn't going to be able to see past all the stuffed animals, I trusted Baby's people to handle their business. I went straight to the apartment and unloaded everything. I spent two hours bathing the youngster and trying to put his butt to sleep, and when I wasn't successful at that, he ended up in Monica's care. I couldn't hold out, and not knowing what happened to the Mustang rider was driving me crazy.

"I have to check on something and I'll be back."

"Sure!" Monica stated continuing to rock the youngster into his coma.

I got out of the house to catch a corner phone booth and hoped like hell Baby had something for me.

"Baby, you come up with something?" I anxiously asked.

"Two things! Little Mama got a mean driving game and she's black, long hair and cute in the face. My cousin down at the Fort Worth

Police Department says the car is registered to a Denise Gray out of Austin, Texas."

"Austin!" I shouted.

"You know this chick?" he asked.

"Bullshittin'' with you is like cuttin' my own neck, Baby; and I'm not with that! I was turned on to the girl by a mutual acquaintance to do some P.I. work on the party I needed the key for."

"Well, brother, sounds like you need to clean your house because you have roaches. If you're a smart man, you'll place this woman and that close acquaintance of yours in the same group with your uncle."

"I'm already there, Baby," I said.

"Look here, Stephon, when those plates came back with an Austin owner, I had to put the old man in your business."

"You did the right thing, Baby."

"Fair warning to you: if anything associated to this Gray chick is going to drip anywhere toward Catalina, she'll know within the hour, Homie," explained Baby.

"I'm not trippin' Baby, and please keep me up on this shit."

"I'm more than sure this chick was thinking my boys wanted her car, so if you get close enough to pull the bitch's fangs, don't blow your chance, Stephon. I would hate for the girl to come back and bite you or Catalina on the ass."

"I need to stop off by the tackle house for some bait," I told Baby before hanging up. It's been over six months since I left Pioneer Park Place Apartments and Denise was placed on me from day one. My question is, has she given my ass up after all this time, and if she has, what's kept James at Bay?

My mind was on rewind...I've got some good news and some bad news for you, youngster. She just got out of college, but a few detectives said the girl didn't cut corners, and is out to make a name for herself, replayed in my head. As I stood in the lot with a brain dysfunction behind all the shit going on, holding on to the door handle on my car, and my shoulder bracing the phone to my ear, I dialed 411.

"Southwestern Bell Information, can I help you?" the operator stated.

"I need a number and address for Gray's Investigators, please."

"One second sir. Sir, would that be in Irving or Dallas?" she asked.

"To be honest ma'am, I'm not sure."

"I'll just check the surrounding cities," she stated while silence stood between us.

"Sir, I'm sorry, but there's no listing for a Gray's Investigators in the Dallas area."

"Before you go, ma'am, can you please give me a location of a phone number?" I asked.

"Sure, what's the number?"

"214-555-3824."

"7106 Castlebend, Highland Park sir."

"Thank you so much, ma'am," I said politely then hung up.

Damn, when does this shit stop? Fran, Tye, Denise and who else is on my ass, I wondered. I'd fought tooth and nail not to bring Catalina's name up in all the shit that was going on, but I was being spread around too damn smooth to exclude anybody from the suspect list.

All I could think about was Monica and the safety of her son. I got in my car and took to the highways around Dallas-Fort Worth area for a thinking session.

"Catalina can be excluded in a sense because she wouldn't sit by and allow me to live with another woman and not say anything about it, so it's clear that she doesn't know about Monica. At least not yet! This could be a move to break Catalina down, but Catalina going back across the border, that would be a waste of time," I mumbled.

It's already understood that I'm not jumping ship when it comes to Catalina, so why hasn't anybody made a move on me? I wondered. Monica and her son can't be the reason because I spend too much time at the Bay. So if anybody wanted to do me some harm, it would be at the Bay! A lot of the details weren't adding up right, and though I'd been tossed up like a dinner salad, I knew bad math when I encountered it, and somebody was stalling. I guess taking Baby's advice is my best move. "You're not following me for nothing, Denise," I said under my breath.

I guess it was time for me to start playing the game since I was smack dab in the middle of it. The question was how do I make myself available to Denise? "Fran," I said out loud to myself.

Sometimes I come in late on Saturday nights, she had said. "Okay people, it's stage call!" I said as I headed back to the apartment. I had no intention of breaking my dinner date with Monica and my boy. As soon as I got back in my area, I started looking for Denise to pick me up. Tonight, I had plans to make shit easy for her, like she said at the Hyatt.

I made reservations for two and a half at my favorite spot and for the first time, I didn't have to wait on a table.

"Stephon, good to see you my friend," said the manager.

"What's with all the smiles, Tony?" I asked.

"Well, when I heard you needed a seat, I thought I'd come out of the office to see the little one. It's very rare that we have to pull out a booster seat, so excuse the dust," he said chuckling. He made sure the booster seat was secure before helping to get my boy settled in it.

"Tony, this is Monica and my godson."

"Nice to meet the two of you, and since the young man is a guest in my place, Monica, your meal is on me," Tony said, extending his hand to offer her a handshake.

"Thank you, Tony," she said.

"Hell, can I expect the same if I bring my other godchildren in for a bite?" I asked. Tony just laughed and walked off.

"I didn't want to get all sentimental back at the apartment in front of my boy, but I can't help being weak about how I feel about you in that dress. I'm not saying that you don't look beautiful every day, but outside of seeing you naked the way that I did, you are turning my world upside down tonight."

Monica blushed. "Thank you, Stephon. I had made up my mind to take it to Goodwill Monday to toss it in their box. I had been fussin' at you from the time we walked out of the house about you not saying anything about this dress."

"What were you saying?" I asked her.

"I spent my whole day off searching for this damn dress just for your black ass, and you don't like it! I ain't gonna lie, I was ready to go back in the house and lock my door."

"Girl, you trippin."

"Boy, I'm serious!"

"Well, I'm happy to see you sitting across from me, and you are beautiful tonight, Monica," I stated as I kissed the top of her hand.

"Fef-fon," said the young prince as he reached out for the small packages of crackers on the table.

"Ask and you shall receive, my young prince," I said turning my attention to him. I took the cracker out of the package and gave it to him.

"Thank you for being his godfather, Stephon," Monica remarked and at the same time she touched my fingers.

"You're not getting sentimental on me, are you?"

"I refuse to answer that question."

I looked into her eyes for a second and agreed, "Yeah, you keep that to yourself."

The youngster made dinner fun, because he wanted to taste everything at the table besides his own stuff. He was the perfect baby until he started passing gas. Monica thought the boy had taken a dump and excused herself to take him to the restroom to change his Pamper, but the boy was only passing gas. After about the third time he did it, it was time to go! The boy's gas had a radius of two tables over and the customers started to smell my boy's wrath.

"Dooky booty," I said to him in a cartoon like voice. I kept it up and he and Monica laughed all the way home.

Once I got them safely settled in the apartment, I was in my jeans, Longhorn ball cap, T-shirt and sneakers.

"Are you coming back tonight?" Monica asked.

"As soon as I get done, okay?" I replied as I kissed her forehead.

"What was that for?" she asked.

"A lovely day," I said as I walked out the door.

After stopping off at a liquor store to purchase a bottle of champagne, I took my time and drove a steady course back to my old apartment. I pulled up and parked at the pool, and though Fran's apartment was at a good distance, I would be able to know when she arrived as soon as she turned on the lights.

I stood outside of my car and undressed down to my swimming trunks. As soon as I went towards the trunk of the car to get two wine glasses that I'd snuck out the apartment earlier that day, I saw the headlights of a car go off. I knew it was Denise. I retrieved the set of wine glasses, two towels and my handgun. Once I settled down into the water, I popped the cork on the champagne and poured me a drink. Five minutes passed before she appeared.

"You expecting company?" she asked.

"What gave you that idea, Denise?"

She pointed and replied, "The extra glass, I suppose."

"Well, I'm not the rude type as you would know. You never know who might show up." I said as I held the extra glass up for her. "You always out this time of the night in this area, or are you just stalking me?" I asked as I poured her a drink.

"Why don't we stop all the bullshit, Stephon," she said and then took a sip of her drink.

"I'll drink to that, Denise." I looked at her posture and saw that she was just as ready to set some shit off as I was. "First things first," I said.

"I'm listening," she said.

"Clothes off," I said.

"You've got to be joking! Does it look like I came here to swim?" she asked.

"Don't take this too personal, but the few bitches I know from Austin stay ready!"

She looked at me for about ten seconds, "Only if you remove your hand from under that towel."

"Right now, I'm a nigga and far from being a gentlemen; so request denied, Boo!" She saw that I wasn't giving in and took off her jacket, revealing her handgun and shoulder holster. She got undressed all the way down to her panties and bra.

"Nice set! Anyway, can I get a look at the back?" I asked.

"To hell with you," she said bitterly.

"Since you have been doing research on my recreational activities, you already know I'm good at that, so watch your step," I said. I held the bottle up to pour her another drink.

"I hope you know this water is cold," she said.

"As hot as I am, I hadn't noticed," I said. "You gonna talk or keep complaining?"

She stepped into the water, and started explaining. "I was asked to find you when things between you and your uncle-"

I cut her off, "James would be sufficient enough."

She continued, "You and James went bad."

"You were the one in my apartment when Catalina called. Was the request to find me out of anger?" I asked.

"You should know that already," she stated.

"If that's the case, then why hasn't he made a move?"

"My guess? Because you're family! But being that we both understand that James is not a fair man, all he had to do was order someone to take care of his problem. He wasn't counting on you to go against the grain this deep. His frat brothers would be facing conspiracy charges, along with countless other charges, and risking it all behind you wasn't going to happen."

"Catalina would have been the first to bring them up. You haven't told him that you know where I lived at yet; why?"

"I figured we can both do business together," she said.

"Why would you come to a conclusion like that?" I asked.

"Here's a little story for you, but first, a gift for you," she said as she got out of the pool to retrieve a photograph out of her jacket pocket. She got back in and handed me a picture of James and Fran having dinner somewhere. Deep down inside, I was furious!

"I haven't jumped on top of finding out yet, but I believe James is my father."

"Get off the bullshit, Denise." She looked at the shock on my face, nodded confirmation, and continued talking. "James, Fran, and my mother all went to college together. Fran was always jealous of my mother behind James. My mother came up dead when I was a year old. My sources and police records indicated that she was involved in a fight. All the clues, plus Fran's cut on her throat suggested that she was in the brawl with my mother, but the authorities couldn't come up with enough evidence to convict the bitch. From the day my mother was placed in the ground, James has looked after me, calling himself my godfather.

"When I graduated from high school, I had enough information surrounding my mother's death that I sought a degree in Law Enforcement to investigate things on my own. That gave me the keys I needed to get a job that would open any door I wanted, and when I got what I needed, I quit! Now I'm a freelance P.I."

"So what's your problem, and what the hell does all of that have to do with me?" I asked her.

"You are the only person that can get into his apartment. In fact, you are the only one who has ever spent two hours in that apartment or who has been so close to him. What I need is to get in his apartment myself, she confessed."

"She had plastic surgery," I muttered.

"Excuse me," Denise said.

"Fran... she had surgery to hide the scar. Yeah, about five years ago. In fact, the woman is a plastic surgery queen. I was eleven when I first saw her in the elevator at the Tower."

"Let's get this straight. If you think I'm going near his place, you're sadly mistaken," I told her.

"I think that you will for two reasons. One, a sixty-forty split on his money; and two, he stays free from prosecution for my mother's death. Having knowledge of a first-degree murder is about twenty-five years in prison," she explained.

"So, what's fifty percent looking like for me?" I asked.

"I don't know the full range of his assets, but I'm claiming two million each."

"You want me to risk my life to get some shit for you and it's sixty-forty! Well, I just added another category to my Austinites," I said.

"What would that be?" she asked.

"I know one bitch from Austin that's crazy!"

"I'll disagree with that. This bitch knows, and understands that this information will ensure that you will not be involved in any accidental accidents; if you feelin' this bitch! Do you think for one minute James or those other brothers are going to allow you or me to just walk away with his money and their information, Stephon?"

"What makes you so sure that I won't keep the shit for myself?" I asked her.

"You took a girl you barely knew who was living in a crack house with her son and provided for them nicely. That's one reason why James doesn't know where you live, Stephon. It's not in you!" she said.

"I gave you a portion of what I should have given you about your nymphos. You see, from the age of three, I've been listening to Francis whisper in my ear, 'Little bitch, you gon' be sorry like your mama.' James was bringing her with him sometimes when he would stop to see me and give my grandmother money. She's not excluded in this shit either! She was getting paid like the rest of them hoes."

Denise broke down what each woman was worth: Ciara Williams, $200 million; Hillary O'Donald, $179 million; Beatrice Ferguson, $135 million; Jacqueline Summers, $145 million; Karen Danelle, $214 million; Amanda Brooks, $160 million; and Francis, $36 million.

"I'm listening," I said pouring both of us another drink as I loosened the grip of my hand off my pistol.

"James has provided young brothers for Fran's little hustle for years. His cut, I don't know, but she won't allow you or anyone else to bring her down or back to the ghetto," she said.

"You beat me to her computer access code that I've been trying to figure out for three weeks," she said.

"You should have tried, 'Stephon'!" She started laughing.

"What's funny?" I asked.

"I thought about that two hours before you went in, and when you came out, I knew you had the information you needed."

I asked her how she figured that out. She told me that there was a disk missing and a file deleted off her screen. All I could do was smile as I asked her what her plans were for Francis.

"Nothing can bring my mother back, and the only way to hurt this tramp is to bring her ass down to my level. That way, I can whisper, "This is for my mother, bitch!" I want you to have fifty percent of the money in her account," she said.

"Why don't you want it all?" I asked.

"I didn't like the way you got played. I'll take fifty percent and a copy of the disc for insurance purposes! Your nymphos would be panicking right now if they knew you had their lives in your hands."

"Fran will be looking for you before noon tomorrow because as far as she's concerned, you are the only person who could have her shit. Let me make one thing clear; if I walk into some bullshit when I get to the Tower, you'll never see tomorrow," I said as I grabbed my pistol and left.

I waited until I got to my car before I dried off because I needed to see if Denise had company or not. It was after ten o'clock and Fran still hadn't made her way down to the ghetto. I needed to be in and out of Austin before Fran found out that her files were gone, and I needed Baby's help again.

It was too late to be out on a pay phone, so I waited until I got home. Monica was lying on the sofa watching a movie when I came through the door. "You waiting up on me or you just wanted to show me those cream lace panties?" I probed her.

"Keep your eyes where they're supposed to be and you won't have to worry about all this," she said in a fly manner, waving her hands over her fine ass body. I shook it off and went straight into my room and called Baby.

"What's up?" he asked.

"Don't trip, playa, but I need you again, Baby."

"I'm not trippin' and won't trip as long as we're cool, Stephon. Talk to me."

"I need to get in and out of the Tower without Carlos or Catalina knowing that I was ever in the building.

"Damn, brother. That's some David Copperfield shit, and the only one that can make some shit like that happen is the old man, Holmes."

"I need to talk to him, Baby."

"Shit better be V.I.P. Stephon, for real playa."

"Get him on the phone, Baby!"

Three minutes later he was wanting to know why.

"Mr. Sias, I need to get into his bedroom and on his computer before the sun comes up. I'll obtain some information that might help us all out. I lived with him for almost eight years, and I was only allowed in his room twice."

"How do you know the information will be there, Stephon?"

"I'm willing to risk my life getting in Mr. Sias. Good enough?"

"When are you leaving?" he asked.

"I need to find out if he's out of town or not," I said. "I'll save you some time, son. He won't be back until Monday about noon."

"How do you know this, if you don't mind me asking, sir?"

"For starters, it's my job, son."

"I'm on my way there as soon as I hang up this phone."

"You park your car on the east side of the building and my people will be waiting to get you in and out of the building."

"Mr. Sias."

"Yes, son."

"Tell Baby if anything happens to me and I don't make it back...tell him to find Denise Gray for me."

"I understand and will pass that on," he said.

I got dressed in some black on black and went to talk to Monica. "Hey, Country, I have to go see a man about a dog, but I'll be back for breakfast."

"You promise?" she asked.

"Promise!" I said as I gently kissed her forehead.

I walked over to where my boy was sleeping on his baby futon and kissed him too.

"You love my baby, don't you, Stephon?"

I looked at Monica and thought about what Denise had told me about the two of them and said, "I love you too, Monica, but don't tell him."

"And why not?" she asked.

"He might get jealous and kick me to the curb," I said then walked out the door.

Chapter TEN

FOOL'S MATE

For me to ever take James for granted was suicide on my behalf. Remembering back on the day that he took me back into the Eastside Projects, the fact that he strolled through them without a worry, meant something to me—even when I didn't understand. Nobody would mess with him because he supplied all the weed in those projects. I never said a word about it after I found out, but there was a thin line between frontin' to be a gangster and James. Catching me in his apartment was all he needed to close the chapter in my book. Whatever was on that computer was enough to say, "to hell with the family".

I made it into Austin without being stopped for speeding. By the time James finds out that his life, his home, personal business, and world has been breached, he'll be checking every source he can, even the Texas Department of Public Safety, just to see if I was within a hundred miles of the Tower. Catalina's people covered me like fine linen as my car was ushered toward a hiding spot. No one spoke a word to me until they got me into the underground service station.

"Stephon, this will not be very comfortable for you, but it is the only way to enter the Tower for you, Señor."

I looked down at the food cart and back at the man talking. "I'm too tall; damn it!" I stated with a measure of frustration.

"No, Señor, look what we did for you. We weld here for back and here for your feet. No fall out, Señor; trust Pablo."

After seeing that a piece of metal was welded on the cart to support my back and at the opposite end to ensure my legs wouldn't pop out, I had no choice but to try it.

"Come, Señor, we must go right away.

It was 1:30 in the morning and the only way I was going up was under that cart! I went from underground to the first floor and then into the take-out section of the kitchen. I sat there folded up like an accordion in its case for ten minutes. Finally, food was being placed on the cart and I was on the move again. Knowing the Tower the way that I did, and listening to the conversations as I traveled to my destination, there were shortcuts taken. I was taken through the main lobby and straight to James' door. I was pushed into the room and the gentleman closed the door behind him and helped me off the cart. He stood with his back up against the door and told me, "I will stay here, Senor." I asked him if he had a weapon, and he raised his shirt to show me that he did.

It was time to find out if old habits never changed. I ran into my old bedroom to retrieve alcohol and a washcloth. James had a spare key to his bedroom taped under a brass statue of a Buffalo Soldier. I had lifted the soldier many times in the past to see if the key was ever moved, and had found it there each time. I then went searching for a roll of electrical tape that was kept in his utility cabinet. I knew when I pulled that old tape up, it was going to leave the old adhesive in place, and the only thing that was going to remove its trace was the alcohol.

"Old fool," I said when I saw that the key was still there.

I removed it from the soldier's grasp, removed the adhesive, placed the old strip and towel in my pants pocket and turned towards his room. I drew my handgun and flicked the safety off as I approached his door.

"It's either you or me, James," I said as I slid the key into the lock. I pushed the door open and stood to one side. I took a few deep breaths and went in. After making sure the area was secure, I went to work.

It's too simple, I thought, looking down at his desk. It was too neat and his computer disks were sitting in a disk case in plain sight, as if he had nothing to hide.

"Bullshit!" I said as I went in search for the real stuff. It took me thirty minutes to find two thin slices in the trim molding around the wall. One touch and the spring-release that held the secret compartment was giving me the booty in this battle without one bullet ever being fired. One by one, I lifted and read the code names, and even though I didn't know what the shit meant, I knew I had what I came for.

I slid one of the disks in his computer and chose one of the ten files that appeared on the screen. What came up was enough for me to exit the program, wipe down the keypad and get the hell out with all nine disks. Whether or not I had what Denise was looking for, the negotiations were definitely going to happen. I placed the key back as I found it and wiped down my every touch to remove my presence.

When I got back to the cart, my escort had eaten half the food and rearranged the items on the cart to make it appear as if it had encountered one of the residents. I was helped back under the cart and wheeled back downstairs to the kitchen so that the dishes and other items could be properly discarded. I was taken back down to the service entry and had to sit on the cart for almost an hour because a bread truck was being unloaded.

I was hurting so bad that I wanted to give up and say "to hell with it," but that would expose Catalina's people and things would be very bad for me. As soon as the bread truck pulled out of the service area, two of the men returned to rescue me from my captivity.

"Please, Señor, you must hurry. Deliveries will start to come in and the workers will assemble around here soon," one of them explained.

"Ayudame, I can't walk right now," (help me) I pleaded, then grabbed a hold of the two men.

"Sir, we will not be able to help you out of the service area because it will draw too much attention. You must try to stand," the other man urged as they dragged me toward a dark spot in the service garage.

"Señor, you make it to the corner and someone outside will help you to your car. If you do not want to get caught, you must leave this minute, Señor," he said nervously looking around while he walked away.

"Come on, Stephon, move your ass, boy," I said to myself as I fought to stand. Seeing two Tower employees being dropped off for work by a female driver let me know that I was running out of time because the people who worked the service area were starting to report for duty.

I gave them just enough room and walked out of the service area like a drunken man in the wrong area. I saw the men who were going to escort me back to my car, but they wouldn't risk leaving their positions because they couldn't afford to be seen with me.

"A little more, Senor, just a little more," one man said as I drew closer to them.

Out of frustration, one of them said, "To hell with it," and came out of the protection of the dark and practically carried me to my car. "You are behind time, Señor. Carlos' people will see your fancy car if you don't leave immediately."

I fought to insert the keys in the ignition as I watched the two men trot off in different directions.

I finally got my act together as best I could, and as bad as I wanted to push down on the accelerator, I knew I had to tiptoe away from the area. Plus, knowing that both Carlos and Catalina's people were many and coming from every direction, wasn't making shit better for me.

I was an hour off my trail, but I kept driving the back country roads because the signs that appeared every five miles continued to read, Waco 15 miles; then Waco 10 miles. It was five o'clock and I was nowhere near Irving. There was one thing that I was glad about. My body functions were finally normal, and though I was experiencing some serious jitters, James was on my mind! I finally got straightened out when I made it into Waco and my only objective was to make it back into my area without getting a speeding ticket.

Out of all the things Monica and I had in the apartment, a computer wasn't a flicker of a thought while we were out spending. That meant I would have to wait until noon before I could be able to purchase one. Well, I had eighty-five minutes to figure out how I was going to best protect myself, Monica, my boy, and Catalina from that point on. I figured by the time I walked out of the mall with a computer, Fran would have already contacted James about her files being gone. With Denise being the target of blame, it would give me some time to look over the disks before James discovered that his were missing as well.

Monday morning was a long way off, and the only safe place to store my new precious jewels were in a safe deposit box. Twenty-seven hours was a long time to be dodging James, Fran, the frat brothers, and every big drug dealer under James' care. So the longer I stalled on closing the books on this shit, the closer I drew to being harmed.

Denise couldn't be in two places at the same time, so it didn't make a difference whether I arrived through my front door in Dallas or my back door in Fort Worth. Denise was in Irving waiting on me. Whether or not we cross paths, when Fran questions her about James' shit, she'll be close by Fran's apartment.

I walked into the apartment smelling my favorite breakfast steak being cooked. Me and the youngster locked in on each other and his arms automatically came up, demanding me to pick him up. I hated to brush my boy off, but I had to hit the shower before coming in contact with him or Monica. By the time I was rinsing off, she knew I was home.

"So you're sneaking in the house these days, huh?" She confronted me as she stood in the door with the little man on her hip.

"Fef-fon," he said as he reached out to me.

"He gave me up, didn't he?" I asked and she started laughing.

"After hearing him call your name about four times while he crawled towards this way, I finally heard the shower," she said.

"We need to talk about some serious shit. Hand me a towel and go set the table." I had made up my mind that Monica was going to be more than just an attorney, but my guardian angel for life. I dried off, grabbed me a pair of shorts and found Monica waiting on me. I kissed my boy and followed it with a kiss on Monica's forehead before sitting down.

"My uncle's hate for me is heavier than what I told you about," I said slowly so that she could grasp the seriousness. I placed the set of disks on the table. "From this day forward, your job is strictly law school. I found out some gangsta shit about him and my only way to get him off my ass was to obtain his whole world," I said as I pointed at the disks.

"What's on them?" she asked.

Monica looked stunned and confused, evident by the wrinkles on her forehead and the squint of her eyes. I looked at my watch and back up at her.

"As soon as I can get a computer hooked up, we'll know. I only had time to look over one file and that let me know that I had what I needed."

"You went to Austin last night? He could have killed you, Stephon."

"We have five hours to look over these things and figure out how to best use them as leverage."

I had no choice but to tell her everything, even about Fran and our dealings.

"So what's on the table, Stephon?" she asked with an attitude.

"You upset with me?" I asked.

"No, but I'm very pissed off at your uncle and that bitch Fran.

"Monica, I'm nineteen, so I got played for my piece, but what matters right now is how 'we' handle this shit. So let's drop the attitude and concentrate on the big picture," I said.

"Stephon, you know that you do not have to do this."

"Yes, I do, Monica! What's on the disks, you asked? My freedom from any future retaliation, about fifteen million dollars, and you being my insurance ticket. As long as he never gets his hands on these disks, I live happily ever after."

"What about us, Stephon?" She posed the question as she looked down at her son.

"You're not in the picture."

"Are you trusting her?" Her question showed that she needed some reassurance from me.

"Where can she hurt me? The livelihood that she's after is sitting right in front of us. I agreed to let her have her way with Fran, and I'm not mad at her. Are you?"

"I'm not feelin' her either, Stephon. I don't need her catching a wild hair up her ass and giving me up."

"Monica, you and I will be the only ones who will ever know where the disks are, so stop trippin'."

"I'm not sittin' here by myself anymore, Stephon."

"I don't want you to little mama," I said.

"Please tell me that we all are going to be all right, Stephon." Her eyes began to water.

"You trust me, Monica?" I asked her as I held her hand and wiped the single tear from her right cheek.

"More than you'll ever know, Stephon." Monica shook her head a few times and rolled her eyes up, I guess to stop any more tears from falling.

"As soon as we get back from buying this computer, I want you to pack some clothes because come Monday, you'll be disappearing," I informed her.

"What about you?" she asked.

"I'll catch up with you when the dust settles," I said.

"So where am I going?" She asked the question, but she seemed a bit more confident in following my lead.

"Where would you like to go?"

"How am I supposed to know, Stephon?"

"Have you ever been to Jamaica, the Virgin Islands, South America? Your mother would enjoy a month long vacation."

"Are you serious?" she cried out.

"You think fifty grand will take care of the three of you for a month?"

I paced myself for her response. She almost jumped over the table getting to me. We tongue danced for a while and I slowly pushed her away.

"Not a good time, Boo." We looked at each other with some serious shit on our minds but I ended those thoughts by kissing her on her forehead. My boy had been playing with his toys, but stopped to look at us. Our intimate moment must have not fazed him because he went right back to playing and banging on his toys.

"Wherever you choose to go, book me a flight to you and pay for a one way ticket. When I get there, we'll decide where we'll be going next. Don't get too damn comfortable. You're still taking your ass to law school."

"With all this shit going on, can I at least choose my own college?" she asked, putting her hands on her hips and smirking her lips.

"Let's put it this way, you graduate and pass the bar, I'll take my name off his account and leave you solely responsible for the fifty thousand dollars. Are we straight?"

"I only have one request though," she stated.

"I'm listening."

"I don't want to work and go to school, my mama stays, she gets a salary for watching over your godson and as your attorney, I handle all your future needs."

"You got that!" I said. "You have until this coming March to tell me where you want to attend. Wherever it is, I'm putting you all up in a high-rise living condition because I'll be comfortable with that, and when you're done with school, I'll sell it!"

"Stephon, the computer!" she remembered and pointed to the grandfather wall clock.

"Get my boy ready while I get dressed." Fran is having a fit, I thought, smiling. Not to mention, me not showing up at my usual time will raise a flag.

We took Monica's car to avoid any unexpected problems. Avoiding Denise was impossible and I wasn't trippin' about that. We were in and out of the mall without a single sight of Denise. That let me know that she was waiting another hour or two to see if James was going to start squealing like a wounded animal.

So I had just enough time to review the disks and move Monica and my boy to a safe place until Monday morning. It didn't take us long to get the computer up and running, and when we started pulling up files, shit started getting too deep and there was no doubt James would kill for what was on the disks. Monica didn't say a word after we opened the fourth file on the first disk. She ran to her room and started packing. I was on my fifth disk when she dragged her last suitcase up to the door.

"Stephon, get ready, boy!"

"I have all I need Monica; keys, gun and bank book!" I placed another disk in and went to the first file and froze as if James had just stepped in the door.

"Mr. Gonzales has been in on the take," I said in a low tone.

"Stephon, it's 1:30, boy; let's get out of this place, baby."

"Not yet, Monica." I had to see if the others were in it also. I searched the disk until I ran across what Denise was wanting. Monica looked over my shoulder at the screen.

"That bitch killed Denise's mama," came from a shuddering Monica.

She started nervously placing the other disks into an empty cosmetic bag, and then bent down on her knees beside me.

"Stephon, please, baby, get us out of here right now," she begged, and I could see fear in her eyes. I looked down at my boy, and closed out the program and removed the last disk.

"One quick phone call and we're out; I promise." I said. She got up, grabbed the phone and gave it to me. "Baby please, this is Stephon."

"Stephon, what's up?"

"I'm coming your way as soon as I hang up this phone and I'm bringing company. She's the young lady that holds down my pad and she has her son with her. I need your people on me as soon as I hit Arlington. I got what I went after and I gave your father my word that I would give him anything I felt he would need. You told me that I had some pests; well, your father needs to call an exterminator."

"Don't bullshit like that, Holmes," Baby said.

"We'll be in two cars, Baby. Do you have us?"

"Like a brother, Stephon! Take the Brown exit off I-360 and I'll bring you and your crew in personally."

I hung up the phone, put my pistol in my waist and started downstairs. I had Monica wait until I had all her shit stored before she came out the apartment with my boy. I had expected to see Denise outside the edges of the complex. It was two o'clock and I knew she was now aware that I obtained what she wanted.

We took Hwy 114 to the north entrance of the D.F.W. Airport to avoid passing through Irving. As soon as we exited the south end of the airport and caught the loop to 360, Baby and his people surrounded us. Looking back at Monica through my rear-view mirror, I could tell that the cars around us frightened her. Nevertheless, she stayed on my tail until we pulled up to the Sias compound. I quickly got out and ran to check on her. She had been crying and I didn't like that.

"Monica, look at me. You told me that you trusted me, so why are you crying, little mama?"

"I was scared, baby," she said.

"These are my people, Monica. They'll face a charging bull for you, me, and my boy. You with me, Boo?" I asked her.

"I'm with you, Stephon."

Mrs. Sias was standing behind me waiting on me to turn Monica over to her and the rest of the females of the house.

"Come, young lady, I will show you into my home. Such a cute baby boy," she said as the youngster reached out to Mrs. Sias. Monica looked back at me as she walked into the house with Mrs. Sias.

"Stephon, she'll be all right. By the time those girls get through with her, she will be calling them sisters!" Mr. Sias stated with a manufactured smile on his face.

"I hope you all are ready for this," I said as I looked at Baby and his father.

"Please, come! Let's go into my office," said Mr. Sias.

Before entering the grounds of the airport, I had already made up my mind that I would set my own standards before turning over the disks to Mr. Sias. With as much dirt as Mr. Gonzales and James were built up on, controlling one's emotions and keeping powerful egos in check would take some help from God when it came down to these people. As I followed a man who was old enough to be my father into his office, I knew I was about to find out where I really stood with this man and I knew that my delivery was going to be the factor in whether I come out of this being a servant to him or being a man.

I had one thing on my mind. Long-term status. Since Baby was next in line to wear the crown, this was between me and him.

"Please have a seat close to me, Stephon."

"Before this conversation starts, Mr. Sias, not out of disrespect, but out of respect, I need to know that my requests will be honored by this family before I leave your house today," I said to Mr. Sias. "No harm intended, Mr. Sias, but I will ask that your son not only respect your wishes as long as you're alive, but honor my requests as long as he and I are alive," I explained as I stared at Baby.

"So, what are your requests, Stephon?" Mr. Sias asked and I could see the wheels of contemplation spinning in his head. There was a glimmer of uncertainty on his distinguished face. Looking at Baby then at Mr. Sias, there was no doubt that they were father and son.

"For starters, sir, this is not about a bargain," I started by placing the disks on his desk. "This is about honor and doing the right thing," I said.

"Is he not your predecessor, Mr. Sias?" I asked as I looked over at Baby.

"Yes, he will be my predecessor!" he said.

I stood. "Then let my respect for this family start for you today and your honor to uphold your word before your father today and way after his death, Baby," I said with my hand out.

"On my father's grave, Stephon, I'll honor your requests," Baby promised with a handshake and a gentleman's hug.

"What are your requests, Stephon?" Mr. Sias asked again.

I began my list of requests:

1. After you see what's on that disk, that you maintain your complete status with all four leaders in the same manner that you have been for years.

2. I ask that you do everything in your power, not the other men, but in 'your power' to get Catalina back on these grounds for me.

3. Regarding the young lady and her child: They are to have the same protection that Catalina has for as long as she and her son are alive. If it weren't for her involvement, this meeting would not be going on.

4. I want it understood by the other families that any retaliation that comes to my doorstep is a disrespect to your family.

5. You must withhold this information from the other families until Catalina is back in the U.S. to avoid any harm to her.

6. I want Catalina's sister and her daughter out of the Tower the very hour Catalina sets foot back into this country in order to avoid any harm to them."

"What about her parents?" Baby asked.

"Parents! What parents?" I howled.

This was a bombshell. I was surprised and shocked. Mr. Sias and Baby looked at each other. They were surprised by my reaction of not knowing about Catalina's parents.

"Delia was and still is nervous about your uncle or Carlos getting a pop at them, so we moved them out of the area. If I had to guess at why Catalina never told you about them, it would be because of Delia's wishes. They had to also find out what side of the fence you were going to be on," explained Baby.

"I'll deal with that later," I said still shaking my head from the news, and continued to my final request:

7. Now my last request; keep them all safe and for closures, you can keep a copy of the disks, but that goes with me," I said pointing to the original. "I give you my word that the other disks that I have, do not have anything to do with any of the other families and this disk alone is related to Mr. Gonzales," I explained.

"Gonzales? No son, you must be mistaken, Stephon," Mr. Sias said in disbelief and began to struggle to feed the disk into the computer.

"Please Mr. Sias, allow me," I stated as I took the disk out of his trembling hands and fed the computer. Baby came over to stand on the opposite side of him as the files jumped up on the screen for their choosing.

"Where to, Stephon?" Baby asked.

"Start with the first file, Mr. Sias."

As the computer followed and obeyed Mr. Sias' commands, it granted him his wish. He stared into the screen and the longer he read, the more his facial expressions changed. He slowly reclined back into his chair, pulled open the desk drawer, and retrieved a cigar. Baby reached into his pocket to retrieve his lighter and held the flame to his father's cigar. He sat for two minutes in silence as he filtered his thoughts about Hector Gonzales.

"We spent three days hiding in the desert's camouflage. Stephon, do you know the cruelties that the desert can deliver to a person?" Mr. Sias asked me as he puffed on his cigar.

"No I don't," I said.

"Please sit, the both of you," he ordered.

"In the daylight hours, the sun penetrates your clothes and cracks your skin until the wounds of its beating shows. It drains you until your feet can't travel anymore, Stephon. When you have nothing to drink and your lips are cracked with severe pain, you consider drinking your own piss or someone else's just to quench your thirst. The snakes hunt you down like wild dogs of the cartels, and the scorpions remind you with every step you take, they are more powerful than you. My people have to fight the meanest of snakes for the rights of one spot of cool shade under a bush because there are no trees to take refuge under. Then the children beg for water and refuse the food because they cannot swallow. Some are so weak, they are carried like lifeless bodies.

"At night, Stephon, it is so cold that our bodies jump uncontrollably. A lot of my people die at night because they cannot see the snakes that sit patiently waiting on them to cross their paths. They are so weak, the snakes strike them multiple times, all over their bodies. Like the glow of the moon at night, so does the glow of the city lights in this country shine from afar, letting my people know that they are closer to a life worth dying for.

"Mr. Gonzales and I spent five days and nights with forty others in the desert. I carried that 'son-of-a-bitch' on my shoulders until my legs could not take another step, then I crawled with his body because I refused to leave him behind.

"Now he has forgotten the sounds of the babies that cry in the deserts. He has forgotten the prayers of the mothers of those children begging God to save them and their dying babies. You have my word, Stephon, that your requests will be honored, and the very hour that Catalina sets foot back into this country, I must remind Mr. Hector Gonzales of the cries of our people. Baby, look deep into my eyes and my heart, son. Stephon has done a very great thing here today. He has saved the dying people from the desert. Do not make my honor toward this man, that young lady and her son a disgrace to me, as I lay in my grave. Do you understand, son?"

"Si Papa!" Baby said as he kissed the top of his father's head.

"Talk to us, Stephon," Mr. Sias said.

"Right this minute, my uncle is trying to find out exactly where his shit is and who has it! I need refuge until tomorrow morning for Monica and her son. She's leaving on a vacation and she's taking her mother who lives in Arkansas," I explained. "I need her out of the way until this business between me and my uncle is concluded. I can't send her on her way until I have the opportunity to withdraw some money out of my account for the trip."

"Nonsense, Stephon! How much do you need?" Mr. Sias asked.

"At least fifty thousand. They'll be gone at least a month and I want each of them to be comfortable," I told him.

"Baby, get the lady a hundred grand, I want her travel plans done. I want her to have ten thousand dollars in travelers' checks, and tell Lucy to wire ninety thousand to whatever bank in the lady's name," Mr. Sias ordered.

"Stephon, I will also make sure that she has direct contact with my wife, and anything that she asks, she will receive!" he said.

"You, too, will stay here at my home until Monica makes her arrangements and I will see that she, her mother and son are away towards their destination," said Mr. Sias.

"I'll speak with her shortly about all of this, but right now, it's James that I need to deal with. I'm drawing him to me and I need some protection around me. Before the day is over with, I plan on talking to him about his property. I will be making a deal with him and for the sake of our agreement. I will record the conversation and turn it over to you because it will also include Hector Gonzales. Mr. Sias, I am fully aware how this is about to affect me and my life from this day forward, and your people according to what's on that disk. I'm telling you up front, I am taking half of his money and the lady I mentioned, Denise Gray, will be wanting quite a bit as well."

"Do what you will, Stephon. I only want his feet off the backs of my people," Mr. Sias stated.

"Whatever you need and whenever you're ready, Stephon, just fill me in and give me ample time to set my men up, and it's on," said Baby.

"I'll need to talk with Catalina right now," I stated.

"We will let you talk in private," said Mr. Sias as he got up from his seat.

"No, please stay. It's okay," I insisted as I dialed her number.

"Hello," she answered.

"Hey Mami! How are you this afternoon?" I asked.

"I am missing my man, of course."

"I'm surprised that you are not roaming the Tower." She started laughing.

"For your information, black man, I just came home. Things were slow, so I came back upstairs to wait on your call. Will you be coming to see Catalina, tonight?" I hesitated before answering because I knew she wasn't going to like my answer.

"Maybe Monday night, mommy." She got quiet on me. "You can wait another day, girl, so don't start that."

"Easy for you to say, mean man."

"I'll call you later on. I have some business I need to take care of," I told her.

"I love you, Poppi."

"I love you too, Catalina," I said.

"She has no idea that something is wrong in the Tower," I said to Mr. Sias.

"Your uncle sits and waits on you to contact him about his property. He is a very cunning man and I am more than sure that he is trying to find out if you have been in the city," Mr. Sias said.

"Baby, I'm riding with you. Denise Gray is very smart and knows what she wants. She'll run your plates once we leave here. I'm about to reveal her to you so that you'll know her face. So if you want to keep this address out of her notepad, make sure your plates or any others that she might spot can't narrow you down," I explained.

"So where do we find this chick?" Baby asked.

"She's looking for me to go to the apartment."

"Ready when you are, brother," Baby said.

"I'll just need a few minutes with Monica and we can get this shit started."

I was led to where the ladies in the house had assembled and I heard Monica laughing her delightful laugh before I walked into the room.

"Ladies, I hate to intrude, but I have to steal Monica away from you for a few minutes, please."

As soon as my boy spotted me, it was, "Fef-fon, Fef-fon," and wanting me to pick him up. I couldn't deny him, so I brought him with us. We were escorted into a den away from everybody else and left there for privacy.

"You're laughing; is that a good or bad thing?" I asked.

"It's a good thing, but I'm still worried about you," she said.

"I have some good news and bad news. How do you want it?" I asked her.

"The good and then the bad."

"I still want you, my boy and your mother on a flight or ship to wherever you're going by Wednesday. You know your mother better than I do, so tell her whatever you have to tell her. I don't want my people scaring her, so they'll be around you, but not in your face. I don't need them camped out in Arkansas waiting on you for days. Get your mother and them out of the city ASAP. I need you to start making your plans and reservations right now for at least thirty days and don't forget about my ticket either."

"All this shit is happening too fast for me, Stephon, but I can handle it. So what's the bad news?"

"Mr. Sias said that fifty thousand was too small for such a courageous woman, and he thought you deserved one hundred grand to play with on this trip."

"What! One hundred thousand dollars?" she squealed with her eyebrows up and hands on both hips.

"I didn't stutter, girl!"

"Baby, how am I supposed to carry all that around?" she asked.

"Listen, country girl! You'll have ten grand in traveler's checks and when you decide where you're going, you'll get ninety thousand wired to a bank there in your name. You'll have confirmation that the money has been deposited in our bank before you leave tomorrow morning," I said. "Stop staring at me girl and let me know that you gettin' all this."

"Don't miss your flight, Stephon."

"Don't worry about me, little mama, you just take care of my boy and don't allow one of those island lovers to take my boy away from me."

She popped me on my arm.

I let her know that I had to go see Denise and get everything off the ground. She then wanted to know how I was going to go about finding her.

"Monica, you know that girl is probably posted up outside the complex right now waiting on me to show up."

"Be careful, Stephon."

"I'm not rolling alone; go get your fine ass on the phone and do what you need to do. Come morning, I want your ass heading to Arkansas by ten o'clock. We clear on this?"

"I'm on it, boy, so stop pushin'! I'll have it all together when you get back here. Can I ask you a personal question?"

"I'm listening."

"Is Catalina all right?" she asked.

I looked at her for a few seconds. "Are you asking me to be nosey or out of concern?"

"Both!"

"She doesn't have a clue about what is going on and James hasn't shown a distress signal yet, so he's waiting on a call from whoever has his shit."

"You're not telling her are you?" she asked.

"No, I'm not, Monica. That's enough! Go do what I asked you to do and let me worry about the rest of this stuff."

Chapter ELEVEN

SIXTY SECONDS

It was after six o'clock when Baby and I left the Sias' compound. Though Baby had a rule about him not carrying a gun when he and so many of his boys were out, it was still me against James. We gave his people an hour head start and as we grew closer to the Las Colinas area, Baby finally told me how to recognize his people. Depending on what time of the day it was, what day of the week it was and the mission, Baby would choose his color of vehicles. Since this had the potential of playing into the night, it was brown from my apartment complex to O'Connor Road. From O'Connor Road to Esters Road, it was blue, and from then on, back to Arlington, the vehicles were black.

We didn't cut corners going into Irving because no one was hiding. In fact, everybody was looking for the white Mustang. By the time we made our rounds around Fran's area, everybody was indicating a "no" on the sighting of Denise and her white Mustang. If she was in Irving or anywhere near my apartment, Baby's men would give up her location before I could stick my key in the door of my apartment. We pulled up at a Stop-N-Go on McArthur Street to get some conversation, a container of orange juice for Baby, and confirmation of Denise darting back and forth from the Bay to the apartment every thirty minutes. Instantly I knew that if her pattern was that easy to pick up, she wanted me to find her.

By the time we got ready to turn into my complex, we spotted her and went straight to her.

"Is my house still safe, Denise?"

"That's always been between you and me," she replied.

"How are things?" I asked.

"The gates of hell are wide open and the gate keeper is calling on everybody that he knows," she said.

"I won't keep you in suspense any further, Denise. You were right about Fran, and James is probably holding it over her head. I'll let the information speak for itself."

Denise had been waiting all her adult life to find out exactly who had killed her mother. The fact that I informed her that I had what she needed made the expression on her face turn stone cold.

"I guess I would be asking a dumb ass question by asking you if you're going to let me have that information," she asked.

I had risked my life to get my hands on the shit I had, and for her to even suggest such a thing was out of line with me. No doubt I had ill feelings about the death of her mother, but keeping my ass safe was priority number one; and as long as I held all the cards, I held on to my life.

"You're disappointing me, Denise, but there's nothing wrong with trying, though. Get in the back seat, but I want your guns. All of them, before you get in."

There was no doubt that Denise had already made up her mind that all was cool between us, but the issue of me not trusting her yet was a bit of a sting. The look she had on her face due to my request, plus the eye-to-eye thing we had going on, was clearly establishing some comments that I didn't want to hear.

"Damn, little mama, you expecting company?" I said when she handed me three pistols.

"You never know when uninvited guests might crash the party," she said, as she jumped into the back seat of Baby's Bronco. One of Baby's men drove Denise's car to the apartment.

The moment one of Baby's men came out of the apartment informing us that it was all clear to come up, we all went in. I reached into my pocket and handed her the disk. She wasted no time getting to the computer to feed it. Baby stood in the kitchen with the fridge wide open, feasting on whatever he found, and watching Denise at the same time.

Though it didn't take a lot of time to look over the whole disk, the fact that it contained original copies of witness statements and key evidence that should have put Fran in prison for the death of Gloria Gray wasn't the killing part of what we both knew. It was the police records that never made it through the process that topped it all off. The moment I saw the tears roll down her face, I knew that her search for the information to redeem her mother's death was over. She sat in front of the computer as a hollow woman. There was no more toughness; no hard edges or stiffness to her character.

It was the sincere love for another soul that drew me to comfort her in her time of need.

"Denise, that's enough. Shut it down," I insisted as I lifted her up from her seat.

Her arms wrapped around my neck and she cried on my shoulder.

"She didn't have to do my mother like that, Stephon. She didn't have to!" she cried out.

Questioning her emotional state stood alone in my mind and having her in such a condition at such a crucial time in the game was unacceptable.

"Are you going to be able to hold yourself together through all of this? Because if you're not, I'm putting your ass on the bench, I can handle Fran and James on my own." I guaranteed her.

"I promise you that these are my last tears," she said as Baby handed her some tissue.

I had to place myself in her shoes for a moment by asking myself, if this were my mother could I be in control? The fact that Denise had gone to hell and back to find out the truth about her mother's killers, well… me asking her such a cold ass question like that was stupid of me.

"Thank you for the tissue, whatever your name is." Her voice was gaining some stability.

Baby never responded back to her, he just returned back to his feeding.

"So how do you want to handle this?" she asked.

"Have you talked to anybody today?" I asked her.

"I talked to Fran about two…maybe three hours ago and you were right; she thinks I stole her shit. She told me that James wanted my black ass in Austin before the sun goes down and if I wasn't there, he was coming to look for me."

This wasn't a time for hasty ass decisions, but a time to be a complete gentleman.

"I want them both inside of the restaurant at the Mandalay Hotel at five o' clock," I stated. "I don't want you to deliver the message. I want Tye to do it!"

I wanted Fran and James to know that the rules of the game also applied to them as well and having the perfect messenger meant first class.

"Does everybody know where you lay your head at night?" I asked her.

"Yeah!"

"Then you stay here tonight. Forget about ever going back to wherever you live, because after Tye delivers your message, you're marked for death. You've got a little time to hit the mall to get what you need, so take this," I said handing her all the money I had.

"And after you are done, stay off the streets!"

"I'm not concerned about Fran or James' ass, and I'm really in the mood to be fucked with," she said.

"I'm rolling with you on this because of what was done to your mother, but if you want to go bump heads with them, then go right ahead. If you miss this meeting behind some, 'I want to get crazy shit'

I'm taking all the spoils of this war for myself! So you're either going to get off this pity shit and join me, or I'll have your ass confined to this apartment until I have my say with them. And by the way, if you have any notions of screwing up my plans with some gun-ho shit, I'll kill your ass myself! "

Denise stared into my eyes as I made that comment. She knew I was dead serious.

Denise had returned from the mall shopping. I needed to give her a more true report of what we stood to gain, and what James and Fran stood to lose.

"For the record, James is worth far more than what you assumed and the fact that I know that, he'll kill me at the drop of a hat. So, we're taking sixty percent of his shit," I said. "Taking everything from him will leave him with nothing to live for, and I don't want to be sitting across the table from that person. Fran, on the other hand is another story. We leave her with nothing!"

"So what do I stand to walk away with?" she asked.

"How's forty-five million?"

"Forty-five, huh?" she uttered.

My sensitive side had taken me down on the mat for a three count and I was now won over by Denise. There was a big part of me that needed to see some redemption unfold and not just for Denise or her mother; but also for the mere fact that James, Fran, and all the police that were involved in this from the beginning had something coming. James was a fool to hold on to such evidence all this time.

"You ready for this?" I asked her.

"Since I was a little girl!" she said.

Baby and I gave Denise a few minutes to freshen up before leaving the apartment. By the time she got her firearms back in her hand, a black cloud covered her entire soul.

"Denise, look at me. If you kill her and spend the rest of your life in prison, what kind of redemption would that be for your mother?" I asked her as she placed her .45 in her shoulder holster.

She walked away and never responded. I couldn't take any chances on Denise going over to Fran's and putting a bullet in her or James, so Baby placed some insurance around Fran's place for the night.

"You think the chick gon' hold up knowing her mother's killer is in the same city?" Baby asked.

"I'm bettin' the house, that the girl is leaning more on seeing Fran suffer through whatever hardships she has planned for her, and once she gets what she wants, there'll be an accident of some sort, claiming Fran's life somewhere down the road."

"What's your take on the other men associated with your uncle?" Baby asked. "You and I already know what my father plans to do."

"I see two pictures, Baby. Catalina informed me that his associates paid him a visit not too long ago, and however that went or whatever was discussed, I can't determine whether or not they're in or out. Secondly, I never met with them, but one thing I do know, they understand the ramifications of a federal conspiracy charge. Whether they knew my uncle was moving the drugs through the Tower, charging twice the price for all that real estate or the shakedowns, they've benefited from it over the years. I know for a fact that they'll be on edge about all this shit.

"So, if you're asking me if they are going to get in the way of how you all deal with my uncle, that remains to be seen, Baby. I'm not heartless at all, but certain things have to happen, and if my part is weakening his infrastructure by taking his money, then so be it! I'm certain that if the bastard comes up dead, no one would get his assets because he's too selfish to have a will and he doesn't love anybody but himself."

"So you understand what's going to happen if he fails to step aside?" asked Baby.

"Clearly!"

As we drove back to the Sias' compound, I questioned how long Baby had been wanting to get the fact that if James caught a wild hair in his ass in any fashion, death was his only choice, into our conversation. I had to realize that all family ain't thick as blood! There wasn't a doubt in my mind that Mr. Sias had left it up to Baby to inform me that my uncle would have to die if it came to it. These people lived by a code like no other, and James was part of some foul disrespect; he had to die.

He waited until we were back into his family's camp before he spoke again.

"Stephon, never underestimate the power of unity that your uncle has built up for many years. You and the chick are about to wound him, and like any wild animal when faced with a decision, your uncle will not hesitate to fight for his livelihood that you are about to take from him."

Baby, nor anyone else for that matter, had to remind me about what type of man James was, and although I had to find out in the manner that I was, he was even more dangerous now than ever before.

"It's either him or me, Baby," I said as I got out of the Bronco.

Monica stood in the window watching me as I approached the house. We both wore emotional faces that were uncommon for the both of us. Deep down inside she knew that all was not well and that I had the world on my shoulders. As soon as I walked in the house, she took me by the hand and led me to the bedroom I had slept in.

"Our flights are scheduled to leave D.F.W. Airport to the Virgin Islands on Thursday morning at six. Your flight ticket will be waiting for you, too. Mrs. Sias has already sent a lady to the airport to pay for everything. I told my mother that I won the trip. I hated to lie to her, but I didn't have a choice."

"You can leave the explanation to me. I'll fix that when I get there."

Monica explained that Mrs. Sias spoke to someone at the bank about traveler's checks and the money being wired. They wouldn't have everything ready for her until nine-thirty or ten in the morning. I then explained to her that she and my boy would be escorted to Arkansas after they left the bank, because I needed them out of the way.

"Aren't you coming to the bank with us?" Her question was more of a plea.

"No."

"Stephon, come on, now," she pleaded and grabbed my hand in

hopes that I would change my mind.

"I have too much to take care of, Monica."

"Can I be nosey?" she asked.

I knew what she wanted to know. "Denise didn't take it too well, but she'll have her time to shine tomorrow, if that's what you wanted to know."

Monica asked James.

"Right about now he's hot as melted steel and headed this way as we speak. Fran knows now, too. Denise is staying at the apartment until this is over with."

"Are you serious?"

"I guess you think James is going to let her make it because I have his shit? The fact that I have it, makes him well aware that I'm going to give her the damn information Monica. She said she didn't tell anyone about my whereabouts, and we're about to find out about that. I assure you if James had the slightest notion that she was there, she'd be dead already. Those police reports are enough to prove that James is working overtime trying to protect an Austin police officer or several police officers. So do you think the man wants to play games right now Monica?"

"Okay, okay, Stephon."

"I want your ass out of the area as soon as you leave the bank. You do anything outside of steering your car towards your hometown and you'll be pullin' up at your mama's tryin' to explain why all those Mexicans are at her house. We straight?"

"Why are you on my ass, Stephon?"

I didn't answer but asked her again if we were straight. When I got the "yes" that I wanted to hear, I kissed her on the usual spot.

"Because I care about you. That's why I'm on your ass! Now, where is my boy?" I asked.

"He's in the next room asleep," she said.

"That's where I'm sleeping, so tell Mrs. Sias you'll need another room."

"Hold on! You taking my room?"

"Girl, you don't own shit in this house, and wherever my boy is at, it's an indication that that's where kings sleep," I said as I walked off.

"I hope you fall your mean ass out the bed," she shouted.

I stopped and turned to look back at her and smiled. "You just jealous that I'm sleepin' next to my boy and not next to you."

"Take two of these with you," she said as she threw me both fingers.

"That's another one of your problems too. You need to fix that before you blow a gasket."

"Why are you worried about it, you didn't want none," she said.

"Get some sleep, Monica."

She called me an asshole and I walked away smiling.

Being at the Sias' should have brought enough comfort to me so that sleep wouldn't be too hard to find; but with all that was going down, I had to welcome the notion of sleep in any fashion that it came in. My boy climbing up on my chest and him trying to open my eyelids with his little fingers awakened me.

"Mama, Mama," he repeated.

"What happened to Stephon, Chump?" I guess I got a little bit of sleep because Monica had brought my boy a fresh set of clothes in my room and laid them across the foot of the bed without disturbing my sleep.

By the time me and the young prince stepped out of the bathroom, my whole childhood flashed back into my memory. I was surely back in El Paso. As I grew closer to the kitchen, I was reminded of the authenticity of a people and a culture that encompassed my beginning stages of life. Even that morning, I paid homage to the very essence that made these people unique. The spices, tortillas made from scratch, peppers roasting in a cast iron skillet, the smell of underground smoked goat. I stood outside of the kitchen in complete silence as I listened to Mrs. Sias hum a Spanish tune. I inhaled one last time before making my presence known, to remind myself of why I reverenced their cooking.

"Good morning, Mrs. Sias, Mr. Sias."

"Good morning to the two of you. Aaah, one time shall I kiss the baby, yes?"

"Have your way, Mrs. Sias," I said and I leaned my boy toward her.

"Monica will come soon to feed the baby," Mrs. Sias informed me.

"Please, come and sit next to me at my table, Stephon," said Mr. Sias. "Today is a good beginning for you, son. When I was no more than seven or eight, my mother read me a story about a young African boy who was about to turn of age. His right to become a man was based on killing a beast that was known as the ruler of the jungle. Today, though, you will not face a lion like the young boy in the story. You will face a very dangerous man, son, and you must face him as a man.

"If he sees any sign of weakness within you, he will kill you! This death may not come at that very minute, but a beast will stalk or wait on his prey for as long as it takes, Stephon. You must secure all that you want today, so that your tomorrows will be strengthened with some stability for a potential war with this man or his people."

"I plan to do just that, Mr. Sias."

"Good! Now we eat and enjoy one of the reasons why I love this woman so much," Mr. Sias said as he kissed Mrs. Sias on her cheek.

Monica came in and said her usual "good mornings" and began to feed the youngster. The way she kept watching the clock made Mr. Sias and I look at her once or twice.

"Monica, are you nervous about traveling so far, or for the safety of your friend?" Mr. Sias inquired.

"I've always daydreamed about going to different places around the world, Mr. Sias, but I didn't figure it being like this and by myself. Stephon has helped me in ways you wouldn't believe, and for a man who is not my boyfriend or husband to care for my child and me out of the goodness of his heart, this is my time to fight side by side with him and I'm not allowed to. So, I'm nervous about a lot of things."

She looked over at me then back to Mr. Sias before continuing, "Today is a day that will change what we do and how we do things. Not only will they affect me and my son, but my mother, your family, Stephon, Catalina, his uncle and the people that work for you. Our lives are about to be shifted because of some bad people and I have to sit and wait to find out—thousands of miles away from here—about the outcome of today's actions. So yes, I am nervous about my friend too!"

Being the mother she was, Mrs. Sias went to Monica. "He will be fine, Monica. This I know because of his good heart," Mrs. Sias stated.

"Are we at a funeral or at breakfast?" I asked, wanting to break the somber mood.

"Everybody, eat, because time draws near," said Mr. Sias.

With so much heritage lingering in the air, surely a man the size of Baby wouldn't miss a meal of this caliber. After hearing Mrs. Sias say a short blessing over the food in Spanish, I looked up at Mr. Sias with one question on my mind and he already knew what that was.

"This Denise girl… you left her at your home, so Baby made sure your home stayed secure. Your uncle is here in the area already. In fact, he arrived to this Fran's home at ten thirty last night. He has met with six men for more than four hours last night, but we will not be able to run their plates until eight o'clock to find out who these people are," explained Mr. Sias.

"Baby has reserved seven tables for you at the Mandalay, and yours will be in the center of my people. So you need not worry about your going or returning back here."

"Has Denise been leaving the apartment?" I asked.

"Only once."

"Please, excuse me."

I walked away from the breakfast table because I had to call Catalina to get a check on the atmosphere inside the Tower. The phone rang five times before she picked up and from the tone of her voice, I couldn't tell if she was glad to hear from me or not.

"This had better be you, Stephon," she said when she answered the phone."

"I feel very important this morning knowing that my girl is awaiting my call."

"I call you at the Bay and at home, but no Stephon. Something is wrong, yes?"

"No baby, everything is okay, Catalina. I had to take care of something very important before you leave."

"This thing makes you not think about Catalina's heart." Sadness dripped from each of her words.

"I always think about your feelings, girl."

"You keep me up all night and I worry about you, Stephon."

"How is everything with you?" I asked her.

"I will feel much better tonight when you arrive."

"And why is that?" I enjoyed toying with her a little bit.

"Stephon, do not forget that my time to leave comes soon for me."

"Three weeks girl, that's a lot of time."

"Maybe easy for you to speak, but for Catalina, that is very short."

"Does anybody know that I'm coming tonight?" I had to pump her for reassurance.

"Only me!"

"Keep it that way."

"You come after work, yes?"

"As soon as I get off, Mommy. I must get some sleep for a little while. I didn't sleep all night, so call me later. I love you, girl."

"You show me tonight and I will forgive you just a little bit."

"Bye, girl!"

Monica walked in on me while I was hanging up the phone.

"Is she okay?" she asked.

"Sounds like it," I said.

"It's time for me to leave, Stephon, and I don't want to leave you here. Funny how life can take a twist, huh? I guess we just have to be ready when it's your turn. Don't miss your flight, Stephon. Please!"

"I know thirty days isn't a long time, Monica, but would you please teach my boy how to say my name right?"

"Boy, you know he's doing his best."

There were some things about me that stood apart from my rough edges and for the most part, kept reminding me that there was something sentimental about me and it showed me that no matter how hard I needed to be at times, I still had a heart. I couldn't bear to see Monica and my boy drive away from me, especially knowing that their leaving the country was because of me and the bullshit in my world.

Two hours had past and the phone rang at least twenty times, but still no word that Monica was on her way to Arkansas. I hadn't eaten my hometown food since I left El Paso, and the only thing I wanted to do was sleep on a full stomach. The phone rang again and from what I was feeling, I sat up and waited to see Mr. Sias appear at my door. Just as I was about to give up my feeling, he showed up.

"She's on her way, her money is already in the bank, and she has her traveler's checks." Mr. Sias eased my mind. I bobbed my head at him with silent communication and I laid back down for some sleep.

Baby had made it back to the house about an hour after I fell asleep and decided to grab him some sleep as well. A couple of hours later he woke me.

"Black man, time to rise, my brother. Monica made it home by the way," Baby said, as he chewed on a sandwich. "The old man said that a soldier who sleeps before battle is a very fierce fighter because he isn't worried about his opponent. Shower, shave and let's crash the fuckin' party, Holmes."

I got up and laid out my gear in a fashion higher than any level James had taught me. As I stood there looking at myself in the mirror, I kept seeing the little skinny kid who had arrived in Austin the day before and never had the chance to feel what it was like to actually be a kid. From the word, go, it was "use or be used". "Kill' em dead, black man," I whispered to myself before I dialed up my apartment to check with Denise. She answered after the second ring.

"Still livin', that's a good sign, little mama."

"Stephon, you sound like you just woke up or something."

"You not sleepin' these days, girl?"

"Too much Fran on the brain," she said.

"So what are you wearing, Stephon?"

"Navy blue pinstripes and the rest of the trimmings."

"You sound like you're going somewhere special," she stated.

"This being our first date, a brother really tryin' to make a good impression for you."

"You tryin' to win, Mr. Wilkerson?"

"Depends on what you talkin' about!"

"You still giving me a minute of your time after this shit is over with?"

"Still plan to, Denise."

"So tell me what you know," she stated.

"James fell through about ten last night and had some company."

"You know who they are?"

"Not yet, but they won't be enough, whoever they are," I said.

"By the way, if I'd wanted some company, I would have asked you to stay!" she said.

From the time Mr. Sias told me that Baby was actually babysitting Denise, I smiled at the fact that she knew they were there before they even took their positions.

"Couldn't just leave you alone. Hell, even big, tough girls like you need lookin' after too!"

"I need some 'me' time right now, so call me when you're ready. I'm trying to catch a live one tonight," she said.

Before I had time to jump out of the shower, Baby had come to tell me that the old man wanted to see me before we left. Getting fresh brought on a new meaning of pre-game warm up. By the time I placed a knot in my tie, Baby came calling for me.

"So how do I look, Holmes?" Baby sported a very nice tailored suit that was perfectly fitted for him.

"You look like a damn mobster, playa!"

"That's all I need to hear. I'm your limo driver for tonight, brother. I needed an excuse to be right outside the front doors of that joint."

"What's up with the dudes that my uncle met with last night?" I asked.

"Some of Carlos' toughest in this area; but no fools! My father runs a tight ship in his area and no amount of money is going to get those fools to cross or disrespect it."

"I just wanted to know."

"Time is growing short and the old man wants us in his office." I grabbed my jacket and pistol and fell in behind Baby as we stood in the door of the old man's office.

"I just wanted to ask you a favor before you left," Mr. Sias said.

"Name it!"

"Monica, out of respect…when she finishes law school, would you mind her looking out for my family's affairs? Please understand that things can get messy at times, but Baby will need someone to keep the motor running in this truck until he gets ready to pass the keys to his son or whoever it may be."

"You talk to Monica about this?" I asked.

"She told me and my wife last night that she was going to law school to look after your affairs and that I would have to ask you if she could."

"To be honest Mr. Sias, after she gets a taste of what she'll be faced with after this, she might just want to take a backseat and watch how you handle Mr. Gonzales. If all you want her for is for some cleanup— no. But, if it's protecting your assets—yes."

From what Mr. Sias was asking for, it didn't take a rocket scientist to know that Monica did some venting. I knew right then that she vowed to look after me and refused to make a move without me knowing it. It was the type of situation that James would have taken advantage of if given the chance. But not me. I had to assure Mr. Sias that the decision would be totally up to Monica and not me.

"Listen, I'll need to borrow a car tonight. I have to go see Catalina."

"Are you crazy, Holmes? At the Tower? Tonight? You lookin' to die tonight, Stephon?"

"If I don't, she'll know something is wrong."

"What's more important to you, some ass or your damned life, man? Call her and tell her that your uncle is down here having a special meeting and you won't leave until he leaves town. I'm telling you, Stephon, you go to his home field tonight after this meeting, and you'll die there! As soon as Carlos finds out or even a rumor that you are in the city limits, he'll contact your uncle and he'll order your death. Mark my words. It does not take a genius to figure that shit out."

"I guess you're right, man."

"Listen, after tonight, I'll go get her and bring her to you and take her back, but until you get your cash man, stay the hell out of Austin!"

After finding out that no one but Denise was in the apartment, I went up and was met with a .357 magnum pointed at my head.

"Is that how a man gets handled in his own house?"

"I thought you were going to call first?" Denise asked as she lowered her gun.

"I'm doing that right now!"

"Real funny, Stephon. You almost got your ass shot!"

"You wouldn't shoot me. Besides, in order to kill me you're going to have to put on more than your sexy ass panties and bra."

"Change of plans?" she asked as she slipped into her dress.

"Yeah, you're riding with Daddy tonight!"

"You got me feelin' special," she said with a crooked smile as she straightened out her dress.

"You violating me in that dress, woman. Damn, you're on tonight." I rubbed my hands together as my eyes took in the sights.

"I have to be a top-notch Diva when I grace the presence of trash. So it's a gift for you and your eyes, black man; and strictly business for anybody outside of you."

I grabbed her handbag, took her scarf and placed it around her shoulder, and led her to the living room.

"Give me a minute," I said as I went into my room to get some extra cash I kept stashed.

"By the way, your phone rung all night." Her comment was nonchalant as she leaned to one side, putting on her earrings.

"Wasn't important. Let's go do this," I said. I took her by the hand and led her down into the car.

We didn't utter a single word from the apartment up to the Mandalay. We checked our weapons, looked at each other and smiled our grimace.

"I'll lead...you follow; and be respectful. You want to kill'em, then kill'em with kindness while they fork over the booty. Are we straight?" I asked her.

She looked at me and smiled as she placed her pistol in her handbag,

"Always the lady, Stephon," she said.

I tapped on the window of the limousine, informing Baby that we were ready to go and he opened the door.

"You lookin' good, my brother from another mother," Baby stated as I straightened up my tie.

"You know, I knew there was something in common about us. Remind me to talk to the old man about that when we get back in."

Baby couldn't help but to laugh.

"Keep that on the low, brotha. Mama find out and there goes her good cookin'," he said.

We laughed the nervousness off the both of us.

"Denise, no disrespect, but I haven't seen a sista as beautiful and fine as you in all my twenty-one years of living," Baby flirted.

"Keep livin', big fella," she said as she shifted in her seat.

"Too late for that, black woman, you've already given me a heart attack," said Baby. He gently helped Denise out of the car.

"You and me, sweetheart," I smiled to Denise.

She placed her hand on my arm and we walked into the Mandalay.

"Good evening sir...madam," said the maître d'.

"Good evening to you, too, my good man."

"The Wilkerson's table please."

"Oh yes, I've been expecting you, sir. This way please."

As we approached our table, I looked toward the other six tables in view with a quick glance and thought to myself those people are too groomed to play hardball. Looking into the eyes of my very distinguishably dressed uncle and his long time murderous piece of game, I killed that notion.

Eye to eye, we played out the shit. Whatever he was trying to communicate wasn't computing with me. By the time Denise and I got to the table, the shit he was trying to sell me was second hand. There was a time in my life when his stone cold ass stares would bring a level of fear in me. But those days were long gone and over with.

"I was taught that a gentleman always stood when greeting a lady," I looked directly into James' face and said to him. "I gather that was just part of the façade too," I stated as I pulled out Denise's chair for her. I then turned to Fran.

"Fran. The last time I had the pleasure of seeing you look so exquisite was when I accidentally came in here for a bite to eat. You and your cronies were raising a toast to my fine ass. But, nevertheless, you are smashing tonight, if I may say so. I don't mean to be rude, but you all remember Ms. Denise Gray, don't you?" I asked them sarcastically lifting Fran's hand and kissing it. "So, which one of the two of you would like to go first?" I asked in a subtle tone. James jumped on the opportunity to speak first, which was no big surprise to me.

"I'm going to ask you one time and one time only, Stephon; where is my shit?" he asked with a high tone of anger as he placed his hand under the table.

His tone of voice reached out—way past the boundaries of the people who were placed around me to protect me. They all turned and looked my way; scanning James' every move like secret service would for the president. Without underestimating him, I knew his pistol was drawn.

My mind flashed back to the conversation that Mr. Sias and I had about the African boy. I knew it was time for me to join that boy in his quest to kill the beast alongside of him.

"Pardon me if I failed to mention that any and all rudeness at my table will not be accepted or tolerated from either one of you. And if you raise your voice at me in anger again in life, uncle or no uncle— nigga—I'll kill you!" I said as I clearly gave him an indication that my pistol was also pointed at him.

"Again, who wants to go first?" Neither of the two wanted to step up, so I did. "I guess there's no need to discuss or even mention how this young lady feels tonight. For the record, James, I now know who I am and clearly know who you are, too. I must admit, I was a bit surprised to know that you would screw me over too; but then again, what is there to expect from a heartless fool! You told me when I get tired of flunkin' to take charge of my life. Well, I'm tired of being a flunky today, James. Use or be used is what you taught me. Out of respect, you respect the game that you created the rules for! I hope that you didn't think that I was going to just sit back and allow the two of you to continue to wipe your funky ass feet on my back.

"To conclude all the talking, this is how you and I are going to handle this. So, if you can't respect it, pull your trigger and let's get this over with; but know this, I'm not going die by myself!" I took a few sips of water from my glass just to make them wait a little longer. "I've reviewed each disk."

Fran and James looked at each other and glanced over at Denise.

"The best is yet to come, ladies and gentlemen," Denise said and smiled at both of them. She then raised a glass of water at them in a personal toast. "I truly believe after looking and weighing all the factors out, we both understand that in the hands of the right people— you and your frat brothers, oh, and certain Austin police officers—can kiss your asses goodbye; or can start killing off each other for good reasons." She took a sip of the water with pure satisfaction.

"For insurance purposes, I'll hold on to the disks in case one of you, the frat brothers, or certain police officers decide you want to get a hard-on for a piece of my ass. Along with that, I'm really kind of disappointed in myself because I have a grain of compassion for your ass. So be gracious that I didn't take after you." I slid a piece of paper over to James and he snatched it from beneath my fingers. "I want twenty million transferred into that account at 8:01 tomorrow morning. Are we clear on this?" He just looked at me and smiled with contempt.

"You have exactly sixty seconds to comply or all talks are concluded with you my distinguished gentleman. Starting now!" I sat there glancing back at him and counting in my head.

"Fifteen seconds, James."

"Touché, Stephon!" He placed the account number in the inside pocket of his jacket. "Damn it, I just lost twenty dollars on you, James. I figured you would let your pride get in the way, but I don't feel bad about it because I'll let your piece of game pick up my tab," I said as I looked over at Fran.

"You fuck yourself," Fran whispered, then sipped on her glass of water.

"Speaking of which… since you so kindly brought it up, you ought to appreciate this last one I'm about to put on you. I want you to know that I'm not upset with you at all, and I thank you for the schooling. Every woman that I've had the pleasure of blessing should be lining up to kiss your ass for teaching me so much," I explained and at the same time I caressed her hand. "What really made me want to screw you instead of make love to you, is when I found out that you gave me the crumbs off such a large table, girl. You made twenty grand every time my piece was placed in use, and all you could toss this miserable peasant was fifteen hundred dollars.

"Again, I'm not mad at you, and I really do want to continue serving your clients up with the best. After today you'll need the work, but if you're not appreciative, I'll just contact your clients at their residence and inform them of your being so uncooperative with their Stephon. Surely, we wouldn't want that to happen now would we? So, if you don't mind, deposit fifteen million worth of great bangin' in that account by 8:05 tomorrow morning." I told her. Without missing a beat, I slid the account number to her. I had to stab a little more, so I added, "I thought you would need a little more time to get your composure together before you pulled your panties down for me this last time."

"Are you going to sit up here and let him handle me like this, James?" Fran asked.

"Shut the fuck up and do as he says, Fran."

She snatched the piece of paper off the table and placed it into her handbag. She looked at James out of the corner of her eye.

"You've always been a weak ass nigga," Fran mumbled.

Denise cleared her throat, "Could we not spoil the mood before the food arrives with all the whining you're doing, Fran? If you're going to keep that up, I'll just take my dinner elsewhere." Then Denise looked over at James with a stiff glance. "I want you to know and understand that technology is advancing every day," Denise stated as she locked her glance down on him.

"I asked Stephon to get me some hair samples, your toothbrush and your shaving razor for D.N.A purposes. I knew you would never consent to a paternity test so that I could find out if you're my father or not. Not like I give a damn right now, but when I do find out, and if you are, count on me paying your sorry ass one last visit, if you feel me! You let this bitch get away with killin' my mother and on top of that, you helped conceal the truth. For what? A nympho ass bitch!"

"Bitch, who do you think you talking to?" Fran directed her glance and her words towards Denise as she tried to get past James holding her down in her chair. Fran's commotion startled quite a few patrons and brought two of Mr. Sias' men, the ones closest to Fran, to their feet. I had to motion them to sit back down in their seats.

"Bitch, sit down and shut your mouth until you're spoken to!" Denise ordered her. "I'm far from being my mama, and tonight I won't have a problem with puttin' my foot in your ass."

Denise turned her attention back to James. "I guess the guilt was too much on you that you felt compelled to take care of me," Denise accused him. "Knowing that this bitch killed my mother, you still allowed her around me, but I can tell by how she's handling you now, that you couldn't help it." She looked back over at Fran and raised her glass of water and took another sip and stated, "Old hateful bitch, you're right about one thing, he is a weak ass nigga!"

She slid her piece of paper over to James as well. "Twenty-five million by 8:02 tomorrow morning. End of discussion! That is, until I find out if you're my father or not." James slowly pulled the piece of paper to him and placed it in his pocket without muttering a single word.

"Now, just for you, Ms. Francis. Since you're special, I saved just a little tee-taste of some good shit for you and I hope you appreciate it. I can remember when James used to drag your bad breath ass over to my grandmother's house when he came to see me. You wouldn't leave me without whispering, 'Little bitch, you ain't gone be shit, just like your mama' in my ear. I thought about having the D.A.'s office pick your stank ass up for the death of my mother, but the thought of you enjoying gettin' your cunt sucked on by jailhouse dykes for the rest of your pathetic ass life wouldn't be justice. So just to make me feel good, bitch, place the remaining twenty million dollars in your account...into my account."

Fran looked over at James with a look on her face that clearly indicated that her life was over and she needed him to rescue her from drowning.

Fran hesitated to respond to Denise's demands two seconds too long. "I really do wish you would give me the slightest indication that you don't like this, because I would rather have you arrested so that I can see you in prison for the rest of your life. On top of that, I'll sue for the whole thirty million, your home and everything else. So, please hesitate, bitch. Please!"

Fran picked up the piece of paper and placed it into her handbag.

"Oh, and before I forget, I have a message from my mother." Denise threw a glass of water in Fran's face as she stood up. "She said, 'Don't ever call my daughter a bitch again!'" Denise said before walking out of the restaurant heading for one of the limousines.

With all the emotional hell that Fran was going through, Denise's dashing a cold glass of water in her face slammed the door on everything she was feeling and brought her back to reality. Such a move brought our protection to their feet, and from the looks on their faces, they were ready for whatever.

"Well, I guess this dinner date is over with," I said to James as I got up to leave. "And for precautionary measures, keep your seats for about thirty minutes. I'll leave my friends here with you to make sure you two kids mind yourselves. You two have a blessed afternoon."

I got up and all the men Baby put in place remained standing while I walked out of the room.

Baby had the door open for me, where Denise was waiting, when I got back to the car. The other limousines pulled off behind us as soon as we pulled off. All five limousines were headed down two blocks of the deserted street. Baby slowed down to allow two of the limousines to pass. By the time all of us made it to Beltline Road, each car took its own route.

Chapter TWELVE

SUNSET

Baby had a whole new set of plans that I would have never thought about. If some gunplay would have gone down and I had to do James, a plane ticket was waiting to get me out of town. We were heading into the south end entrance of the D.F.W. Airport instead of taking Highway 183 back into Arlington. I've learned not to question Baby's decisions, so I sat back and chilled. We pulled up into the valet of the Hyatt Regency West Hotel. As soon as Baby opened the door of the limo he handed me a key.

"Suite 741. The old man is waiting to hear that tape," Baby said.

Denise and I were escorted upstairs, and once I opened up the door, our escorts turned and left.

"The fact that the both of you made it here without incident is good," said Mr. Sias. "Please, the both of you sit while I pour you a drink to celebrate your victories this day. I ask you to excuse my rudeness, Denise, for not introducing myself."

"No harm taken, sir," Denise replied.

"Stephon, the tape please. I only want to feel the conversation."

"I can tell you this, there wasn't much conversation on his part and he never questioned how far the disks have been passed on," I updated him at the same time that I gave him the recorder.

"Can I take this with me, Stephon?" Mr. Sias asked.

"Please do!" He stepped into the next room to listen to the tape. "You holdin' up all right?" I asked Denise. "I'll answer that question about eight thirty tomorrow morning."

Mr. Sias returned and handed me the recorder and shook both our hands. "You have no reason to question this young lady any further, Stephon. I strongly advise the both of you to become as a braided rope because you'll need each other from this point on," Mr. Sias advised.

He continued, "As long as the two of you possess this man's freedom in your hands, he will continue to search for a weak spot between you until he gets his freedom back. I want you two to stay here until your business is conducted tomorrow. If either of them refuses to comply with your requests by noon, then your lives are at risk. If staying in the same suite is or will be against your standards, Denise, I have another room reserved right across the hall."

"I have also placed my people on each side of this suite and on both sides of the suite across the hall. If you want to request food, you are listed as Mr. Jimenez, so put on a Cuban tongue. You'll have to leave here tomorrow with the same clothes, but if things go your way, you shouldn't care. Stephon, if you need me, you know how to find me, son, and congratulations to the both of you. You've done a great thing today," he said then walked out the door.

The very first thing I did was order food for the both of us. I hung up the phone. Denise never gave me a "yes or no" on the food I had ordered, so I took that as a good sign. I walked over to her and removed her shoes and placed an ottoman under her feet. I chose the room I planned on sleeping in and decided to take a view of the luxuries it had to offer. I wasted no time getting out of my clothes and into one of the hotel robes to relax. One look at the phone and I had to call Catalina.

"Ms. Malano, please."

"This is Ms. Malano."

"And how is Ms. Malano doing tonight?"

"Aaah, Poppi, I am very tired, and my feet…they hurt."

"Why don't you go rest then?"

"There has been a lot going on today. Stephon, I was told today that your car was parked on the eastside of the Tower the other morning, really early. This is true?" I told her that it was true and she wanted to know if my presence there was important since I didn't come to see her and I had kept my visit so quiet.

"Yes, it was, Catalina!"

"If you do not come to see Catalina and keep it very quiet, this thing that you do was very important, yes?"

"It was very important, baby!" I knew what was coming next.

"We talk tonight if you wish," she said.

"Catalina, James is here and it is not safe for me to come to the Tower tonight."

"Poppi, noooo!" she cried out.

"Catalina, I said it is very dangerous for me to come tonight."

"Then I will come to you, yes?"

"I have made arrangements for you to come here, but you have to give me time to see what James is doing. By noon tomorrow, I will let you know how you will get here, so pack some things."

"Poppi, can I stay a little while, maybe three days; please?"

"Will that make you happy?" I asked.

"You are cruel. My feet hurt…I need my man…and you want to play with my heart."

"It's 'emotions' Catalina," I said, correcting her English.

"Okay, 'emotions' then! Whatever the term is, Poppi,—you are play-ing with my feelings."

"Go pack and I'll call you around noon."

"I will be there, Poppi," she said.

I walked to the doorway of my room, leaned up against the door-frame and stared at Denise as she looked out the window.

"So what's on your mind?" I asked her.

"I've been on this quest for so long that I'm standing here trying to figure out what I'm going to do with myself once it's over. Nothing else has really ever mattered to me except justice for my mother. I don't see either of them allowing their pride to get the best of them; do you?" she asked as she continued to stare down on the constant flow of traffic from the airport.

"What other choice would you have, Denise?"

"I'm trying to convince myself that I have a reason to stay around, but when it all boils down to it, I have no parents; Grandma's gone; ain't had a man to call 'my man' since I was in the academy and he ended up being gay," she said with a smirk on her face. "Life is crazy," she stated turning to face me. "What about you?" she asked.

"Don't know yet. You want to hear some crazy shit? All my associates that I have are old nymphos, gangsters or people with some type of crisis," I admitted.

"So, where do I fit in all of that?" she asked.

"What! You're a damn gangster, hell," I said making both of us laugh.

"I'm a sister who only did what she had to do."

"Give me a break with the Betty Boo scenario."

"So I gather you're in the 'crisis' category?" she asked.

"So you would not agree with that at all. Right?" I asked with a grin on my face.

She started laughing at me. A knock came to the door and the first thing that she did was retrieve her gun and threw me mine. "See, that's the shit I'm talkin' about, right there, Ms. Gangster. I whispered. Hell, just take both of them," I said as I tossed her my pistol. "And you just start regulating like you do best, girl."

I picked up the phone and dialed up the room next door. "I have someone at my door," is all I said and hung up my phone. About ten seconds later, I heard my name.

"Stephon, you make an order for food?" the voice said from the other side of our door, and I opened it.

"Thank you, brother," I said to the Hispanic man. His voice alone had his entire crew out in the hallway frowned up and begging for something to go down. I went to each of them and shook their hands without saying a word to them. It was understood that my gratitude was high. I pushed the food cart in and closed the door.

"Girl, I'm glad you're here to protect me." Sarcasm dripped from my voice.

"Boy, please!" she said, as she brushed me off and sat the guns down.

"I'm serious, Boo! If you would have seen that look on your face and how you just glided to get your heat, and mine too, at that. That was some gangster shit if I ever saw any."

We both started laughing again.

"It's been a while since I've been able to do that," she said.

"What? Going after your pistol like you did?"

"No silly!" she laughed.

"Get off the bullshit. Don't stand there trying to convince me that it's been straight grind for you," I said as I sat her food down on the living room table and gave her a glass of wine.

"It's been straight business, Stephon."

"You women get a thorn in your ass or build up enough of a reason to shut down your personal life and it's a wrap." I couldn't help giving her my observation.

"I guess you talkin' up under my dress now, huh?" she asked.

"Hell, that comment means a lot of things. It just so happen that your little cookies fall in the category," I said.

"Typical!" she said. I walked over and took both pistols and moved them out of her reach.

"So what's that for?" she asked.

"I don't want this conversation to get too far off base. One thing I've learned, never mention or remotely hint that a woman's love spot is gathering dust on it because she'll shut down to do something else. Don't need you catchin' an attitude. Do we?"

"Negro, I know you're not implying that..."

"I'm not implying anything. You asked me and I told you why I moved the guns. Typical!" I said in a fly ass way.

"Hell, naw, put my pistol back over here because I see now you going to make me fire one off at your ass before 8:01 in the morning." We both started laughing.

I got quiet and started thinking about what Mr. Sias said about Denise and me uniting for our own safety. The fact that she was a bit more advanced in the game than I was, had me feeling as if my thinking that I was the one getting ready to be a babysitter was wrong in every way. In fact, she would be the one looking out for me!

"Atlanta," Denise whispered.

I turned to glance her way and saw a hollow look on her face as she continued to stare out on the airport's activities.

"What about Atlanta, Denise?"

"It's enough blackness in that city to hide us for a while. I'm starting a security firm—as high tech as I can get, and I'm not sparing anything. We'll both need it after tomorrow."

It didn't take me long to realize the importance of her venture because we didn't strip James of the most important thing—his power! To me, it was just like removing the rattles of a rattle snake; but not his fangs.

"My sister lives there. I want in on the business, fifty-fifty, and I'll stay out your way, but your protection will need to umbrella Monica and her son as well."

"Stephon, I already knew that."

Dinner ended with the last drops of wine, and for me, I was glad—my buzz was on. Without it, sleep wouldn't have come. I clearly remember having to help Denise to her bed and going back to place her gun on her nightstand.

The phone ringing near my head awakened me. I picked it up on the third ring and heard Baby's voice on the other end. "Big timer, wake up."

"What's up, Baby?"

"Got the call from the bank five minutes ago. My cousin said every dime is there and tell Denise hers is too!"

"Baby, you know I'm going to need you all day today, brother."

"Give me some time to make my rounds and I'll come through."

"Do you know if James is back at the Tower or not?"

"I've gotta make some calls," he said.

"Monica called last night about midnight. Mama told her you were doing fine and to be patient."

"Get you some more sleep brother and I'll get with you later on. I haven't forgotten about your cravin' for Catalina, Holmes."

"Stop playin' around, Baby. Too damn early!"

He started laughing at me and hung up.

Denise was lying in the bed across from me in her panties and bra. I could tell she meant to sleep in the hotel's robe too, but it probably got in the way of her having a good sleep. I sat up to watch her sleep, and at the same time, admire her body. Her breasts were perfect, she had a slim waistline, and for a woman that wasn't exercising her goody on the regular, she sure spent countless hours keeping it toned to perfection.

It was time to wake her fine ass up and what better way than a good arousal. I gently dragged my index finger across the top of her breast and started down the center of her stomach. I knew I wasn't going to make it to the rim of her panties, so I stopped and dipped the tip of my index finger in the hole of her navel.

"What are you doing?" she asked.

"You want the truth?" I said as I dropped lower and drug the tip of my index finger under the elastic of her panties. She laid there with her eyes closed and whispered, "Yes."

"I'm dusting," I teased.

She opened her eyes and reached for her gun. "Dust this then!" she said while in the process of trying to grab her pistol.

I reached over her, covering half her body with mine.

"Sensitive so early in the morning, aren't we?," I said, looking into her eyes.

"You started it," she said.

"Please tell, old fine ass woman, whose bed are you in?"

"I was too paranoid to sleep by myself."

"I got a rule about women sleepin' in my bed." In an instant, my robe came untied and the little separation that I did have between the terry cloth and Denise's panties had disappeared. I had seen this same ass scene played out on television and at the movies, where the horse playing led to some bomb ass sex and my piece was ready even before the shit played out.

"Why do I get the feelin' that you're going to tell me?" she teased back.

"I'll take that as an 'I'm dying to know' since you twisting my arm," I said. "No clothing allowed!" I continued.

"So why do you have some on?" she asked.

"Because this is my damn bed so it's my damn rules." She took her index finger to my chest and ordered me off her by pushing me gently.

"I'll make sure I read your manual the next time!" She never moved or covered herself up and I wasn't trippin' about it either.

"Your money is posted in your account," I told her. She sprung up so fast and without even the smallest bit of modesty. Her legs came so far apart that she exposed more than she wanted me to see.

"All of it, Stephon?" The excitement showed in her eyes.

"Every dime!"

She sat up in the bed and looked at me. "Yours?" she asked.

"Every dime!"

"I hope this doesn't sound crazy, Stephon, but I have to go to Austin for a few days."

"What's so important?"

"I want my mother and grandmother moved to Atlanta."

"Girl, you don't even have a clue where in Atlanta you're going to be."

"That doesn't mean that I can't go ahead and pay for it now though. When can we get away from here?" she asked.

"You're not being held captive. Just call next door, tell the man what you want to do and it's done."

She leaned towards me, kissed me on my cheek and got out of bed. "Thank you so much, Stephon."

"For what? Not knockin' the dust off that thang!" I said laughing.

She had her pistol in her hand and pointed it down toward my soldier.

"Keep playin' with me. Hear? For helping me get the information, asshole."

"Buy me a car if you're grateful woman."

"What kind, Stephon?"

"Whatever kind you want to see this sexy ass black man in," I said as I stood up in the bed with my hands on top of my head.

"Silly ass," she said smiling. "Let me know when you're ready for it. I got you," she said as she went back to her room. Denise was in the wind and it was already after twelve.

All I could do was sit and think that I'm heading towards twenty years old and I'm sitting on thirty-five million dollars without a clue as to what I'm going to do with my life.

I sure as hell wasn't going to rush and tell Mama, Honey, Marie or my Uncle Thomas because I had no way of explaining how I came up on the money. I had already informed Mr. Sias that I had no plans of informing Catalina about the money or the whole ordeal because I didn't want a leak to get back to San Antonio or become a target for some sort of kidnapping. Nevertheless, I was sitting on some change and the only worry I had was revenge. I had stayed up the night before the meeting trying to figure out where I was going to stash all of the disks and when I couldn't come up with a good enough spot, I just decided to send them with Monica.

Monica's call at midnight was a message telling me that the disks were in my safe deposit box already. Now that the money was in my account, I had no further need for Monica to have access to my safe deposit box. The cleaning ladies were in the room doing what they do, and I was in a rush to get to the bank to secure the disks and grab me some pocket change. I had already made up my mind about spending three days in the same hotel, but on a different floor and under a different name.

A knock came at the door and I allowed one of the cleaning ladies to answer it. I didn't give Baby the opportunity to take five steps into the room before turning him back out of the door.

"Let's leave this joint, playa. I've got some serious issues outside of your Catalina jokes."

"I thought we were family, Holmes?" Baby asked.

"We are, big boy," I said.

"I can't tell by the way you're handling a brother."

I didn't respond to his playful antics because we had outside guests taking the elevator down with us. As soon as we got off the elevator and walked toward the front doors of the hotel, I saw Catalina sitting in the back seat of the limousine we were in last night.

I stopped Baby in his tracks. "So you want to play, huh?"

He started laughing and placed me in a light headlock and walked me out to the car. I gathered that the girl in the front seat was Baby's girl.

"Hi, Stephon. I'm Carman, Baby's girlfriend."

"It's strange knowing somebody would put up with his ass, but it's nice meeting you Carman."

Catalina got out of the car with tears in her eyes.

"So are those happy tears?" I asked her.

"Very happy tears, Poppi!"

I kissed her in a way that told her that I missed her too, and we were off. After about five minutes of private foreplay in the backseat with Catalina, I had to set my course with Baby. I let the partition down to inform him that I wanted to go to the bank. Then it was back to Catalina.

"So when did you leave the Tower?"

"About seven thirty this morning, Carman knocked at my door and told me who she was. I was very shaky."

"You mean nervous!"

"Poppi, let me talk! So I went into my bedroom and called Mr. Sias to confirm. He told me that his son came to pick me up as a surprise for you. So, is not my man surprised?"

"I'm very surprised, Catalina! Who else knows?"

"Me and Carman leave the Tower in the taxi and Baby wait for us at the Holiday Inn, and then we come here in this car. Poppi, I have no clothes or my things, so we go to store, okay?"

"You bring me some money?" I asked.

She dug into her purse and pulled out three rolls of money wrapped in a style that I recognized. "Is that the money I told you to use in an emergency only?" I asked.

"It was seven thirty in the morning, Poppi, and I cannot go to the bank for money. So yes, it is the emergency money you speak about."

"So when you're up here with me, I don't take care of you?" I asked.

"Do not start, Poppi."

"I guess I'll just let you take care of me in my city and yours too," I said, trying to put on a sad face.

She let down the window and was about to throw the three rolls of money out and I caught her arm. "You, crazy woman!"

"If Catalina does not have the money, you have to take care of me, black man."

"And you were just going to throw the money out just like that, huh?"

"Just like that!" she said with a straight face.

"When you get back to the Tower, put the money back, okay!"

"Yes!" Despite all the attention that I was receiving from Catalina, my mind was steadfast on my business at the bank.

As we approached the bank, Catalina started her usual mirror primping, which was an indication that she had intentions on following me.

"Catalina, sit tight until I get done with my business. I won't be long." I could tell by the expression on her face that I had scared her. When I got out of the car, my intent level was running high and extending my gratitude to Baby and his father was at the top of my list.

I tapped on Baby's window, "Step outside the car for a second."

"What's up, Holmes?" "I want to give your father a million of this money."

"That wouldn't be wise of you, brother. If you ever want to disrespect or spit in my father's face, do it by saying anything bad about my mother or by stepping on his generosity. Since you brought that piece of information to him, he wakes up with you on his mind. You didn't have to do what you did, Stephon, and my father understands

284 • Johnny A. McDowell

that clearly. Mr. Gonzales has probably made over half a billion off the backs of his people. My father wants, and will get every dime of that money back for his people and he has plans to take his assets as well. So you keep your money and continue to hold my father's respect."

"What about you? Will you take the money instead?"

"I can't, Holmes. As bad as I need a new ride, my old man would flip. But what you can do... you can show my boys some love by doing something for their children."

"Anything in particular that I can do?" I asked.

"It's your money, black man." He wasn't going to guide me, but insisted that I make my own choices.

"I want you to establish a halfway point between the entire crew and find me a building so that I can get it turned into a learning center."

"No shit, Holmes?" Baby said with a huge smile on his face.

"I'll fill it up with the latest shit and after school or on the weekends, they can hang out there. I'll name it the Juan Sias Learning Center. Will your father trip behind that?"

"That will bring him to tears, Holmes. We'll keep that between us. I'll get on it and we'll surprise the old fart," Baby said as he gave me a bear hug.

"We'll have to set up accounts for depositing and withdrawing, with both our names on it so that we can transact business in my absence."

It took me about five minutes of red tape before I got into my safety deposit box, but everything was intact. Monica had also left me a quick reminder to not miss my flight. I smiled at the thought of her and my boy leaving out the next day.

Before leaving the bank, I spoke with my personal account representative about having my piece of change transferred to an Atlanta bank. She was surprised to hear that I was leaving the area and asked if Monica would be leaving as well. Though I threw her off with the nosey ass question, she let me know right then that she was a gossiper too.

Baby had remained outside of the car until I exited the bank. He stood his post as a body guard on duty.

"You expecting some trouble, big boy?"

"From the time you stepped out of the Mandalay, Holmes."

"Relax, Baby! James is no fool right now. Listen, I need a new room and you can tell your crew to check out. Put me under an English name on another floor for three days. I need to stop by the apartment, grab some things, change and I'm back out. I hope you don't plan to trip, but Catalina is not going to sit back and shop and your girl ain't buying nothing. We got to change that, so take this and let her do her thing," I said and gave him five grand.

"Since you insist, brother."

As soon as we made it up into the apartment, Baby was on the phone barking out orders, having my rooms switched around. Catalina was captivated by the contour of the apartment, and it was a job keeping her in my eyesight. Monica and Denise's presence were all over the other side of the place. Hell, not to mention my boy's shit too! So I knew the quicker I got what I needed and got out of there, the better chance I had of avoiding Catalina's questions. By the time Baby got off the phone about my room changes, I was locking my bedroom door and dragging Catalina behind me.

Four hours later, we were back at the Hyatt listening to Ron Isley and his "brothers" breakdown the codes to "In Between the Sheets." After a long awaited interlude, we showered and ordered food.

"Poppi, we talk right now, yes?"

"Do I have a choice about what I want to talk about and what I don't want to talk about?" I asked her.

"Always, Stephon!"

"Yeah, we can talk, then."

"You have not been at work nor do you care about your work. Why?"

"I no longer care to work there because I'm planning to move out of Texas when you return."

"Stephon, look at me. Do you tell me that you do not want us anymore?"

"Why would you say something like that?" I asked her.

"You say that you will leave when I return, but you say nothing about Catalina being with you. Why is this?" Concern for our future dictated her words.

"I don't want you to say one word to anyone, do you understand?"

"Yes, Poppi!" she said eagerly.

"I don't want you to take Carlos' place at the Tower when you return. I don't like living the way I do and I don't like the way you have to live. Look at all the shit you had to go through just to spend three days with me. Do you like living like this, Catalina?"

"No, because you are not with me, Stephon!"

"When you return, you do what you have to do to get someone else to take control of the Tower."

"So you wait on me to return before you leave, yes?"

"I'm not leaving without you, girl," I reassured her with a kiss. "Will I be able to go with you to see you off?"

"Oooh no, Stephon! If people see us, they get mad because I betray the Honduras man. When I walk back across the bridge that separates the borders, I must be a poor and struggling Honduras woman, and when I walk back to you, I will be a poor struggling Honduras woman in the presence of the police."

"Why haven't you told me about your parents?"

As soon as the question was asked, her eyes widened and her head swung low into her chest.

"They are still afraid of your uncle's presence and they are old-fashioned believers. They say that I need to be with a man of my own kind."

"They don't trust me, do they?" I asked.

"They wait for the opportunity to prove that they are right about what they say about you because of your uncle. Don't be mad at them, okay? Sometimes this is hard to do because they do not know my Stephon the way that I do."

"It doesn't matter, Catalina."

"Why did you come to the Tower and do not come to see me?"

"I don't want to talk about that!"

"I will not interfere with your business, Poppi."

"Mr. Gonzales: why do you meet with him alone and not with the others?" I asked her.

"Because he speaks for the others on some things."

"Are you comfortable with him?"

"Sometimes, no Stephon; because he tries to push me into what he wants me to do." Hearing this made me see how Hector Gonzales was trying to soften up Catalina slowly. Though she hadn't mentioned it, I had a feeling that he had crossed the line with her and forgot who was running the show.

One fact that set the stage for an overseer at the Tower was that Catalina wasn't rescued by James or by her people. So she owed them nothing! There was no doubt that James and Hector had to find a crack in Catalina's exterior and they knew that if they didn't find that she had a bad side that was willing to take the dirty money, they could stand to get shut down.

"Do you allow him to handle you?" My curiosity had gotten the best of me.

"Not one time, Stephon. Once he tried to give me extra money as a gift and I refused to touch it. I tell him never again to do that with me."

"Let's eat and stop with the talking because I want to love you over and over again," I sang in a botched attempt.

Catalina covered her ears and begged, "Ooooh noooo, Poppi, you are no Isley Brother. Never do that again, black man."

The three days had come full circle and brought on some ups and downs in my world. While Baby drove us back to Austin in the limo, the events of the past days played back in my head. I had just sent a mother and child half way across the world, and because of that, I was about to lose someone I love to a beast of a country. So me having a few hours with Catalina before we reached Austin was much needed.

She really wasn't trippin' about me not going upstairs when we got back to the Tower because I had made plans to see her again before she left for Honduras the following week. Baby and I really didn't do much talking because he knew I was on the Catalina fumes. As soon as we made it back to my apartment, I had to tell him about Mr. Gonzales.

"Before you go, tell your father that Gonzales tried to push up on Catalina by offering her extra money. She said she checked his ass about it, but didn't want to make a big issue out of it. He's met with her three times without the others. Whether that's standard or not, I want your father to know."

"It's done, Holmes. You going to be all right here on your own?" Baby asked.

"I'll be okay for a few days, and I'll sneak to Austin to get at Catalina again before she leaves."

"If you need me, black man, call me."

"I'll get with you in a couple of days," I said as I hauled all of my belongings upstairs.

One look around the living room told a story of the past week. It was also a sure sign that Monica wasn't around because the house was not kept up to either of our standards. So, I started straightening and cleaning, starting with my own room.

I came across two checks from the Bay that I hadn't cashed and I promised myself to do so because I'd worked for that money. I finally got around to calling Steve and giving him my deepest apologies for leaving him high and dry. Despite telling him that I wasn't coming back, the brother offered me a whole five dollar an hour raise just to keep me. It took me two days of off and on cleaning before I made it into Monica's room. As soon as I saw Denise's things still on the floor on the other side of the bed, I knew that she had just come back and jumped into her car and burnt off.

I thought I would start with gathering Denise's things and setting them in the living room. As big as the tote bag was, you would swear she was smuggling something. After being nosey, hell, I discovered all it was, was a huge purse. I guess having to live in her car on different assignments, she just carried everything she could in one place. Looking at all the zippers and compartments, I drug the bag into the living room and took another nosey break while Luther Vandross filled the room. After running into a few of her panties, I couldn't imagine all of her body fitting into such tiny spaces. I had to confess, if she would have had on either of the two pair that I found, I would have surely done some spring cleaning on her ass.

As soon as I unzipped a side panel on the bag, the first thing that caught my eyes was Beatrice Ferguson coming out the front doors of the Bay. I reached in and retrieved the entire stack of 8x10 photos. Not only was the girl a good P.I., but one hell of a photographer! The more I went through the photos and thought back at where she was held up as she took the pictures, the girl was totally invisible because according to the posted time on some of the photos, I was at the front desk.

Suddenly, I it seemed as if a rope of some sort wrapped around my neck, and whatever force that tightened it, had cut off my air supply and I fought with all my might to breathe. My mind was racing through so many memories and past encounters with Catalina that the closer I came to the ones that really mattered, the more the photos started to come alive right before me.

Catalina, who are you loyal to, my James or me?

You of course, Poppi! Stephon, I will never lie to you. One day you ask me something, I tell you the truth and it hurt you, but you will know that Catalina tell you the truth. You bastard, I will tell you again, I will never lie to you! Poppi, I do nothing wrong; trust me!

I felt a presence in the room with me, coaching me back to my normal state and telling me to breathe.

Breathe! Breathe, Stephon! It repeatedly ordered me. I finally had the strength to rip free from my own consciousness. I found myself on my knees and hands, staring down at a photograph of Fran, James and Catalina toasting over a joyous matter of some sort.

"This bitch!" I shouted.

I pulled myself up off the floor and began to pace like a lion in a cage.

"Think, think, think, Stephon," I said out loud. "What is she after? What do I have that she wants? Is it the money or the disks? This funky ass bitch! Okay, so you want to play, my Honduras Bombshell," I said as I grabbed my car keys and drove over to a local post office.

Before going in, I wrote a small and short message to send to Catalina, along with the photograph. "I told you not to fuck with me!" is all I wrote on the piece of paper. I went inside the post office, bought a large envelope, postage and sent it to her certified express mail. I went back to the apartment and started packing my suitcases. I was due back in Austin the same day the photo was to arrive at the Tower, so I had just enough time to figure out what I was going to do. I had to remind myself that I was sitting on thirty-five million dollars.

Once I finished packing the things I needed the most, I placed Denise's shit back like I found them; just in case she showed up to pick up the stuff. I drove over to the bank to obtain some traveler's checks and went back to the apartment. I got comfortable on the couch with both pistols posted up and begging to be fired because if Catalina knew where I was, so did James. As the day ended, her calls started to come in. I was hoping like hell she told James where I was—which wasn't at home—so that someone would overstep their bounds that night.

All night she called and I continued to wait. Her calls finally stopped around four in the morning. If I was lucky, somewhere around ten in the morning, I would receive the call from Catalina that I was patiently waiting for. The counter attendant told me that the package could make it to the Tower before ten or after two in the afternoon. I cleared my phone recorder and recorded a new message for her.

"Tell me, Catalina, what is the reward for your betrayal?"

It was eight o'clock when her first call came in and she heard my new message.

"Stephon, I don't know what you ask of me, but please talk to me." Thirty minutes later she called again! "Stephon, you begin to worry me. Please explain to me this 'talk' you leave for me."

It was a quarter to ten when she received the package.

"Stephon...Poppi...noooo! Please answer the phone, Stephon!"

I answered the phone and paused before speaking.

"I told you not to fuck with me, Catalina," I said in my normal tone of voice.

"Stephon, please listen to me, mi amor. This picture is a lie, Poppi.

Never do I sit with James or this woman. I do not know this woman, Stephon. Please Poppi, I tell you the truth," she said as she cried uncontrollably.

"Please tell me, Catalina, tell me one thing that I have done to you? After today, you mean nothing to me, Catalina Marie Malano, nothing!"

"Poppi, nooo, please do not do this. It is not true; I tell you the truth, Stephon."

"Who the hell do you think I am, Catalina? Look at the picture, damn it," I shouted at the top of my voice. "I told you not to fuck with me!"

"Stephon, I know, Poppi, but this picture is not the truth. Listen to me, mi amor; I swear this on our children."

"What! Bitch, go to hell," I said and snatched the phone cord from the wall.

I was brutally beaten down by Catalina. I put my bags in the car and just started driving. It was three thirty in the afternoon and I was going nowhere. My going to a hotel meant that Baby would eventually find me. The only person I knew I could trust and probably find some needed refuge at the same time was LaShonda.

I drove to the bank and when I walked in, I guess the shit was written all over my face because the moment she saw me, she closed her counter. She held up her hand to indicate five and tapped on her watch. I went back out to my car and just leaned up against it. I looked up and saw her car pulling up next to mine. She got out of her car and walked up to me.

"Stephon, baby, you don't look too good. What's wrong?"

"LaShonda, I have twenty thousand dollars in my pocket. If I could find some peace at my apartment, I wouldn't be here. If I knew I could find some peace at a hotel without being found, I wouldn't be here."

"Get in your car and follow me over to my place."

"I'm not looking for no shit, LaShonda!"

"Stephon, let's go!" I had no idea what part of Dallas we were in, but when we pulled up into the driveway of a modest home, both of the garage doors came up and we both went in as the doors came down in unison behind us.

"You don't have to worry about anyone coming by. Don't worry about the phone and if you don't want to talk—cool! But if you do, I'm easy to find in this house."

"Can I stay for a couple of days?"

"If it's going to get you back to being you…yes!"

"Can you cook?" I asked her.

"Boy, do you think I'm packing around an ass like this eating on some diet shit!" she stated to bring some humor to my situation.

I reached into my pocket and pulled out about two thousand dollars in one hundred dollar bills. "If you don't take it, I'm leaving."

"What do you want me to do with it?" she asked.

"I like red wine and champagne and anything you want to cook for me."

"Your room is down the hall to the left. You'll find everything you need in the bathroom. I don't have a robe that will fit you, but I won't trip seeing you stroll around in some of my oversized boxers."

"I'll have to see these things before I agree to that," I said as I walked toward my assigned quarters. I heard LaShonda pull out of the garage and speed away. After a quick shower, I wrapped my towel around me and went to my car to retrieve one of my suitcases. On my way back to my room, I quickly came to the conclusion that this was not LaShonda's house.

Though LaShonda's presence was everywhere, it was most likely her mother's house. I put on some shorts and a tank top and stretched out across the bed. It was seven that night when LaShonda woke me up.

"Whatever's on your mind carried over into your sleep because you were having a full-fledged conversation with yourself when I got back from the store."

"What did I say?"

"Let's put it this way, somebody lied to you!"

"Enough said," I stated.

"Where is your mother?" I asked her.

"She's on vacation with her boyfriend. She'll be back in a week, so don't trip."

"So what about your own place? Who's looking out for your stuff?"

"Stop with all the questions and wash up for dinner."

Dinner turned out to be a venting opportunity for LaShonda. She was really trying to get me settled on the cool. Hell, after two or three glasses of champagne, I wasn't doing too much talking anyway! We cleaned up our mess and caught in on a movie. Poor girl was doing all she could to get me to talk, but it was a lost cause.

"I can't take any more of this movie and I don't mean to be a bore, but I'm going to bed," I stated.

"Don't get lost," she said.

I heard the shower running after about ten minutes into my restless thinking. Minutes after the water went off, LaShonda knocked at my door.

"Come on in."

"I just wanted to tell you that I'm leaving for work in the morning and if you wanted to leave, I'll leave the extra garage door opener with you and you can drop it off to me," she mentioned behind the door.

"Why are you talking to me with the door closed?"

"Because I just got out of the shower!"

"You still stink," I said jokingly.

"How would you know?" Before she could say another word, I opened the door and pulled her near to me.

"I don't know, and I won't know until you let me smell you," I said to her as I drew closer to her lips.

"Start smellin' me then," she murmured as she rose up on her tip toes to meet my lips. As I found some compassion on the layers of her tongue, I slid her bathrobe off her naked body and led her to my assigned bed. Whether she wanted me to bang her spot up or not, I was giving her my "Fran Degree" and then some. Making love to her started with a seduction of glances from the both of us. I stared at her smooth, honey-tinted body as she found her spot in the bed. She, in return, watched my every move as I undressed and never made a sound until I reached for my wallet and pulled out a Trojan XL condom.

"You make it a habit of traveling with those?" she asked but kept her stare focused down at my piece. I never responded to her question as I slid the condom down on my cock. It was three thirty in the morning before we gave in to sleep. Whatever time she left the house for work, I refused to wake up for anything besides draining my piece.

It was four in the afternoon before I showered and pulled myself together. I was going to have dinner fixed before LaShonda got in because I was going back to the apartment afterwards. Catalina was leaving in the morning. LaShonda pulled in with more wine and champagne. I took that as, "I gotta have some more of that!"

"I did all that rushing to get back here to cook you dinner, and it's done already." She came into the kitchen tasting everything. "Lord and he can cook too!" she said with a smile on her face.

We sat down to eat without saying a word. She saw that the sheets on my bed had been changed, towels washed and placed back in the cabinet, and my suitcase missing. So she knew I was leaving.

"So, how was your day?" I asked her.

"It was horrible and it was all your fault!"

"How was it my fault?"

"Because my stuff stayed wet all day!"

"How is that my fault?" I said laughing.

"I couldn't help thinking about last night. I haven't had sex in nine months."

"Well, you damn sure filled your tank up last night," I said with a smile.

"Stop teasing me, boy."

"I'm leaving Texas, LaShonda, and I don't know when I'll be back; but I would like to buy you a gift if you don't mind." We sat quietly for several minutes. I could tell she wasn't happy about my announcement, but didn't want to add drama to my situation. She simply asked when I was leaving.

"I'll drop your gift off before I leave."

"You promise?"

"Yeah!"

I made it back to the apartment about nine and found Denise sitting in the living room watching a movie on TV.

"You know this can be called breaking and entering. Right?" She held up the spare key. "You've got people looking for you."

"How would you know that?"

"I watched them and after they felt that you weren't coming back, they stopped making rounds and I slipped in. After they knew I was in here, the big guy came up and asked me to have you call him when you got in. What's wrong, if you don't mind me asking?"

"You don't want to know!"

"I'm all ears, Stephon."

"I was snoopin' through your shit and ran across a picture of Catalina toasting with Fran and James."

She jumped up immediately. "Stephon, what did you do?" Hysteric was in her voice and on her face.

"What the hell do you mean what did I do?" I was confused, and I'm sure it was evident in my voice and on my face. We stood staring at each other, both full with different emotions.

"What did you do, Stephon?" she asked again, but this time more demanding.

"I cancelled her ass! That's what I did!"

"Damn it, Stephon. Listen to me. James had the picture manipulated to look like she was with them. The night I was in your apartment and she came down to be with you, I took the picture of you and her eating dinner. He had the picture fixed and told me to find your new residence and place it in your door, but I wasn't going to do it. So I just put the damn thing in the bag. I'm sorry, Stephon, but it's not her fault; it's mine!"

I rushed into Monica's room to call Catalina's apartment and got no answer. So I called the main desk and was told that she left the country earlier in the morning. I dialed Baby.

"Who's callin'?" he asked as he answered the phone.

"Where is she, Baby?"

"Damn, black man, she couldn't take it anymore and she left. She drove down here on her own and showed the old man the picture. The shit was disturbing to him too, but after she wouldn't calm down, the old man called our contact at the police department."

"She took the picture to the department and within an hour, she told the old man it was rigged up. Catalina was messed up about it too, black man. I felt real bad for her, and I couldn't imagine how you were taking this shit."

"I need to get to her, Baby."

"That's a for sure no-no, brother. A black man fallin' on those streets trying to get with one of their own, you'll die and so will she."

"Don't give me that shit, Baby. I need to get a message or something to her, man!"

"Calm down, brother."

"How in hell am I supposed to calm down when my whole damned world has been shifted? There's a damn shift in my world, Baby!"

"Stephon, we'll get to her, black man; I promise you this."

"What about Denise, can I send her?"

"She'll draw too much attention on Catalina. Brother, I'm telling you, if you want her back quickly and safely, let us handle this shit for you."

"Baby, I need her back over here, man. Whatever it takes! You feelin' me?"

"Stephon, let my father handle this shit. Trust me, man, he's feelin' your pain, brother."

Chapter THIRTEEN

ONE REASON

Two weeks had past. In fourteen days, I had sent Catalina two letters by two different people. One of the ladies was only in Honduras for three days and stated she handed the letter to Catalina personally. She also stated that Catalina read the letter and afterwards, ripped it up and threw it to the ground with anger. The second letter was also delivered and it was torn up without Catalina ever opening it. Word was sent back every week concerning Catalina having a date posted for a review hearing for the renewal on her work visa. What drags matters even deeper is that she'll still have to wait on the proper authorities to grant her renewal.

Baby had enough compassion for both me and Catalina that he would contact me to inform me if someone was going to Honduras. That was just to keep me from worrying him to death. Not only was Mr. Sias trying to push Catalina's process for me, but also for his opportunity to deal with Hector Gonzales as well. Denise was already in Atlanta trying to find a perfect building to call our headquarters or some property on which to build.

298 • Johnny A. McDowell

I asked her to find me a high-rise apartment and a home that could be modified and made difficult for an intruder to get to me if I were playing with kids in the yard. I had talked to Marie three times and had been wanting to tell her about my status, but it had to be done in a way that she wouldn't go running off at the mouth. Hell, she was worse than Honey at times. There had been enough going on in my life to remind me that I hadn't had the opportunity to live life or experience it as a normal teenager. Whether it was lost for me or not, being in Atlanta with my marble shooting buddy was my way out of a life that I never envisioned.

So if being in Atlanta meant being normal for me, even though I had no earthly clue what that meant, at least I was making my own paths!

I had no preconceived notions that Catalina would put all the shit that happened in the past and start living a normal life herself, but if she wanted to discard our friendship, she was going to do it on her own. I had no plans on luring her to me with my money, my future plans or my desire of making her my wife. So on the cool, I had begun starting a life for myself and under no condition was I going to allow her or anyone else to get in the way of it.

There was no doubt that I cared for Catalina and I can openly state that it was my compassion for another person that kept me trying to make things okay between us. I realized that the whole ordeal was not my fault, but for Catalina on the other hand, it was all about trust! The fact that I didn't trust her is what was eating her alive.

I finally had everything in the apartment shipped to Atlanta and placed in storage, contemplating Monica staying around me. In the meantime, I had found myself a nice, safe house out on Lake Dallas to live in until I got ready to leave Texas. The only things I had in the place were my bed, curtains, a television, phone, and my weapons. With my neighbors being a hundred yards away from me on both sides, if ever my security alarm went off, so would I!

It was time for me to catch my flight to check on Monica, and I was hoping that Denise had found Monica a place to settle down in before I left Irving, but that wasn't happening. Denise was thrilled about me doing what I was for Monica, and she saw the benefit of the both of us having her as our attorney. So she was really being picky about where she wanted Monica located within the city.

I got the address to the house that Monica had lived in and drove by to get a few pictures of the place. I had some schooling I had to put down when I got to the Virgin Islands. My flight was scheduled to depart at 4:30 Wednesday afternoon and since it was only Monday, I had ten thousand things to do. Mondays were my scheduled report days on Catalina's status and I was headed to see Baby.

As I pulled up into the Sias compound, Baby was out front washing his Bronco.

"Have I ever told you that you could pass for a rapper out of New York called, Big Pun?" I asked. "What you know about 'Pun', black man?"

"Don't let this smooth taste fool you, Baby!" I said as we hugged each other and laughed.

"I can't believe you're cuttin' out on me like this, brother," Baby said.

"I'll be more useful to you in the long run, Baby. With what Denise is setting up, you'll need the best of her when the time comes."

"I don't mean to be a pest concerning Monica handling my legal issues, but you got me, right?" Baby asked.

"I'll talk to her, Baby, and I'll stress the family issue too, so chill, playa!"

"I just see me callin' on some dick-head to rep me and once he or she finds out what's going on, then they will flip the script on me. At least there are no surprises with Monica since she knows the deal," Baby mentioned.

"I hate that the old man is out of town and I'm leaving, but I'll see him soon enough. Catalina still refuses to send word back. A close source gave her your message and Catalina went on to talk about something else. From what my mom is being told, Delia is supposed to be picking her up at the border when she gets cleared."

"You giving up on her or what, Stephon?"

"I gave her my word that I would be there before all this shit went down and though I'm making the moves I'm making, I do intend to be there, whether she needs me or not."

"One thing you can count on, when I find out she's been granted her pass back, you'll know within minutes," Baby said. "I've got some rounds I need to make."

"So what's up on the center?"

"My boys are working around the clock on it and it should be functional in about another three weeks or so. I got a call from the computer supplier. She wanted to see the sight to determine the space for each station. So, I'll be having my girl taking her around," Baby said.

"Just don't let the woman sell you some shit you don't need," I stated.

"I got this, playa! So go vacation and when you get my call, have your ass ready to roll out with the 'Baby Squad.'"

"The Baby Squad!"

"Yeah, Big Pun has the Terror Squad in N.Y. and I got the Baby Squad in Texas."

I grabbed the water hose and started wettin' his ass up for that bullshit. "Man, shut your corny ass up!"

"Okay, trick, you gettin' the best right now. Yeah, go ahead and run, coward," he said dripping wet from head to toe. I got in my car and drove off.

My next stop was to visit with LaShonda and Cathy at the bank. It had been two weeks since I last saw LaShonda and I knew she was probably steamed about not hearing from me after getting her world rocked like that. I took my time strolling through the entrance and stalled so that she could get a good buildup of steam. I saw that she had about six people waiting in her line, so I went to talk to Cathy.

"Hey sexy," I stated.

"Hey, Daddy, you come to take us to lunch."

"I'll do better than that if you and my girl can take off for the rest of the day."

"Stephon that will take a miracle."

"I'll give you that Jaguar sitting out front if you can make that happen and to show you I'm not bullshittin'. Here's the title to it; already signed. All you have to do is sign your name at the marked spots and it's yours."

"That Jaguar right there?" she said as she pointed at my car. She grabbed the title and went upstairs. She stayed gone for about ten minutes. The whole time I stood down at Cathy's counter, LaShonda was trying to watch me and serve her customers at the same time.

I just continued to wave at her, which was pissing her off because she wanted me in her line and I wouldn't come. Cathy reappeared with two purses on her arm and a white lady in-tow. As soon as Cathy made it to LaShonda, she grabbed her by the hand, shoved her purse in her direction and headed my way.

"Miracles do happen; now let's get the hell out of here!" Cathy said. She was breathing fast and was trying to catch her wind.

"Where are we going?" asked LaShonda.

"Bitch, stop with the questions because you're off the clock and we're rollin' out with Stephon," Cathy said as we walked out the door.

I held the keys to the Jag out in front of Cathy and she danced around as if her name was called on the Price Is Right game show.

"Oooh thank you, thank you, thank you," she said as she continued to kiss on my cheek. "LaShonda, he gave me his car!"

"What!"

"Don't hate, redbone, just get your fine ass in the car and let's go do lunch at my place."

"Cathy are you cool enough to drive or do you want me to?" I teased.

"I got it, Daddy! Ooooh, thank you, Jesus," she said and hopped in the front seat.

"You just gave her this car?" LaShonda asked in disbelief.

"My way of saying, 'thank you' for what you did for me concerning my money that day," I told Cathy.

LaShonda turned back around to face the front of the car. "You're leaving aren't you?" asked LaShonda.

"I told you I would come to see you before I left." I couldn't look into LaShonda's face, but I could hear it in her voice. She was about to cry.

"Oooh noo, you ain't about to start that shit right now, bitch!" Cathy said as she looked over toward LaShonda.

I had been aching to ask Cathy why she was constantly referring to LaShonda as a "bitch", but I declined to when I kept hearing LaShonda refer to her as "hoe".

"What are you crying for, Red?" I asked.

"Because I don't want you to go, Stephon."

"I know the both of you don't keep secrets, so I'm just going to say what I want to say! If I stay around here, your shit gonna stay wet and it ain't enough panty shields in the world to handle that."

LaShonda turned around in her seat and started swinging at me while Cathy laughed out of control.

"Tell it. Tell it, Stephon!" Cathy continued to shout.

"Don't be telling my business, boy," she warned. She sat back in her seat with a smile on her face.

"Bitch, you told me you were sprung on Stephon the next day," Cathy said.

"Oh, so you tellin' my shit too, huh?" LaShonda said.

"Cathy, did she tell you that she came so hard, she didn't know if she was peeing or cumming?" I couldn't help but rag on her.

LaShonda was out of her seatbelt and shoes all in one motion and in the back seat with me, swinging. After some tear dropping laughter, I ended her stares at me with a long kiss.

"Now get your red ass up off me before I have you callin' out my name in the back of this woman's car."

"Shut up!" she said as she kissed me on my lips before crawling back up front.

We pulled up to the restaurant and I told the girls to stay in the car. I ran in, grabbed my take-out order and set up an open account for LaShonda so that she could dine at the place on special occasions.

"Cathy, please let me drive for a few." She looked apprehensive but let me behind the wheel. I drove to the house and parked out front. "I want you to sit tight, LaShonda, and Cathy...please help me inside with the food," I continued while handing LaShonda a large envelope out of the glove box. "I don't want you cryin' all over my clothes," I said as I closed the car door.

The envelope contained the deed to the house and the spare keys. I didn't pull into the garage because I didn't want to show her the new Cadillac that I bought for her as well. It took me fifteen minutes to show Cathy around the house and the breath-taking view of the lake from the patio deck.

"I know that bitch ain't still out in the car," Cathy said.

"She's out there cryin' with her sensitive ass. I just gave her this house and a Cadillac in the garage." Cathy took off running toward LaShonda. I looked out the living room window and they both stood out in the front of the house crying. I went to the front door and talked my shit.

"If you gon' be doing all that damn cryin', stay your ass out there," I shouted from the front door.

"To hell with you!" came from both of them at the same time."

"You two been around each other too damn long," I said as I went and grabbed LaShonda by the hand and pulled her into the house. "I asked you if I could buy you a gift before I left and you told me, 'yes'. So this is what I picked out and your car."

"Thank you," she said as she cleaned up her face.

"Now, can we please eat," I said. I had stocked the refrigerator with both of my favorite drinks. We ate, drank and enjoyed each other's company.

It was time for Cathy to move around. LaShonda had made arrangements to drive Cathy's car back to her house and Cathy would bring LaShonda back to the bank to pick up her car. LaShonda had already talked about coming back to put me between her legs one last time, but not explaining why I did it the first time, she took me saying "no" to her offer respectfully. She made plans to take off Wednesday to take me to the airport so that she could kick it with me the whole morning.

I spent all day Tuesday on the phone talking to my mother, Honey, Marie, Denise and drinking champagne straight out of the bottle. LaShonda stopped by to bring me dinner and to switch cars. Her mother was back in town and she couldn't wait to talk about her new fortune. We talked, had lunch at my place and she took me to the airport. Our departure wasn't really a goodbye thing because it was agreed upon that I could always have a room in her house whenever I came to visit Texas.

Though I hadn't been in the airport but a couple of hours, I already knew that Monica had called to see if I had caught my flight out. My flight was that of a King's cart. First class was the shit and for a brother who had never flown before, that form of transportation was really on point! I smiled at the thought of meeting Granny from the Beverly Hillbillies. I thought about how I was going to explain my financial ability to do what I was about to do from the time I got off the ground. With Monica telling her she won the trip, hell, we all can't be winning all this damn money. I needed another story.

Informing her mother of her relocation from "down in dem der hills" to a high rise condo was going to take some snappy talking! Denise told me that she found what I was looking for in a home and in an apartment for Monica too, but the owner had two apartments in the building he was selling as a package deal, but not separate. I immediately thought about Marie and asked Denise to put the guy on hold until Monica and I touched down in Atlanta. The stewardess brought me three shots of brandy, and I found a pillow behind my head, my seat reclined, and the shades drawn on my window while I found a cloud to sleep on.

The stewardess had to call my name several times to inform me that we were landing in about forty minutes. She apologized for waking me, but I had to place my seatbelt on. Monica was on top of her shit when it came to my arrival. As soon as I walked into the terminal, I was being flagged by a native gentleman holding up a board with "Mr. Wilkerson" written on it. As I got into the back of the limousine there was a bottle of champagne on ice and a card,

Stephon,

I don't see you coming straight to the hotel. I told the driver that you would probably want to stop and shop before coming here. But if you're coming straight to the hotel, we're out back on the beach. Your boy is about to worry me to death about playing in this sand and want-ing to go into the water. Ooooh, come and get him, please!!!

~Country (smile)

Passing up all the men's clothing stores took a lot of restraint on my part, but I was too eager to see Monica and the young prince so I headed straight to the hotel. As soon as I arrived at the hotel, I grabbed the card and champagne before getting out of the car. The concierge handed me my room key and ordered the bellhop to take my bags to my room. I requested two containers of mixed, fresh fruit delivered to my room. By the time I had changed into my gear, the fruit was delivered. I took the fruit, three champagne glasses and the champagne out to meet Monica. I was directed to their location and heard my boy crying and an elderly lady holding him. He saw me coming and knew who I was off the jump.

The lady didn't know who the hell I was, but the little man fell down in the sand about five times scrambling to get to me. All I heard was, "Boy, you bring your butt back here," from her.

And, "Stephon," coming from him. Monica reached out and grabbed the lady by her hand and stopped her from pursuing my boy. I bent down and scooped him up over the champagne and glasses that I car-ried and stopped him from crying.

"They got my boy out here cryin' like this. Who did it to you?" I asked him as we stood there watching Monica and her mother.

"Mama, Mama!" he said pointing. As we got closer, he stopped cry-ing. Monica took the items from my hands and set them down onto a small beach table. She stood on the tips of her toes and gently kissed my cheek.

"Stephon, this is my mother, Ms. Annie Cobbs, and Mama, this is Stephon."

"Stephon, it's my pleasure to finally meet you, and I want to thank you for being so kind to my baby."

"Ms. Cobbs…"

"Please call me Annie."

"Annie, there is no need to thank me; and what I do for Monica,

I do it from my heart. Now if anybody owes me anything, it's your daughter and what she would owe me would be an apology," I said in a serious tone.

"For what?" she curiously asked.

"Because you got my boy out here cryin'. You know what he wants. Who did it, little man?" I asked him again as I wiped his face.

"Mama," he replied still pointing to Monica.

"Don't sweat it, baby boy, Stephon got you." I saw a man pulling his motorboat into the shallow waters. I whistled to get his attention. "You have a lifejacket his size?" He held up the smallest he had. "Come on, Little Daddy, I'll take you where you want to go."

My boy and I rode around the edges of the shore for two hours. By the time we got back, the fruit and champagne was gone, and Monica and her mother were doing the female bonding thing. It was evident that my boy had been riding on their last nerves, and my having him gave them a break. We docked for fuel at a mini-market on the water's edge and my boy spotted some shit he wanted and I did the fool for him. Monica didn't give me a chance to sit down before she started in on me.

"I'm tellin' you right now, Stephon, I'm not packing all that stuff."

"You don't have to; I'm leaving his butt here. He found a girlfriend that was about nine and he cried his ass off because he didn't want to leave her." We all started laughing.

My wanting to go in for a nap before dinner brought everybody in. Annie told Monica that she would take care of my boy while we rested. Her subliminal message was coming in loud and clear. I could read her mind saying, girl, don't let this man get away. Give him some!

"I'll take my boy and give you two a break. Bring me his things," I told Monica.

"You sure about that, Stephon?" Annie asked and shifted her glance toward Monica. I smiled and tried handing him to Monica and he wasn't having it!

"That lets you know he's coming with me." Whether or not Monica told her mother that I was running on fumes or not, any type of excuse wasn't good enough for Annie because she had one thing on her mind: Seeing Monica and me get together.

Monica followed me down to my suite so that I could give her my key so that she could bring my boy back something to put on after his bath. By the time she made it back, my boy was bouncing arund in the bed with a towel around his neck like Super Man and butt ass naked.

"That's how playas act under some A.C. after a bath," I told Monica.

"I've never seen you do it," said Monica.

"I'm not a playa," I said as I looked at her sideways.

"So how is my baby one?" Monica asked.

"Women can't keep their hands off the boy. From nine years old to gray headed on a cane," I said.

"He's not a playa, he's just cute!"

"We'll see if you sing that same tune when he turns eighteen. So what did you tell Annie?"

"I told her that you inherited your money. She can't believe you haven't tried to mount me."

"I can tell that. She practically begged me to bring you up here and do you."

"You heard that too, huh?" We both smiled. It was good to see Monica.

"Everything went okay?"

"Very smooth," I said.

"Catalina?" she asked, looking away from me.

"That's a story that I'd rather not talk about right now. Listen, I know I told you that you could choose your own college, Monica, but I want you in Atlanta. That's where I'll be going when I leave here.

"The apartment is still good in Irving if you want to go back to it, but I'll have a high rise condo by the time we make it to Atlanta, if you're going. I've joined up with Denise for better reasons and she's turned out to be a real sister like you! She's in Atlanta waiting on you to come and look over the place before I buy it."

"Where are you going to be?"

"I haven't found a home yet and this isn't about me. Are you coming with me to Atlanta or going back to Irving?"

"Atlanta!" she said.

"It's still law school. You'll have a salary, no bills and I got your mother. You pass the bar, I'll give you a million dollars to start your firm and you look out for me and Denise. As far as the Sias', I'm leaving it up to you."

"Mama is going to want to go back to Arkansas to shut down her house."

"Tell her to give it to someone who needs a home for free!"

"So when are we leaving?"

"As soon as you book the flights," I replied.

"Are we going to be able to see each other? Atlanta is huge, Stephon."

"We've got the best guide in the city- my sister! She's in college too and she'll be living in the same building with you, so don't trip. To answer your question, 'yes we will'. As far as I'm concerned, I'll always be around. You think my boy is going to let you handle him all the time?" I pulled up his underwear. "Tell Mama who's the man."

"Stephon!" He giggled.

"You hear that, girl? I'll be headed back to Texas whenever Baby calls. Catalina is back in her country and waiting on her paperwork to be issued. Something went down and a misunderstanding brought some drama between us. If we both can pull through the shit, I'm going to marry her. If I get the slightest indication that we can't, I'm walking away."

"It's that bad?" she asked.

"Yeah, but enough of that; what's up with you, girl?"

"I'm still trippin' on how my life has flipped. I've wanted to talk to you about something for some time now, but it seems like every time I get ready to, you're either off and running, or I'll be the one who backs down because the timing isn't right-"

"I want you to have something I brought you as a keepsake. It's in my bag. Get it!" I interrupted her. As she scrambled to get the package out of my suitcase, the first thing she noticed was the wrapping on the package.

"You've been to Dillard's?" she asked.

"Before opening it, tell me how you know it's from Dillard's?"

"How do I forget something like that? That was my job at one time, Stephon."

"So what is your job now?"

"To go to school!" I patted a spot on the bed and gave her the indication that I wanted her to sit down next to me on the bed. I had my boy cradled in my arms and she saw that he was almost asleep.

"Have I been good to him?" I asked her as I looked down at her sleeping son.

"Yes! You're more of a father to him than his father will ever be."

"My mother faced some very, very hard times and like my boy here, my father was never around to hold me in his arms like this. Have I not been good to you?"

She looked at me with tears in her eyes, leaned over towards me and kissed my cheek as tears ran down her face.

"I don't mean to make you cry, girl."

"I'm crying because I'm so happy, Stephon."

"Before you open that, I want you to know that this gift that I'm giving you isn't in that package, but a reassurance to you that no matter how our lives end up, I'll always be here for you, Monica. But there is one thing I also want you to do for me, and that is never forget about your past. To constantly remember it will help you strive even harder to be a strong person."

"I want to see this gift in your office every time I walk in there and I want you to be proud of who you are, Monica." I leaned over to return the kiss she gave me.

"I love you, Monica." She opened the package and started to cry as she laid her head on my shoulder. I had her son in one arm and Monica in the other.

"Thank you so much, Stephon, and I love you too!" she said. She looked at an 8x10 size photograph of the crack house that she and her son lived in for more than a year. The memories flowed with her tears, as did the thoughts of perseverance.

"How?" was all that came out of her opened mouth. Monica was shocked. She stared at the photo, then at me, and then back at the photo. Her head was shaking side to side in disbelief.

"Denise. When she started looking for me on James' order, she found out about you and followed you back to the house. It was because of you, my boy and what I was doing for the both of you that made her lie about not being able to find me after we moved in. So, she's a good girl, Monica."

"Yeah, she is!"

"Hey look, my boy is asleep." He was sleeping peacefully and snoring softly. I couldn't help the grin on my face caused by just looking at him.

"He loves you too, Stephon."

"What? You tellin' me something I don't know? Girl, I'm the man!" She kissed me on my cheek again and crawled off the bed.

"Where are you going?" I asked.

"I'm going to my own room because I'm tryin' to avoid hearing that bullshit about you being the man! The real man got you strained up right now," she said as she pointed at her son and walked out laughing with her picture in hand. I sat back in my bed looking at my boy and wondering if I'd ever have a son of my own.

We couldn't catch a scheduled flight out for two days, but that gave me time to sit down and have a heart-to-heart talk with Annie. I guess certain things ran in the family because Annie cried a lot too!

We landed in Atlanta during the nighttime hours and the Cobbs women were glued to their windows as we descended down on their new environment. Denise was there to pick us up by limousine and we all found refuge at the Hyatt. Sleep took us south and all of us, including my boy, slept until about five the following afternoon. We cancelled our appointment for that day and made arrangements to see the apartments the next morning. I decided to wait until Monica chose the apartment she wanted before meeting up with Marie. Once we got together, there was no way to separate us. Morning came again and we all ate breakfast downstairs in the restaurant. I sat back and thought to myself as Monica, Denise and Annie carried on about life in Atlanta. My boy and I looked at each other a few times because we both knew we were outside of the conversation circle.

Walking into the Barlington Tower quickly reminded me of Austin, but with a flash for flavor. I was learning why Marie was saying how country Texas was. Once we made it upstairs to see the first apartment, Monica didn't want to go any further. She pulled me to the side and stated, "I don't need to see the other one." It was a very beautiful setting and bigger than any living space I'd ever seen.

Four bedrooms with full baths, two living areas, a dining area, a bar that sat six, and though the kitchen was compact, the views from two of the bedrooms and the living rooms were breathtaking. After walking into the second apartment, which only fell below the standards of the first apartment by a bedroom, I knew I was going to have to surgically remove Marie's tongue to keep her from talking. I pulled Monica and the owner of the apartments into one of the rooms and told the guy that I was sold on them. Because of the location and all the amenities the place had to offer, Monica wouldn't have to leave the area. All the colleges in Atlanta were minutes from the downtown area.

The bank was serene and elegant in its appearance. We entered the loan officer's office to finalize all of the paperwork. I allowed her to sign on her own dotted line and I signed mine on the other. She looked at me before signing her paperwork as if to say, Are you sure about this?

"Monica—graduation gift!" I said.

Her hands were shaking so bad that I had to hold her hand so she could sign the paperwork. I followed Marie's directions to her apartment after the owner and I left our meeting at the bank. I was introduced to half of her apartment complex before we made it into her apartment. I wasted no time in sitting her down to tell her about everything that had happened and what it all turned out to be.

Her only response was, "To hell with his low-down ass!" She agreed that if Mama, Honey or Uncle Thomas found out, they would kill him.

"So that's the real reason you're here?" she asked.

"No! My real reason for being here is because I wanted to be here with you. We have to move slowly about how we're living because Mama won't ever understand thirty-two million dollars being in my possession."

"I'm changing my major," she said.

"To what?"

"Do you think I'm going to sit back and let this Monica girl look out for my brother by herself? Plus, that will be my way of accounting for a nine hundred and fifty thousand dollar condo."

She stared at me for a few and shook her head in disbelief. "Damn, I can't believe this shit!" she said. "Where are you going to live?" Marie asked.

"Hell, with you! I'm not too concerned with living quarters right now or not until this Catalina shit is over."

"Well I'm telling you right now, you can start by looking for a dummy apartment so that Mama and Honey can come too. At least until graduation."

"Can I help you furnish the place with some shit I like?" I asked her.

"Hell, it's your money, boy!"

"Girl, do you think for once that I'm going to sit on all this money and not break my sister off?" I said as I popped her up against the head. Graduate and pass the bar and I'll deposit a million into your account."

She popped me back upside my head and said, "Get ready to pay up, chump!" After introducing everyone to Marie, I chilled out at Denise's apartment, which was also located on the north end of downtown.

Two days had gone by when I got the call from Baby.

"Stephon, she got approved, Holmes, but it's going to be at least two days before she gets the paperwork in her hand."

"I'm on the next flight available, so pick me up. Is the old man in town?"

"Yeah, and waiting to see you."

"Pick me up," I repeated before I hung up.

Not knowing where to find the girls, the best that I could do was to leave a note. I caught a cab to the airport and waited about thirty minutes before the next flight was accepting boarding passes. Within three hours, I was walking through the doors of the Sias' camp.

"Good timing, son. The both of you will need to hustle if you want to be there when she comes across."

"Question: Are you putting Hector Gonzales on hold?" I asked.

"Our agreement was until Catalina is safely across, Stephon."

"Then you are preparing to relocate Delia and Catalina's parents at this time?"

"Stephon, it will not be too wise to start moving or stirring up any smoke signals. I promise you that the very minute I land on Hector's front yard, the Malano's will be relocated at the same hour. One thing: Delia should be a day ahead of you. She is being taken to pick up Catalina as well. I cannot inform her or Delia of anything until Baby and his men know she is safely across. Baby will call me to tell me that Catalina is safe and then I will proceed with my business."

"Mr. Sias, I told you and your partners the first time that I met you that if either of you placed her in any danger I would step in. This is what is about to happen. If it's my call when I see her, you all can find someone else to oversee the Tower because I'm removing her. If she refuses to abandon her position, I'm walking away from this ordeal because I can't live in Texas anymore. As soon as you visit Hector, Catalina won't be safe anyway. So I hope you understand. Lastly, if James refuses to comply, there will be no hard or ill feelings between us!" I shook hands with both Mr. Sias and Baby and then left.

Baby and I already assumed that if Delia were already in El Paso, it meant that Catalina was either on a bus from Honduras to Monterey or coming to Mexico City from Monterey. Either way, a fourteen-hour drive was ahead of us so we left Arlington five vehicles deep. Baby and I remained speechless the closer we got to El Paso. He wasn't too thrilled about his old man dropping in on Hector when he wasn't there, but like all the men under Mr. Sias, you do as you're told.

"So you walkin' away. Just like that, huh?"

"If she stays to help you all out, she has to live in the Tower, Baby. You and I know this. It wasn't your father who betrayed my trust, but I refuse to allow Catalina to stay after what is about to happen. Now, if she stays, I want you to take me to the airport in El Paso immediately so that I can get back to Atlanta. I need you to promise me something, Baby."

"Talk to me, brother."

"If she ever needs me, you call me."

"Without hesitation, brother," said Baby.

We pulled into El Paso at six thirty in the morning. We couldn't count on Catalina's people to collaborate with us, because she was making the calls from where she was. Whatever Mr. Sias had said to the person who informed him of Delia's departure, it was day-old news and Catalina's influence was standing strong. We had no intentions of searching the city for Delia's location. Catalina was still pissed at me and most likely gave strict orders not to inform me of anything. Though the sun was slowly rising, my home city was alive. I felt saddened at the notion that I couldn't call or see my grandfather. It was strictly business. We found a spot to chill, and one that would give us a good view of the people coming into El Paso or waiting to cross over.

It was seven thirty when Baby spotted Delia. I reached for my door handle and Baby placed his hand on my shoulder.

"Not yet, brother. When you see Catalina, then we go. Let her make it safely across first."

It was eight fifteen when I saw her. I had to look twice to be sure. Catalina was looking as if she had just walked out of hell itself.

"Now you can go," Baby said. As soon as I got out of the Bronco, she spotted me and kept walking my way.

"Catalina, Catalina," Delia continued to call her name as Catalina's escorts were running up behind her. I was hoping that she would run into my arms, but the closer she got to me, her facial expression told another story.

"Catalina," was the only word that I could get out of my mouth before my face was met with a fierce slap.

"Never call me a bitch!" she softly whispered as she slapped me again.

"Catalina," was all I was allowed to say before I received another fierce slap.

"And never tell me to go to hell!"

The fact that I stood there humbly and took those body-rocking slaps and didn't respond with anger pissed her off even more.

"Catalina."

She tried to deliver another blow to my face but I caught her wrist.

"You and I both know that this is not my fault," I reasoned with her.

"I told you I would never lie to you, you bastard!"

"It was my mistake, Catalina and I apologize."

"You're sorry is no good to me!"

"Please, Catalina, don't do this."

"Do not dare blame this shit on me!" I had never seen her so angry.

"I apologize to you, Catalina, and this will not happen again. Please, let's leave this place."

"You treated me like I was no good, and you disrespected me by calling me a bitch. Give me one reason, one damn reason why I should go with you?" I looked at her with a lot of regret on my part and much disappointment on her part.

"I am speaking to you, bastard, and release my arm," she said as she pulled away from me.

"Catalina, I've given you more than a single reason," I said to her and I walked off. I got halfway to the Bronco, took the ring box that held Catalina's engagement ring and held it tightly in my hand. I was going to give it to her after asking her to marry me. At that point, my mental state was confused. I didn't feel whole anymore. It was as if everything that stood between me and Catalina played out in slow motion and seeing it crumble in my mind made me sick to my stomach. I felt my life end as the ring box slowly released itself from my grasp. I had no reason to hold on to it and I left it where I left Catalina.

All I heard behind me was, "I'm talking to you. I'm talking to you, you bastard." When I finally blocked her out, I was climbing back into

316 • Johnny A. McDowell

the Bronco.

"I'm done! Take me to the airport, Baby. I'm done here!" I never looked back.

Chapter FOURTEEN

DILEMMAS, DILEMMAS

"Mama, Daddy cut his finger and it's bleeding real bad."

"So you're telling on me now, huh?"

"But Daddy, you're bleeding, though!"

"When you were playing ball in the house and broke your mother's vase, did I say, 'Mama, Devon broke your vase'?"

"You're the one who missed the ball Daddy, so don't go there with me on that one!" he said as he tossed me a towel. His hollering for his mother brought his grandmother on the scene.

"Stephon, you got blood on my floor! Let me see what you've done. Boy, you need some stitches in this one. Devon, get my keys, tattle-tale."

"You're going to have to take my car because the girls took yours to the store."

"Mama, what was wrong with Marie's car?" I asked.

"Boy, you know Honey likes to ride in your convertible."

"Daddy, I'm going with you; can I drive?"

"This isn't the right time, son."

"So what's up, you going to tell me or what, Daddy?" Devon asked as we pulled out of my mother's driveway.

"Tell you what, boy?" I said as if I had forgotten about his question.

"About you and Mama meeting?"

"Come on, Devon, I'm fighting for my life at this very moment and that's all you have to talk about? What did your mother tell you?" I had to ask him to see if he had found out something he wasn't supposed to.

"Daddy, I've never asked her!"

"Since you're so insistent, I met her out at the mall. She was jockin' a brother's style. Hell, she practically tackled me down on the floor and begged me to marry her and have her children!"

"Daddy, stop trippin'!"

"I'm serious, boy. These could be my last dying words so hush and listen. I was real close to callin' the po¬lice on her butt until I saw how fine and pretty she was."

"I see now that I'm talking to the wrong person," he said as we pulled up into the emergency room parking lot.

By the time Devon and I walked through the emergency room door and a nurse spotted the bloody towel that was wrapped around my hand, filling out paperwork was going to have to wait. It was straight into an examining room. As I was getting my much needed stitches, I heard my baby's voice from a distance and the more she inquired about my whereabouts, the bigger my smile became. There was something about how she rolled Stephon off her tongue and past those lips of hers that really turned me on.

"I'm looking for Mr. Stephon Wilkerson's room please."

Devon peeped his head out my room door when he heard her voice and turned to tell me.

"Mama's coming and this is not my fault either! And since you won't tell me the real scoop, I'll just ask her."

"Boy you act as if I was lying. She'll tell you herself," I said with puffed up pride.

"So whose fault is it this time?" she asked. Devon and I pointed at each other. "So what happened, little daddy?"

"Mama, I just asked Daddy how the two of you met and he cut his hand. That's all and we weren't playing around either."

"Stephon, look at your pants and shoes, they have blood on them," she said in a fussing manner.

"Stop fussing, girl!" I told her as she kissed me on my lips. "You know I'm going to need a nurse and a sponge-bath tonight." The emergency room doctor that was stitching me up started laughing. "Damn, Doc, this is a serious moment, brother," I stated.

"Yes, sir!" he said with more laughter.

"Look at your clothes, they're probably ruined, Stephon!"

" ¡Cada vez yo le dejo dos en la cocina juntas, algo siempre sucede!" (Every time I leave you two in the kitchen together, something always happens!) Catalina said as she wiped the blood off my shoes.

" ¡Esta vez, la culpa no es mía a mamá)"! (This time, it's not my fault, Mama!)" Devon said.

"This is your fault, tattle-tale," I said.

"How is this his fault, Stephon?" Catalina asked.

"You don't want to know!"

"Mama, I asked Daddy how you and him met and he cut himself, that's all that happened."

"Oooh my," Catalina said as she smiled at me. "So did your daddy tell you?" she asked as she gave me the beady-eyed look.

"Si Mama, but I don't believe him." We stared at each other for a few seconds before she made up her mind. "Whatever he told you, that's how we met," she said and he started laughing.

"I told you boy, I'm the man, little daddy!"

The way Devon carried on with his boyish laughter, she knew whatever I told him was far from romantic. Catalina and I had discussed "what if scenarios" if, and when our children asked such a question and it was Catalina who insisted on the all-out romantic thing out of a fairytale book; but since I was asked first, that's what it is!

"We'll talk when we get home, yes?" she said with her hands on her hips as she looked at me. "Something just isn't right about your story, Stephon and if it's not what we discussed in the past, there will be no sponge bath for you mister or the sounds of Gerald Lavert if you catch my drift."

More from Johnny A. McDowell

The Settling

Ten years ago I made up my mind to stand for what I believed in and that nearly cost me my life. I opposed the wrong that my Uncle James, his secret brotherhood, some dirty cops and the De Leon cartel from Honduras placed on my wife's people. The information I obtained about these people would surely place them in prison for the rest of their lives. Deep down inside I knew one day they would come to collect what was rightly theirs and the calling card they left, let me know that no one was safe.

The video my mother received of my sister's badly beaten body was more than an idle threat. I have seventy two hours to return what they want or she dies. The fact that they took my sister right from under my nose, in-forms me that they would continue to kill off my family if I refused. Well from where I stand, they have no plans on allowing us to live anyway. There is only one thing to do, get my sister back and settle this once and for all!

Raising Hope for Darius

Authored by acclaimed writer Johnny A. McDowell, this novel is the first published book among his six other works.

Raising Hope for Darius is an intriguing murder mystery about two-year-old Darius, who is the only witness to the untimely death of his mother, Hope. In an attempt to cover the crime, the murderer changes his life's course, never imagining the possibility of the witness being capable of solving the case with the help of the award-winning journalist named Trey who happens to be Darius' uncle.

Narrated from one of the characters' point of view, this gripping novel takes the reader through numerous twists and turns where love, fear, loss, justice, and redemption collide.

Johnny A. McDowell

About the Author

Resisting the notion of being tied down to a certain genre is not a battle that Johnny A. McDowell has to deal with as a writer, publisher and owner of The House Of Legacy Publishing. His breakthrough release, "Raising Hope For Darius," earned him a 41/2 and two 5 STAR RATINGS. Presented with The 2011 Distinguished Author Award by the Reflections Book Club and was a featured author at the 2013 National Book Club Conference in Atlanta, Georgia.

The release of "A Shift In My World and it's sequel, The Settling," is Johnny's way of informing the literary world that he possess the ability to be a "Chameleon" when it comes to his style of writing and should place him in the company of other nationally known authors.